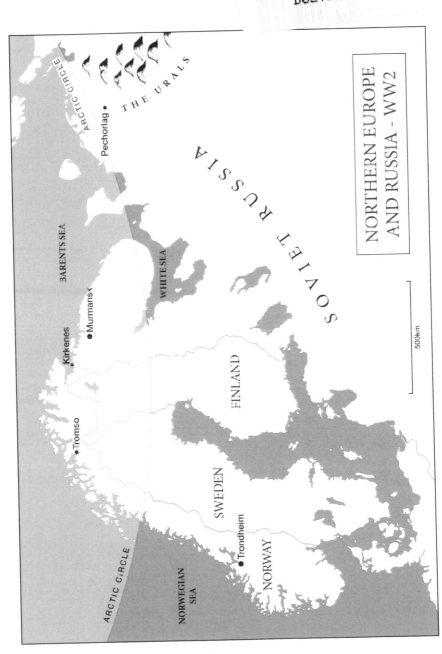

NORTHERN EUROPE
AND RUSSIA - WW2

SOVIET RUSSIA

THE URALS

ARCTIC CIRCLE

Pechorlag ●

BARENTS SEA

WHITE SEA

Kirkenes
●

● Murmans<

● Tromso

FINLAND

SWEDEN

● Trondheim

ARCTIC CIRCLE

NORWEGIAN
SEA

NORWAY

500km

THE
RING
AND THE
SWASTIKA

THE
RING
AND THE
SWASTIKA

SANDY JENKINS

Matador
9 Priory Business Park,
Wistow Road, Kibworth Beauchamp,
Leicestershire. LE8 0RX
Tel: (+44) 116 279 2299
Fax: (+44) 116 279 2277
Email: books@troubador.co.uk
Web: www.troubador.co.uk/matador

ISBN 978 1785892 127

Editing and front cover by Oxford Editors
266 Banbury Road, Oxford

Maps by Nial Smith Design
nial@nialsmith.co.uk

British Library Cataloguing in Publication Data.
A catalogue record for this book is available from the British Library.

Printed and bound in the UK by TJ International, Padstow, Cornwall
Typeset in 10.5pt Palatino by Troubador Publishing Ltd, Leicester, UK

Matador is an imprint of Troubador Publishing Ltd

To David Kilpatrick
A fishing and travelling companion for over half a century

Gather ye rose buds while ye may,
  Old Time is still a-flying:
And this same flower that smiles today,
  Tomorrow will be dying.

Robert Herrick c1650

ACKNOWLEDGEMENTS

The Lofoten War Memorial Museum in Svolvaer and the Tirpitz Museum at Kafjord were both rich sources of information about the German Occupation. The former in particular houses extensive military artefacts including weapons and uniforms but also many everyday items that would have been familiar to those involved in the conflict.

The Tirpitz Museum on the shores of Kafjord close to where the battleship was anchored provided unrivalled insight into what happened to the ship there including the heroic attack by British mini submarines.

Many individual Norwegians also provided useful information but special mention must be made of Leif Jessen whom, in 2009, I chanced to meet at a ferry near Tromso. As a thirteen-year-old boy he had witnessed the final sinking of the *Tirpitz* and he gave me a vivid description of the event, the details of which he wrote in my diary.

The later part of the novel features life in a Soviet gulag but, thankfully, having had no direct experience of what went on in the camps my eyes were opened by reading *Gulag Boss, a Soviet Memoir* by Fyodor Vasilevich Mochulsky, who was a guard in sub-arctic Pechorlag. He describes the appalling conditions and casual cruelty that existed there.

I am so grateful to my daughter, Kate, who solved many computer glitches which arose during writing the manuscript with only occasional exclamations of, 'Oh Dad, you are so stupid!' She also gave useful advice on aspects of the story.

Thanks are also due to my daughter in law, Maryanne, for her help with computer problems.

Finally, my gratitude goes to David Kilpatrick who consistently prodded me and encouraged me to write the story, which is set mainly in a part of the world where, on numerous occasions, we have fished and travelled together for more than half a century.

*Most of the characters in the novel are fictional,
as are some of the place names.*

CHIDDINGFOLD, SURREY, ENGLAND: 1939

The couple studied the tray of rings, which had been laid on the counter. The young man's fair hair and blue eyes looked strikingly Nordic but his fiancée, for clearly that was what she was, was attractively dark. They spent five minutes making a choice. Then, after a final murmured discussion, they selected a broad, plain gold wedding ring.

'It's a present to me from my fiancée,' explained the young man to the jeweller.

'An excellent choice, sir.'

The young man tried the ring on and was pleased to find that it fitted his left fourth finger perfectly. He held up his hand for his fiancée's approval then asked for their initials and the date to be engraved on the ring's inner face. At the jeweller's request he wrote their names, Erik Kingsnorth – Anna Forteith, in an order book, followed by their initials and the year, 'E.K. 1939 A.F.', before explaining exactly what they wanted.

'Just the initials and the year, please.'

A week later the couple returned. The jeweller smiled a welcome to them as they walked in and taking out the engraved ring he gave it a final polish it and, as he showed it to them for their approval, remarked, 'It's beautiful isn't it?' Then he placed the ring in a small blue box with a white satin lining.

'I hope it will bring you long life and happiness,' he added as he wrapped the box and handed it to them.

However, neither the jeweller nor the couple could know that, although the ring was given as a token of love, hidden within its golden circle lay a dreadful tale of future desperation in war, of treachery, flight and finally of monstrous events in a far-off land too awful even to contemplate.

1

THE FADING PEACE: 1939

Gunnar Torkelsen's farmhouse in northern Norway still stands on a knoll in a steep-sided valley not far from the shores of Lyngenfjord. A bumpy farm track, branching off from the road running round the fjord, leads for 300 metres up a slope through hay meadows to reach the farm. A stone's throw in front of the house a small river charges among scattered birches to reach the fjord, and behind the farm a waterfall cascades thinly over a cliff. On windy days it sends a veil of spray into the hayfields but in dry summers when the valley is green it shrinks to a mere trickle and then its gentle voice hardly intrudes on the consciousness.

In winter the valley is transformed. On the lower mountain slopes a filigree of frosted silver birches sparkles against the dark rocks, like diamonds on the black velvet of a jeweller's display. Sometimes in the cold of this glittering landscape, the waterfall freezes into a motionless ladder of ice hanging from the lip of the cliff, but later, in spring, great blocks of ice break away and crash to the rocks below.

From the door of the farmhouse the view stretches over the hay meadows to a distant barrier of mountain peaks cradling snow-covered glaciers. In summer, when warmth returns, the mountains shrug off much of their snow, and cuckoos, warblers and other migratory birds return to fill the valley with birdsong and once again the landscape smiles.

In this beautiful part of north Norway Gunnar and his wife, Birgitta, both in their fifties, managed to wrest a living. Gunnar's deeply lined face with its thatch of pale straw-coloured hair was classically Norse. In his face were written years of struggle against the elements and his blue eyes seemed to reflect a steely resolve to survive in that often inhospitable northern land. His powerful sinewy frame, honed to fitness by constant toil, held not a scrap of fat. Birgitta, on the other hand, was a tender, homely soul, with a matronly fullness around her middle. She was a fine-looking woman, no longer beautiful, but she radiated the calmness of a hard-working wife who had devoted her life to the family she loved. The couple did not have an easy life but there was enough to eat for themselves and their two children, Bjorn and Lara, often with something left over to barter with neighbours. The farm was not large, in fact it was more of a smallholding than a farm, but it supported a cow, some hens and a flock of six sheep. The family subsisted partly on milk, from which Birgitta made a delicious white cheese to go with her home-baked bread. Mutton was a rare treat but most important of all were fish from the fjord and river.

Across the hay meadow, near the mouth of the river, Gunnar kept a small open fishing boat, which he could see from his windows. Usually he fished for codling but when mackerel were in he caught so many on a hand-line that he salted some and smoked the rest for winter use. But the real bounty came with the arrival of salmon in June when he and Bjorn fished hard on the river to supplement the family diet with delicious pink fresh-run salmon, full of the goodness of arctic seas.

Compared with their neighbours there was nothing unusual about Gunnar and Birgitta except for one thing – they had an English nephew. Twenty years previously Gunnar's sister, Alice, had left Norway and had married Andrew Kingsnorth, a doctor in England. Their son, Erik, an only child, kept in close touch with his Norwegian relations and when he came to stay with them, he felt as much Norwegian as he did English. His mother had made a point of chatting to her son in her native tongue and used to read him Norwegian folk tales at bed-time so that by the time he went to the local kindergarten in England he was bilingual.

During summer visits to his uncle and aunt, Erik played happily with their children, Bjorn and sweet-natured Lara. Most of all the boys liked to take Gunnar's boat out onto the fjord to fish, usually leaving a protesting Lara behind. The children played and chattered in Norwegian, although Erik tried to teach his cousins a little English as well.

Erik's life back in Surrey was very different from the carefree existence in Norway. He lived with his parents near Chiddingfold in the English home counties in a rambling white house whose walls in summer were festooned with mauve wisteria. Lawns shaded by ornamental trees swept round the building and at its west end there was an annex from which Erik's father had run his medical practice until his recent retirement on health grounds. He had a reputation as a kindly and much loved practitioner. His upright military bearing was perhaps a legacy of his service in the Great War, in which he had seen appalling mutilations of the human body. He found it hard to believe that the world was about to be plunged into yet another conflict.

When Erik reached the age of thirteen he was sent to a boarding school in Dorset. It was an uncompromisingly strict school, and Spartan in the manner of most private establishments of that time, but he enjoyed the company of his fellow pupils. With his fair hair and strikingly blue eyes he stood out among his peers, but soon earned a reputation as a rebellious prankster and, consequently, was often in trouble. When aged fifteen he acquired considerable prestige among his school-mates when one of the masters caught him in a shrubbery during a school dance in a highly compromising position with one of the visiting girls from a neighbouring school. He was rewarded with a headmaster's thrashing, although, when he later inspected his bruised behind in a mirror, he reflected ruefully that it had been worth it.

After leaving school, Erik's father insisted that he should begin studying for a proper career. Erik had no firm idea what he wanted to do but, as he used to enjoy building crystal sets at school, he ended up enrolling on a physics and radio-communications course at University College, London, and travelled there daily by train.

By the time Erik was eighteen, war with Germany seemed all too probable. Since childhood he had been fascinated by aeroplanes and, as the likelihood of war approached, he was excited to see increasing numbers of aircraft appearing in the Surrey skies. Twin-engined Armstrong Whitley bombers lumbered overhead along with Hurricanes and even, on one occasion, a Spitfire. These sights stoked his enthusiasm for everything to do with aeroplanes and, in the summer of 1939, he began taking flying lessons on a Tiger Moth biplane at an aerodrome near Cobham. It was a wonderful aircraft, easy to fly and gave him an exhilarating sense of freedom.

In spite of these commitments he still found time to

devote to Anna, a charming girl, the daughter of Colonel and Mrs Percival Forteith who lived not far from his parents' house. The two of them enjoyed going for walks together in the surrounding heath and woodlands which gave them plenty of opportunities for intimacy of which they were happy to take advantage – time and again. This agreeable way of life continued for many months until, one day, Anna, looking worried, told Erik that she had missed two of her monthly periods. They both knew what that meant – disgrace by the standards of the day which, Erik knew, could be averted only by marriage. At first he was greatly disturbed by what that would do to the freedom which he currently enjoyed, but both were genuinely fond of each other and agreed that they should tell their parents without delay.

That same warm autumn evening Erik found his father and mother sitting on the veranda in the gathering dusk enjoying their usual Martinis. He pulled up a chair and sat down to join them.

'Have you had a good day, dear?' asked his mother. 'Fetch a glass and join us for a drink.'

Erik went through to the pantry, helped himself to a splash of Bells whisky and returned with the glass to the veranda. As soon as he sat down his mother noticed that something was bothering him. She was always like that and could almost read his mind.

'What's the matter, dear?' she asked. 'You seem all on edge.'

'That's because I am,' replied Erik. 'I've got something to tell you, something important and you may be furious with me, but Anna's pregnant.'

For a few moments there was a stunned silence.

'Oh!' exclaimed his mother as she knocked over her Martini.

'Good God!' spluttered his father. 'How far on is she and what are you going to do about it?' he demanded.

'We think it happened about three months ago and we've decided that we definitely want to get married.'

'Well, that's something,' replied his father. 'Thank God for that!'

'But what about her father, dear, have you spoken to him – about getting married, I mean?' asked his mother. She was already working out that the baby might arrive in six months' time and that she would be a grandmother. Far from being angry with her son, the prospect of a grandchild filled her with secret delight, which she took care to conceal.

Their drinks forgotten, the three of them discussed the need to arrange an early wedding, which, in view of the likelihood of war with Germany would have to be a low-key event. After a long discussion both his parents finally gave their blessing to their son's plans. They knew the Forteiths well and liked the girl who seemed destined to become their daughter-in-law. For his part Erik felt mightily relieved to have unburdened his mind but at the same time he was embarrassed that his parents now knew what he had been up to on those heathland walks; nonetheless he felt proud of what he had achieved.

On that warm summer evening, as pirouetting moths circled the light on the veranda wall, Erik sat with his parents discussing his future. A tawny owl began to hoot softly and insistently in the garden dusk. Its calls went on and on with unusual persistence. An omen? wondered his parents, thinking of the imminent war, and they were overcome with a feeling of dread. They had only one son.

The next day being a Sunday Erik and his parents spent a quiet morning making a list of things to do in preparation for a civil wedding. Alice, Erik's mother, brought a tray of coffee and biscuits through to the drawing room and the three of them settled down to listen to the Home Service on the wireless. Almost at once their worst fears were realised when, in his familiar measured tones, Alvar Liddell, the announcer, made a statement.

'At 11.15,' he said, 'that is, in about two minutes, the Prime Minister will broadcast to the nation. Please stand by.' The wireless fell silent.

'Well, this is it!' said Erik's father while the three of them waited for Neville Chamberlain to speak. Then the solemn voice of the Prime Minister came on the air.

'I am speaking to you from the Cabinet Room in 10 Downing Street. This morning the British ambassador in Berlin handed the German Government a final Note stating that unless we heard from them by eleven o'clock that they were prepared at once to withdraw their troops from Poland a state of war would exist between us. I have to tell you now that no such undertaking has been received and that, consequently, this country is at war with Germany.'

2

THE TORKELSENS, LYNGENFJORD

Eight hundred miles away in northern Norway, Gunnar and Birgitta also had heard the momentous news on the wireless and they too wondered how many parents would lose their offspring in the war which would inevitably follow. They hoped fervently that the conflagration would not spread to Norway.

After their own marriage they had tried unsuccessfully to have children. Each month they had waited anxiously for Birgitta to show signs of pregnancy, only to be disappointed. Together, on several occasions, they had attended a clinic in Trondheim but the doctor there could find no reason why they were unable to conceive. Finally they had decided to try to adopt and in 1922 were lucky to have found a year-old baby boy called Bjorn through an adoption agency in Trondheim. The prospective parents made the long journey by bus and ferry to see the child and to hear something of his background. On arrival they were ushered into the home for orphans and were greeted by the superintendent who took them through to her office.

'Please sit down while I tell you about little Bjorn,' she said, pointing to a pair of chairs while Gunnar and Birgitta looked around them. It was like a hospital room, clean and smelling faintly of carbolic soap, but the lady superintendent was friendly enough. She put her head out of the door and called down the corridor for a nurse to bring the infant. After a few minutes the baby, wrapped in a small, blue, woollen blanket, was brought in. All Gunnar and Birgitta could see was a pink face with a pair of blue eyes peering crossly at them. At once the face crinkled up and the infant began to bawl and shriek. Undeterred, Birgitta reached out and took the small bundle from the nurse and, surprisingly, the shrieking stopped almost immediately and the blue eyes gazed up at her. Calm was restored.

It took two hours to deal with the initial formalities and the superintendent explained how to go about applying for formal adoption. All of Birgitta's suppressed maternal instincts began to blossom as she felt the young body squirming against her breast. She was sure that things were going to work out well. The superintendent went on to explain something of the child's background.

'His mother was a local girl who went to the European continent to work as a home help for a wealthy family, but things didn't turn out well and within six months of her appointment she developed morning sickness and turned out to be pregnant. Her employer was thought to be responsible. That was the end of her employment and she was sent back here to Norway. The pregnancy itself was uneventful but after the birth she developed a high temperature as an infection took hold in her womb; "puerperal sepsis" they called it, and tragically the young mother died soon afterwards. Her elderly mother was not a fit woman and found she couldn't cope with a baby and that's why Bjorn is here. He's now almost exactly one year old and is a lovely, healthy child.'

The superintendent took the infant and removed the blanket.

'Look,' she said, 'he can almost stand if he has something to hold on to!'

Birgitta turned to her husband, her eyes bright with hope. 'That means he's almost the same age as Erik your nephew and once the adoption goes through they will be first cousins.'

Two months later, when the adoption formalities were complete, Gunnar and Birgitta again travelled to Trondheim to collect Bjorn and this time they brought him back to his new home on the shores of Lyngenfjord. As the youngster grew up Birgitta sometimes ruefully reflected that the name Bjorn, or bear, was entirely appropriate in view of his rough and tough assertiveness.

Having accepted that their family was then complete, something extraordinary happened. Six months after the adoption, Birgitta began to experience a feeling of nausea in the mornings and in due course her abdomen developed into a smooth round swelling. The couple were overjoyed that the seemingly impossible had happened, and the result was a beautiful baby girl whom they christened Lara. She grew up into a sweet-natured and attractive young girl with limpid brown eyes and dark hair. Gunnar would sit her on his knee, gazing at her admiringly saying, 'With both of us having fair hair isn't it strange that hers is so dark?' Birgitta would reply simply, 'Yes, and is it not beautiful?' She had always longed for a girl and never divulged how the miracle had happened.

Ten years previously, when her married life with Gunnar had looked as though it was not going to be blessed with children, Birgitta had become depressed. However, in spite of the adoption of Bjorn her maternal instincts only seemed to grow and she was overcome by an emotional storm of longing to carry and to give birth to a child of her own. Often when she was alone she pondered about the possible reasons why she should unable to conceive but she could find no answers. She and Gunnar often talked over her moodiness and they both understood the reason for it. Then suddenly it came to her that perhaps her body was not at fault after all and that the problem might lie with Gunnar. From then her thoughts slowly began to take a quite new direction. At first she was shocked and felt guilty about the ideas that came into her head because she loved her husband. But what if she could try for pregnancy with another man whom she could trust? For a time she was consumed with guilt about the idea, but at the same time her thoughts kept returning to a neighbour, Nils Anders, whom both she and Gunnar liked. No one else would need to know about it, least of all Gunnar. Essentially Birgitta was a good and faithful wife, but a single carefully timed clandestine episode with Nils Anders, who was such an obliging young neighbour, just might serve its purpose.

At first this outlandish idea gave her some hope but later when she had time to think about it she had to admit to herself that agreement by both Nils and his wife, Helga, was almost out of the question and that such an extraordinary suggestion might cause offence and the breakdown of the friendship between the two families. With this in mind she rejected the whole idea as a flight of fantasy and tried to forget about it; but she could not forget about it. The urge to nourish a child in her own body grew to an almost unmanageable level and she returned to the original idea.

Nils Anders and his wife Helga lived on a small farm a kilometre to the west and, on a bright spring morning in

1924, Birgitta went to visit them carrying a small present of half a dozen eggs. She was nervous and was relieved to find that Nils was out in his fishing boat. She and Helga sat down on a seat outside the house in the sunshine and chatted about everyday matters.

'Birgitta, are you alright?' asked Helga, who had noticed her friend's unusual anxiety. 'You're a bundle of nerves today. What's up? Do tell me what's troubling you because something certainly is.'

Then it all came out: the reason for her recent depression, her longing for a baby of her own and her feeling that it might be Gunnar who was unable to father a child, even though the doctors in Trondheim had found no fault in either of them. The two women talked for a long time but still Birgitta could not summon up courage to broach the question of the role that Nils could possibly play. Then suddenly she decided to take the plunge. Now was the time!

'Helga, what I am going to ask is something that may seem to you disgraceful but I hope it won't spoil our long friendship. If Nils would give his agreement would you allow him to try on just one occasion to achieve with me what Gunnar cannot?' There was a stunned silence as Helga took this in. She could hardly believe what she had just heard. The trilling call of a curlew from the shoreline and the gentle sea-murmur were the only sounds which filled the silence. At last, after two or three minutes, Helga turned to Birgitta.

'Birgitta, we have been good friends for a long time but I cannot possibly give you an answer just now: I want time to think. What you ask is something that would go to the heart of my family. If I feel able to agree I will then tell Nils about it and will let you know our decision. I hope you will understand that, just now, I feel appalled at the idea.'

A month went by with no response to Birgitta's proposal and then at last Helga appeared with a small present of home-made cheese. The two women went for a stroll together and Birgitta was relieved to find that their friendship did not seem to have been shaken. And then, almost unbelievably, Helga said that she and Nils had discussed the idea at length and that he would not object to trying to help out on one occasion only. So it happened that, after careful timing, Birgitta called at the Anders's house at a time when Helga, by arrangement, was away buying provisions at the store in Olderdalen.

Birgitta, Nils and Helga never again referred to what had been done even after the pregnancy became obvious, and Gunnar never for a moment suspected that he was not the father.

The addition of a little girl to the family brought great happiness to the household and Lara proved to be a particularly affectionate child. As a toddler she loved to sit on Gunnar's knee to feel the rough bristles on his chin and squealed if they hurt when he kissed her. Soon she was helping her mother with little tasks in the kitchen and liked to sit on the draining board of the sink with her feet in the soapy water helping with the washing up. She and Bjorn usually played happily together but also quarrelled like all siblings of their age.

Their childhood and most of their teenage years passed untroubled despite warlike growls from Hitler's Germany. Then in 1939 Germany savaged first Czechoslovakia and then Poland and six months later, on April 9th 1940, went on to invade both Denmark and Norway. Gunnar would always remember the date as it was his fiftieth birthday. The Norwegian coastal defence fortress of Oskarborg promptly sank the German pocket battleship *Blücher* as she approached Oslo and the following day British RAF planes from Orkney sank the *Königsberg* at Bergen. The war had come even to peaceable Norway. Bjorn, just nineteen years old when Norway was invaded, was excited, rather than alarmed.

'How will it affect us?' he asked. 'What will happen now?' Nobody could answer those questions because, quite simply, nobody knew.

Arne and Inga Petersen, a couple from a neighbouring farm, hurried round to the Torkelsens' soon after news of the invasion was broadcast and they sat together around the kitchen table listening to the wireless.

'Heaven help us!' said Gunnar as he poured everyone a glass of akavit. 'We are going to need this,' he said downing his measure in one gulp.

Things went from bad to worse. As the weeks went by King Haakon was evacuated from Tromso to form a government in exile in England and two days later on June 10th the Anglo-French forces withdrew from Norway altogether and the Norwegian 6th Division finally surrendered.

'Now we really are on our own,' said Gunnar.

Two months later the realities of Occupation became all too clear. In June Austrian paratroopers landed near Tromso. People said they had arrived with bicycles along with their weapons and gradually the enemy tide extended up the whole of Norway to Kirkenes in the far north near the Russian border. The German-led Administrative Council declared it an offence to listen to BBC broadcasts, and all wirelesses were to be handed in at designated collection points. Public gatherings were banned and a pass had to be obtained to allow travel out of the applicant's home area and, worst of all, food rationing began.

In the scattered farms around the fjord people began to secure extra food supplies as shortages seemed certain. Once a month a coastal supply ship called in at the fjord bringing items people could not produce themselves. Since the invasion, however, many of these imports were no longer available in the local store in Olderdalen, but gradually a scanty amount of German produce began to appear on the shelves.

The Torkelsen family's lifeline was fish: fish from the river and fish from the sea. Each June grilse, young salmon, ran up the river from Lyngenfjord in their quest to find the spawning grounds where they, themselves, were reared. Gunnar operated a sea net a short distance from the river mouth and it was Bjorn's job to check this regularly and to remove the accumulations of jellyfish and weed which spoilt the net's effectiveness. When the fish were running, they could catch around ten a day, some of which they ate fresh but most they salted and then smoked in an old barrel perched over a smouldering fire on a bank at the back of the house. With food rationing and food shortages looming these salmon would assume great importance to the household and Gunnar with Bjorn worked hard to lay in a good reserve supply. Sometimes they fished on the river as well, using a thick bamboo cane to which Gunnar had wired a series of rings for the line and bound an old brass reel onto the butt. He made effective lures out of small kitchen spoons and, after cutting the handles off, drilled holes for the nearly invisible gut and the hooks.

On an especially beautiful day in June 1940 when the Occupation and the war seemed far away Gunnar was fishing on the best pool quite near the track leading up to the farm. A torrent of water pouring down from rocks above sent the flow surging for thirty metres down to the middle of the pool. Towards its lower end the water quietened, releasing its suspended bubbles and there, in the crystal depths, he could see salmon hovering above the gravel. Gunnar cast the spoon across the middle of the pool and felt the vibration and pull as it turned and swung across the current. Suddenly a salmon took the bait. Most of the fish at that time of the year were small, around two kilos, but this one was a different matter. It raced across the river, silver flanks flashing in the sunshine as it leapt from the water near the opposite bank, disturbing smaller fish which jumped in alarm. Clearly it was much bigger than usual, about eight kilos, thought Gunnar. In his concentration and owing to the sound of the river he did not notice the olive green motorcycle and sidecar approaching along the farm track. Suddenly, with a start, he became aware of someone standing behind him. He turned and was startled to see two German soldiers in field grey uniforms watching the fight with the salmon. One of them, with fair hair, greeted him with a friendly smile and nod of encouragement. Gunnar reflected that these were the first German invaders that he had seen. However, he continued with the task in hand and after five minutes he carefully brought the tiring salmon towards the gravel beach. Exhausted, it turned onto its side while Gunnar walked backwards drawing it to into the shallows at the water's edge where, half stranded, it lay flapping. The fair-haired soldier stepped forward and with both hands scooped it out onto the gravel. He seemed to know what to do and kneeling on the struggling fish, he quickly dispatched it with a stone. It was the biggest that Gunnar had caught for a long time, a particularly fine fish for such a little river.

The soldier who had helped was only about nineteen. His cropped fair hair and cheerful face reminded Gunnar, a little, of his nephew Erik. He seemed most friendly and with a broad smile held out his hand in congratulation. Without thinking, Gunnar shook the proffered hand, too late remembering that this agreeable young man was an invader, an enemy of Norway. Quickly pulling his hand away Gunnar gave a curt nod and asked the man what he was doing here in Norway. The young soldier replied in German, smiling in his lack of understanding. Mutual incomprehension was complete. The second soldier created a quite different impression. He seemed to be a non-commissioned officer, an NCO. Below his forage cap his face was thin and sallow with a narrow nose supporting a pair of wire-framed spectacles. Once the fish was landed his initial tight-lipped smile did not reappear and he made no attempt at friendliness: he looked as disagreeable as his colleague was agreeable. He said something to his companion while pointing at the motorcycle and together they returned to the track, mounted the machine and drove off. The fair-haired soldier in the sidecar turned and waved a hand in farewell as they disappeared towards the fjord.

Gunnar was stunned at this first meeting with the invaders, at least one of whom seemed so pleasant and friendly. When the motorcycle had departed he realised with a start that not only had he shaken the German's hand after landing the fish but had also acknowledged his departure with an involuntary wave of his own.

This won't do, he thought. Is this the way that fraternising with the enemy begins? He rinsed his hand in the river as though trying to remove some contagion. As he walked back to the farmhouse carrying the fish he decided that he and his family should have an urgent discussion about what their attitude to the Germans should be.

'*Stor laks*, a big one!' exclaimed Bjorn admiringly. 'Eight kilos, I bet,' as his father dumped the salmon in the kitchen sink while recounting his meeting with the Germans. Birgitta was greatly alarmed that the Occupation had reached so far north already but Bjorn was excited and wanted to see for himself what the enemy actually looked like.

'You'll have plenty of opportunities to see them soon enough,' said his father as he scraped off a cluster of sea lice from near the fish's tail. Then, using a razor sharp filleting knife, he opened and cleaned the fish while pink eggs spilt into the sink. Then he filleted the salmon leaving two halves ready for salting and smoking, all the while turning over in his mind his meeting with the Germans.

'Bjorn, can you come here for a minute?' he asked. 'I would like you to call on the Petersens and the Anderses as well. Try to get them to come here tomorrow morning for a meeting because we ought to agree how to behave towards these Germans. Try to get old Leif Jessen, too, if he can manage it.'

Leif, a widower well into his seventies, lived alone in a tiny wooden house two kilometres down the fjord. His wife had died of stomach cancer five years previously and since then his neighbours helped with his small patch of hay and the half dozen sheep. He did not get out and about much but when he had to pay visits he turned up on his ancient grey Icelandic pony. His dislike of Germans was well known locally even though he had never actually met any.

That evening in the kitchen, Birgitta and Lara rubbed coarse salt into the pink flesh of the salmon, while discussing the possible consequences of the Occupation. Lara was a beautiful girl and with a shiver of fear Birgitta thought about the threat to her daughter from a horde of foreign soldiers deprived of the company of women. She was also unsettled by Bjorn's opinion that the war was already lost and that Britain didn't stand a chance as Germany was unstoppable. Statements like that greatly annoyed Gunnar and gave rise to tension between himself and Bjorn and they had had several shouting matches over it.

3

THE APPROACHING MENACE

The following morning dawned bright and clear. The fjord shone turquoise in the sunlight and far across the water a mountain, piercing a layer of cloud, held up its glacier as if making an icy offering to the heavens. Although the view looked peaceful enough Gunnar knew that a menace was infiltrating their beautiful country like a cancer spreading through the body of its victim.

At mid-morning the Petersens arrived, pushing their bicycles up the slope of the farm track towards the house. Arne Petersen and his wife, Inga, owned a sizeable piece of pastureland at the head of a small inlet two kilometres away but most of their livelihood was derived from their stout sea-going fishing boat moored nearby. They had long been good friends with Gunnar's family and the two households regularly bartered fish and occasionally mutton and helped each other at hay-making time and with the sheep shearing. In the evenings Gunnar and Arne sometimes enjoyed a drink or two together though Birgitta scolded them if they over-indulged. Both Birgitta and Gunnar had come to know and like their neighbours well.

The Petersens had had their share of tragedy. Their first child, a girl, had been born mentally subnormal. Privately, some neighbours thought it was because the couple were related, albeit distantly. Both parents had adored the child, but one day when she was four years old she had wandered off and had later been found drowned near the boat's mooring. For a time Inga had been inconsolable and for two years she had vivid dreams of the little girl in which she could hear the childish voice chattering away, and sometimes she seemed to hear the patter of her feet. When healthy twin boys, Per and Pal, were born a year later her sadness resolved and she was able to accept what had happened, but she never forgot her little girl. For many years a framed photograph of the child stood on the bread bin in the kitchen.

Half an hour elapsed before the other neighbours, Nils and Helga Anders with their teenage sons, Lars and Kristian, appeared on bicycles. Nils apologised for being late but explained that they had been delayed on the road by a long convoy of German trucks filled with troops moving north. The Anders family lived half a kilometre to the west along the shore in the opposite direction from the Petersens. The boys often visited Gunnar's family and sometimes went to fish on the fjord with Bjorn. Lars, the oldest, had just turned eighteen when the Germans invaded Norway. He enjoyed fishing but most of all he liked shooting and sometimes took along his father's rifle to shoot seals which might be unwise enough to poke their heads out of the water to inspect the boat. When the Germans occupied the country possession of weapons was forbidden, and their father had wrapped the rifle in layers of oiled cloth and had hidden it in a dry space beneath a flat rock on the farm.

The three families settled themselves in the kitchen, and were pulling their chairs up to the table, when old Leif Jessen appeared on his pony, ambling along the track up to the house. Neither Leif nor his pony ever hurried. He dismounted outside the door, unwound a short rope from his waist and tied the animal's forelegs together. This allowed it to graze but not to go far since it could only move with an odd looking leap. Leif was known in the community as a wise and shrewd old man and since the death of his wife he had lived alone. In his youth he had spent a year on an Icelandic farm and had picked up some customs of that country, including his frugal habits and simple way of life, and had given his smallholding the name 'Bakki' meaning 'riverside field' in Icelandic. His few luxuries included what he called his 'neftobak', a kind of coarse Icelandic snuff which he sniffed from the 'anatomical snuff box' made by extending his thumb to form a little hollow between the tendons on the back of his hand. His leathery skin, weather-beaten face and sparse grey hair were legacies of his life as a farmer in Arctic Norway; he was old but tough.

'I'm glad that you have all come,' said Gunnar, who was accepted as spokesman on community matters and was held in considerable respect. 'Help yourselves to coffee from the pot and make the most of it as we won't get any more. I'm afraid these are bad times. It's obvious that the Germans are going to occupy the whole of the country and I think we should decide together what, if anything, we can do about it and what our attitude to them should be. Is it to be cooperation or should we actively oppose them by every means possible?' There was silence for a moment then Bjorn spoke up in his typically impulsive way.

'We should fight them and kill as many as we can!' he said.

There was a murmur around the table while Arne and Nils glanced at Gunnar to assess his reaction.

Huh! The intemperance of youth, thought Arne Petersen, shaking his head. 'Steady on!' he said aloud. 'How could we possibly do that and what would their reaction be if we did?'

His wife, Inga, agreed that reprisals would be inevitable.

'We must face the fact that Germany has really won the war,' she said. 'The whole of Europe except England has been beaten and I think that we'd be wise to cooperate and even show some friendliness.'

The safety of Per and Pal, their two young teenage twin boys, was uppermost in her mind when she said this though, later, when she had time to think about it she certainly did not want to be known as a collaborator. Arne did not often disagree in public with his wife but he did this time; her suggestion was too much for him and he looked angry.

'Don't ever say that we'll cooperate, Inga! We are Norwegians and must behave honourably and that means no dealings with the Germans and no cooperation at any time. They say that people in Tromso refuse to sit next to a German on the buses and even get up and stand if one of them takes the next seat. If they can do that in the towns then surely we, too, should be able to think of some way of showing them our resentment.'

The Anders family took the same attitude as Arne but Leif Jessen remained silent. He sat there occasionally sniffing his neftobak from his gnarled hand and blowing his nose into a tobacco-coloured handkerchief.

'Come on, Leif! Let's hear what you think about it,' said Gunnar.

The old man was finally persuaded to give his opinion but not before a lengthy pause as he considered what to say.

'This war,' he finally said, 'will eventually come to an end one way or another and at the end of it all there will be those who helped the Germans, those who did nothing for or against them and those who opposed them to the best of their ability. It may be that if the Germans win then the first group will be best off and some of the last group may be dead. However, I have no wish to be amongst the best off.'

There was a thoughtful silence in the room broken only by a soft snort from the pony outside. The slow tick of the large wooden wall clock emphasised the silence while the neighbours thought about what Leif had said. They agreed with him that the choice of action was an individual matter, but perhaps not all thought that it was inconceivable ever to help the Germans in occasional small ways. Gunnar passed round small glasses together with a half bottle of akavit, telling the men to help themselves. For nearly an hour the families chatted together until, finally, chairs were pushed back as the company prepared to depart, each having decided how they would behave towards the invaders.

The Anderses were last to go. Birgitta walked with them for a little way down the farm track and after she finally said goodbye to them she stood watching the sunshine glinting in Nils Anders's dark hair, exactly as it sometimes did in Lara's.

As the weeks and months passed, life gradually became more difficult as food rationing almost eliminated supplies of everyday items such as meat, sugar, flour and butter. Farmers and smallholders were in a relatively fortunate position of being able to produce food from their livestock and fish remained a major source of protein for those living along the Lyngenfjord. In view of the German order that wireless sets should be handed in most locals thought it prudent to comply, but some did not. Gunnar lifted two kitchen floorboards, hid the family wireless in the space beneath, and covered the loose boards with a mat. The newspapers were controlled by the collaborating Quisling government, and broadcasts by the BBC provided the only reliable news of what was really happening. Retaining an illicit wireless set was the only, albeit risky, way of keeping in touch with the war news.

Gunnar and his neighbours avoided contact with the German troops although no one could think of any reasonable way of demonstrating their outrage at the Occupation, and it fell to one of the fourteen-year-old Petersen twin boys to take the first small step of active defiance. The youngsters had spent a morning in a dinghy out on the fjord fishing for codling with a hand line. They had just secured the boat back on its moorings and were walking home carrying their catch of half a dozen fish strung through the gills on a piece of twine, when a German open-backed truck carrying a number of soldiers sped by showering the boys with dust and gravel. A few moments later a second truck appeared and, impulsively, Per picked up a handful of stones and hurled them at the departing vehicle. The stones rattled against its rear and immediately there were shouts from the soldiers sitting in the back. The truck skidded to a halt and two grey-clad soldiers leapt down onto the road and made for the boy. There was no time to run. A sickening sensation of fear held him like a limpet as a soldier caught him by the back of his jacket and dragged him behind the truck. Pal heard angry shouts in German followed by his brother's pleading voice, and then silence. A moment or two later there was the sound of two strokes of a belt striking flesh followed by a stifled whimper, then the truck moved off leaving Per in the roadway pulling up his breeches and wiping away tears of pain and humiliation. He was the first of the local Norwegians in the Lyngenfjord district to suffer reprisal from the occupiers.

4

OCCUPATION

Two weeks later the weather turned warm and sunny and Gunnar and Bjorn were cutting hay at the front of the house. Their scythes fell into an easy swinging rhythm as the warm sun drew out sweet perfume from the lengthening swathes of cut grass. After half an hour, their shirts darkened with patches of sweat, they paused for a rest. A column of German military vehicles passing along the shore road caught Gunnar's attention. Shading his eyes against the sun he watched as a motorcycle and sidecar turned into their farm track. Three or four hundred metres away it stopped beside the river, and two German soldiers dismounted. They walked down to the water's edge and stood there discussing something. The sun was hot and they had taken their forage caps off and Gunnar watched as one of them with fair hair pointed to the salmon pool. The other returned to the motorcycle, reached down into the sidecar and, taking out an object, walked back to the water's edge. In a moment they seemed to come to a decision and backed away from the river, whereupon the soldier carrying the object lobbed it in a low arc into the middle of the pool. In a few seconds a mound of foaming water and spray rose from the surface followed almost immediately by the deep thud of an exploding grenade. One of the men took off his boots and waded into the shallows among a number of stunned or dead salmon floating on the surface which he began to retrieve using the broken branch of a tree. Appalled, Gunnar and Bjorn dropped their scythes and ran down the farm track to the pool, shouting at the Germans whom Gunnar recognised as the pair who had watched him landing the big fish several weeks beforehand.

It was an act of pure vandalism. Some salmon floated, belly-up, out of the pool towards the sea and scores of immature fish a few inches long lay dead or stunned at the edge of the gravel beach. By the time Gunnar and Bjorn reached the scene the bespectacled German had thrown four salmon up onto the gravel. Enraged, Gunnar ran up and grabbed the man by his lapels, shouting insults at his face and gave him a hefty push. The man stumbled backwards, tripped and fell into a few inches of water losing his glasses in the river as he did so. The German, equally enraged, stumbled out of the water in his bare feet while Gunnar continued to shout at him. Pulling a pistol from the holster at his side, the man levelled the weapon at Gunnar's chest. Bjorn heard the click as the safety catch was released and instinctively leapt forward to pull his father away. Simultaneously the other soldier lunged at his colleague's arm, deflecting the shot.

Gunnar and Bjorn froze. It took them a second or two to realise that the bullet had missed its intended target. A violent argument began between the two Germans; Gunnar noticed that the hand of the soldier with the weapon was shaking and there was sweat on his forehead. The blond soldier waved Gunnar and Bjorn away and, picking up the boots, led his colleague back to the motorcycle. He started the machine and the two of them departed without a backward glance, leaving behind numerous dead salmon and a pair of spectacles in the river. Gunnar's legs suddenly seemed to give way and he sat on a rock aware of his thumping heart. It had been a close thing.

In the distance, up at the house, he could see Birgitta and Lara shielding their eyes against the sun as they tried to see what had happened down on the river where the confrontation had taken place. They had heard the concussion of the grenade and had seen the altercation with the Germans.

Gunnar waded into the pool and pulled out four more dead salmon while Bjorn went to fetch the hand cart to transport eight fish back to the farm. Birgitta and Lara were horrified to hear about the shooting while they gutted and split the fish in preparation for salting. Gunnar remarked that he thought it was only German officers who carried side arms but, while the bespectacled soldier did not look at all like an officer, he had a weapon all right.

*

A few weeks after the hay had been stacked and thatched Bjorn started to become restless and was often argumentative at home. Now that summer would soon give way to autumn there was less work to do on the farm. He wanted a real job. He wanted independence. For some time he had talked about the need to get a proper job. As a fit young man he naturally wanted to see something of life away from the family farm and to earn some money for himself. Other than Lars and Kristian Anders and the young Petersen twins there were few young people living within easy reach along the fjord. Most importantly, apart from his sister, Lara, there were no girls. Bjorn heard that there was work to be had 300 kilometres away at Svolvaer on the Lofoten Islands, at a fish oil extraction plant which had become especially busy since the Occupation. He was sure that he would be able to find some kind of employment there. Fortunately one of Gunnar's distant relations, a widow, lived on the harbour front in Svolvaer. He sent her a letter asking if she could give advice to Bjorn about jobs at the plant and if she could provide lodgings for him. Gunnar knew that he could not stand in the way of his son's plan to leave – after all a young man needs to see the world and he could probably manage the farm on his own, with help from neighbours at busy times.

Ten days later Gunnar received a letter confirming that there would be a good chance of Bjorn finding a job at the plant and that the widow would be pleased to have him as a lodger. Later that week Bjorn took the local bus along the fjord to the Fridalen police post and applied for a permit to make the 300-kilometre journey by bus and ferry. Two weeks later the permit was ready for collection and a date for the journey was set. Lara was upset at the thought of her brother's departure and she, too, began to think about finding work of some kind. The store at Olderdalen ten kilometres away sometimes took on young girls to help behind the counter and to sort the incoming stores from the supply ship. She thought that, in summer, she should be able to manage the daily bicycle ride to and from the store while still living at home. Winter would be another matter and she would see if Hans Larsen, the storekeeper, and his wife, Hilder, could give her lodgings.

Without further delay Bjorn left for the Lofoten Islands and shortly after that Lara reported for her first day's work at the store. The bicycle ride along the fjord was a pleasure in the late summer sunshine. There were plenty of German vehicles on the road and soldiers in the open-backed trucks often shouted and waved to the attractive young girl on the bicycle as they passed. She was careful not to respond in any way and tried to keep her eyes firmly on the road in front of her. Sometimes, however, she glanced up involuntarily and would catch sight of pleasant young men who smiled and waved in such a friendly fashion. In the immediate vicinity of her home there were so few young males apart from the Anders boys and the Petersen twins, who were far too young to catch her attention.

Hans Larsen and his wife, Hilder, were glad to have Lara's help at the store. They explained her duties, which included stacking shelves with what little in the way of stores now seemed to be available. Although scanty tins of food from Germany began to take the place of Norwegian produce many of the shelves remained unfilled. Food rationing had come into full force and distribution of stores to customers was regulated by what their ration cards allowed. Lara's first morning at work was quiet and only a trickle of locals called in to buy what they could, but she soon discovered that the store also served as a social meeting place. People came in to gossip as well as to buy things. Customers were happy to meet Lara and to have news of her parents and neighbours.

Towards the end of her first week at work Lara, gazing out of the window, was disturbed to see a German army staff car drawing up on the gravel outside. It was an open vehicle and the two officers sitting in the back got out, leaving the young driver in the car, and pushed open the store door. Lara was aware of her quickening pulse as she faced two enemy officers alone and at close quarters for the first time.

They both wore long coats with insignia at the collars, but seemed quite friendly and surprisingly unthreatening. Taking off his peaked cap, one greeted her politely.

'*Guten Abend, Fräulein,*' and then, to her surprise, he began to speak, haltingly, in Norwegian, very poor Norwegian, but nevertheless she could understand the gist of what he was trying to say. He said how much he liked Norway, that he came from Düsseldorf and wanted to buy some Norwegian birchwood carvings as souvenirs and, if she had any, a piece of 'stokfisk' or dried salt cod. Lara went through into the back shop to fetch one of the pieces of fish hanging in the store room while the Germans wandered about the shop looking at the small collection of locally carved wooden figures, mostly odd-looking gnomes and trolls.

Lara had never spoken to a German before and as she returned to continue serving her unexpected customer she reminded herself not to be too friendly. But what else could she do but serve him? Besides, both the Germans seemed very pleasant and cultured and were not at all like the Germans that she had imagined up till now – threatening and boorish. They were nice! The officer thanked her politely as he took the wrapped fish. He paid for it and for two small carved figures which he had chosen and the pair returned to the car. Thoughtfully Lara watched the departing vehicle through the window as it disappeared up the gravel road and along the shore of the fjord.

Later Hilder Larsen came through from the back shop and told her that German soldiers had often been coming to the store. They were courteous and always paid without demur. She told Lara that they should be served like anyone else but it would be best to avoid any suggestion of undue friendliness. Apparently some Norwegian customers walked out if a German came in.

As the weeks went by and summer turned into autumn, the countryside began to glow with colour; russet, brown and yellow. The birches on the slope above the store turned to gold and one morning the mountain tops were white with new snow. The mornings and evenings were starting to get dark, and, when the bicycle ride to and from her parents' house became impractical, Lara moved into a room above the store. It was a simple but warm room with a small double-glazed window and a bed tucked into an alcove beneath a sloping part of the ceiling. A Bible lay on a pinewood table by the bed and in a corner was a comfortable chair. Hans Larsen and his kindly wife made her most welcome and said that, of course, she should take her meals with them downstairs. Before long she began to feel like one of the family. She found out that the Larsens, too, kept a hidden wireless set in the house and were able to keep up to date with the war news by tuning in to the BBC. The news, however, did not sound reassuring. London was suffering from heavy raids though the British Royal Air Force had managed to shoot down a number of bombers. In November, a big city called Coventry which Lara had never heard of was devastated by bombing and it seemed only a matter of time before Britain, too, would be invaded.

Lara had heard nothing about Bjorn in his new home in the Lofoten Islands and was therefore excited when a forwarded letter arrived which he had sent to their parents. She took it up to her room and unfolded the creased sheet of paper torn from an exercise book. She glanced at the pencil-written lines and read:

October 21st 1940

Dear Father and Mother,

I am getting on well at Svolvaer and am lodging with good people not far from the harbour. Dag and Liv Gunstensen are kind and luckily she cooks well and I get enough to eat even though it is mostly fish. Dag works as the harbour master's assistant and he showed me round the docks. He also took me to meet the German harbour administrator, Herr Altman, who was very friendly and seems to be on good terms with him. Although we see the Germans every day they mostly keep to themselves and don't bother us. Apparently they say that Germany has won the war in Europe and that England will soon be finished off. If that is true it looks as though the Occupation is going to be permanent and that we will just have to live with it.

Dag and Liv have an attractive daughter. We get on well and sometimes we go round to meet her friends. One evening we went to see a cinema film in the town hall. It was mostly about how young people in Germany get together in the countryside and help on the farms. They seem very keen on physical exercise usually in organised groups. Perhaps it's a way of preparing them for military service but some local people did not approve of the film and walked out.

I have to say that I feel some admiration for the Germans. They are so well organised and it seems that life just now is really good in Germany.

I hope you are both well and that you are managing on the farm alright. How is Lara getting on at the store?

Your son, Bjorn

Back on the farm, without Bjorn's help, life turned out to be more difficult than Gunnar had anticipated and the winter of 1940 was long and tiresome. There seemed to be Germans everywhere and it was around this time that events took on a more troubling and sinister turn.

Birgitta had been preparing a midday snack of salmon and freshly baked bread when, through the kitchen window, she saw a German army car turn up the farm track. It stopped outside the house and, leaving the driver in his seat, an officer got out and banged on the door. He was polite enough but indicated that he had come to carry out 'an inspection'. He went through the whole house looking into all the rooms and cupboards. He did not say what he was searching for but Gunnar was acutely aware of the wireless hidden beneath the kitchen floorboards. When the officer was finished, without explaining what he had been looking for, he returned to the car and was driven away. The unexpected visit had left Birgitta shocked and pale. She pleaded with her husband to do something about the wireless set.

'You must get rid of it. Why not throw it into the fjord or bury it in the hay field? You know what the penalty is for listening to the BBC and it's just not worth the risk. I heard that someone at Storslett was arrested and was sent to a prison camp in Germany for having a wireless. The authorities are obviously suspicious for some reason, otherwise why did they single us out for a search? We might even get shot!'

Gunnar, however, had developed a routine which he did not want to change. Each evening at 7.30 pm he brought the wireless out from its hiding place and tuned in to the BBC's Norwegian Broadcast. The sinister four drum beats reminiscent of Beethoven's Fifth Symphony introduced the news and Gunnar relied on this link to what remained of the undefeated world. To be on the safe side, when they were listening, one of them always sat by the window with a clear view down the farm track to warn if any Germans were approaching.

'No, I want to keep it,' said Gunnar obstinately, 'and anyway don't call the Germans "the authorities". We mustn't think of them like that.'

Birgitta had to accept, albeit unhappily, that the wireless would stay where it was whether she liked it or not, but her worries remained.

Some months later on a dark January evening, when the landscape was covered with half a metre of crisp snow, Gunnar and his wife, together with their neighbours, Arne and Inga Petersen, were huddled round the wireless in the warmth of the kitchen. It was just after 7.30 pm. The BBC newsreader was reporting the shooting down of German bombers by the RAF over southern England when suddenly there was banging on the front door accompanied by shouted demands in German. No one had noticed the military vehicle approaching in the darkness with its lights off.

For a moment the two couples were frozen into horrified immobility. The Germans continued to bang apparently trying to break the door catch. In seconds they would be inside! Gunnar scooped up the wireless, ran through to the back bathroom, opened the window and dropped it into the snow against the outside wall of the house. In a panic Birgitta pushed the two floorboards back into place and pulled the mat over them just as two Germans broke in. One wore a black leather coat over civilian clothes and was accompanied by a junior officer, who was evidently there as an interpreter. The civilian sauntered up to Gunnar and stood unpleasantly close to him, staring into his eyes, while the interpreter translated the man's aggressive-sounding German.

'We will search your house. You know well what we are looking for.' This was not posed as a question but implied a statement of fact.

'What do you want?' Gunnar asked thickly, finding that his mouth had become curiously dry.

'We know you have a wireless,' the man retorted, and then the search began. The two couples were made to stand against the kitchen wall and had to watch while every cupboard was turned out and every room searched. Finally the junior officer pulled back the matting on the kitchen floor. It did not take him long to find the two loose boards and, on lifting them, he gave an exclamation of triumph when the space beneath was revealed. However, examination with a torch revealed nothing: the space was empty. The floor of every room and a shed outside were examined but nothing else untoward was found.

Clearly frustrated, the senior of the two men stood threateningly in front of Gunnar and, with his face only a few inches away, demanded to know why the boards were loose and what had been hidden there. To Gunnar's disgust a faint spray of spittle settled on his face as the man spoke.

At that instant Gunnar decided that a half-truth would be more likely to satisfy the Germans. He replied that when keeping a wireless was made illegal he had indeed hidden theirs in the space beneath the floorboards but after a short time, realising the risk of severe punishment, he had taken it out onto the fjord in the boat and had dropped it overboard which was why the space was now empty. The German, clearly angry, warned Gunnar that if he was found to be lying the consequences would be serious. To reinforce his threat he warned that Gunnar would no doubt understand what that would mean. The Germans then departed in their vehicle. As soon as they had gone the two couples slumped into chairs round the kitchen table, shocked by the experience.

Later that evening, after the Petersens had left, Birgitta wept out of fear and frustration. She felt helpless in a world dominated by men – men who started wars, who invaded other people's homes and men who decided whether a wireless was to be kept in spite of the danger it posed to their lives. In silence Gunnar looked out a screwdriver and hammer and repaired the twisted door bolt. It really was time to get rid of the wireless, but who had told the Germans about it? Their neighbours would surely not have indulged in careless talk about it but he and Birgitta, Bjorn and Lara were the only others who knew of it.

5

COMMANDOS PREPARE: 1940

For the British population, the war news had not been good. Six months previously, in the spring of 1940, Germany had invaded Denmark and Norway. The Norwegian collaborator, Vidkun Quisling, had been established as Norwegian head of state and a Nazi SS head of the police was appointed. Germany occupied most of Europe from Norway to the Spanish border, and now London was being bombed. Many people in Britain thought it only a matter of time before Britain itself was invaded, although RAF Fighter Command's success against the bomber fleets over southern England gave a glimmer of hope, and later that autumn the prospect of imminent invasion receded.

Erik's proficiency in spoken Norwegian had impressed the conscription interviewers and without having any idea for which branch of the services he was being interviewed he was ultimately assigned to a 'Special Services Unit'. Initially he was sent to a radio communication centre at Little Norwood in Buckinghamshire with instructions to report to a Major Arbuthnot. As soon as Erik arrived at the unit he was shown to the major's office. The major's lean frame and aquiline nose reminded Erik of a vigilant bird of prey, but, engagingly, he wore a monocle in his left eye and had a pleasantly informal manner. He pointed to a chair at the side of a large desk piled with files and documents behind which hung a picture of the King facing, on the opposite wall, a photograph of Winston Churchill. The major settled down to read through a file which, Eric assumed, was about himself. Once or twice the reader stopped, polished his monocle and peered thoughtfully at the young man in front of him, the silence broken only by the faint cawing of rooks in the elm trees outside. They reminded Erik of Sunday church in his boyhood days when commotion from the local rookery used to fill the minutes of quiet contemplation between prayers.

'Welcome to Norwood,' said Arbuthnot at last as he put down the papers. 'It's my job to explain that you have been selected to carry out a particularly important task. Your experience in radio communication and your ability to speak Norwegian, and indeed to look like a Norwegian, seem to have attracted the attention of the selectors.' The major paused and peered again at Erik.

'Tell me a bit about yourself; I gather that you are married – any children?

'Just a little boy called Neil, but I haven't even seen him yet. He is at my parents' house, with my wife'.

'It's good to have children,' replied Arbuthnot before getting down to the business in hand. 'Now, what I am going to tell you is strictly confidential and you must reveal it to no one whatsoever and you will remember that you are, of course, bound by the Official Secrets Act.'

The major looked again at Erik who, sensing that some kind of assent was expected, simply nodded.

The major went on: 'Churchill is worried about the massive build-up of German troops and shipping in Norway. We think their purpose is two-fold: first, to safeguard the supply of Swedish iron ore which is sent through Norway to Narvik and on by sea to Germany. Secondly we believe the Germans intend to gain control of the North Sea and Western Atlantic. Consequently we can expect major capital ships of the Kriegsmarine to show up in northern Norway at any time and they are likely to use bases there as springboards for attacks on Allied shipping. Any questions so far?'

'Only the obvious one; how can I help?' replied Erik.

Just then an attractive, young, uniformed secretary knocked and came in with two cups of tea and two digestive biscuits. She smiled at Erik, put the cups on the desk and took a tiny bowl of sugar from a shelf and put it beside the cups. Arbuthnot had stopped speaking and, after thanking her courteously, waited for her to leave before continuing.

'We need your technical and linguistic skills to help the Norwegian Resistance to organise radio transmissions from three centres in northern Norway. Come over here and look at the map.'

The major led Erik across to a brightly coloured wall map.

'These are the Lofoten Islands off the Norwegian coast, just above the Arctic Circle. Svolvaer on the Lofotens is the first of the three centres. Then there is Tromso 260 miles still further north and most important of all Alta, which is in the far north of the country on the edge of a region known as Finnmark. We want to know about all shipping movements but especially if German capital ships appear in Norwegian coastal waters. Your British radio contact will be the SIS, the Secret Intelligence Service, in England. The local Norwegian Resistance is already watching out for shipping movements but they need better radio equipment.'

Once again Major Arbuthnot paused and looked questioningly at Erik.

'I see a big problem,' ventured Erik. 'The distances involved will make transmissions from those northern parts of Norway difficult.'

'Exactly,' replied the major, 'and that's where you come in. We've a standard, compact and well-tried transmitter which weighs only nine pounds and has been designed to fit into a suitcase. It can be dropped by parachute to resistance personnel and is known as the "Whaddon Type III Mark II". It's currently being used successfully in Occupied Europe where the distances are not so great. Because it can be delivered by parachute it has acquired the name "Paraset". The trouble is that it has a limited power output with a range of only about 500 miles and agents using it in north Norway will be constrained by this. Alta, by the way, is well over 1,000 miles from Britain. Now, here is the interesting part – our boffins here in Little Norwood have developed a vitally important improvement. The provisional name given to this latest gadget is the "B2-Z". If it works as it should it will enable agents in northern Norway to communicate easily, in Morse of course, directly with SIS in Britain, which will allow us to react quickly to a German naval threat.'

`The major pushed back his chair, got up and sat on the corner of his desk.

'You will undergo initial training here on the use of these devices and later you'll be posted to Thame Park near Oxford where they specialise in wireless and coding. Once your technical training is complete you will be sent to HQ Commando Special Operations Centre run by Special Operations Executive or SOE at Inverailort Castle in the Scottish West Highlands. They train agents for covert operations. Finally you will be sent to Norway to do whatever's necessary to help the "Hjemmefronten", which is what they call the Resistance, to use the transmitters. We have reliable contacts in the three places which I mentioned. Of the three the most southerly is Svolvaer in the Lofoten Islands and we will get you there, but after that you will be on your own. Next is Tromso, 260 miles up the coast and, finally, Alta is 200 miles beyond that. Each contact will have received a receiver-transmitter by the time you arrive and your job will to ensure that they are familiar with the workings and can use it properly. Of the three centres Alta is considered the most important and it is likely that you will be there for an extended period.'

The major returned to his seat behind the desk.

'Now, let's have a short break to drink this tea, which is getting cold and, anyway, I need a smoke.'

Both the major and Erik enjoyed a ten-minute break during which they talked about things unrelated to the war. Erik found himself liking this eccentric officer and the two of them chatted about their shared interest in country pursuits, including Arbuthnot's love of fishing. He was proud of a twenty-pound salmon which he had caught in the River Awe in Argyll several years previously. At the end of the break they got back to business, continuing with the matter in hand. After a further half hour the major stubbed out his 'Abdullah' and got up.

'Now, that's all we have time for today,' he said, 'but in five weeks you will be posted to Inverailort Castle. I have to tell you that the training there will be tough – seriously tough. I want us to have another meeting here in three days' time to tell you some more details about your mission.'

Three days later at the second meeting Arbuthnot told

Erik how to contact the three members of the Norwegian Resistance whose reliability was assured. Erik was intrigued the hear that there was to be a top secret raid on the Lofoten Islands, of which he would be part, and that he would remain behind once the raiders withdrew. The major emphasised that should the battleships *Bismarck* and *Tirpitz*, or the battle cruisers *Scharnhorst*, *Gneisenau* and *Prinz Eugen* among others succeed in breaking out from Keil into the North Sea and from there into the Atlantic, they would pose a deadly threat to Britain's shipping lifeline. Erik was left in no doubt of the importance of the assignment or the nature and extent of the risks that he would run. The major finished by telling him that he must be able to recognise the German ships which he had mentioned as well as some others and that he would be given silhouette pictures of the vessels to commit to memory.

Finally, on a sombre note, he was told that if he was caught he should not expect to survive, and he left the meeting in a pensive mood. On one hand he was stimulated at being a key figure in the plan, but was also troubled by thoughts of what would happen to his young wife and baby son should he die. Quite apart from that he admitted to himself that he was also a little afraid: the whole thing seemed a dangerous undertaking.

*

On a cold October day in 1940 a chilly wind blew along the platform at Fort William in the Scottish West Highlands. Soldiers in a variety of uniforms surrounded by heaps of kitbags waited for the train to take them on the thirty-mile journey westwards to Lochailort at the head of a remote sea loch. It was a journey that Erik on his annual holidays as a boy had made many times and he knew each sweep of the single-track railway as it wove its way amongst rocks and stunted oak woods, and which now and then gave way to long views out across sea lochs. Things were very different now and on the drab wartime station platform he had time to reflect on those holidays when, from the age of ten, his parents had taken him to stay with friends at Arisaig House a few miles beyond Lochailort. For a boy the journey was always thrilling with the prospect of a fortnight's exploration of the burns and hill lochs of the Highland estate: it was always an adventure and on calm days he and his father used to row out among the islands of the sea loch to fish for mackerel. He remembered a time when the estate workers had 'splash netted' the mouth of the little river which ran through the home policies. Using a rowing boat, they had stretched a net across the river mouth while several men waded down the lower part of the river, stamping and splashing with sticks as they went. Nearly two dozen silver sea trout trying to escape back to the sea had ended up in the net, but the real prize was a beautiful six-pound salmon which thrashed about on the bottom boards of the boat until it was despatched by the farm manager.

Erik was jolted back to reality as a fellow soldier brushed past him, heaving a large kitbag. Those idyllic days were behind him and in 1940, with the war in its second year, life had assumed a grimmer aspect. He knew that Arisaig House with its beautiful gardens had been taken over by the military authorities for Special Operations Executive training and his destination, Inverailort Castle, was being used as a base for commando training.

The train, pulled by a venerable locomotive, belched

clouds of black smoke and steam as it pulled out of Fort William station. The compartments were packed with jostling soldiers with rifles and kitbags and Erik had been lucky to squeeze into a window seat. He had already met some of the men on the long train journey up from London and a good camaraderie quickly developed, as most of the troops were assigned to what they called 'special ops'. Most were destined for training at Inverailort, but two were going on to Arisaig. Despite their varying backgrounds the men were already beginning to feel a sense of togetherness and most of them keenly anticipated their forthcoming training. Cheerful banter filled the smoky fug of the compartments and the inside of the windows streamed with condensation.

'Where are you from, mate?' enquired Erik's seated neighbour, offering him a Woodbine from a crumpled packet.

'Surrey,' he replied, 'near Chiddingfold.'

'That's a posh area, innit? I'm Bert by the way, from East London.'

Later, Erik heard that Bert's home near the docks had been destroyed by a bomb which had killed his young wife when he was away, and he was desperate to wreak vengeance on the Germans.

Surprisingly it transpired that most of the men were from London and the south east of England. In civilian life some had been artisans: plumbers, joiners and builders' labourers, but there were also clerks and university students among whom, oddly, was a second year theology student from Cambridge.

A lively discussion ensued about where, ultimately, they would be sent. Some thought it would be France while others reckoned on Norway though only Erik knew for certain that Norway was, indeed, their destination.

'At least we've got a padre with us to pray if things get tough,' remarked Bert, pointing with his Woodbine at Ronald Smith, the divinity student.

'You're well past praying for, Bert. I bet the Lord doesn't even know you,' came the quick reply through the thickening smoke and chatter. Erik found himself enjoying the lively company of these straightforward men. Their sometimes coarse directness and openness appealed to him and provided a welcome contrast to the secret nature of his own status. Besides, they took his mind away from the disturbing thoughts which he had been having since Major Arbuthnot's warning of the certainty of being shot if the Germans caught him. Erik was musing about this as the train pulled out of the station when his wandering mind was brought back to the present by a dig in the ribs from Bert.

'Hey, I was talking to you! You've been daydreaming.'

★

As soon as the train left the station and picked up speed horizontal streaks of rain on the windows partially obscured the view, but, through the billowing clouds of engine smoke, Erik could still glimpse the familiar West Highland hills: Loch Eil, the sea loch, on the left and the tawny-coloured mountains streaked with cascading burns on the right. After half an hour the train passed along the shores of Loch Eilt, a beautiful freshwater loch, where, aged fourteen, he had caught a sea trout of nearly ten pounds on a fly that he had made himself especially for that year's holiday. Just beyond some small islands topped with pine trees the loch narrowed as the current pulled away to form the River Ailort. The autumn rains had transformed the river into a peat-stained torrent which went charging down the glen. Together the railway and the river, never far from each other, led ultimately to Lochailort.

The station was little more than a platform and small waiting room. At the head of the sea loch, the castle, grim and forbidding, crouched beneath the shoulder of a mountain, its towers and turrets the fantasies of some long-dead architect. As soon as the train stopped, the men crowded to the doors, threw out kitbags and gathered into a chattering crowd on the platform. Almost at once a burly sergeant-major brought order with a bellowed command. He wasted no time in telling the men that for the next month or two they were in for a tough time and then he formed them up and marched them out of the station, past the local inn, across the River Ailort on a wooden-decked bridge and on down to the castle.

As the ranks of marching men approached it, the grey building was momentarily lit by a shaft of sunlight but the trees behind it still huddled round in a gloomy backdrop. In normal times and in good weather it might have looked impressive but now an ugly rash of military tents and Nissen huts in front of the castle destroyed any such pretensions. Beneath the turreted façade the driveway widened into a sweep of grey gravel where four camouflage-painted Bedford lorries were being unloaded by a group of soldiers and, near the massive oak front door, stood a pair of army staff cars.

Once the new arrivals had gathered, an officer emerged from the front entrance. He was a tall, striking figure in a kilt and wielding a swagger cane. Lord Lovat, in his capacity of Commanding Officer, welcomed the newcomers to Inverailort and to the Special Forces' training course which, he said, would be demanding. He stressed that standards were high and the recruits would be required to learn a new approach to warfare with emphasis on skills involved in personal combat and physical fitness. He said that they were going to make a special contribution to attacks on German forces by unconventional means and followed this with details of their forthcoming period of training. It was going to be arduous and clearly they were in for a tough time. With that the new arrivals were dismissed and directed to their billets in the Nissen huts.

Erik reflected how different things had become: as a boy, he had once been invited over from Arisaig House for afternoon tea at Inverailort. The castle looked darker now, though perhaps that was just part of the gloominess of wartime which seemed to pervade most aspects of life.

The weeks spent training at Inverailort brought the men to a peak of physical fitness under the watchful eyes of two tough field instructors, Major Bill Fairbairn and Captain Eric Sykes, who specialised in personal close combat. The extreme regime included a weekly training run up the steep slopes of An Stac, a nearby 2,500-foot mountain. The rugged and wild terrain of the area was well suited for training across all manner of assault courses and deep river crossings, which had to be mastered in full kit under fire from live ammunition. Seaborne assaults from landing craft and small boats were practised by both day and night. German light weapons such as the Schmeisser MP40 9mm machine pistol were provided until live firing of these became second nature. The recruits spent many unprotected cold and wet nights in the mountains navigating between set points and often suffering unexpected training ambushes. It was hard going.

Erik surprised himself by enjoying this unremitting regime and none of the men proved unequal to its rigours. Morale, camaraderie and general fitness improved the harder the men were pushed; they vied with each other in achieving peaks of toughness and came to feel invincible.

One of the field instructors, Donald Cameron, a head stalker from an estate in Wester Ross, specialised in personal concealment and the use of cover in open country. He used red deer far up in the mountain corries as the enemy and demonstrated how to approach them unheard and unseen.

As a boy Erik had been stalking on several occasions and the principles of concealment were familiar enough to him. Many years had passed since his last day out with the Arisaig Estate stalker, and he relished the idea of a whole day on the hill with Donald. It would be a welcome break from the usual training routine. It was a clear crisp December day when Donald took Erik with his rifle up the mountain behind the castle to stalk hinds.

'You'll ken hinds are much mair canny than the stags at this time o' year,' said Donald, 'and they're difficult tae get close tae. Not that we are actually going to shoot onything anyway. The laird would be fair scunnert if he heard the military'd been killing his beasts so you'd better just stick to Gairmans!'

Donald led the way up the steep hillside using the shallow ravine of a burn as cover. Several times Erik's legs sank into patches of bog covered with a solid looking blanket of green sphagnum moss. Then, to avoid being scented by the hinds, the pair swung east to allow an up-wind approach to any beasts that they might encounter. After a further half an hour they were near the top and a fine view opened up over the sea loch. The Island of Eigg lay far out near the horizon with its unmistakable 'Sgurr,' a massive block of protruding pitchstone, and away to the right were the mountains of the Island of Rum. Donald took his telescope from its leather case and, lying on his back, rested it on a raised knee. Apart from the sound of innumerable rushing burns there was complete silence while he scanned the slopes. Erik could see no sign of deer on the mountain slopes or in the high corries.

'There's a party o' hinds below that far cliff wi' a stag among them,' said Donald quietly. 'He's lying down but I can just see his points above a rock. The hinds are grazing, so they are, but they'll be canny and difficult to stalk.'

'Where? I can't see them,' replied Erik.

'Take my glass and hae a look just below that small cliff, yonder.'

Erik lay back and rested the telescope on his raised right knee. When he examined the slope below the rock face the grazing hinds suddenly came into view as they occasionally lifted their heads to look for danger.

Using all the guile of a professional stalker, Donald led the way, crawling out of sight in dead ground and along burns. As they crept around a hill loch Erik noticed a stone circle, five feet in diameter, set flat into the short turf, in the centre of which lay a cross fashioned with elongated rocks.

'I've always wondered who put that there,' whispered Donald.

Half an hour later, they were within fifty yards of the hinds. Donald handed the rifle to Erik, who edged himself forward and eased into a firing position. He slipped the rubber cover off the muzzle and selected a hind which had become suspicious. Her head was up and her long ears were pricked as she stared directly at them. With the rifle's open sights trained on the heart Erik gently squeezed the trigger. That hind never knew how lucky she was. The click of the empty weapon made her wheel round and, coughing with alarm, she and the rest of the beasts careered round the hillside and out of sight.

That day for Erik was like being on holiday. Donald was more than satisfied with his fieldcraft and Erik had enjoyed the well-earned break from routine training. He reflected that, before long, there might well be a German soldier in his sights rather than a deer. A distant target would not be so bad but he imagined that it would be difficult if he could see the face of the German as he killed him. However, Erik knew perfectly well that his present training at Inverailort was designed to dispel such thoughts and to train him to kill without hesitation.

6

THE NORTH ATLANTIC: 1941

The spring weather had been foul. Heavy snowfalls blocked roads in northern Britain, schools were shut down and conditions on the Orkney Islands were even worse. On February 21st, the commando troop ships, HMS *Queen Emma* and HMS *Princess Beatrix*, with an escort of five destroyers towing windblown streamers of black smoke, left Scapa Flow accompanied by squalls of sleet, and set course for the Faroe Islands. There the Special Service Battalions would receive final training and be re-designated No. 3 and 4 Commando. 'Operation Claymore' would be a surprise attack on installations in the Lofoten Islands off the coast of occupied Norway. Svolvaer, the island capital and a focus of fish oil production, through which the Germans obtained ingredients for explosives, was singled out for destruction. The plans included a simultaneous attack on Henningsvaer, another key Lofoten port.

In Britain, the war news had been almost unremittingly bad until the population's spirits were lifted by more RAF successes against the Luftwaffe in the skies of southern England. Winston Churchill, in an effort to maintain morale, was adamant that Britain must attack the Germans wherever possible.

Erik came up on deck of HMS *Princess Beatrix* as she

approached the Faroes. The sea was breaking white against the rocks and cliffs of the islands, and the summits of the craggy hills were lost in dense, drifting cloud. Erik gazed at the desolate landscape but could see no sign of human habitation and, as he watched the rhythmic surge of waves slamming into a rocky headland, he wondered how people could spend their lives in such a place. Shortly afterwards, watched by a small crowd of locals, the two ships docked at Torshaven. The people there were welcoming even though Britain had not been invited to occupy their islands, the decision to do so having been taken when Denmark and Norway were invaded.

The two commando groups spent nine days on the islands participating in last-minute training for the forthcoming attack. The landscape reminded Erik of some of Scotland's Hebridean Islands, but there was little time to appreciate the wild beauty given the intensity of preparations. Bert from London's East End thought it was a godforsaken place, 'Like the end of the world,' he said. Erik was cheered to find a number of Norwegian sailors among the crews of the two ships with whom he could chat easily in their own language.

At last, on March 1st, the ships and escorts set off on the final leg of the voyage to the Lofotens. It did not take long for the vessels to move out of the shelter of the Faroes and soon the full force of a North Atlantic gale hit them and all loose equipment had to be lashed down. The three-day journey was, for Erik and many of the troops, a misery of seasickness as the weather worsened, making it impossible to go on deck. With a sickening repetitive rhythm, the ships' bows burrowed deep into huge waves, shedding seething white water as they rose to meet the next onslaught. For many of the men the journey was an ordeal and for some it was impossible to keep any food down.

By the time that darkness fell on the third day the seas had calmed. Ammunition and equipment were checked and the landing was scheduled for the early hours of the following morning. The lights of Svolvaer were clearly visible as HMS *Princess Beatrix* together with two of the destroyers rounded a headland and began to close in on the port. It was clear that the Germans were not expecting an attack, and on the way in one of the destroyers stopped and boarded the *Krebs,* an unsuspecting German trawler.

Half a mile from the landing point Erik and the rest of the troops were transferred into landing craft. The passage to the shore was rough and as ice-cold spray lashed over them many said a silent prayer for their safety. Despite the apparent lack of German activity the men were far from sure that their arrival would be unopposed.

The landing craft headed for a small beach beside the port and as the troops stumbled out with weapons at the ready they found that the beach was frozen like concrete under their boots. Erik, bitterly cold, found that his spray-drenched outer clothing had frozen on his back and it crackled like eggshell when he moved, but he was grateful to be active again. Parties of commandos fanned out through the port as they made their way to their objectives, the main target being the fish oil factory. Almost at once groups of Germans taken by surprise were rounded up and placed under guard while sappers laid demolition charges in key buildings and in the fish oil factory itself. There was no organised resistance and not a shot was fired. Parties of commandos moved through the town, their previous studies of the street plans leading to rapid control of the enemy garrison.

Erik, following his instructions, made his way to the main harbour, passing groups of commandos on the way, some herding German prisoners before them. Local residents watched from doorways, some shouting a welcome to the unexpected visitors, and some just staring, bewildered by the sudden activity. Erik hurried round the waterfront and found his objective: a narrow footbridge leading to a small rocky islet where four fishing boats were moored. According to his briefing *Nordfisk* should be among them. Just as he was crossing the footbridge, the demolition charges at the fish oil factory went off in a series of jarring explosions followed by flocks of gulls shrieking in alarm and a pall of acrid smoke. When he reached the boats, all four were deserted and there was no sign of the name *Nordfisk* on any of them, but one, an elderly boat about 40 feet long with a varnished wooden hull, had the correct registration number, S-150S, painted near the bow. The boat's general features left no doubt that this was indeed the *Nordfisk*. His briefing had confirmed that the skipper, Olav Birklund, a fisherman, was a reliable 'jossing' or Norwegian patriot and was to be the first of his Resistance contacts. Erik climbed onto a small concrete jetty built into the rock where *Nordfisk* was moored and stepped onto her deck, which was covered with a clutter of fishing lines, floats and general paraphernalia. Clearly the boat was a working fishing vessel, but there was no sign of anyone on board.

Sporadic shouts of the commandos still came from the town and were accompanied by an occasional burst of cheering from local Norwegians as more Germans were rounded up, along with a number of Norwegian collaborators, all of whom were herded down to the main harbour. Evidently the raid had succeeded in taking the garrison by surprise. Erik stepped off *Nordfisk* and made his way back along the narrow walkway when a man emerged from a wooden house thirty metres away. His demeanour was not friendly as he asked Erik what he was doing on his boat.

'I'm looking for Olav Birklund,' replied Erik.

'That's me,' said the man.

'I'm Erik Knudsen,' replied Erik, using his assumed name for the first time. 'I think you are expecting me.'

'I am not expecting anyone. What do you want?'

'Perhaps you know Axel Porsanger,' suggested Erik. The man's expression changed as soon as this fictitious name supplied by the British Secret Service was mentioned.

'Come inside quickly,' he said, ushering Erik into the house and through to a low-ceilinged room with wood-lined walls, dark with varnish. Bric-a-brac connected with the sea lay on every flat surface: coloured glass floats, models of boats and one or two large metal fish lures with enormous hooks. On the wall hung a painting of the *Nordfisk* in a choppy sea.

Erik knew that his contact was an established member of the 'Hjemmefronten' who, for six months, had been supplying information to the British using a wireless transmitter hidden on his boat. He had sent details of German shipping movements and had reported the strength of the German garrison at Svolvaer. His code name was 'Rev', the Norwegian for 'fox', and his immediate task was to transform Erik into a typical Lofoten fisherman with forged identity papers in the name of Erik Knudsen, which had already been obtained from a trustworthy source. An hour later Erik did, indeed, look like a genuine fisherman in old clothes appropriately smelling of fish and wearing a wool sweater ragged with holes while his discarded military apparel, boots and underwear smouldered in the living room stove. If, by chance he was searched, no trace of his British origin would be found. In a wallet were personal details including a tattered photo of his fictitious late wife outside their home in a fishing village near Hammerfest in the far north of Norway. Olaf Birklund also handed Erik a membership card for the pro-Nazi Nasjonal Samling party and had already clipped to it one of the two photographs which Erik had brought with him.

'If you are stopped and searched, this card might help as members of the NS Party receive favourable treatment from the Germans,' he explained.

Erik's transformation was complete. So far all had gone to plan. The details of life in his home village in north Norway had been imprinted into his brain before leaving Britain. His wife had died of tuberculosis two years ago and since then he had taken odd jobs aboard fishing vessels. There had been no children. He had little interest in politics but, if questioned, he would admit to some sympathy with the German cause if only because the Germans seemed to be winning the war. The reality was very different. His primary task was to link with agents as far north-east as Alta and to ensure that they were familiar with the new Paraset transmitters. The Alta resistance group had unaccountably ceased transmissions two months previously and it seemed possible that it had been infiltrated by the Germans and the members arrested, or worse.

During his training Erik had spent many hours learning to recognise the silhouettes of German battleships and cruisers, including the *Tirpitz, Bismarck, Scharnhorst, Gneisenau, Admiral Scheer, Lützow,* the *Hipper* and *Prinz*

Eugen. He fully understood that his reports and those of his Resistance colleagues were to concentrate specifically on the movements of these ships which could pose such a serious threat to British shipping if they appeared along the north Norwegian coast.

★

The danger of detection and arrest would be ever present. He would be able to trust few people as even those sympathetic to his cause might indulge in idle talk which could reach the ears of the Norwegian police or even the Germans themselves. The great majority of the population were strongly opposed to the German invaders, but a few were passively pro-Nazi. Most dangerous of all was the small number who were members of the collaborating Nasjonal Samling Party.

Erik spent that first day hiding and resting in the house. As the day wore on the town became quieter and Birklund went out to see what was happening. He returned at four with the news that the British raiders were departing, taking with them over 100 German prisoners, some Norwegian volunteers and a number of known Norwegian collaborators. In the darkness of that evening the British raiders re-embarked and silence enveloped the town as the inhabitants waited apprehensively for the inevitable reappearance of German troops. When reinforcements finally arrived by sea twenty-four hours later German military control was quickly re-established and a curfew was announced.

7

THE AFFAIR BEGINS

Two hundred miles away at the Olderdalen store, news of the Lofoten raid was picked up on the Larsens' illegal wireless set. Hans was delighted at the news.

'This is only a start,' he said to Hilder. 'I think that the English will invade sooner or later. Even though that may not be for some time the Germans will, in the end, be thrown out and I expect that there will be more raids to come.'

'That's all the more reason not to do anything rash now,' replied Hilder, his ever cautious wife. 'We must make sure that we survive, because if Norwegians start to kill Germans it is all too obvious what the reaction will be.'

At that point Lara came down from her room and joined the discussion round the kitchen table. She had heard the news of the attack with oddly mixed feelings: her mind was in a state of confusion. Of course she was patriotic and wished that the Occupation would end, but she had met a number of charming and polite Germans at the store. She could not imagine that killing them would be desirable. The very first officer whom she had met there, the one who had bought a piece of stokfisk, had become a frequent customer and every week Lara found herself looking forward to his visits. He was unfailingly courteous and she found herself admiring his athletic-looking figure in the smart uniform. He had very fair hair and a kindly face with little wrinkles round his eyes as though he smiled and laughed a lot. His Norwegian was better than it had at first seemed and the two of them could almost chat together, although he always stopped whenever any local customers came in. She understood why he did this and was grateful to him. He seemed so sensitive and cultured. One day he had come in when the store was quiet and he clearly wanted to chat to her. He told her that his name was Willi Schmidt and that he had been studying law before joining the Wehrmacht in 1938. Shyly, he explained that he loved nature and was an amateur botanist. The word 'botany' was difficult for Lara and she did not know what he meant until he went over to the window where there was a potted plant and pointed to it and then to some yellow coltsfoot flowers which were beginning to push through the gravel outside.

'Each summer before the war,' he said, 'I used to go to the Black Forest for two weeks to look for some of the rare plants which grow there, especially the mysterious ghost orchids. Although they are not beautiful in a showy way, they are interesting plants.'

Lara was disturbed by her feelings for this German officer. Of course he was an enemy, but once or twice she found herself daydreaming rather than attending to her duties in the store and Hilder had to remind her to get on with restocking the shelves with some of the scanty German tinned produce which had just arrived.

Gradually spring returned and the days lengthened. The little birch wood behind the store burst into a mist of pale green leaves and, on calm evenings, their sweet smell drifted into the open windows. The fjord no longer looked grey and, on calm days, the snow-topped mountains cast their inverted reflections onto the glassy surface.

Lara had not seen her parents for nearly four months and, one morning in May, on one of her days off, she decided to make the journey home. She wheeled out her bicycle, pumped up its tyres and set off along the gravel road beside the fjord. The view and scents of spring made her feel how good it was to be alive. Yellow flowers dotted the grey gravel at the edge of the road, and on the hillsides a flush of green was replacing last summer's withered grass. Summer migrant birds were returning and she could hear the sweet piping of willow warblers in the birch thickets. High up above her head against the azure sky a solitary buzzard circled on motionless, outspread wings, its mournful mewing just audible above the steady crunch of the bicycle tyres on the gravel.

To Lara everything in the world seemed perfect, except when she thought about the Occupation. As if to remind her of it, an open-backed military vehicle passed her and the seated soldiers wolf-whistled and waved. She tried to keep her eyes on the road in front but could not resist glancing up at the departing vehicle. Through the dust raised by its passing, she could see the young men who looked so fine and... even friendly. Before the Germans came she had never in her life been so close to so many vigorous looking young males and she was aware of a curious stirring within her. Although she had long been friendly with twenty-one-year-old Lars Anders and his younger brother Kristian, no emotional attachment had developed. The family, being neighbours, knew her mother and father well and she liked the Anders boys in the way that one likes brothers. They both had chestnut dark hair, and were not bad-looking. She was still mulling over these thoughts by the time she had almost reached home. She passed a boat secured to a small jetty, and up the slope on the other side of the road stood Arne and Inga Petersen's house. She had always thought it a rather grand building for the locality with its balustraded balcony above the front door and its downstairs astragalled windows. In a distant field she could just make out one of the twin boys working on a fence. Was it Per or Pal? She could never tell them apart even when she was close to them. She rode on, and, in ten minutes, she arrived at the turning to her own home.

She rode up the bumpy track running alongside the little river which served the family so well with its annual supply of salmon. She pushed the bike up the hill and, on reaching the house, laid it on the ground and pushed the front door open, calling out as she went inside. Her parents, seated at the kitchen table, broke off what seemed to be a serious conversation.

'Oh, what a lovely surprise: we weren't expecting you, but how wonderful to see you!' exclaimed her mother. 'You do look well. Come and sit down and tell us all about everything and then I'll get you something to eat.'

Lara gave her father a hug and commented that he looked thinner than when she had last seen him.

'It is the wartime diet,' he said, 'No one really has enough food though we are lucky here.'

'What were you discussing when I walked in?' she asked.

'It's your brother,' said her father. 'I'm worried about him. The bus driver who comes from Svolvaer told me that Bjorn is getting very friendly with the Germans and a rumour is going around that he wants to join the Nasjonal Samling Party. If he does, it would make him a collaborator.'

Later on, she joined her parents in a meal of vegetable soup and bread and afterwards went outside to think about things. The farm looked the same as ever and Sigil, the milk cow, lay on the fresh grass contentedly chewing the cud. Lara loved the sense of permanence and security of her home in a world that seemed to be changing so dramatically. The sun shone on the fjord and on the distant glaciers in the mountains. The waterfall beside the farm looked a bit smaller than usual owing to the dry spring but otherwise nothing much had changed.

As she wandered about the flowered meadows she decided that from now on she had better discourage Willi's friendliness or, indeed, familiarity with any other German who came to the store. She didn't want to be called a collaborator. She had been alarmed to hear that her brother was getting so friendly with the Germans. What had got into him? On the other hand it certainly looked as though the Germans were winning the war and might stay permanently in Norway. If that was the case, perhaps it did make sense to accept them and to work constructively with them. But then that was collaboration, wasn't it? Oh dear, she did not know what to think. It was all so confusing.

8

WILLI SCHMIDT

Two weeks later, in June 1941, Lara decided that the days were light enough for her to live at home again and to use her bicycle to travel to the store each day. Twice Willi had come in to the store recently, ostensibly to buy some small item, and Lara tried to serve him as dispassionately as possible but knew that her face flushed when he spoke to her. She was aware that he looked at her wonderingly at such times and, when it happened, she tried to turn away to some invented task.

Things came to a head one day when she was cycling along the fjord on her way home after work. As she rode over some loose gravel she was startled by a loud bang as the rear tyre burst. The steady rhythm of the wheels on the road changed to a jolting ride and she got off to inspect the damage. The tyre was certainly flat and only then did she realise that the puncture mending kit was not in her small leather saddle-bag. She turned the bike upside down and wondered what to do as it was another seven or eight kilometres to her parents' house. The road was quiet at that time of day and only two German lorries sped past but did not stop. She sat down on a patch of grass and waited to see if any locals would stop to help her. Presently, she heard a motor engine in the distance and from round a bend appeared a German staff car followed by a military motorcycle. Unusually, the car driver was the sole occupant. On seeing Lara beside the road the driver followed by the motorcycle drew up alongside. Only then did she notice with a start that the driver was Willi, 'her' German officer.

'Hello, Lara!' he said in surprise, evidently having found out her name from the store. 'You have a problem?' and not knowing the Norwegian word for a puncture he added, 'Your bicycle it is unwell?'

'It's all right. I don't need help,' replied Lara mindful of her earlier decision not to talk to Germans, unless it was absolutely necessary.

'I think you do need help. You have long way to go?'

There was a silence as Lara pondered before answering. Unaccountably she felt her lower lip beginning to tremble, which she knew was a sign that tears were on the way. Yes, of course she needed help but, not from a German. She didn't even want to be seen with one of them. She looked up at Willi, who seemed so concerned for her and she shook her head. For a moment she was unable to speak, and a tear rolled down her cheek. She wiped it away in annoyance but Willi had noticed and placed a comforting hand on her shoulder. Angrily she shrugged it off. The motorcyclist, still astride his machine, watched impassively from a short distance away. The silence between the pair was interrupted only by soft mewing of eider ducks at the nearby fjord. Suddenly Willi strode forward and, picking up the bicycle, carried it across to the car and dumped it on the open rear space.

'Come.' he ordered. 'I will take you wherever you want to go. Get in.'

It seemed to Lara that this was an order rather than an

invitation, but should she get in? Willi was already standing at the passenger door which he held open for her, a kindly smile on his face. He was one of the hated Germans but, on the other hand, he was so kind and was obviously trying to help her and she certainly did not hate him. Reluctantly she climbed in while Willi went round to the driver's side, reached beneath the seat and produced a German army forage cap.

'Put it on,' he ordered, and Lara did as she was told.

As they set off towards her parents' farm, she tucked her hair into the cap admitting to herself that its real purpose was to hide her identity. Fortunately, on the way, they did not meet any locals and soon, after passing the Petersens' farm, she asked Willi to let her out as she would like to walk the rest of the way pushing the bicycle. The last thing she wanted was for her parents to see her in the company of a German. Her father, especially, would certainly be angry and would not understand her explanation. As she wheeled the bicycle up the farm track she saw her father coming down to meet her and was thankful that he had not seen her getting out of a Wehrmacht vehicle.

Lara found it oddly difficult to settle back at home with her parents. She knew that she was becoming moody and that only made her cross with herself as she realised that her moodiness affected them and she had no wish to bring unhappiness into the home. However, thoughts of Willi kept coming unbidden into her mind in spite of all she could do. It happened especially at night when the house was quiet and she was alone, alone in her bed. She had never felt anything like this before. Sometimes, in the privacy of her room she imagined that he was there with her and then, with a gathering momentum of their own, her thoughts burst into the most intense physical sensations that she had ever experienced. The next day she would be filled with a sense of shame, but as the days and nights passed the thoughts became a longing, a yearning to see him again.

A week or two later, she was working in the store when the Larsens had gone out to meet the supply ship and the shop was quiet. Presently, a German lorry stopped and four soldiers came in. They wandered round the store but only bought one bottle of akavit before leaving. Then a German staff car drew up on the gravel. Lara, looking out of the window, saw an officer getting out, leaving the driver in the vehicle. Her heart seemed to stop as she saw the familiar tall figure saying something to the driver before walking towards the store entrance. By the time the door opened her heart was pounding in her chest and she felt the familiar embarrassing flush coming to her face. Then Willi stood in front of her, beautiful handsome Willi, with his gentle smile and laughter lines round his eyes.

'Oh, hello!' was all that Lara could think of saying.

'Hello. It is good to see you and how is your bicycle?' enquired Willi in his oddly phrased Norwegian. There followed a few minutes of self-conscious conversation then the German, who had not been able to get thoughts of Lara out of his mind, experienced a sudden desire for this beautiful dark-eyed Norwegian girl. Putting his thoughts aside he asked if she had any more of the stokfisk which he had once bought from her. He really did not need any more of the dried fish but it seemed a reasonable excuse to go on chatting. Lara turned to go into the inner store room to fetch what he wanted, aware that Willi had followed her in. The store room was a secluded place and once inside they turned to face each other. It was the moment when they looked into each other's eyes that any pretence of indifference vanished and the mutual attraction which welled up was obvious to both. Willi held out his arms and Lara almost collapsed into them. His embrace gently tightened as she reached up and encircled his neck with her arms. She gazed up at his face as he bent forward tenderly kissing her on the lips. Low down she felt the masculine firmness of his body pressing against her own and his tongue gently explored between her lips. Somewhere deep inside her a spasm of desire blossomed like an opening flower.

'Oh, Lara,' murmured Willi.

The ecstasy of the moment was cruelly interrupted by jangling of the entrance doorbell as it shook on its spring mounting. The couple, taken by surprise as there had been no sound of a vehicle arriving, quickly stepped apart and Lara, flushed and breathless from the encounter, hurried through to serve the customer. It turned out to be her parents' neighbour, Nils Anders, who had borrowed old Leif Jessen's Icelandic pony to visit the store. For some reason Nils always seemed to be so concerned for her and interested in what she was doing.

'Hello, Lara. How are you getting on?' he enquired, glancing through the window at the waiting car outside. 'I see that you have a German customer today.'

Lara busied herself at the counter, arranging things, to control her sense of panic.

'I'm well, thank you,' she replied, acutely conscious of Willi still in the store room as she went over and shut the door. She was terrified that he might appear and that Nils would realise what had been going on. She was unable to think clearly. What should she do? Her hands trembled as she felt perspiration forming on her forehead.

'Are you sure you are feeling all right?' enquired Nils, noticing her anxiety. 'When I arrived there was just a driver waiting outside in the vehicle. I hope that you are not having trouble from the Germans?'

Before she could answer, the stockroom door opened and Willi emerged carrying what looked like all the stokfisk that was in the store. Ignoring Nils he brusquely dumped the armful on the counter.

'I have selected these,' he said curtly to Lara in a formal tone without any suggestion of familiarity. 'How much to pay?'

Lara, thankful for the subterfuge, counted the pieces of fish and duly received the correct money whereupon Willi left without further comment. The door-bell jangled again as he walked out and Nils gazed wonderingly at the departing vehicle.

'The officers' mess must be fond of our Norwegian delicacy. He has bought enough to feed dozens of people. Why did you shut the door back there when he was inside?' There followed a short silence as Nils glanced at Lara's face.

'Are you quite sure that he hasn't been causing you trouble?'

'No, no,' she protested but she did not try to explain her actions.

She had always felt quite close to Nils but nothing could make her even hint to him what had happened in the store room.

9

SVOLVAER. NORDFISK HEADS NORTH

Four days after the British raid on Svolvaer, Olav Birklund began preparing *Nordfisk* for sea. Fishing was not the only reason for sailing. As a member of the Resistance he had to take Erik to Tromso to meet his next contact. After the raiders had departed he had been surprised to find that a suitcase containing what turned out to be a Paraset B2-Z transmitter-receiver had, without explanation, been left on *Nordfisk*. Erik remained hidden at Olav's house following the raid and used the four days to explain to his host the detailed workings of the set and how to contact SIS in Britain. He made sure that Olav was confident in its operation before explaining the codes and single use ciphers which, for ease of concealment in clothing, were printed on silk. The ciphers used a very secure system based on poems and once each line had been used it was torn off and destroyed.

'As you can see,' said Erik, 'the B2-Z is comparatively heavy, so you'll have to think carefully where to hide it here in Svolvaer.'

On the day of departure Erik boarded *Nordfisk* along with Ivan, Olav's longstanding fishing partner, whose ancestors had been traders from Archangel in Russia. Ivan was a tough individual who, despite having lost three fingers of his right hand, could still repair any machinery to do with boats. He would never admit his age, perhaps because he didn't know it, but looked well into his seventies. At noon they cast off and slowly moved out of the harbour. Even after four days a haze of smoke and a smell of burning from the destroyed factory still hung over the town but Erik was grateful to be out of doors again after being cooped up in Olav's cramped house for so long.

He stood outside the wheelhouse taking a last look at the town while the boat chugged past the wooden piles of the harbour. A group of locals idling on the outer harbour wall were watching a boy pulling up small fish with a hand line. They looked down at *Nordfisk* as it passed, but when Erik glanced up at the faces, his heart seemed to miss a beat. One of the watchers was a young fellow of about his own age whose face was joltingly familiar. As *Nordfisk* drew away their eyes locked in recognition. There was no doubt about it. It was his Norwegian cousin and boyhood playmate from Lyngenfjord. Bjorn Torkelsen of all people! An expression of amazement came over Bjorn's face as he raised a hand to wave but he then hesitated as though unsure of himself before lowering it again to his side. He continued to gaze at the departing boat but by that time Erik had turned his face away and had quickly stepped out of sight into the wheelhouse.

The last thing that Erik wanted was to be recognised but the likelihood of coming across Bjorn, or any other of his Norwegian relatives, had seemed impossibly remote. However, he was virtually certain that he had indeed been recognised. If Bjorn talked about the sighting and the Germans got to hear about it and if they realised that a British agent had just sailed out of Svolvaer a massive hunt would follow. If he was caught Erik knew only too well what his fate would be; it was not a good start.

Erik was deeply disturbed by the event at the harbour. He hoped that his cousin would have the sense to keep the incident to himself, but he knew that Bjorn was an impulsive and sometimes intemperate individual. He told Olav that he had almost certainly been recognised and once again reminded himself that he was simply a deckhand who worked on boats around the coast. At least he had convincing papers in his assumed name of Erik Knudsen which had been produced for him in Svolvaer along with the Nasjonal Samling membership card with his photograph at the bottom left corner which implied sympathy for the Nazi cause. The only personal item on his body was the ring inscribed with his own and with his then fiancée's initials. He was emotionally attached to the ring and not wishing to be parted from it had ensured that his assumed surname of Erik Knudsen conformed to the ring's 'E.K.' engraving.

In other circumstances the journey through the Lofotens would have been a pleasure. Soon after leaving Svolvaer *Nordfisk* turned northwards up the narrow Raft Sundet channel where steep cliffs like gigantic walls soared up from the water-line on each side, hemming the boat into the narrows. Here and there stunted saplings, defying the laws of gravity, clung in the high crevices. Later, on the port beam, Trollfjord opened into the channel from a deep cleft in the mountains, its gloomy depths bereft of life save for the solitary speck of a sea eagle soaring on thermals above the cliffs.

Two hours after leaving Svolvaer the boat emerged from the confines of the Raft Sundet into open water and it was then that Olav thought he heard the sound of a distant plane.

They both listened but could hear nothing definite owing to the noise of the boat's engine. Ivan shut the engine down and in the silence they both clearly heard what sounded like a small plane. It seemed to be circling over the coastline somewhere ahead. Olav scanned the area with binoculars and after a few minutes picked up what appeared to be a Fieseler Storch, a reconnaissance plane commonly used by the Germans. 'It's a Storch all right', he commented as he put down the binoculars, 'and it seems as though he's looking for something. I doubt he's interested in us but it would look less suspicious if we got under way again.'

After about ten minutes the Storch headed away south but then the pilot appeared to catch sight of *Nordfisk*, abruptly changed direction and came straight towards the boat. It was obvious that they had been seen but all they could do was to maintain their course. After a few minutes the plane closed in on the boat and began to circle round it before making three low passes overhead. Olav waved to the pilot who clearly was inspecting them with more than a passing interest. Then the Storch broke away to the south and finally disappeared into the distance. There was nothing to be done but hope that no action would be taken against them and to press on, keeping to their planned course. For four hours nothing further untoward happened. They passed an occasional fishing boat but as *Nordfisk* emerged from the Lofoten Islands near Harstad, they heard a low, throbbing sound of a powerful boat engine, audible above the sound of their own engine. Olav scanned the channel towards Harstad then muttered an oath as he put the binoculars down.

'We are in trouble,' he said. 'It's a big motor launch, one of those German "Schnellboots", and it's making up on us fast.'

Soon the launch was easily visible with the naked eye. The spreading white plume of the bow wave showed how fast it was moving and it did not take long to reach them. It looked seriously threatening with a manned machine gun mounted at the bow and a black and red swastika flying at the stern. An officer with a loudhailer came out on deck and ordered them to stop and to prepare for boarding. Olav told Ivan to cut the engine and *Nordfisk* drifted to a stop. The launch drew alongside and three Kriegsmarine sailors, two carrying Schmeisser rifles, swung themselves aboard while another two armed Germans watched from the launch. The Germans were not taking any risks and one of the sailors remained behind the mounted machine gun at the bow.

Olav presumed that they had been intercepted because Erik had, indeed, been recognised as they left Svolvaer harbour. He couldn't think of any other explanation. He had the necessary permission to fish north of the Lofotens and their papers were all in order.

The three of them were lined up on deck and checked for weapons. Erik was specifically picked out and was ordered to transfer to the launch, leaving Olav and Ivan aboard *Nordfisk*. Once on the launch, Erik was taken below and was questioned by the officer about his movements in the Lofotens. He replied that he came from a village in the north of Norway, that he had no permanent home since his wife had died and that he was working out of Svolvaer on *Nordfisk* to try to make a living.

'We are taking you to Harstad where you will be further questioned,' announced the officer.

Two Germans were left aboard *Nordfisk*, which was ordered to follow the launch to Harstad. It took an hour to reach the port while Erik was kept under guard in the tiny cabin below. The young sailor guarding him was relaxed and friendly and offered him a cigarette. When the vessel tied up Erik was taken ashore and was escorted a short way along the main street where passers-by stared at him and his armed escort with curiosity. He was taken into a wooden office building and was seated at a trestle table and told to wait. The inactivity only compounded his anxiety and he hoped that his fraying nerves would not be noticed by his captors. About half an hour later a German wearing civilian clothes came in, along with a Norwegian interpreter and both sat opposite him. Then the questioning began.

The ordeal lasted for an hour during which he was asked where he had come from and how he came to be working on *Nordfisk*. Erik's account of his movements and his ability to speak perfect Norwegian seemed to satisfy his questioner. He denied ever knowing anyone from Svolvaer and stated that he had certainly never travelled out of Norway. He knew his statement that his original home had been in the far north of the country and that his wife had died years previously would be difficult to check and finally the presence of his Nazi NS card in his wallet seemed to allay any residual suspicions. Besides, with his fair hair and blue eyes he looked genuinely Norwegian.

Suddenly the SS officer stood up, evidently having decided that his suspicions were unfounded.

'You are free to go,' he said. 'Your boat will be here in an hour.'

Erik got to his feet while trying not to show enormous relief at his reprieve and found himself thanking the officer. At the same time he was shaken by the belief that Bjorn must have talked about seeing him on *Nordfisk* as they left the harbour. He found it difficult to believe that his cousin would knowingly have betrayed him and thought it to be more likely that unguarded talk had done the damage. At any rate he felt lucky to have got away with it. He whiled away the time sitting on a bollard at the harbour's edge and in due course *Nordfisk* appeared, motoring into the harbour and, manoeuvring alongside the German launch, tied up to the dock. Olav looked mightily relieved to see Erik standing unguarded at the dock side. A Norwegian member of the harbour police emerged from the building where Erik had been questioned. He walked over to *Nordfisk*, and spoke to the two German guards on board. He evidently told them that the boat should be allowed to go on its way and, nodding briefly to Olav, turned and went back to the police post.

Within half an hour *Nordfisk* set off once more, heading towards Tromso on a course which would take them through some of the best cod fishing grounds. On the bulkhead near the stern hung an array of large metal lures for use on hand lines. The presence of fish in the hold would be useful if the boat was again inspected and would allay suspicions that they were anything other than genuine fishermen. Erik could hardly believe that he had survived the recent episode and was shaken by the experience. He sat back against the wheelhouse watching a pair of gulls following the boat while the coastal mountains, lit with patches of sunshine, slid steadily past the starboard beam. Even in wartime, he reflected, there were moments of beauty and peacefulness and his Norwegian half acknowledged its affinity with this northern landscape. As they sailed north Erik and Olav discussed the interrogation, and why the Germans had come to suspect Erik in the first place. It was inescapable that Bjorn must have talked about recognising his cousin, but was it just an unguarded word or an intentional betrayal?

Once *Nordfisk* emerged from the shelter of the northern tip of the Lofotens, a steep swell driven by the west wind drove into her port side, causing her to pitch and roll. Erik had never been a good sailor and all too soon felt the familiar uneasy sensation in his stomach. Olav and Ivan were quite unaffected but nodded sympathetically when he ran to the starboard side and was painfully sick while the brisk wind whirled the results towards the Norwegian coast.

After about an hour Olav cut the engine and turned the bows into the oncoming waves and at once the boat's motion became easier to tolerate. Ivan fetched two hand lines and, attaching a metal lure to each, gave one to Erik. They let out the lines until the lures touched the bottom, then, after retrieving a short length, began to fish, jigging the lures to and fro. Within two hours they had caught a dozen good-sized cod, which they laid in fish boxes and covered with crushed ice from the hold.

The following day *Nordfisk* entered the channel leading to Tromso. The town looked quite big and busy and on docking Erik saw at once that there were plenty of German troops on the streets. Leaving Ivan on board Olav took him ashore to meet Magnus, Erik's Tromso contact, a marine engineer and a personal friend of Olav's. As they walked through the town Olav quietly explained to Erik that Magnus worked actively in the Resistance and regularly reported German shipping movements. He would also find reliable lodgings. As they walked through the busy streets Erik noticed that some Germans attempted friendly nods to Norwegian passers-by, who for the most part ignored them. Most of the population was outraged by the Occupation and he had heard that some people walked out of a shop if a German came in.

They continued for a few minutes along narrow streets hemmed by wooden houses, before coming to a boatyard on the waterfront. The sound of hammering came from a ramshackle building and inside they found Magnus, a powerful-looking man wielding a long-handled hammer, who recognised Olav immediately. He put the hammer down and greeted him with a broad smile and a hefty handshake. Olav introduced Erik and explained the need of reliable lodgings and then took Magnus aside for a moment and spoke quietly to him.

'Lodgings', said Magnus, 'will not be a problem, but have you heard the news? An illegal wireless picked up a report that on June 22nd, that's last Sunday, Germany attacked Russia. As far as I can find out their advance seems unstoppable and they are already bombing Russian cities. The news is spreading fast and people are in quite a state of excitement about it.'

Apparently nobody was forecasting what the outcome would be though Magnus thought that Germany had taken on too much and would pay for it in the end. He followed this up with the additional news that the *Bismarck* and *Prinz Eugen* were known to have left the Baltic in May, and had appeared in southern Norway.

Both Olav and Erik were most surprised by the news of the attack on Russia, which gave the war in 1941 a whole new dimension. Suddenly events were moving quickly. *Bismarck* and *Prinz Eugen* having broken out of the Baltic might well move up to the northern Norwegian fjords. If that happened Erik's wireless communication skills and the new transmitters would become crucially important. Magnus took Erik's arm and led him over to a small open fishing boat which had been pulled up the slipway into the workshop. He removed a panel below a seat and in the cavity lay a large, slightly battered, suitcase which, he explained, had been brought clandestinely from Shetland by fishing boat. He pulled the case from the hiding place and when he opened it Erik recognised immediately what it was – another long range B2-Z Paraset.

'A Resistance man I know well delivered it yesterday. He also told me that you will be going to Alta when you leave here.'

After replacing the set in its hiding place Magnus gave Erik the address in Tromso of a lodging house near the harbour that would be able to take him in.

'My sister runs it,' he said, 'and if you tell her that I sent you she will be happy to have you.'

Before they parted Magnus stressed how important it was for Erik to register his arrival in Tromso with the authorities and then, when the time came, to obtain permission to move on to Alta, 'in search of work'. 'Once you have permission to travel, local bus will be the best way of getting around. If anyone asks why you are travelling tell them that you are looking for work on the fishing boats.'

With regret Erik said goodbye to Olav and to old Ivan who had brought him safely from the Lofotens to Tromso, and then followed the directions to the lodgings run by Magnus's sister. A short walk along the main street and up a narrow side street brought him to the white-painted wooden house. He knocked on the door, which was opened by a woman in her fifties with striking henna-dyed hair. Erik began to explain that Magnus had sent him in the hope that he could be given lodgings for a short time, but before he could finish he was immediately ushered in as though he was expected. Her greeting could not have been friendlier.

'Welcome to Tromso. I'm Helga, Magnus's sister and, yes, of course I can give you a room.' Looking at his rucksack, she went on: 'Give me any washing that needs doing and in half an hour I'll have a meal ready for you in the kitchen, but first I'll show you your room.'

Erik could hardly believe his luck as he followed Helga up the steep pinewood stairs and looked into the room. It was small but comfortable. The window looked out over the street and above the rooftops he could just see the harbour and the masts of fishing boats. Helga was not only welcoming and kind but clearly realised that he needed a good feed. When he came back downstairs she seated him at the kitchen table and put a large bowl of vegetable and fish soup in front of him followed by a big slab of black bread, pickled herrings and cheese. After the meal Erik felt his body relaxing as he stretched his legs in front of the stove. He was warm and comfortable, and for that he was grateful.

He asked Helga about the German presence in Tromso and she told him that occupying forces tightly controlled life in the town and that the police station was staffed by German as well as Norwegian police. Some of the Norwegian police were all right but it was better not to trust any of them. She repeated Magnus' advice that if he wanted to travel to another area he would have to obtain a travel pass but this would take time to be issued.

Later on that evening Magnus called in, greeted his sister and sat down in the kitchen with Erik while Helga busied herself in the adjacent living room. When they were alone Erik told Magnus that he would need several sessions with him to demonstrate the new B2–Z Paraset and to explain new codes and ciphers. They made arrangements for Erik to come back to the boatyard over the next three or four days which, Erik thought, should be sufficient to teach Magnus about the codes and the workings of the new transmitter. After one of the sessions Magnus commented that the Resistance further east, round the top of Norway, could well use the powerful short-wave B2-Z as just now all they had was a device with a range of only about 800 kilometres.

'I have a friend, Sven Svensen, who has a boat repair yard in Alta,' he said. 'He is short staffed just now and, if you were to go there, he will be able to take you on. You will find his boatyard at the far end of the harbour. Sven is a reliable man, much respected in that community, who for some time has helped previous agents in Alta.'

When Magnus mentioned Svensen's name, Erik immediately realised that, by lucky chance, this was the very man who had been designated as his third contact in Norway and who hopefully had already been supplied with a B2-Z transmitter with accompanying codes and ciphers – or was it by lucky chance? Things seemed to have been prepared for him wherever he went.

'If you do go there,' said Magnus, 'you should know that, for some reason, the Germans have stepped up security at Alta and are particularly vigilant about illegal radio transmissions. Something is going on in Alta – there's a rumour going about that the Germans are building new harbour facilities near there.'

10

LYNGENFJORD.

Two months after the Lofoten Raid, when Lara was once again living at home, she noticed one day that her father was unusually silent and preoccupied. That morning she found him sitting in the early summer sun outside the front door reading what looked like a letter written in pencil on a page torn from a notebook. Although the paper was crumpled she recognised her brother, Bjorn's, spiky handwriting. Gunnar pushed the letter into a pocket but Lara's curiosity was aroused.

'What's that letter about, and why are you trying to hide it from me – it's from Bjorn isn't it?' she asked.

Gunnar took out the crumpled sheet, put it on his knee and smoothed it out before handing it to Lara.

'Yes, it's from Bjorn in Svolvaer,' he replied. 'And it has been delayed in getting here. Read what he says but don't talk about it to anyone outside the family.'

Lara glanced at her brother's untidy handwriting with its usual spelling mistakes and read:

Dear Father and Mother,

You will never believe it but I am fairly sure I saw Erik, Erik Kingsnorth, on a fishing boat which was leaving the harbour here. It was a few days after the

English raid on Svolvaer. I am not sure if he saw me or not but he looked like a real Lofoten fisherman. I noted the boat's registration number and found out that it belongs to a man who lives here down by the harbour. I really don't know what to think but if it wasn't Erik it was a young fellow who looked exactly like him. I haven't told anyone else about it.

After reading some normal pleasantries Lara read on –

When the British raided the town the oil factory was blown up and is still not back in operation. Most of the workers there lost their jobs, including me. Some people in Svolvaer think that Norway should accept the German presence here and that we should cooperate and I am beginning to think that they're right. The British have done me no favours and when the assistant harbourmaster asked if I would join the Nazi Nasjonal Samling party I agreed and I am now a full member. The advantage is that you can sometimes get special concessions from the Germans.

The letter continued with small items of news from Svolvaer and finished with Bjorn's good wishes. Gunnar was obviously distressed by what he had read. His own son collaborating with the invaders; how could he do such a thing? Lara saw how distressed her father was and decided not to mention, even in passing, Willi, her German officer friend back at the store, who had a smiling, kindly face and who loved plants and flowers.

'How could it have been Erik on a fishing boat?' she

asked. 'Erik's in England and anyway, how could he have got to Norway? I think that Bjorn's imagining things as usual.'

★

In spring 1942, life on Gunnar's farm proceeded relatively normally. In spite of the ban on wirelesses, news of the war's progress somehow seemed to reach most of the households in the district. No one enquired just how they heard the news though clearly someone had a set hidden somewhere.

One April morning Gunnar rode to the store at Olderdalen to try to buy some more paraffin. He parked his bicycle and inside found a group of serious-looking locals discussing something that, judging from their expressions, was bad news. As he walked over to join them he heard the name Telavag mentioned, which he knew was a fishing village about forty kilometres from Bergen. Hilder Larsen was standing behind her counter listening to the exchanges.

'What's going on?' he enquired.

'Haven't you heard?' she replied. 'The Germans have burnt Telavag to the ground in revenge for the shooting of two Gestapo men. They executed some of the villagers and deported all the rest to Germany. Even women and children have been put in prison. There is no one left.' She paused to draw breath, and continued, 'There's a rumour that some people who had nothing at all to do with killing of the Gestapo men have also been shot in reprisal. They even sank or took away all the fishing boats.' Hilder, breathless, fell silent and slumped down in a chair.

This terrible reaction by the Germans was clearly

intended as a warning that any attack on the Occupation forces would be met with devastating retaliation.

By this time a considerable group of locals had gathered in the store; enough to induce a reaction from any German who happened to come in as gatherings were forbidden. Hans Larsen began to look anxious. Standing beside Hilder at the counter he appealed for attention.

'I know that we are all good Norwegians and we would do anything to help end the Occupation but this news shows what would happen if a German was to be killed in this district. I am sure that I speak for all of you when I say that on no account should a member of our community attack a German. Such action will not affect the outcome of the war and will only bring us misery.'

There was a murmur of agreement from most, but not quite all, of the company and gradually the group began to leave.

Gunnar retrieved his bicycle and cycled home in a thoughtful mood. He crossed the bridge over the river and cycled up the hill to the farm, where he met Bjorn who, together with Lars and Kristian, the two Anders boys, was walking down towards the main road.

'Hello Father!' exclaimed Bjorn, 'I'm taking a few days away from Svolvaer and I wanted to come to see you and mother. I've just had a good chat with mother and I'm just going out with Lars and Kristian in the dinghy for a bit of fishing. I'll tell you all my news when we get back.' With that, the three boys set off down the farm track. At the bottom they were just about to turn left along the road when they heard the howl of a fast approaching vehicle.

'Wait. Keep back!' shouted Bjorn to his companions. A moment later a speeding Wehrmacht lorry rounded the bend and charged far too fast towards the bridge. The driver tried to straighten up to cross the decking, but the right wheels skidded off the hard surface and the vehicle lurched half off the road. The driver over-corrected the steering in his struggle to align the wobbling vehicle with the crossing. In a cloud of dust the wobbling became uncontrollable and it was all to no avail as Bjorn caught a fleeting glimpse of the driver's face, teeth clenched, struggling to regain control. A split second later the lorry missed the bridge decking and careered down the slope towards the river and with a shattering crash, ended up on its side in the water. For a moment there was silence while the engine smoked and steamed.

'Come on!' shouted Bjorn and, followed by the others, he ran down the slope and plunged into the water to reach the wreck. Through the cracked windscreen they could see the driver in the cab, slumped against the wheel. Bjorn climbed up onto the skyward facing side of the cab, wrenched the door upwards and peered inside. The young driver was lying on his side while water flooded in and swirled around him. Blood streamed from a laceration in his face but he showed signs of life and began to mutter, '*Mein Gott, mein Gott!*'

Bjorn and Kristian lowered themselves into the cab and inspected the man's injuries. His left leg below the knee lay at an odd angle and was clearly broken. The facial wound was still pouring blood and, tearing a piece off his own shirt, Bjorn tried to staunch the flow. Then they started to work out how to lift the man out of the wreck. Both had attended first aid lessons before leaving school and remembered the importance of protecting a broken leg from further damage. They could find nothing to use as a splint so, with Kristian holding the leg as straight as possible, the two others lifted the man's body out of the seat. In spite of his groans and shouts of pain they managed to manoeuvre him up and through the open door. They then slowly eased him down against the now vertical chassis to the river below. As they did this Bjorn caught his foot beneath the driver's seat and there was an audible crack from his ankle as his body turned, but in spite of that Bjorn lowered himself to the river bed to help evacuate the injured man.

After a struggle to keep him clear of the water they finally managed to lie the German flat on the grassy riverside bank. The driver looked about twenty years of age and, with a sheen of sweat covering his deathly pale face, seemed in a bad way. With one hand he was clutching his abdomen where his jacket had been torn. Bjorn gently moved the hand away and lifted aside the ripped material to find a massive pink stain on the underlying shirt. That, too, he pulled aside and was horrified to find coils of pink intestine which, having escaped through a laceration in the abdominal wall, were lying on the surface of the abdomen where they writhed and twisted with an innate peristalsis of their own. Bjorn, ignoring his own pain, took command of the situation;

'Kristian, go onto the bridge and stop any vehicle that comes. This fellow's injuries are serious; we must get him to hospital where he'll need a surgeon urgently. Lars, go and find something to splint his leg with – a bit of wood from the shore will do. I'll stay with him here meantime.'

A few minutes later another Wehrmacht lorry appeared, driving north. Kristian waved it down and it pulled up just short of the bridge and two non-commissioned officers jumped out and hurried down to where the injured man lay on the riverbank. No explanation from Bjorn was needed for them to understand what had happened and they indicated that they would take their wounded colleague and send him on to Alta where he could be treated. The injured man was lifted into the back of the lorry and, after shaking hands with Bjorn and the Anders boys and nodding their thanks, the two Germans drove off with their patient.

11

COLLABORATION

Five months after the lorry crash, Gunnar and Birgitta Torkelsen were sitting warming themselves by the stove in the living room. The days had shortened quickly and there had already been a sprinkling of new snow on the mountains across the fjord. The previous day Lara had left to go back to live at the store as the mornings and evenings once more were too dark for making the journey by bicycle.

Gunnar had found the farm work tiring without Bjorn's help. He was worried about his son who wrote only rarely, and who seemed to be working too closely with the Germans in Svolvaer. He couldn't bring himself to tell his neighbours that Bjorn had joined the NS Party, the only political party allowed by the Occupation, and he felt depressed in spite of Birgitta's cheerful support.

'We've got a lot to be depressed about,' he remarked to her. 'The Occupation is bad enough and now we have Bjorn cosying up to the Germans to worry about. I miss Lara already, and I'm worried about her too. I didn't mention it at the time, but two or three weeks ago I was talking to Nils Anders who was buying something at the store. Lara had just been serving a German officer and a sixth sense told Nils that there was something going on between the two of them, though he couldn't be more specific.'

'What do you think Nils meant by "something going on"?' asked Birgitta. 'Surely she wouldn't be so silly as to get involved with a German but, if it did turn out to be true, it really would be absolutely awful.'

Another week passed by when Birgitta, who was preparing a meal in the kitchen, called out to her husband that there was someone walking up the track to the house.

'Come and look,' she said, 'I think it's Bjorn.' Even at a distance they could see that it certainly was Bjorn with a haversack on his back and together they walked down to meet him.

'Oh, we weren't expecting you dear,' exclaimed Birgitta. 'Is everything all right?'

'Yes, of course and it's great to see you!' replied Bjorn, giving his mother a hug. 'I've got so much to tell you.' Gunnar put an arm on his son's shoulder and looked at him quizzically.

'Are you really all right?' he asked.

'Of course I am, except for my ankle which is still sore,' Bjorn replied.

Bjorn was pleased to be home and to find that everything looked the same but in some subtle way things did not feel the same. Although there were no outward signs of change he had felt a new confidence in himself since starting work for the Germans and reasoned that the change must be within himself. For one thing his opinions seemed to carry more weight than before, but at the same time he had also noticed that some people in Svolvaer had become wary in his presence and avoided getting into arguments with him. A few would not even speak to him, though with his new-found confidence he was able to brush this aside.

Over a simple meal the family inevitably discussed the

Occupation and Bjorn asked how Lara was and whether there had been as many salmon in the river as usual.

'I hope that no more Germans have been fishing with grenades,' he remarked. 'That was a bad moment when you nearly got shot after pushing that soldier into the river, Father.'

'How long can you stay?' asked Birgitta.

'Only a few days. The Svolvaer police have told me to go to Fridalen and from there I'll be involved with driving Russian prisoners up north to Kafjord, ten kilometres this side of Alta. It seems that a big construction project is underway there, something to do with harbour facilities. The construction labour work is to be done by Russian prisoners who are being held in a big camp in Fridalen. I and some other members of the NS Party are joining up with Organisation Todt and I have been put in charge of the transportation of the work parties.'

Gunnar was aghast. His face flushed with anger.

'For God's sake!' he shouted, thumping the table with his fist. 'What's got into you? You can't work for the Germans.'

Birgitta, upset by the prospect of an argument, got up from the table and left the room.

'How can you bring yourself to join the Todt? Where is your sense of patriotism and have you no shame?' demanded Gunnar. Here was his son, a collaborator, working in an official German labour organisation of his own free will and openly travelling in German army vehicles. How has this happened? he wondered. At the beginning the boy was always advocating violent action against the invaders and now he was going to transport prisoners for them.

Bjorn, seeing his father's distress, explained that his

friendship with the harbourmaster in Svolvaer, an NS member, had led to his selection for this new job and that he was trusted by the Germans. After all, the Occupation was likely to be permanent and they might as well make the best of it.

'You are nothing but a damned collaborator and one day you'll have to face the consequences!' shouted Gunnar.

Bjorn jumped to his feet, stormed out of the room and a moment later Gunnar heard the outside door slam.

Birgitta, hearing the commotion of Bjorn's abrupt departure, came to join her husband. She was worried about him and, although his anger had subsided, she found him sitting alone at the table with a sheen of sweat on his brow. Arguing with Bjorn made him feel unwell.

Two days later Bjorn had to leave and, shouldering his haversack, he took the local bus to the junction where the road from Finland runs down through Fridalen to join the coastal road. Since the argument with his father, their relationship had been cool and he was glad to escape from the house. He found himself looking forward to reporting to the camp where large numbers of Russian prisoners were being held.

There was no difficulty in getting a lift in one of the numerous trucks which passed. The driver, a fellow Norwegian employed in bringing construction material to the prison camp, told him that the war in Russia must be going well for the Germans as huge numbers of Red Army prisoners were arriving almost every day and were being crammed into the camp.

'The Germans are going to use them to build what they are calling the "Lyngen Line" which is meant to stop the Russians if they ever attempt to invade Norway from the north. Other prisoners are being sent to Alta as slave labourers where something else is being built,' he said.

Twenty minutes later they arrived at the camp. Bjorn had never seen anything like it. Inside an enormous stockade, and surrounded by a high barbed wire fence, thousands of Russian prisoners were crammed together without shelter, some dressed in little more than rags or the remains of uniforms. Some wore old boots but others simply had cloth binders round their feet. Many were lying on the bare ground and looked as though they might well already be dead, and a foetid stench of excrement hung over the place. A strange murmuring rose from the mass of despairing humanity while, outside the fence and watch towers, armed guards patrolled with dogs.

The driver stopped and let Bjorn out beside a wooden administration building. The pungent, resinous smell of its freshly sawn timbers provided relief from the stench of the stockade. Before going in Bjorn glanced again at the packed mass of prisoners. He could not imagine how starving men such as these could possibly do useful labouring work at any construction site. He found two other Norwegians waiting in the building who told him that they, too, were waiting for instructions to take truckloads of prisoners north.

After a few moments a German, a Feldwebel, came in and sat down at a desk. He spoke in Norwegian and was very polite.

'Good afternoon, gentlemen,' he said, smiling pleasantly, 'do take a seat. We have important work for you which will involve driving Russian prisoners up to Altafjord where there is a shortage of labourers but, before we go any further, I have now to ask you to show me your Nasjonal Samling membership cards.'

He took the cards and noted down their details in a ledger on his desk and assigned the three of them to an overnight accommodation hut, then in a nearby canteen, they were given a meal of soup and fish stew.

The next morning Bjorn and the other two drivers were each provided with a truck which they were told to drive to the gate of the prison compound which was opened for them by an armed sentry. The drivers were told to halt the vehicles beside a group of Russian prisoners who were ready for transfer, and twenty were loaded into each vehicle. Although some of the strongest of the prisoners must have been selected, those who climbed aboard looked half starved, with the bones of their heads standing out revealing contours of the underlying skull. Bjorn, standing at the rear of the truck, helped the prisoners to climb up and was immediately assailed by the pungent smell of their unwashed bodies. The smell clung to his hands and once loading was complete he rinsed them at a tap outside the administration building. Shortly afterwards they set off in convoy for Alta, 270 kilometres to the north, with armed motorcycle escorts driving in front and behind.

12

THE AFFAIR DEVELOPS

Lara would never forget the summer of 1942. She was happy in her work at the store and the Larsens had become very fond of her. When the summer months became light and warm she again moved back to stay with her parents, using her faithful bicycle to travel daily to and from the store. Once her parents had remarked that the journey occasionally seemed to take a surprisingly long time: it was true that she sometimes stopped off to visit the Petersens on the way home. She enjoyed chatting to Inga and the twins, Per and Pal, now 15 years old, who, if they were not out working, often came to join them in the kitchen, but even then she was not always sure which twin was which.

However, such visits did not always account for Lara's late appearance back home. Near the end of June, Willi had called at the store and in a moment when they were alone he had passionately embraced her. Lara had let him enfold her in his arms and, dreamily gazing up at him, she felt a desperate longing for this handsome man with his blue eyes and his laughter-lined face. With ears alert for the sound of other customers they had kissed and the rest of the world faded into insignificance as she felt his hands exploring her body.

'Not here, Willi!' she exclaimed breathlessly, realising

that she had used his Christian name for the first time. 'Someone might come in at any time.'

'Lara, I love you,' he said running his finger along the tip of her nose and round her lips.

'Let's meet where we can be by ourselves,' he continued. 'I know a track leading off the road about a kilometre from here which used to lead to an old quarry. There's a birch wood by a little stream up there where we wouldn't be disturbed. Take your bicycle fifty metres up the track where you won't be seen from the road and I could meet you there on Friday. Could you manage around six o'clock in the evening?'

Of course Lara would manage to be there; she could easily invent some believable reason for being late home that evening.

After Willi left she felt almost giddy with expectation, and for the rest of the day, her whole world seemed brighter and her heart seemed to sing within her. The fjord and mountains looked unaccountably more beautiful than ever before as she cycled home. She smiled to herself as she rode delighting at the thrill of her secret, a secret which, although she did not know it at the time, would transform her life in ways which she could not imagine. Once she arrived back home her high spirits were noticed by her parents and, as her mother prepared the evening meal, Lara saw her give her father a knowing look.

At last Friday came. In the afternoon, Lara left the store as usual and set off along the road but, instead of continuing home, she quickly turned off along the track that Willi had told her about and, in moments, the dense birch woods hid her progress. She soon found the stream with the thicket beside it, dismounted and laid the bike among a bank of ferns and waited.

For about ten minutes nothing happened, and then she caught the sound of a motor engine coming slowly along the track. Her heart pounded as the vehicle emerged from among the trees. It stopped and suddenly, there he was!

Willi jumped from the car and, without a word, they ran to each other and embraced, not in the anxious way which they had done at the store but with a complete abandon which Lara had never known before, as she buried her face in his neck, savouring the manly smell of his skin. He tilted her face up towards him and with great tenderness kissed her on the lips. His tongue slipped into her mouth and she felt not only physically joined to him but actually part of him.

They sank down among the soft ferns, as Lara abandoned all thoughts of prudence. Willi was gentle as he removed her clothes, until she lay naked among the fronds. Feverishly he stripped off his uniform and they clasped together feeling the thrill of unclothed bodily contact. Willi knelt upright beside her and gazed at her beautiful body with its perfect breasts while Lara, as in a dream and with surprise, saw for the first time in her life the sign of urgent male arousal. This was Lara's first experience of love-making and an involuntary gasp of surprise escaped her, as she felt her body being entered. Then the two of them seemed to melt into one as the rhythm took hold until it ended, after a few minutes, in a surge of ecstasy.

Time passed and the only witness to their exertions was a little olive green willow warbler busying itself in the birch trees above them. It had migrated in spring all the way from tropical Africa and had perhaps seen forest apes behaving in the same way.

Afterwards, as they rested, Lara knew that she had passed

a milestone in her life and nothing would be quite the same again. Although she had felt a little pain at the time it had quickly passed and she had felt great fulfilment in the act. She was a new, confident Lara.

That summer was one of the happiest that she could remember. She met Willi almost every week in the same fern-covered spot in the birch woods. The indentation in the greenery, from their previous visits, became a welcoming bed.

Their meetings continued in a similar manner until one day, in late summer, when Willi seemed unusually quiet. After their love-making, he helped Lara to lift her bicycle from among the ferns, took both of her hands and looked into her eyes.

'I have some news,' he said. 'I've had orders to move further north with some of the army group. I have to leave in four days' time and so this will be the last of our regular meetings. You know that I love you and will find a way of seeing you again as soon as I can.'

Lara was devastated. She could not imagine life without Willi's weekly visits and tears ran down her cheeks while she sobbed in his arms. The parting was acutely painful for both of them.

Lara returned to her old summer routine, commuting between home and the store but each morning she awoke with a numb feeling that something unpleasant had happened, until she remembered what it was. Her listlessness was noticed by her parents until, one evening, her mother took her aside and asked her outright if she had been having an affair. She could not deny it.

'Who is the man?' her mother asked.

Then it all came out.

'He's a German officer but he is a good man who used to be a lawyer in civilian life. He hates the war and I really love him.'

For a few moments Birgitta was speechless with shock.

'Why does it have to be a German?' she demanded. 'You know perfectly well that they are our enemies and, if this gets out, our friends and neighbours will never understand. You will be shunned, in fact the whole family will be shunned. If you promise not see him again I won't tell your father about this.'

Lara found herself agreeing to do as her mother wished, but, at the same time, knowing it was a promise she would be unlikely to keep.

In September she decided to move back to live at the store, as the evenings were getting darker. Gradually, winter extended its grip over northern Norway with a light snowfall in mid-September. For solace, in the dark evenings, Lara sometimes stood outside the store in the darkness and cold to watch the aurora borealis in the northern sky, its massive, folded veils of green and red light flitting silently across the heavens. On such occasions she felt comfortingly near to her maker and wondered if her lover too might be watching the sky. She desperately missed Willi and, alone in her room at night, her thoughts often turned to their time together. Most Norwegians she had talked to since the Occupation thought that all Germans were truly evil but Willi was clearly not evil. He was a kind and considerate man and his interests in literature and nature, did not suggest anything warlike in his character. She could not imagine him shooting anyone, although she did wonder what he would do if his senior officers told him that he had to.

She knew that somehow or other she would have to meet him again and at night she prayed fervently that it would happen soon. However, six weeks after Willi had gone away, her prayers were required in quite a new direction. She had come down to join the Larsens for breakfast in the kitchen when a sudden feeling of nausea had overcome her and she had to rush out of the room and was sick in the bathroom. For two weeks she had been worrying about her monthly period, which had failed to appear, but she had put this down to her disturbed emotions. Suddenly, the awful realisation came to her that she must be pregnant.

After a few minutes, Hilder Larsen hurried through to see if she was all right and, somehow, the kindly soul had guessed what the matter was. At first Lara, white-faced, could not bring herself to confess who was responsible but after four or five days the whole truth came out. It was a great shock to both Hans and Hilder when they heard that the German officer they had seen at the store was responsible, but they had become very fond of Lara and made it clear that they would support her throughout the pregnancy.

Lara dreaded the thought of telling her parents the news and kept putting off the inevitable day. At last, one evening in January, she looked at herself in her bedroom mirror and admitted that the smooth bulge of her abdomen could not be hidden much longer and she could no longer put off breaking the news at home. She told the Larsens that she needed a few days off to go home to see her mother and father.

The next morning, muffled against the cold, she stood outside the store in the darkness waiting for the bus. Lara was terrified of the forthcoming meeting and she fretted with anxiety during the short journey. All too soon the bus reached the farm track leading to her home. She got out and trudged up the slope.

When she reached the house she pushed the door open to find her parents busying themselves about the house. They were delighted at her unexpected appearance and gave her a warm welcome, but anxiously asked if everything was all right. However, with a mother's intuition Birgitta knew that it was not. She guessed why her daughter had come and her fears were confirmed when Lara took off her coat. There was no longer any possibility of concealing from her father who was responsible for the pregnancy.

Through her tears Lara could see that her parents were heartbroken as the truth came out. Gunnar was more upset than she had ever seen him and he hardly spoke to her for the rest of the day, although, by the following morning, he seemed to have come to terms with the situation. Despite everything, her parents loved her dearly and there was no thought of rejection. They told her that when the birth approached she would have to come home to the farm and they would support her.

'I think,' said her father, 'that friends and neighbours will accept the situation when the baby arrives, after all, these things do happen, but, inevitably, they will wonder and will ask who the father is. My advice is that, on no account, should you tell anyone that the father is a German.'

After spending the three days at home Lara took the bus back to the store. She told the Larsens that her parents would have her back home later on in her pregnancy when working at the store was no longer feasible.

As the weeks went by some customers began to notice Lara's enlarging abdomen. Most treated her kindly but then something awful happened that was to change Lara's life for ever.

Hilder Larsen was in the habit of opening up the store first thing in the morning but, on one occasion, which she would never forget, she was horrified to find daubed across the outside of the door in large, red-painted letters TYSKERTOSER – German whore. She called out to Hans who hurried through to see what the matter was. Aghast at seeing the graffiti, he ran to fetch a rag and turpentine and immediately started to remove the dreadful word. But before he could obliterate it, Lara, having heard the commotion, appeared and saw the smudged, but still legible, letters. She sank to her knees with shock, her face deathly pale, and slowly subsided onto the floor, her head spinning. Hilder hurried to attend to her while Hans scrubbed more turpentine onto the door until all that remained of the insult was a reddish smear on the woodwork. They had no idea how the truth could have had got out, nor who could have painted the word.

The Larsens had already heard that the dreadful word 'Tyskertoser' was being used in parts of Norway, but even worse was the term 'Naziyngel' – Nazi spawn – which was applied to children born of such a relationship. Apparently in some towns the German authorities had set up hostels for Norwegian girls made pregnant by a member of the occupying forces and consequently rejected by society.

Lara was far too distraught to work that day. She remained sobbing in her room until Hilder came up to talk to her. She was persuaded to return to the store counter the next day but, as time went on, she became ever more aware of a certain coldness of some customers towards her. After a few weeks, antagonism towards her became overt and even some of the regular customers walked out rather than be served by her. The situation had become impossible: she and the Larsens agreed that she would have to stop working and, reluctantly, Hans ended her contract.

The following day, she returned home but never found out who had discovered and spread her guilty secret. She soon found how it felt to be an outcast in her own community and remained closeted in her parents' house, not daring to face the world at large. Soon after her return some neighbours, the Petersens and the Anderses, arrived together to pay a visit. They had heard through gossip that a German was involved and had kindly come to give moral support to Lara, in her time of distress. When they arrived Lara shut herself in her room and only with great difficulty did Gunnar manage to persuade her to come down. When, at last, she did appear, in her misery and shame she tried to hide her face with her hands and could not look her neighbours in the eye. She looked gaunt and, with her face tear-stained, she was unrecognisable as the happy girl that they had once known. Birgitta was near to tears as she tried to talk to the guests, but took some solace from their sympathetic support. Oh, my beautiful daughter! How can it have come to this? thought Gunnar.

13

ALTA

Erik's stay in Tromsø was well spent and Magnus quickly understood the workings of the B2-Z Paraset along with the ciphers and codes. It was time for Erik to move on to his final and most important destination: Alta.

He was sorry to have to say goodbye to Helga, his landlady. She had looked after him with great kindness and had never enquired about the reason for his travels around Norway.

The ten-hour bus journey to Alta was uneventful until a German patrol blocked the road at Storslet. The bus was waved down and two soldiers came aboard to check the passengers. They examined all identity cards and travel permission documents. When Erik held up his Nasjonal Samling card for inspection, it was seen by his seated neighbour, who immediately got to his feet and roughly pushed past him to find somewhere else to sit. At the back of the bus an altercation developed between one of the Germans and a Norwegian youth whose papers, apparently, were not in order. White-faced, the boy was taken off the bus to a nearby sentry box while a soldier carried his haversack in one hand and in the other, a wooden box, which seemed to be the problem.

After half an hour the bus got under way once more,

but without the youth. The road crossed the Reisenelv, a beautiful fast-flowing river, which in peaceful times was renowned for its prolific runs of salmon. Further into the journey, magnificent views of mountains and fjords rolled past. Then, forty kilometres from Alta, the road crossed into Finnmark where occasional herds of reindeer, attended by Sami herders, grazed on the tundra.

Signs of military activity increased as the bus approached Altafjord. There was a further security check and then suddenly on the left, the wide expanse of the fjord opened up. There were about half a dozen small construction sites mostly on headlands overlooking the fjord but one of them, quite close to the road, gave Erik the chance to see what was going on: it looked as though an observation post or a gun emplacement was under construction by workers who could have been Russian prisoners. They were dreadfully thin and were dressed in bits and pieces of old uniforms, while being supervised by German guards.

The road followed the shoreline and continued around Kafjord, a narrow secondary fjord, which branched off from Altafjord itself. There, on a flat area on the Kafjord shore, buildings were being erected as two small ships unloaded cargo at a temporary dock, while labourers manhandled crates ashore. Erik craned his neck as the bus passed a white church on a knoll overlooking the narrows, from where he had a good view of the developments. The road then rounded the head of Kafjord and continued along the shoreline for eighteen kilometres, beneath a steep, wooded mountainside, to Alta itself.

There was plenty of evidence of the Occupation in the town and, when the bus arrived there, Wehrmacht lorries were parked nose to tail along one side of the main street, and German soldiers wandered around the few shops. As the bus drew up opposite the local store Erik pulled his haversack from beneath his seat, got to his feet and, along with most of the other passengers, stepped out into the street. From the side of the store he could look down on the whole of the harbour. Most of the boats were moored far to the right, near some ramshackle sheds and buildings. He set off straight away for the waterfront and wandered along towards the place where Sven Svensen's boatyard should be. Sure enough, the name 'Svensen' was painted in red on the front of the largest building, but there were no sounds of activity. A somnolent Alsatian dog lying there eyed him indifferently, but no one seemed to be about. He pushed open a small side door and found himself in a huge workshop, amidst a clutter of dismantled engines, machinery and bits of boats. Light shone from the window of a cabin built into a corner of the main building, which evidently served as the office. He knocked at the door and, after a few seconds, it was opened by a strikingly beautiful, blonde, blue-eyed girl of about eighteen years of age.

'Hello, I'm looking for Sven Svensen,' he said. 'Is he around?'

The girl eyed him with curiosity. 'That's my father: he's not here just now,' she replied, 'but he should be back in an hour. Do you want me to let him know that you called?'

'Please, tell him that Erik came. I've been sent by Magnus from Tromso, who said that your father might be able to give me work. I'll come back in an hour if that's all right.'

As he turned to leave the cabin he found his eyes drawn to the girl, dressed so alluringly in blue working overalls, then self-consciously averted his eyes and wandered back to the waterfront. As he had an hour to spare, he climbed the steep slope above the harbour and sat on a rock to get his bearings and to take in the view.

The wide expanse of Altafjord lay in front of him. The day was calm and the blue sky was reflected in the water. Some forty kilometres away, Stjernoya Island guarded the fjord entrance. Two local fishing boats, leaving the harbour, were making their way towards the open sea and, on the left, a coastal ship, its deck laden with what looked like crane gantries, was turning in towards the opening of Kafjord, where the Germans were so busy building docking or servicing facilities. As he sat, he studied the entrance to Kafjord. A layer of cloud hung against the steep mountainside on the south side and, half hidden beneath it, the activity along the shores suggested that a naval base of some kind was being built there. The fjord would certainly make a secure refuge, since an air attack on ships anchored there would be difficult, owing to the steep mountainside rising from the south shore. In addition, cloud cover, which often hung over the heights, would give ships added security. It would be an ideal lair for German warships intent on preying on Allied shipping in the North Atlantic.

After an hour, Erik wandered back down the slope to the waterfront and along to the Svensen building. Once again he went through the side door into the workshop. Light still shone from the office window through which he could see the girl talking to a man whom he assumed was her father. Before he could knock, the man glanced through the window, got up and opened the door.

Sven Svensen's eyes were wary as he gazed at Erik.

'What can I do for you?' he asked.

'My name is Erik. Magnus in Tromso told me to look

you up,' he replied. 'He says that you know him well. I'm looking for a job on the boats or in a repair yard and wondered if you could help me. By the way, do you know Axel Porsanger?'

At mention of the fictitious name Sven visibly relaxed.

'Welcome,' he exclaimed, 'we have been expecting you. Come in and sit down. I understand that you have already met my daughter, Else. If we are nice to her she will arrange some so-called coffee for us. It's German but it's all we have.'

The girl eased herself off her high stool and went over to a brass paraffin-fuelled Primus stove sitting on a shelf in the corner. She filled and lit the spirit holder and after a few moments pumped up the pressure, then lit the hissing jet of paraffin vapour and put on a blackened kettle. While the stove roared softly, Erik again found his gaze drawn to the girl's figure as she adjusted the heat.

'Tell me about yourself,' said Sven. 'You don't speak with a local accent.'

Erik, confident that he was in safe company, spoke frankly about who he was and that he had been sent by the British SIS. He explained that he had landed in Norway as a participant of the Lofoten Raid in December 1941.

Sven sat forward in his chair, his eyes widening in surprise as he listened to the tale.

'But you sound and look like a real Norwegian,' he remarked.

Erik gave a brief account of his personal history without mentioning his Uncle Gunnar's name or where the farm was.

'I know that you already have an effective organisation of coast watchers here and I've been instructed to liaise with you and to assist in any way I can. Also I'm required to report the types of protection which the Germans are using for their ships in north Norway, including anti-aircraft batteries, minefields and anti-submarine nets. On the way here I saw the facilities which they are building at Kafjord. I presume that they are planning a naval base there and it's obvious it will provide a very secure anchorage. The steepness of the surrounding mountains would certainly make an air attack difficult.'

Erik's account of himself dispelled any doubts that Sven might have had about him, and the three of them relaxed over mugs of what passed for coffee. He told Erik that a few days previously a transmitter of a type new to him had arrived through the Resistance by fishing boat. He presumed that it was to do with Erik's visit but so far had not examined it closely.

'By the way, don't worry about my daughter listening to our conversation. She knows about the things I do around here and she is very useful in many ways, and I don't just mean making coffee!

'You should know that there is some risk to yourself working with us. We keep up regular surveillance of German activities in the area. There is always the chance that some local Norwegian with German sympathies might discover what we are doing. I am afraid to say that even in Norway we have traitors, though it is not easy to identify them. I should add that all of us involved in this work carry a suicide capsule for use in case we look like being forced into giving away other members of the group'. There was a long silence. Erik felt Sven's gaze upon him, assessing his reaction to the implied stark warning. The silence continued until Erik nodded his understanding, then the moment passed and Sven went on – 'but first of all it's important that you find somewhere to stay. I can give you several addresses of possible lodgings and then you must register your arrival at the police station. You can tell them that you'll be working at Svensen's as I can, indeed, take you on, though the pay will be very modest.'

Erik expressed his thanks, before Sven continued.

'Come back tomorrow as I want you to meet a member of our "fjord watchers" who has just resumed transmitting reports on German shipping movements.'

With the help of Sven's directions, Erik found lodgings in a small house further up the slope behind the town. It was owned by Olga, a widow, who had lost her husband in a drowning accident at sea a few years previously. She was a kindly, elderly soul who welcomed him and showed him to an upstairs room with a view over the fjord. Her evident loneliness was emphasised by numerous photographs of her late husband, some taken on the deck of a fishing boat, and of her children at various stages of their lives. A large cat was her only companion.

Olga proved to be a useful source of information about local wartime conditions. She said that that there had been a recent influx of German military and police personnel to the region and that this seemed to be connected to the developments at Kafjord.

'You'll notice that the Germans have requisitioned a lot of the private houses in Alta where officers and other troops have been billeted, so I advise you to stay well clear of those. You must also take care if you use the road along the fjord as it's often affected by check points, especially near the construction site on the north shore.'

Erik was glad to have her advice but reflected that she

seemed to be aware of what he would be doing in Alta. The following day he returned to the boatyard to meet Sven once more. He found him in the office talking to a weather-beaten young Norwegian, but to his disappointment, there was no sign of Else. The newcomer rose to his feet as Sven introduced him.

'It's better that you don't know this man's real name,' he said, 'but for our purposes he is called Bernt.'

Sven began by explaining that, although the resistance group responsible for sending radio reports about shipping had been broken by the arrest and suicide of one of the members, Bernt had started transmitting again, mainly about the activities in Kafjord.

'We have a radio transmitter-receiver hidden in the pine forest above the Alta River. One of our men operates it while another with a sten-gun acts as lookout. Three weeks ago the Germans stopped the lookout as he was coming down through the forest and, unfortunately, he still had his weapon with him. He was arrested and was turned over to the Gestapo. We've since heard from a contact that he committed suicide rather than give them any information. Fortunately the Germans didn't find either the transmitter or Bernt, who had been operating it.'

Sven paused briefly before continuing, 'So you'll see that we have lost a man in recent months. His arrest did not seem to be by chance and we feel that that there may well be an informant in the community.'

'How do you think that I can help?' asked Erik. 'You seem to have a good organisation already in place.'

'I'll come to that in a moment,' replied Sven. 'Apart from our own activities here we have our own local informer who is employed at the construction site at Kafjord and he tells us what's going on there.

'Now, I'll come to what you can do,' he continued. 'Without meaning to seem ungrateful for your offer of help, we ourselves can manage meantime to cope with surveillance at Kafjord; however, we need to know what is going on in quite another place: a place near the tip of Svartfjell Peninsula which is about eighty kilometres from Alta. It's a very remote area but, for some reason, the Germans have ordered a land and sea exclusion zone there. The few local fishermen who lived there have been forcibly resettled elsewhere and for some time blasting has been heard coming from the peninsula. Clearly something major is being prepared but we don't have the manpower to investigate it ourselves.'

There was a long silence as Sven and Bernt studied Erik's reaction to this information. Sven produced a map from beneath the table, spread it out and showed Erik the remote peninsula in question. Cut into its tip were three narrow fjords facing north out to the open Barents Sea.

'We know what's happening right here at Kafjord where they are clearly establishing a secure harbour, but why are they preparing yet more facilities on Svartfjell Peninsula – if that is indeed what they are doing? Having lost a member of our resistance group, we are over-stretched and could do with your help to find out what's happening there. Do you feel that you could take that on?'

There was a long silence while Erik considered the proposition. He was aware of Sven and Bernt watching his face, waiting for his reaction. It sounded to him as though the ring might already have been penetrated by the Germans and that it would be a dangerous undertaking. He also knew that Hitler had ordered that all captured commandos be summarily executed. At last Sven broke the silence.

'Erik, there's another quite different matter you ought to know about and that's what we call the "Vorgsund Question". Something strange has been going on in the Vorgsund region which is also on the Svartfjell Peninsula, but a good fifteen kilometres down its western side. That coast is particularly remote. There used to be a very small fishing community there which could be reached by boat, although a rough track now exists along the shoreline. Very few people live there now but we've discovered that a special detachment of German police, apparently including members of the Gestapo, has been questioning the few people who remain there. There's something odd about the whole thing as it seems to have no obvious military relevance. They are looking for something and we don't know what.'

Erik pondered for a moment. 'Are there any clues at all about what they're after, and why on earth should the Gestapo be involved?'

'We don't know the answers to those questions, but we'd like to find out just what they are up to. A local fisherman there has been passing us a little information and tells us that the police have been showing a curious interest in that shoreline for about six months.'

After further thought, and with some misgivings, Erik said that he would do his best to help.

Sven finished off the discussion by asking Erik to give priority to finding out what the Germans were doing at the tip of Svartfjell Peninsula before, at a later date, going on to investigate the 'Vorgsund Question'.

14

SVARTFJELL

During the winter of 1942 Erik felt almost redundant. There was an effective group of Norwegians, including Bernt and others, already observing and reporting German shipping movements at Altafjord.

In March, however, the reason for the German preparations at nearby Kafjord became clear, when the biggest battleship in the world, the *Tirpitz*, pride of the German fleet, sailed up from Trondheim along with nine cruisers. Soon after arriving in Altafjord, she moved to the almost impregnable anchorage which had been prepared for her in Kafjord. There was no doubt that a formidable naval presence had arrived.

Shortly after the arrival of *Tirpitz*, Sven asked Erik to come to his office in the boat shed. His face was grim, as he closed the door behind them.

'I'm afraid that I have bad news. The German police arrested Sigurd, one of our key resistance men, in his home in the early hours of this morning. Someone must have betrayed him and he is likely to be shot. Apart from the personal loss to us, it's a disaster for our group as he may be tortured to make him reveal information about us.'

'How did the Germans get wind of him?' asked Erik.

'We are suspicious of two local men, but, to complicate

matters a number of Norwegian workers have been moved to Alta from further south to help with the construction at Kafjord and it could have been any of them. Ten days ago, Sigurd had been using his binoculars during his regular surveillance of the fjord from the woods above the town, when, suddenly, he felt that he wasn't alone. Apparently he quietly put the binoculars down and, with one hand on his pistol, looked around. It was then that a man, a stranger who, Sigurd said, looked like a worker judging by his rough clothes, appeared from among the trees. The man stopped, called out a greeting and, without another word, hurried away down the slope and disappeared. It all seemed a bit odd at the time. He was a youngish fellow Sigurd had never seen before and it is possible that he may be the one who reported what he had seen to the Germans. He may or may not be one of the incomers from further south.'

'Was Sigurd able to give a description of the man before the police picked him up?' asked Erik.

'Nothing very helpful, except that he seemed to walk with a very slight limp. Rest assured that I will do everything possible to find out who he is. Apart from that there is nothing much that we can do to help our man. We can only pray for his safety.'

★

The following week, Erik started to prepare for his first major espionage undertaking. After a discussion with Sven, he agreed to try to find out what was being constructed near the tip of Svartfjell Peninsula. This would involve taking the regular bus to the head of Langfjord under the pretext of attending to a boat engine repair job there. Then he would leave the bus and travel on foot over open hill and tundra for thirty or so kilometres to the far end of the peninsula where sounds of construction activity had been reported. Sven showed him a map of the area, which he memorised as best he could. Several narrow fjords cut into the tip of the peninsula and it was in one of these that the Germans were thought to be working. The map showed a rough road leading around the coast to the area, but this was apparently closed to all but German construction and military traffic.

Erik prepared for a six-day round trip. As well as food, he packed a waterproof sleeping bag into his haversack and a change of woollen socks.

Sven told him that, although it was usually better not to carry a weapon, which would inevitably compromise him, on this occasion his very presence on Svartfjell would compromise him anyway so he might as well take a gun. Sven went across to a boat which had its engine partially dismantled and, from inside the engine casing, produced a German Mauser pistol along with twenty rounds of ammunition. It was a model that Erik had used during his training at Inverailort and as he took the weapon from Sven it felt reassuringly familiar in his hand.

'I must tell you', said Sven, 'that this is a highly dangerous operation and that, if you are caught with this, you will probably be tortured for information and it's therefore essential that you don't let yourself be taken alive.'

Following Sven's advice Erik made a holder for the Mauser out of one of his socks which he stitched with a needle and thread borrowed from his landlady. It fitted closely into his crotch along with the rounds, a place where it might be missed at a cursory physical search. It was uncomfortable but bearable.

'You should practise a few shots with the pistol,' advised Sven, 'and you can do that here in the workshop. Come back tomorrow morning when I'll be test-running a boat engine and the noise from that will be more than enough to hide the sound of shots.'

When all preparations had been made, Erik told Olga, his landlady, that he would be away for a few days, visiting friends. He packed his haversack, secured the pistol with its rounds inside his underwear, and walked a little awkwardly down to meet the bus.

Ten minutes after setting off, the vehicle was waved down at a German checkpoint where a red-and-white-painted pole barrier blocked the road. Two soldiers climbed aboard. They were only youngsters, possibly about eighteen years of age, and seemed bored with their task. They counted the passengers and asked for papers from each of them and when Erik's turn came the haversack beneath the seat was not even noticed.

Half an hour later the bus rounded the head of Kafjord and drove along the north shore past the white church. Then, just beyond a low spit of land, Erik saw it – the monster, the *Tirpitz*! The huge ship, malevolently beautiful and bristling with guns, looked incongruous in its geometric white and grey dazzle camouflage. There was a lot of activity around the ship as numerous small craft plied between it and the shore. In the distance, at the mouth of Kafjord, lay what looked like a battle cruiser.

The bus retraced the route along which Erik had first come to Alta three months previously. Some of the stone-built observation posts looking out over Altafjord were not yet finished and Russian prisoners were still working on them. It took the bus an hour and a half to reach the head of Langfjord, the next major fjord, where, pulling out his haversack, Erik asked the driver to set him down at a small village by the shore. There were no signs of Germans in the isolated little community and, after the bus drove off, Erik was struck by the complete silence of the place. There were no bird calls and no sound of rivers or of the sea. The possibility of a body search having passed, there was no longer any need to keep the Mauser in its uncomfortable hiding place and Erik transferred it, along with the rounds, into a trouser pocket.

He walked quickly along the road for a short way, keeping a sharp lookout for traffic, before setting off to the right across the rocky tundra in the remaining early evening light. The landscape, without any tree cover, was rough and intersected by numerous streams and dotted with small ponds and lakes and it was clear to Erik that progress was not going to be fast. He quickly decided to abandon any thought of gathering information about the Vorgsund Question on his way to the tip of the peninsula as that area was away to the west – well off his route.

Although the spring weather was still quite chilly, the steady exercise kept Erik comfortably warm but he knew that he would have to spend at least one cold night on the tundra before he reached the north coast.

Occasional glimpses of the sea, towards the north, helped to keep his sense of direction. After at least two hours of walking he started to look for a sheltered spot where he could have something to eat and spend the night. He found a place on a small knoll among some jumbled slabs of rock, where the ground between the stones was soft with lichen and moss. Between the rocks he could glimpse the sea to the north and the huge expanse of the tundra around him. He laid out his sleeping bag, took some bread, a piece of smoked fish and some cheese from his haversack. The fish made him thirsty and cupping his hands he managed to drink from a nearby rather stagnant-looking pool before settling down for the night. For a long time he lay on his back looking up at the sky thinking of his wife and little Neil, his young son whom he had never seen. The boy would be three now and it was sad that he would not know his father if they were reunited. He wondered how Anna was coping with life in wartime England without news of him. Was she missing him? Was she being faithful? Gradually, as the sleeping bag warmed him, he felt his limbs relaxing and he slipped into a dreamless sleep.

In the early morning light, Erik was abruptly woken by an outlandish shriek, closely followed by another. His heart thumped in alarm. What could have made such a ghastly noise? It took him a few seconds to realise that he had heard the bird call before in the Scottish Highlands. It was none other than a red-throated diver, an attractive and almost amphibious bird! He scrambled out of his sleeping bag and noted with satisfaction that the weather was fine. After a brief breakfast of more fish and bread he once again set off northwards. He calculated that he still had another ten kilometres to go before reaching his objective and he pushed ahead at as good a pace as he could manage, given the terrain. He paused only once to drink from the beautifully clean water of a stream, which settled his thirst.

Gradually the land began to slope towards the north coast and, for the first time, he heard the unmistakable throbbing sound of a distant heavy diesel engine. In the absence of tree cover, he pushed on with increasing caution, drawing upon all the fieldcraft skills taught to him by Donald Cameron in the hills above Inverailort. Then he breasted a rise in the terrain, and suddenly the whole fissured north coast of the peninsula lay before him. In the far distance, a grey-painted naval ship lay at the mouth of the nearest of the three narrow inlets, which seemed almost too small to be called fjords. A haze of smoke rose from somewhere near the head of the nearest inlet before being dispersed by the onshore breeze.

Erik settled himself against a rock and pulled out his binoculars. Fortunately, as an overcast of high cloud had formed there was no danger of reflection off the lenses and he started to examine the ship and the inlet with meticulous care. He could just make out the tiny figures of sailors working on the deck. Five small vessels lay at moorings, whilst others were busily moving between the ship and the shore. Most seemed to be going to and from the head of the nearest fjord, which was still partially hidden by a knoll of high ground. Erik lay quietly for half an hour while watching the activities before cautiously dropping into a small ravine, containing a stream, well out of sight of possible observers. From there he crawled downhill towards the shore. As he crept forward, more and more of the opposite shore of the fjord came into view, along with a grey ship of about ten thousand tonnes and several small craft moving around it. Astern of the ship there was a black, low-lying object in the water at the foot of the rock face. A few more yards of crawling and there was another immediately astern of the first. Suddenly he realised what they were – U-boats! With reptilian menace the evil-looking pair crouched low in the water at the foot of the cliff, with naval ratings moving about the deck of the nearer of the two. Erik trained the glasses on them and their numbers sprang into view. 'U30' and 'U25' were painted in white on their conning towers.

'So that's what it's all about,' he exclaimed to himself, 'They are building a U-boat base!' He knew, at once, the importance of the discovery and as far as he knew, the local Norwegian Resistance had no knowledge of what the Germans were up to in this isolated fjord. The possibility of a submarine base had never been raised, and a haven for U-boats in this part of north Norway would pose a deadly threat to Arctic convoys sailing to Murmansk in North Russia. Erik lay back and scanned every inch of the surrounding landscape.

Such a sensitive area must have a defensive screen, he thought.

The binoculars soon confirmed that, on the opposite side of the inlet, there were at least three anti-aircraft gun positions on the high ground above the U-boats. They were well hidden by walls of rock, behind which he could just make out occasional movements of the gun crews.

In light of what he had seen Erik was alarmed by his relatively casual approach to the area. There was no evidence that he had been spotted, but that was through luck alone. With great caution, he eased himself back up the ravine until he was out of sight of both U-boats and the gun positions. Working his way further uphill, he came across a rock outcrop and crawled round the back of it so that he could no longer be seen by observers around the shore.

He was just beginning to relax when, to his alarm, from no more than twenty metres to his right, a brief laugh was followed by a snatch of conversation in German. Erik froze, lowering himself face-down into the bilberry leaves growing between the rocks. He lay there, unmoving, for fully fifteen minutes hearing continued snatches of German conversation. There must be similar gun emplacements, or observation posts, on this side of the inlet too and he realised that he had almost blundered into one of them. Presently, the talking stopped, but Erik heard the sudden clink of a nailed boot on rock no more than ten paces from where he lay. One of the soldiers was approaching.

Oh God, he thought, gripping the loaded Mauser, This is it! He froze, expecting a challenge, but instead heard a splashing sound as the German relieved himself against the other side of the intervening rock. Instead of returning to the gun position the soldier then wandered up the hillside and began collecting bilberries which were growing so prolifically among the rocks. Out of the corner of his eye, and hardly daring to blink, Erik watched as the German, engrossed in his gathering, now and then stood up to swallow a mouthful of berries. The man, who had reached a point a little above where Erik lay, suddenly straightened up and turned around to gaze for a moment across the inlet, directly over the spot where Erik was lying in full view.

Erik, hardly daring to breathe, pressed his face into the bilberry leaves expecting a challenge at any moment. But nothing happened and, miraculously, the man simply strolled out of view to rejoin his companion in the gun position.

With sweating hands Erik cautiously pushed the Mauser back into his pocket. He had seen enough and he needed to escape undetected from this exposed hillside with the vital information that the fjord was going to be, or perhaps already was, being used as a staging post for U-boats.

He decided that it would be safest to wait until dusk and then to strike back inland, retracing his steps of the previous day. For several hours he continued to hear snatches of conversation from the anti-aircraft gun crew then, at last, all became quiet.

Could they possibly be asleep? he wondered, and as the light faded he crawled up the hill, keeping the rocks between him and the Germans. It seemed unlikely that he would be seen by watchers on the opposite side of the inlet in such dim light, and after about 200 metres it seemed safe enough to walk upright.

He had gone another few hundred metres when, against the fading light of the western sky, he came across the silhouette of a low rock outcrop. As he skirted this he saw that it was, in fact, a circle of built rocks. Suddenly he was startled by an exclamation, in German, from within. At the same time he saw the barrels of an anti-aircraft gun protruding from what was, evidently, yet another gun position.

There was a shout of '*Halt! Halt!*' from the gunner but there was nothing to do but run. Using the dusk and what little cover there was, Erik made off as fast as he could. He got no more than twenty metres when he stumbled on a rock and fell on his face just as several rifle shots whip-cracked over his head. There were renewed shouts of alarm from the Germans as he picked himself up and, bent double, ran for his life. There were no more shots and he silently thanked the gathering darkness for saving him.

For a long time Erik kept running. His pounding heart pleaded for a rest, but he kept going, putting as much distance between himself and the Germans as possible. As the darkness deepened, he continued at a walking pace for about two hours. With no continued sounds of pursuit, he judged that it was safe enough to rest for at least part of the night in an area of frost-shattered rocks which would give him temporary cover. In spite of his still-thumping heart he found a sheltered dry patch of ground, climbed into his sleeping bag and, after eating a slab of dry bread, pulled his clothes tightly round him and tried to sleep.

The night was particularly cold and, after only a few hours of fitful dozing, he rolled up his belongings, shouldered his haversack and set off once more towards the road. At first he stumbled along in the half-light but it was not until late afternoon that, far ahead, he glimpsed the road which he had left three days previously. There was no sign of traffic and he felt that he would have time to take cover should a German vehicle appear. The regular bus would not pass for another day and his best hope would be to hitch a lift from a passing local.

He had walked for half an hour when he heard a vehicle approaching from behind. At that point there was no cover where he could hide by the time the lorry reached him: there was nothing for it but to stand his ground and give the impression that he was an innocent local. The lorry, heading towards Alta, was a Wehrmacht vehicle with a closed canvas cover at the back. Erik waved as it swept past while the driver, who looked like a Norwegian, raised a finger in acknowledgement but did not slow down. But Erik's brief glimpse of the driver was enough. He was sure that it was his cousin, Bjorn – again! A German soldier, sitting beside him in the cab, turned his head to inspect Erik as they passed, but still the vehicle kept going. It was closely followed by two similar lorries, each driven by a civilian but with a German soldier in the cab.

While Bjorn had given no sign of recognition, Erik was deeply disturbed at seeing his cousin apparently working for the Germans. There was nothing he could do about it but he found it difficult to understand how Bjorn, his boyhood playmate, could have come to work for the enemy.

Erik, although weary after the long trek from the peninsula, kept on walking. After half an hour he heard another vehicle approaching from behind him. This time he decided to try to get a lift and turned to face the oncoming vehicle. An open Kübelwagen appeared round a bend and the driver seemed to be the sole occupant. Erik stood his ground and flagged it down. To his mild surprise the car slowed and drew up beside him. The driver, a German NCO, studied Erik for a moment then nodded and indicated that he could get in beside him.

'Alta,' said Erik as he threw his haversack in, got in and sat down. The German nodded again and drove on. Suddenly, Erik remembered the Mauser in his left trouser pocket and cursed himself for his carelessness as the outline of the weapon was clearly visible through his clothing. Worse still the front seats were so close together that the bulge of the pistol was almost touching the German's leg. Erik put his hand down in an attempt to make the weapon less obvious but as he did so one of the rounds which he was carrying fell out of his pocket and, with a clink, ended up under the wooden floor slats between him and the driver. The brass object was all too visible to Erik where it lay deeply between two of the slats. The German glanced down to see what had fallen but from his angle he could see nothing suspicious. With rising panic Erik tried to distract the man's attention by using some of the few words of German which he knew. The driver looked at him curiously, evidently not understanding what Erik was talking about, and continued to drive on as before. At last

Erik was set down in Alta's main street and, as he watched the Kübelwagen depart, he thanked God for his luck and wondered what the reaction was going to be when the Mauser round was discovered.

15

LARA'S TORMENT

At Lyngenfjord Lara was having an unhappy pregnancy. She continued to live with her parents and would not see anyone else. Gunnar seemed to have aged visibly since he had learned the truth about the pregnancy. Birgitta, too, had taken the news badly but, as the months went by, she began to show increasingly sympathetic interest in her daughter's condition.

'How are you feeling, dear?' she began to ask each morning. 'You really ought to take a rest each day on your bed.'

She encouraged her daughter to eat whatever nourishing food she could provide, and Lara was aware that her mother was beginning to show concern, not only for her, but also for her unborn, half-German grandchild.

By late winter the pregnancy was very evident and one evening Lara asked her mother to come to her bedroom to look at the smooth swelling of her lower abdomen. Part of her simply wanted reassurance, but, most of all, she wanted to share what was, for her, a deeply emotional experience. She felt the bitterness of Willi's absence and longed to share with him this most important event in her life. Often, at night, she dreamed of him and, at other times, in her sleep she imagined she could hear a child's chattering voice.

Their nearest neighbours, Arne and Inga Petersen and Nils and Helga Anders, were sympathetic and supportive of Lara in her predicament but, when they came to visit, Lara hurried up to her room to avoid meeting them. One morning, old Leif Jessen appeared on his faithful pony. He did not manage to call often but he was always a welcome visitor. Gunnar saw him coming from a distance, moving slowly past the river and up the farm track. Gunnar called through to Birgitta and together they went outside to greet the old man. Without speaking, Leif dismounted and after gravely shaking hands with Gunnar and Birgitta, as was his habit, he unwound the usual piece of rope from his waist, tied the pony's forelegs together, smacked it on the rump and left it to forage.

'Come away in. It's good to see you, Leif,' said Gunnar as he ushered the visitor into the house and sat him down in a comfortable chair in front of the stove. 'Birgitta will make us a hot drink – ersatz of course, but it's all we have.'

When the steaming cups were brought through, they settled down to talk.

'How is Lara?' Leif asked after a time. It was clear that he knew about her pregnancy and that the father was a German. Gunnar explained that she did not want to meet visitors, but, nevertheless, called to her to come down to join them by the stove.

'Lara, come down! It's Leif. He's come specially to see you.'

After a moment or two they heard the door opening and Lara came slowly downstairs keeping her eyes on the floor and not even glancing at the visitor. She was a picture of abject shame and misery. Gone was the happy cheerful girl they had all once known. Her face looked shrunken and ill.

Rather than joining Leif and her parents at the stove, Lara sat down alone at the wooden table by the window absent-mindedly tracing the grain of its scrubbed surface with a finger.

Leif was disturbed at what he saw. The local blacksmith, Jon Gerstenberg, who lived five kilometres away, had two sons who sometimes helped to shoe his pony. Leif had overheard the youths discussing Lara and they, like most of the locals, knew that a German was responsible for her pregnancy. The youths evidently thought that she should be ostracised and humiliated in public. What was worse was their reference to her as the 'the Nazis' whore'. One of them said that she should have her head shaved as a warning to other Norwegian girls. It was not the first time that Leif had heard people saying that kind of thing.

Leif was disturbed at the state Lara was in and when the unhappy girl later excused herself and had returned to her room, he asked Gunnar what he and Birgitta planned for their daughter's future.

'I think she will have a difficult time in Norway,' said the old man. 'There's widespread hatred of girls in her situation. In the long term I'm sure the Allies are going to win this war, but until then things will be very difficult for Lara and probably afterwards too. The problem will not only be Lara's but the child's as well.'

The three of them fell silent while Gunnar opened the stove and threw in several birch logs. In the silence the burning wood crackled within the blackness of the stove and a faint coil of sweet-smelling smoke drifted out into the room. Gunnar was pensive but Leif noticed that Birgitta's eyes were shining with welling tears.

Gunnar was the first to speak.

'Leif, you are an old and trusted friend and I would like to ask what you would do in our situation?' He paused and added, 'Lara won't hear what you say if you keep your voice down.'

The old man did not reply right away, but shook some snuff onto his hand and sniffed briskly.

'Since you ask,' he said, 'I don't think there's much you can do so long as the Germans remain in occupation. It's at the war's end that she's likely to suffer persecution. People are already calling the blameless children born in such circumstances "Nazi spawn." Human beings can be very cruel,' he added. 'Perhaps people who say such things are those who have done little or nothing against the Occupation and feel that they must make a show of patriotism.'

'Yes, I know that but what do you advise?' persisted Gunnar.

'I think that her life will become impossible in Norway, but have you thought about...'

Before he could finish Birgitta suddenly broke down in tears. Gunnar got up and, putting his arm round his wife's shoulder, gently guided her through to the kitchen, murmuring some words of comfort before closing the door and returning to rejoin Leif.

'I'm sorry about that. Birgitta is so upset – well, we both are. What were you about to say?' asked Gunnar as he returned to his chair.

'I know,' continued Leif, 'that Birgitta has a sister in England and that her boy, Lara's cousin Erik, used to stay with you in summer. Have you thought about sending Lara and the child over there to live with her once the war is finished?'

It was certainly an idea worth considering, thought Gunnar. He lapsed into silence, as he contemplated losing his beloved daughter.

Leif apologised for giving such blunt advice and said that if he could help in the future then Gunnar only had to ask.

At last, after a long discussion about the war, Leif rose to leave and the two old friends went outside to find the pony, which had managed to wander round to the back of the house. Leif untied the hobble rope which he replaced round his waist, mounted the patient beast and, amid thanks from Gunnar, set off at a slow walk down the farm road.

A month passed. Lara remained withdrawn and rarely chatted with her parents. The normally happy house had become a gloomy place.

In May the days lengthened so that there was almost no night. The grass on the farm flushed to a brilliant green and migratory birds again appeared. Even the birdsong, which Lara had always loved so much, did not lift her depression. As the evenings lengthened she started to take walks by herself, often sitting alone by the river for hours. From a distance, her parents, with tears in their eyes, would catch sight of the solitary hunched figure, their Lara, their beloved Lara, alone, always alone.

The unhappy girl began to go for longer walks and her parents became used to her absences but they would have been more worried had they known what was passing through their daughter's mind.

Lara could see no way out of the trap which she had woven. Life had lost all meaning. She despised herself and could see no future for the baby after it was born and she was already an outcast from society.

One day when her parents were out she took a sharp fish-filleting knife from the kitchen and imagined putting an end to herself. She filled the sink with hot water and immersed her hand in it, then turning her wrist upwards she placed the sharp edge of the blade against her skin pressing it into the flesh. She hesitated before drawing the steel across her wrist, nauseated by the sight of the blade on her skin. Then her courage failed her and, shaking, she put the knife away.

A few days later she found herself wandering along the fjord shore. She was barely aware of the beautiful mountain scenery, which no longer brought her comfort; neither did she notice the flotillas of eider ducks which mewed so softly on the placid water. With mild surprise, she realised how far she had wandered when she came upon Arne Petersen's two small boats moored close to the shore. At the sight of these she suddenly made up her mind. Yes, she would do it – now!

She stepped out of her shoes, waded into the shockingly cold water and found that she could just reach the nearest boat. It was secured to an anchored float by a stout hemp rope and all it contained was a single old oar and a rusty fishing knife which lay under a seat. She picked up the knife, sawed at the hemp rope and dropped the cut end into the water. Suddenly the boat was free. She pulled it towards her and, with difficulty, put her leg over the thwart and rolled herself on board where she lay for some moments gathering her breath. Then she sat up and, using a mixture of poling and paddling, she drove the boat as far as she could from the shore. She stood up in the wobbling craft looking about her and, as she did so, she felt her unborn child moving in her belly.

Could it really be that somehow it knew what she was about to do? Still, she had made up her mind. She would take herself and her child to a place beyond suffering.

She put a foot on the thwart. The boat dipped unsteadily as she took a leap over the side and was engulfed by the icy waters of the fjord.

★

Obergefreiter Hans Meyer and Gefreiter Kurt Richter, NCOs of the Wehrmacht's 196th Infantry Division, were thankful to have been posted to Norway. They were driving a truck along the Lyngenfjord shore, having been detailed to report to the administration office of the prisoner of war camp at Fridalen. The journey from their depot in Narvik had been a pleasure on that sunny June day. An alternative posting could easily have been the Eastern Front where the most appalling butchery was going on, the 'Mincing Machine' some were calling it. Kurt's elder brother had been killed when the Russians had finally encircled, then annihilated, the Germans at Stalingrad. The recapture of the city by the Russians had come as a great shock to all Germans; it was an almost unbelievable event. It was said the Russians had fought like devils and had captured General Paulus alive. A hint of unease about the war's outcome had begun entering the minds of many soldiers of the Third Reich.

Those events seemed part of another world as they drove along the peaceful Lyngenfjord shore. There were few locals about as they passed the scattered farms. Presently they crossed a wooden bridge spanning a clear river near where a track led off to a distant farmhouse. It was a beautiful spot and the glassy fjord to their left was unruffled by wind. A little further on, round a sweeping bend in the road, Hans Meyer suddenly gave an exclamation and pointed to a small boat a hundred metres offshore. Something was odd about it. A figure, apparently a woman, was standing upright in the craft, which was rocking dangerously. Then, without warning she put one foot on the thwart and deliberately leapt into the water. The empty boat wobbled wildly for a short while before quietly drifting off, leaving the woman floundering.

Hans Meyer braked hard and the truck skidded to a halt close to the shore, not far from where the other boat lay at its moorings. Both men leapt out. Meyer told his colleague to wade in and to untie the boat. The oars were secured to the seat with cord but it took only seconds to free them. Richter quickly poled the boat in, picked up Hans Meyer, and rowed as fast as he could to the drowning woman.

She was still afloat but moving only weakly when they reached her. They grabbed her clothing and tried to pull her aboard. She was clearly alive but semi-conscious and it proved strangely difficult to drag her into their boat. She was unexpectedly heavy and, it was only when they tried to lift her on board that it became clear that she was pregnant.

With difficulty they at last managed to place her on the bottom of their boat and rowed to the shore while she coughed and choked. She was confused, pale, cold and barely coherent as the Germans lifted her out and carried her over to the truck where they laid her down in the back while her body convulsed with shivering. They wrapped her in an army greatcoat and, after pulling the rescue boat ashore, started to drive to a nearby farmhouse. At that point the woman, regaining her senses, sat up and when she saw where she was being taken, she became agitated.

'No, no!' she protested weakly and, pointing in the other direction, said, 'Home!'

Her meaning was clear enough and, after a brief discussion, the men turned the vehicle around and, prompted by their passenger, retraced their route to the bridge and up the farm track leading to the house which they had seen earlier. Gunnar, who had watched the Wehrmacht truck driving up to the farm, emerged in alarm as it stopped at the door. Hans Meyer jumped out and beckoned him round to the back of the vehicle and showed him Lara, soaked and shivering.

'Oh, my God!' exclaimed her father. 'It's my daughter. Lara, what's happened?'

Without waiting to explain, the German NCOs gently lifted the girl out and, under Gunnar's directions, carried her into the kitchen. They laid her on the floor in front of the stove, whereupon Birgitta appeared. She was shocked and horrified at what she saw and, ushering the men out of the room, she stripped off Lara's clothes. After drying her with a towel she rubbed her down to restore the circulation and wrapped her in several blankets.

When the two Germans made to leave, Gunnar began to thank them. Only when he was interrupted by the men explaining by way of signs, gestures did he realise that they had actually seen Lara's suicidal leap into the fjord. He went back into the house, indicating that the Germans should wait for a moment, and returned with a pencil and two pieces of paper. On one he asked them to write their names and on the other he wrote his own and Lara's names and gave that piece to them. He tried to thank them for what they had done and shook hands with both. Then the Germans drove off and Gunnar went back into the house to find his daughter sitting up, swathed in blankets in front of the stove. She was still shivering but, despite her tears, was beginning to recover from her ordeal. Birgitta helped her to take some sort of hot drink and she smiled weakly at her father when he came in.

'I'm sorry, Father, sorry, sorry,' she sobbed as he put his arm round her shoulders. 'It won't happen again, I promise.'

'Where was it, Lara?' asked her father gently.

'At the Petersens',' she replied though her tears. 'I took their boat.'

Gunnar felt his chin trembling and tears pricking in his own eyes as he hugged his daughter, his remembered little girl, ever beloved with her tumbling dark curls. He found that his voice had choked up and he could not speak. He took a deep breath, stood up and fed more logs into the already roaring stove. After some murmured reassurances, he beckoned to Birgitta to come out of the room with him.

'What about the pregnancy?' he asked quietly. He did not know what to think and did not mention to Birgitta what was in his mind, but would it not solve a lot if the near drowning were to lead to a miscarriage?

'It's far too early to tell,' she replied, at the same time realising that a miscarriage was the last thing that *she* wished for. She hoped and prayed that, ultimately, she would be presented with a grandchild even if it was to be half German.

After an hour Lara had recovered enough for Gunnar to leave her alone with Birgitta. He took the bicycle from the shed and rode over to the Petersens to explain what had happened to their boats. The twins had already noticed that someone had pulled one of them up onto the shore and that the other was missing. They were down at the waterside trying to work out what had happened and were busily rearranging the moorings. They soon located the missing boat, which had drifted half a mile down the fjord, and rowed off to retrieve it. Gunnar then cycled on up to his neighbours' house where he could see Arne watching his sons rowing down the fjord to the distant boat.

★

After Lara's suicide attempt, life gradually settled into a more normal rhythm. Her parents nursed her back to her usual physical health but remained worried about her moodiness. Between them they agreed not to leave her alone for longer than was absolutely necessary: if she could do it once she might try it again.

Spring had turned into summer and, when Gunnar stepped out of the house one morning, he heard the first cuckoo of the year. Its soft notes repeated again and again announced that summer had, at last, returned to that northern land. Gunnar left the house in good spirits and walked the 400 metres down to the road to see if any mail had been left in the box. The early sun warmed his back as he strolled along. On his right the river was running at a good level and he stopped for a moment beside the main pool to see if the salmon had yet come in from the sea. He stood watching the water sliding smoothly down into the rapids below. Then something momentarily caught his eye in the white water at the head of the pool. It was a single fish repeatedly jumping as it tried to mount the falls. They had arrived! Gunnar spirits immediately rose still further as he knew that his family's diet could be supplemented once again. He would catch and smoke as many salmon as he could.

He wandered another fifty yards to the post box, which had, so often, brought welcome and happy news of family and friends but this time it was different. There was a single letter in the box addressed in Bjorn's familiar, untidy writing, but why did his heart sink when there was a letter from Bjorn? He lifted the letter out, held it pensively for a moment, and then slit it open. The single sheet of paper read:

Dear Father and Mother,

I hope that you are both well. Since I last saw you I have been busy as a driver, taking Russian prisoners to Fridalen.

It's not a bad job but it's a bit boring and when the German authorities there asked if I would volunteer to join the military, I said that I would think about it. Apparently, two other Norwegians that I know have volunteered and will be sent to Sennheim in Germany for training. That will last six months and then they will join the newly-formed SS Skijeger Bataljon, Norge. which has German officers but, apart from that, it's purely Norwegian. All the men will be specially trained to use skis, which would be easy for me as I already ski well, and then the Battalion will probably be sent to the Finnish front to face the Russians. I have not yet offered myself as a volunteer as I need more time to think about it.

I know that you are very anti-German but I have found that they have always treated me well and are not the monsters that some people think. They say that there is a real danger of Russia invading Norway and they make the point that we will be fighting for Norway alongside other Norwegians against an enemy which may well attack us.

The letter went on in a chatty vein, with enquiries about Lara's well-being.

Gunnar was appalled. His daughter being pregnant by a German officer was bad enough but now his son seemed to be playing with the idea of joining the Wehrmacht, which had invaded Norway! Gunnar knew that Bjorn had always been impressed with military might in a way in which most Norwegians were not. Perhaps this is just another of his passing enthusiasms, he thought.

One thing after another seemed to be building up to upset Gunnar. Now he would have to tell Birgitta about Bjorn's letter. She seemed to have come to terms with Lara's situation but it was difficult to imagine a similar reaction to their son's ideas.

16

WILLI RETURNS TO LYNGENFJORD: 1943

On a sunny June morning in 1943 a group of Wehrmacht soldiers were standing outside a shop which sold newspapers in Alta's main street. The men were enjoying a brief rest and a row of them, sitting on a low wall outside the shop, were scanning copies of *Germania,* one of the official publications of the Occupation. The paper made much of the news that a new Wehrmacht unit, the 'SS Skijeger Bataljon Norge', a ski battalion, had been created by the successful recruitment of Norwegian nationals loyal to the Nazi cause. However, the paper gave no indication that many ordinary soldiers of the Wehrmacht were beginning to have private doubts about the overall progress of the war and there was no mention at all of the catastrophic German defeat at Stalingrad five months previously. News of that defeat had struck the ranks of the Wehrmacht like a thunderbolt. Many would not believe that General Paulus had surrendered the city and had been taken prisoner by the Russians. Hitherto, that Germany might actually lose the war had been unthinkable, but doubts were beginning to creep in and there was a feeling that the tide of the war was beginning to turn against Germany. Not that such feelings could be openly expressed in Hitler's Reich.

A short way off, two officers sat drinking coffee at

a sunlit table outside a café, each scanning whatever real news there was in the paper. They did not look at all like men of war. One was stocky and dark and the other tall and fair with fine lines round his blue eyes. The taller of the two was leafing through the newspaper which he had just bought when, with a sudden exclamation, he leant forward and peered closely at an article on an inside page. There was a photograph of two smiling German NCOs and above it ran the headline:

HEROIC SOLDIERS OF THE WEHRMACHT RISK THEIR LIVES TO SAVE DROWNING NORWEGIAN WOMAN.

There followed a short article describing how Obergefreiter Hans Meyer and Gefreiter Kurt Richter had saved Lara Torkelsen, a young pregnant Norwegian woman, from drowning in Lyngenfjord.

Willi Schmidt was thunderstruck. This must be his Lara! He had not been able to get any messages to her since he had left Lyngenfjord, but 'pregnant'! He made a mental calculation on the lapse of time since their love-making. There was no doubt about it: the unborn child must be his.

'What's wrong, Willi?' enquired his brother officer. 'What have you found in that paper?'

Willi explained only briefly that he had met the woman described in the article, but said nothing about the truth of their relationship. Then he lapsed into silence. He had never stopped longing to see Lara since the day they parted, and had always hoped that his future posting might allow them to meet again. His thoughts were in turmoil. When was the baby due? Would it be a boy or a girl? Was Lara staying with her parents? How could he make contact with her and even see her?

He looked again at the article, which placed much emphasis on the 'heroic role' of the German rescuers. The authorities were obviously using the event to show the occupiers in a good light. He carefully folded the newspaper and slipped it into his pocket.

Willi's chance came on June 10th with the news that, in five days time, Reichskommissar Joseph Adelbrecht, together with other, as yet unnamed, high-ranking officers, were due to come north to inspect the Lyngenfjord defences which were being prepared to block a possible Russian advance down the length of Norway. Two officers were needed to help ensure that the visit went smoothly. Great importance was being given to the inspection and quite exceptional activity seemed to be developing around the visit. As two officers from the Alta region were required to take part in the preparations, Willi volunteered to go. He knew that the assignment would take him close to Lara's home and he knew, too, that he would inevitably try to see her.

Rumours had reached Alta that the inspection party would include the new Commander of German Forces in Norway, General von Schirach, and there was a suggestion, albeit barely whispered, that the Führer himself might be in attendance.

Willi, being an educated man, had not accepted so unquestioningly as had some of his fellow countrymen the National Socialist propaganda about the moral rectitude of Nazi Germany. Since before the war, he had been having serious concerns about the effects of National Socialism on German society. The appalling treatment of Germany's Jewish population had affected him deeply. Although the persecution had been politically inspired, the general population had either remained passive or had taken part in it wholeheartedly. In 1938 Willi himself had seen a Berlin mob ransacking a Jewish-owned shop and had done nothing to show his opposition. He had just walked on, although what could he have done? Now, closer to hand in Norway, events such as the Telavag massacre had destroyed his belief in the system and his doubts had grown into a certainty that Germany had rejected all thoughts of civilised behaviour. What, he pondered, will the world have to say about Germany when it's all over? Despite these feelings he had no idea how he could now opt out from being part of the whole dreadful juggernaut.

Willi made a conscious effort to cast off these thoughts, and spent the next two days in mounting excitement at the prospect of seeing Lara again. However, he could not think of a way of doing so without having to meet her parents. How would they react when they realised that it was he who was responsible for the pregnancy? He had so many questions. When was the baby due and would Lara herself be happy to see him again – or not? He felt no guilt in attaching more importance to Lara and to their child than to the fate of German forces in Europe. His priorities were changing.

Two days later, he, his brother officer Hans Schreiber, and a driver set off from Alta on the 200-kilometre journey to Lyngenfjord. It was a beautiful early summer's day, and in due course they were rounding the glassy-calm waters of Kafjord where the *Tirpitz* was anchored. The huge battleship with her massive sixteen-inch guns lay close against the steep, southern shore, with the mountain soaring above her. A screen of anti-torpedo nets, held by lines of floats surrounding the ship, emphasised her strategic importance. A second warship, the *Prinz Eugen*, lay two kilometres away at the entrance of Kafjord and, on some flat ground of the nearby north shore, extensive servicing port facilities had been developed.

The road led them along the west shore of Altafjord before following the long narrow Langfjord, at the head of which a branch road to the right leading to the Svartfjell Peninsula was heavily guarded. It seemed to be a highly restricted military zone and a red-and-white-painted barrier manned by armed troops prevented unauthorised access. Willi had heard rumours about a U-boat base being established there and he knew that large numbers of Russian prisoners had been drafted in to work on the project.

The rest of the journey was uneventful and, after three hours, they were back on territory which was familiar to Willi. Soon they came to Olderdalen and he suggested that they should tell the driver to stop at the store. Hans Schreiber, too, was more than happy to stretch his legs and the pair went inside.

Willi was surprised at his own nervousness at finding himself back where he and Lara had first met. His heart was thumping when they opened the door and stepped inside. He did not feel at all ready to meet Hilder yet, but there she was, arranging the shelves behind the counter. She looked up as the two officers came in and immediately recognised Willi. Suddenly he was tongue-tied and did not know what to say. Hilder stood looking defiantly at him, but did not speak. With her hands on her hips she waited and waited, her expression hardening as he came to the counter. Clearly she was not going to make it easy for him.

At last, in his awkward Norwegian, he blurted out, 'Please tell me, where is Lara? Is she again with her parents?'

Hilder bristled with hostility and for a time, still with hands on her hips, remained silent and stony faced.

After what seemed like minutes to Willi, she at last answered coldly, 'Why do you want to know?'

'Please do tell me how she is. I know she expects a baby. Has it come yet?'

The shop was empty apart from the three of them. Hilder glanced around her and continued: 'It has and thanks to you the poor girl is now known as the "whore of the Nazis and a lot of people won't talk to her; she's an outcast.'

Hilder had grown red in the face and her voice was raised. 'And do you know what they call her baby, your baby?' Then she spat out the dreadful word –"Naziyngel" – Nazi spawn.

'The baby is blameless, but you are not. You should be ashamed of yourself!'

Before Willi could duck his head she leant across the counter and struck him a stinging blow across the face with the flat of her hand.

Willi stepped back, shocked by the force of the blow. He was humiliated in front of Hans Schreiber – who quickly understood that Willi had been less than honest with him.

'Come on Willi, let's get out of here!' exclaimed Hans and, grabbing his arm, pulled him out of the store to the waiting car.

'What was all that about? You must report that woman for striking a German officer.'

'No, she is in the right,' he replied. 'The fault is mine.' Willi gingerly fingered his smarting face where a reddening imprint of a hand had appeared.

The driver, who had not seen the assault, was told to take them the final few kilometres to their billet in Fridalen, while Willi ruefully gave his colleague an explanation of the confrontation in the store.

'Nevertheless you really must report that woman, Willi. That was clearly an unprovoked attack and you can't let her get away with it. German honour demands it.'

'Now look here, Hans,' replied Willi. 'We've marched uninvited into that woman's country and I know that our troops have committed atrocities here. Against that how much does a slap on the face count for? Also I know that Hilder Larsen is a good woman and we will forget about the incident.'

Presently they passed the half-hidden track where he and Lara had so often lain and loved together. Birches still arched over it and Willi wondered if there was still a trace of their bed among the ferns where their baby had been conceived. The same longing to be with Lara was as strong as ever, but there was an added dimension, the emotional pull of fatherhood.

Willi, deep in thought, hardly noticed the beauty of the mountains as they drove along the Lyngenfjord shore. The car tyres rattled across the timber-decked bridge over the little river and thirty metres further on, the farm track to Lara's home branched off up the hill. He was so close to her but he could not conceive how he was going to see her. He had to admit to himself that he, a German officer of the Wehrmacht, was terrified of the inevitable confrontation with Lara's parents. In his mind Lara's name had come to mean gentleness, softness and beauty. He adored her above all else; he was hopelessly and completely in love. Suddenly, Willi made his decision.

'Stop!' he shouted to the driver and the car pulled off the road on the far side of the bridge.

'Wait here,' he ordered, 'I will be back in about half an hour.'

Without explanation to either Hans or the driver he got out and set off up the farm track. Hans was furious with this off hand treatment but all he could do was to shrug his shoulders as he glanced at the driver.

No one seemed to have noticed Willi walking up to the house, and as he reached the door, he wondered if everyone was out. Then, in the silence, the notes of a sweetly sung plaintive lullaby floated out from somewhere inside the building. He stood for a moment, listening, spellbound. Then a baby cried, the lullaby stopped and a female voice began to soothe the fractious infant. It was Lara's voice: it was his baby!

He breathed deeply and rapped softly on the door. The singing stopped and he heard someone moving inside. There was a brief clatter from some dropped kitchen utensil, then the latch rattled – the door was pushed open – and there she was – Lara!

Lara was transfixed with surprise at seeing him, and for a moment the two of them just stared at each other. Then Willi held out his arms and Lara collapsed into his embrace just as she had done so many times before. He kissed her lips and nuzzled into her neck. The faint sweet smell of her skin was just as it used to be. How he loved her!

'The… the baby?' stammered Willi at last.

'Your daughter of course,' replied Lara and after a brief pause: 'Her first name is Lill but we've called her Lilara which really means "Little Lara".'

Then she clung to Willi sobbing quietly.

'I thought that I would never see you again.' The dam burst and her tears flooded out. Willi held her tightly to his chest until the emotional storm subsided. Having recovered her composure Lara disentangled herself from his embrace and beckoned to him.

'Come and meet your little girl,' but noticing Willi's hesitation, she continued, 'It's alright – my parents have gone to visit neighbours and won't be back for an hour or more. Come on through.'

With some trepidation, Willi followed Lara into the kitchen which was evidently used as a living room as well. There in a corner was a crib decorated with pink ribbon and in it squirmed an equally pink-faced baby. For a moment her blue eyes gazed up at him and then her face crinkled up as she burst into tears at the sight of the tall stranger. Willi had no idea what to do, but he placed one of his fingers in the tiny hand which responded by gripping him surprisingly tightly. The bawling increased to a crescendo and the little legs thrashed about beneath the covers in protest at the intrusion. Lara, murmuring reassurance, picked up the shrieking infant and peace was restored.

After admiring his daughter, Willi broached the subject that was really troubling him. 'What do your parents think about me; surely you must have told them?'

'Yes,' replied Lara, 'I have told them. Mother has accepted that we are a couple, especially since Little Lara was born, but Father is still upset about it. At first he was angry, actually angrier than I can say but sooner or later, Willi, you will have to meet them and now is as good a time as any. They will be back presently and if you don't want to see them you'd better leave at once.'

Willi put his arm round Lara's shoulder. 'I want to

keep you as my own forever which means that I have to go through with the meeting. Tell me, Lara, about something else. I've been very troubled about a newspaper report which I saw of your near-drowning in the fjord. How did it happen – though I think I know? You must have had a terrible time because of me: you poor girl and it's all my fault! Now, listen to this: I want you to promise to marry me once the war is over and we will live together always.'

For half an hour they talked together until voices outside jolted them back to reality. Gunnar and Birgitta walked in. Willi jumped to his feet prepared to face the onslaught.

Gunnar had seen the Wehrmacht vehicle at the bottom of the hill and stood staring at this enemy German officer.

'What do you want? What are you doing in my house?' he demanded.

Willi was speechless for a moment and in the silence Lara glanced anxiously up at him.

'Well?' persisted Gunnar.

'I… I have come back to see your daughter, for whom I have much love and also to see my child.'

Gunnar uttered an oath. 'Swine!' he exclaimed.

'You wish me to leave?' replied Willi.

Gunnar grabbed the front of the German's uniform and with considerable force pushed the interloper to the still-open door. Willi staggered backwards and, falling heavily, struck his head on the door jamb. The blow was hard enough to daze him and he lay on the floor, momentarily confused as to what had happened.

Birgitta rushed to pull her husband away from the prostrate officer while Lara burst into tears. The commotion was soon accompanied by renewed shrieks from Little Lara.

'No, Gunnar! No!' entreated Birgitta as she planted herself between her husband and Willi. 'Leave him alone!'

With Lara's assistance she helped Willi to his feet and, pulling him over to the table, sat him on a chair. Lara, her mind in turmoil, dampened a cloth and mopped the trickle of blood from her lover's face.

Gunnar could not bring himself to stay in the room with this foreigner; with this enemy officer who had defiled his daughter. Without another word, he barged out of the room and went outside. He noticed that his hands were shaking and reflected that this was the second time he had assaulted a member of the Wehrmacht and that he had better not push his luck too far. Fortunately his victim had not responded with aggression.

Birgitta, with a woman's instinct, waited for a few minutes and then went outside to persuade Gunnar to come back in. She found him on the seat just outside the door staring across the fjord. She sat beside him and gently broached the subject of his attitude to Willi. After ten minutes the pair of them returned indoors with Gunnar looking calmer. Birgitta turned to Willi, with what amounted to an extraordinary peace offering and using his first name, said:

'Willi, for that is what I shall now call you, we accept your relationship with our daughter as we want her to be happy, and I know that, one day, this may even mean having you as our son in law. We also know that Little Lara needs a good father, but you must know how difficult this is for us.'

At this point Lara burst into tears of relief and threw her arms round her mother's neck and hugged her.

Gunnar within himself was not untouched by the emotion of the moment, although no one noticed because his face revealed nothing. Willi, almost overcome with relief, detached Lara from her mother's embrace and, right there in front of her parents, kissed her on the lips.

At last Willi removed himself from the domestic scene and hurried down the farm track and back to the car where Hans Schreiber was impatiently waiting. Willi tried to apologise to his angry colleague and the onward journey was completed in silence,

Seven days after the reconciliation, Willi was informed that the Reichskommissar's visit had been postponed until the following summer when he would again be needed. Meantime he was ordered to return to Alta. Later on Willi heard the reason for the change of plan was the outcome of the huge tank battle at Kursk in July 1943 which had been a disaster for the German forces. The growing might of the Russians was steadily eating away at the Wehrmacht's earlier territorial gains and many plans would henceforth be changed.

17

KAFJORD. THE THREAT FROM BELOW

In July 1943 the Norwegian Resistance learned that the Allies were becoming more effective in their anti-submarine activities and that a United States Air Force bomber had sunk a U-boat at Trondheim. In addition, the discovery of the U-boat staging port at the Svartfjell Peninsula had produced a vigorous Allied response with intensive and repeated mining of the sea approaches to the fjord, which effectively prevented access to the port.

Erik had reason to feel satisfied that his activities were contributing to the Allied cause. He had ensured that the Resistance in Svolvaer, Tromso and Alta knew how to use the new Paraset B2–Z and the new codes. He had reported the presence of the U-boat base on the Svartfjell Peninsula and he had continued to help Sven's 'fjord watchers' in the forest above Alta. Then a new opportunity arose. Notices posted by the German authorities appeared in Alta stating that skilled marine engineers were needed to work on small boat engines at Kafjord, not far from where the *Tirpitz* was moored. Applicants were instructed to report to the Kriegsmarine Office in Alta for interview. Erik thought that, with the help of his Nasjonal Samling membership card, he could present himself as a German sympathiser and might be taken on. A job in Kafjord so close to the *Tirpitz* would be a good way of gleaning information about the anchorage, if not about the ship herself. Without delay he handed in his application.

Five days later the interview took place. The Kriegsmarine officer spent thirty minutes questioning Erik making notes about where and for whom he had worked previously. He took Erik's NS membership card and an hour later this was stamped and returned along with a pass allowing the bearer access to the small boat repair facility in Kafjord. The officer made it clear that access to the facilities servicing the battleship itself was strictly forbidden.

Erik reported to the office in Alta the next day at 6.30 am and was taken, along with another Norwegian engineer, by a military van to the boatyard. On the way the German driver expressed his surprise that he had managed to be taken on for work in such a sensitive area.

'I'm an NS member,' Erik replied and continued, 'Also I have a good deal of admiration for the German forces.'

'It was the same with me,' said the other young engineer, 'and I find that NS membership is a good deal.'

The driver nodded as they drove off.

The road wound round the head of Kafjord and back along its north shore. The narrow fjord below the mountainside was dominated by the massive bulk of the *Tirpitz*. As the van passed the white church and the road gained a little height, the protective anti-torpedo nets around the ship were clearly visible. Higher up on the slopes Erik noticed several anti-aircraft gun positions and some German foot patrols were threading their way through the sparse woods. Clearly the Germans were taking no chances of an attack on the ship from the land, sea or air.

Erik's work in the boatyard was routine enough,

consisting mainly of small boat engine repairs and general maintenance. On September 23rd, the sixth day of his employment, an extraordinary event took place. He was on his usual journey to work when the van was proceeding round Kafjord. Suddenly, shortly before 7.30 am, there was a flurry of activity on the *Tirpitz* accompanied by a crackle of small arms fire. Almost at once a foot patrol emerged from the woods, halted the van and told the driver that the road was now closed. The place where the van had stopped was directly opposite the battleship's anchorage.

Erik opened the van door but was immediately warned not to get out by the driver. He moved over to the seat nearest the fjord, opened the window and heard the ship's alarm klaxons blaring across the water as dramatic events unfolded. Groups of sailors clustered at the *Tirpitz*'s port side, began to shoot at a black, low-lying object in the water about one hundred metres from the ship. The rifle fire was clearly striking what appeared to be a midget submarine, when its hatch suddenly opened and a figure waving a white cloth scrambled out and made an attempt to climb onto a nearby fixed floating raft. The firing stopped just as the submarine started to sink, though whether it was damaged or was actively diving, Erik could not be sure.

After a few minutes, a motor launch from the *Tirpitz* raced out to where the mystery vessel was sinking and dragged on board the flag-waving submariner. Suddenly a second figure appeared in the water and was also pulled aboard the launch, by which time the submarine had sunk without trace. Erik, the other Norwegian engineer and the German driver watched in amazement as the launch sped back to the *Tirpitz* with the two prisoners, who were taken on board the ship, and were quickly surrounded by

Kriegsmarine sailors. It was difficult for Erik to make out what was happening to them, given the distance, but it looked as though they were being questioned by some of the *Tirpitz* officers.

'What's going on?' Erik asked, but the driver, also baffled, simply shrugged.

'Attack; maybe English,' he replied.

Suddenly two military vehicles passed them on the road at high speed driving towards the battleship's port facilities. Ignoring the stationary van, the two vehicles swept past, raising a trail of bouncing gravel which clattered against the van sides. Several more vehicles sped past. Clearly, a major emergency was under way and Erik knew that he was witnessing a surprise attack on Germany's greatest capital ship and that he was uncomfortably close to the action.

The drama continued as a second miniature submarine surfaced and was also met with a fusillade of small arms fire. Two crew members evacuated the craft and were picked up, and finally a third submarine came to the surface. By this time gunners on the *Tirpitz* were ready and this one was blown out of the water leaving no trace of survivors.

Erik and his driver watched frantic efforts, both on board and around the ship, apparently aimed at freeing her from her present moorings. Gradually the bows began to swing out to starboard.

Minutes later, Erik was glancing at his watch when there was a huge detonation followed by a shock wave which seemed to drive all the air out of his lungs. A massive explosion had occurred beneath the *Tirpitz* and seemed to lift her stern by a metre while the fjord waters below her boiled into foam.

After the explosion the ship settled back and, surprisingly, did not appear to be mortally wounded. Her alarm klaxons shrieked and wailed for a further five or ten minutes as the crew readied themselves for possible further attacks. None came, but several small boats which seemed to be bringing in damage assessment teams raced out to the ship.

Erik could see that the submarines had somehow penetrated the protective screen of nets around the ship. The attack was an amazing event to have witnessed and although the *Tirpitz* looked relatively normal, he felt sure that major damage must have been inflicted by such a massive explosion.

Four hours passed before the van was allowed to get moving again, but it was directed back towards Alta. News of the attack spread quickly around the town and most Norwegians found it difficult to hide their delight at this sign of what was assumed to be English action against the Occupation. On the streets of Alta the gossip was all about the attack. 'Have you heard the news about the *Tirpitz*?' was on everyone's lips.

The town was alive with rumour and some people even managed to convince themselves that the Germans were about to be beaten. There was new feeling of hope in the air.

The *Tirpitz* did not sink but remained in Kafjord looking superficially as malevolent as ever. However, the seriousness of her hidden wounds was revealed by the intensive repair activity which followed the attack and the Resistance lost no time in informing the SIS in Britain about the likely damage.

Immediately after the event the Germans tightened security around the *Tirpitz* anchorage, which led to Erik and other Norwegians losing their jobs in the Kafjord boatyard.

18

KAFJORD. AIR ATTACK

The year 1944 started well for the Allies in Norway. In April a clandestine wireless operating somewhere in Alta received word that a Norwegian submarine had sunk a German U-boat off Stavanger and there was a growing feeling that German plans were beginning to show signs of disarray.

On April 30th there was a further shock for the Occupation. In the early hours of the morning, the crew of the already wounded *Tirpitz* was awakened by shrieking klaxons. Those not already at their posts tumbled out of their bunks and raced, half dressed, to their action stations. They did not have long to wait. At 5.30 am the battleship's radar had detected a huge flight of planes, which appeared to have come from carriers out to sea, and which was heading straight for the ship. Before full defences could be mobilised there were at least a hundred planes overhead. Wildcat fighters came in low, repeatedly strafing the decks and were followed by Barracuda bombers. Several heavy bombs scored direct hits, damaging the superstructure and radar installations, causing many deaths among the anti-aircraft gun crews. None of the bombs, however, penetrated the armoured deck. The giant ship was further injured but not mortally so; the new damage, however, combined with that sustained in the submarine attack, was destined to put the ship out of service for months.

Erik, asleep in Alta, was awakened by the gunfire and bombing in Kafjord. He threw on some clothes and hurried out into the street. Other townspeople were spilling out of their houses and were standing about in groups discussing what was happening, while the concussion of huge bombs reached them. There was plenty of speculation, but most correctly assumed that the *Tirpitz* was again the target.

After a rushed breakfast Erik went straight down to see Sven at the boatyard. When he got there Sven beckoned him through to the office to discuss the attack but he also wanted to talk about some new recent developments. Else was in there too, having turned a chair round and seated herself astride it with her arms around its back.

'Come in, Erik,' said Sven. 'Take a seat. That was obviously a major attack this morning, and the target, I presume, was the *Tirpitz*. I've had no direct reports about it so far, but the planes must have come from carriers out at sea. No doubt we'll get some news about it soon.'

Sven broke off to ask Else to brew up some 'ersatz' and then continued. 'However, I really want to talk to you about what we have called the Vorgsund Question. As I mentioned to you previously a detachment of German police has been showing a curious interest in part of the Svartfjell Peninsula. We don't think it has anything to do with U-boat facilities. They seem to be more interested in the almost inaccessible far west coast of the peninsula, which is shielded by a small glacier. The only way to get there is either by boat or by a long trek overland around the glacier.'

'What do you think it's all about?' asked Erik. 'In spite of what you say, could they in fact be prospecting for another bunk hole for U-boats? I know that the base at the north tip of Svartfjell has been mined and is perhaps unusable.'

'I think that's highly unlikely,' replied Sven. 'Servicing a base there would be impossible and, in any case, a police unit would not be involved in such work. If a similar facility was started on the same peninsula they know that it would get the same aerial mining treatment. What I would really like to know is why on earth the German police are so interested in such a remote part of the coast.'

There was silence in the office.

After a few moments they heard someone coming through the main workshop. Sven opened the office door and peered outside to find Bernt waiting there.

'Come in, Bernt; any news about *Tirpitz*?'

'That was a big raid,' Bernt replied, 'but unfortunately the beast is still afloat although there's a lot of damage above decks. One of our friends there says that quite a lot of Germans were killed and the bodies are being brought ashore right now.'

'Thanks for the news,' said Sven. 'No doubt we will hear more as the day goes on.'

Sven waved Bernt to a chair. 'Come and join us. We are having a discussion about another matter which I had already mentioned to Erik. Just now I've just been telling him about the German police interest in part of Svartfjell Peninsula. Two months ago Roald Bratland, a fisherman from Valanhamn, made the twelve-kilometre journey across Kvaenangen Fjord to visit his old friend Otto and his wife, Ingrid. They lived at Tovik on the west coast of Svartfjell – the very place in which the Germans seem so interested. When he got there he found that the old fellow had apparently been poking around the shoreline for several weeks, and was in quite a state of excitement. However, neither Roald nor Otto's wife, Ingrid, could get out of him what it was all about...'

'Just a minute,' interrupted Erik. 'Why did you say "lived" rather than "live"? Has something happened to the couple?'

'That's just it,' went on Sven. 'Shortly after Roald's visit Otto simply disappeared and is presumed to have drowned, though how it happened nobody knows.'

From his previous visit Erik knew the general layout of the peninsula.

'Where that old man lived,' he remarked, 'is exceedingly remote and it would be difficult to imagine anything exciting ever happening there. The northern part of the peninsula is remote enough, but it's nothing compared with wildness of the Tovik coast where this old fellow stayed. I gather that, apart from his widow, Ingrid, no one lives or even goes there now. I was told that an archaeologist once lodged with Otto while researching nearby ancient Sami stone circles, but that was well before the war. Has anyone asked Ingrid what could have caused her husband to get so worked up?'

Sven nodded. 'We gather from Roald Bratland that when he sailed across for a second time there was still no sign of Otto. Ingrid said her husband had refused to reveal anything, saying that it would be best if she did not know. During Roald's second visit, a Kriegsmarine boat arrived at Valanhamn and somehow the Germans seemed to believe that Otto had found something of importance. Roald did not, and indeed could not, give them any help.'

There was silence in the office while they mulled over the story while Bernt looked puzzled. Else disentangled her legs from the chair, scraped it back and got up to heat some water for a brew of ersatz. Erik watched her overalls tightening over her hips as she pumped the primus stove and was aware of the involuntary response of his body. She lit the stove and put some water on to boil while a faint smell of paraffin drifted through the room.

Sven stood up.

'I think that this is worth looking into further. It's odd that the Germans are paying so much attention to the area and it sounds as though they are looking for something which they believe to be important. I think we should try to find out what it is.'

'I certainly agree with that,' said Erik, averting his eyes from Else and returning his mind to the problem in hand. 'That means going to see the old man's widow. Perhaps she might give some clue to the mystery.'

'Exactly, but there's a difficulty,' said Sven. 'After today's raid on the *Tirpitz*, the road round Kafjord will certainly be closed to civilian traffic for a long time. However, I know of a track which bypasses Kafjord and would get us to the coast opposite Tovik. Once there we'll then need a local boat to take us across but that should be no problem.'

The discussion ended when Sven looked at his watch and got up. 'I have to stay here to cope with the work at the yard, but I think that you, Erik, should go along with Else. The presence of a woman might reassure Ingrid who, it seems, is still very upset at what has happened.'

19

THE TOVIK QUESTION

Two days later, Erik and Else were ready for the journey. They would have to go by bicycle for about eighty kilometres which would help them to avoid German check points. They packed enough provisions for the cycle ride and for the boat crossing as well.

The track bypassing the *Tirpitz* anchorage in Kafjord was little more than a rough path but Else, clearly physically fit, managed to maintain a good speed. Erik asked her to take the lead, ostensibly out of courtesy to let her set the pace, but in fact, he enjoyed watching her hips moving rhythmically on the saddle in front of him. After two hours both were tired and hot and as they rode along a clear stream Else looked over her shoulder and pointed to the inviting water.

'Let's stop!' shouted Erik.

Else's bike wobbled to a halt. She dismounted, and together they wheeled the machines a short way off the track and dumped them behind some juniper bushes. It was a beautiful day, they were hot and their clothes stuck to them with salty perspiration. They removed their shoes and peeled off their socks. Else sat down on a flat rock beside a clear pool and, with a look of bliss on her face, dangled her feet in the water.

'Come on,' she called, shuffling along to make room for Erik. He sat beside her and let the stream revive his own hot feet. After five minutes their feet started to ache with the cold and Else lifted hers out.

'Now I need to warm them,' she said, tucking a foot against Erik's upper calf. A frisson passed through Erik's body at this bodily contact. 'It's an icy foot all right,' he said and bent down to feel the other one. They lay back to rest on the carpet of crowberry leaves. Erik felt Else's foot gradually move up his leg, followed by her hand. An image of his wife flashed through his mind. He loved her dearly but it was nearly two years since they had been together and he had been celibate since then.

He rolled over to face Else and kissed her lips. Her hand had moved up to his groin. With a sudden surge of urgency they tore off their clothes and lay with their arms around each other while a faint breeze wafted lightly and deliciously over their naked bodies. Else pulled Erik's hips onto her and then there was no going back. Like a dam bursting Erik's celibacy ended as he entered this beautiful girl's body. In a few minutes a wave of ecstasy completed the act and they lay back, panting from the exertion.

'I shouldn't have done that,' said Erik at last, 'Back in England I have a wife that I love and a little boy called Neil that I've never even seen.'

'You're lucky. What's your wife's name?'

'Anna. She has lovely fair hair and is very pretty. I've always been faithful to her – until now that is. Do you have a boyfriend?' he added.

'Mind your own business!' she replied, laughing.

Caressed by the sun and the breeze they lay there for a few more minutes until the cool air made them reach for their clothes.

'Time to get on,' said Erik and, having retrieved the bikes, they set off once more.

The journey to Valanhamn, a small fishing village lying ten kilometres opposite Tovik, took until evening. On arrival they freewheeled down to the harbour to try to find someone willing to take them across to Tovik the next day.

Leaving the bikes, they wandered along the harbour where half a dozen small fishing boats were moored. A healthy smell of fish filled the harbour air. Two men stood chatting and smoking outside the wheelhouse of one of the boats. Erik called out a greeting and Else explained that she was Sven Svensen's daughter and that they wanted to cross over to Tovik the next day and did they know who would be the best person to ask about this. Sven was well known in the locality and one of the men introduced himself as Roald Bratland and said that, for a modest sum, he would take them across the very next morning.

They found lodgings in a small house almost on the harbour, where they were given a room with two beds. They were both exhausted after the ride and after a simple meal collapsed into bed, too tired to think of anything except sleep.

In the morning they pushed their bicycles round to the side wall of the house and left them propped there. They found Roald waiting for them on his boat, and by ten o'clock they were on their way.

'Why do you want to go over to Tovik?' Roald asked, 'There's nothing much there.'

'We want to visit old Otto's widow,' replied Else.

Roald looked surprised. 'That was a sad business, him disappearing like that. Are you related?'

They chatted on for a while, then Roald remarked:

'Strange things have been happening over there. Normally the Germans don't come near us here as we are so remote, but during the last few weeks a Kriegsmarine patrol boat has been seen cruising along the Tovik coast. I heard, too, that German police from the boat have been up to Otto's house and talked to Ingrid, which frightened her dreadfully. Not only that, they say that parties of Germans have been seen combing the shoreline, but no one knows what they are looking for.'

With that Roald stepped back into the wheelhouse, leaving Erik and Else alone on deck. The sun came out, lighting the distant coast and mountains with a brilliant glow, while streaks of snow dazzled white on the higher peaks. Wheeling gulls gleamed in the sun as they followed the boat, hoping for discarded scraps of fish, but peeled away in disappointment as land became more distant. As Valanhamn receded from view Roald banged on the wheelhouse window and pointed to a school of pilot whales crossing their bow, their black backs shining in the sun as they arched above the waves.

Amid such a peaceful scene it was easy for Erik and Else to forget about the war and that men were dying in those deadly northern seas. Far away to port they caught a glimpse of the open sea where it was all happening, where Arctic convoys taking military hardware from Scotland to Russia were being harried and, all too often, cut to pieces by U-boats and German bombers.

After an hour and a half, the boat approached Tovik. Erik had imagined a settlement of some kind but all he could see was a small house with a turf roof of living grass, standing on its own above a stone-built landing stage. Nearby, pieces of net, long dried by the sun, were draped over the skeletal poles of a dilapidated fish-drying rack. As they neared the landing stage, a young man emerged from the cottage and, shading his eyes, examined the visiting boat before walking down to meet them. As they came alongside, he called out a greeting and deftly caught the mooring rope thrown by Roald. They obviously knew each other well and Roald explained that this was Ingrid's nephew, Hans, from Valanhamn, who had moved in with Ingrid for a while to help her after Otto's disappearance.

The four of them walked up to the house and Hans called in through the open door to his aunt, announcing that they had visitors.

'I'd better tell you', he said quietly, 'that my aunt has been badly frightened by some German police who asked her a lot of questions… Ah, here she is,' he said, as an elderly lady emerged cautiously into the sunlight.

Erik and Else explained who they were and that they would very much like to hear about events surrounding her husband's disappearance. Ingrid looked far from happy but nevertheless ushered them indoors and sat them down at a table in a low ceilinged room. Erik looked around. Several faded, sepia photographs stood on the mantelpiece, from two of which a young man, presumably her late husband, smiled.

'My nephew will boil a kettle for you,' she said, 'We are lucky to have a little tea left.'

Over several cups of weak tea Else asked the old lady if she could tell them just what had happened over the last few months and what she thought had so excited her husband before he disappeared.

'I've told the German police everything I know,' she replied, as her nephew and Roald together got up and wandered back down to the landing stage. 'I don't know what they wanted to find out, but they were frightening.'

'Well, please try to tell us all over again,' coaxed Else – and then the story came out. There was a short silence, then Ingrid began to speak in a quiet voice.

'Everything was alright until six weeks ago, when one of my husband's sheep went missing. That's when it all started. We couldn't afford to lose the animal and he went to look for it. There was no sign of it near the house so he went to search amongst the rocks along the shore. Sometimes the sheep break their legs there.

'After four hours I began to worry when he hadn't come back, thinking that he might have fallen. The rocks on the shore are very difficult around here with lots of deep crevices and previously we have had sheep falling into them from the cliff.'

Erik and Else listened intently while Ingrid, staring out of the window, went on with her story.

'I was just setting out to look for him when I saw him walking back home along the cliff top. As soon as he came close I could see that his trousers were soaking wet and I asked him what had happened. He was in a great state of excitement about something or other but all he would say was "I can't believe it!" over and over again. I began to get angry with him but he wouldn't say what had happened. Gradually, things settled down and I got tired of pestering him about it but he never said whether or not he'd found the sheep.

'After a few days when I was tidying up, I came across a smallish flat stone which had fallen down the side of his favourite chair – the one that you are sitting in. It was like any other small stone from the beach and I was about to throw it out when I noticed that he'd made some careful pencil marks on it. I thought nothing of it and threw it out anyway. Otto usually carried a pencil stub in his pocket but often no paper and afterwards I thought, perhaps, that he had copied something that he had seen onto the stone as a kind of reminder note.

'His behaviour for the next week or so remained very odd and his mind seemed to be somewhere else.

'Soon after that I found him sitting at the table writing a letter. He hardly ever wrote and wasn't good at it. I noticed that he put the letter in an envelope without addressing it and took it away with him when he went out in the boat the next day. He wouldn't tell me anything about what he had written, other than it would be better if I didn't know about it. I got very angry with him for keeping the secret from me and now that he is gone I will never find out what it was all about.'

The old lady stopped as her mind seemed to jolt back to the present.

'And that's all I can tell you.' She drew her hand wearily across her face, obviously finding it tiring to talk for so long.

There was a long silence in the room while they pondered about the strange story, broken only by the soft murmuring of the sea and the melancholy cries of gulls.

'That's a really strange story,' said Erik. 'It certainly sounds as though your husband found something extraordinary somewhere and, as you suggest, not having any paper he tried to make a reminder note about it on the stone.'

'Where did you throw the stone?' asked Else.

'I tipped it off the rocks into the fjord, along with the usual rubbish,' replied Ingrid.

There was another silence.

'What did your husband do with the letter?' asked Erik. 'It might tell us something.'

'I never saw it again after he went away with it. He probably took it in the boat, around the coast, where they sometimes take in letters for posting.'

'Did he, by any chance, keep a diary or a notebook in the house?' asked Else.

'He used to make an occasional note in an old school exercise book, but it certainly was not a diary,' replied Ingrid, by now visibly fatigued.

'Could you find it and let us glance through it, please?'

Ingrid wearily got to her feet and went across to an old chest in the corner of the room. She pulled out a small drawer and, after rummaging about, produced a tattered blue notebook and handed it to Else.

Else took it over to the window where the light was better and, pushing aside a pot plant, opened it out on the cill. Erik came over and stood beside her and together they went through the pages. Only the first six pages had notes on them. The writing was difficult to read and was generally about trivia of everyday life by the sea and on the boat. There seemed to be nothing that could help them. Then, on the sixth page, written, in pencil, was a curious symbol with the word 'Россия' beside it enclosed in a pencilled oval frame. Erik wondered whether this could possibly be the mark that Otto had copied from the stone? It was the last entry in the book so it might well be.

'Ingrid,' said Else, 'he drew this on the last page. Have a look. Do you think that could be the same mark that you saw on the stone?'

'I really can't say,' replied the old lady. 'I just glanced at it at the time and it didn't make any sense to me. '

Else and Erik spoke quietly together for a moment and then asked if they could be allowed to take the book away with them.

'Yes, but I would like it back sometime; if you give it to Roald he will see that it gets to me.'

Soon after that they thanked Ingrid for her help and said goodbye.

'If we solve the mystery we'll let you know,' they promised as they walked down to the boat where Roald and Hans were chatting. Erik glanced back at the cottage. The old lady was watching from the door – a sad, forlorn figure as she pushed from her eyes strands of grey hair blown across her face by the sea wind.

20

THE HIEROGLYPHIC STONE

Erik and Else sat on deck and studied the exercise book as they crossed the fjord back to Valanhamn. Some of the writing was indecipherable and included some names, presumably locals whom Otto had met, and there was a reminder to get some more fish hooks. There seemed to be nothing relevant until that last page where the strange symbol appeared together with the word 'Россия'.

Erik was sure that it was 'Russia' in Cyrillic script, although neither of them could think how it could have come to the attention of an old Norwegian fisherman and why he had attached such importance to it.

'The secret to the puzzle must lie in these pencil markings,' mused Erik, gazing at the tantalising scribbles. 'When we get back to Alta we may find someone who knows what they mean; we really need help.'

When they landed back at Valanhamn harbour they thanked and paid Roald and, as it was now far too late to make the return journey, they walked back to the lodgings.

After an evening meal they hurried upstairs to their old bedroom but this time they eagerly pushed the two beds together and pulled the headboards away from the wall. Erik realised that this girl was becoming addictive, like a drug, and an intensely enjoyable one too.

The next day they set out, by bicycle, on the return journey. When they came to the spot where they had made love on the bed of crowberries two days before, Erik slowed down and pointed to the little stream,

'Come on,' he cried, 'let's go back to our special place.' Else, however, would have none of it and they rode on leaving Erik disappointed – and frustrated.

When they got back to Alta they cycled down to the boatyard and found Sven working on a boat engine in the workshop.

'Welcome back,' he said, putting down a spanner and wiping his hands on a rag. 'What luck did you have?'

'We've quite a lot to tell you in fact,' replied Else, 'but first we really need something to eat and drink. It was quite a tiring ride.'

Within fifteen minutes they were seated in the office tucking into sandwiches and mugs of ersatz.

'Well?' enquired Sven. 'What news?'

They recounted their experiences without mentioning their overnight stay in Valanhamn, though for a moment, Sven glanced wonderingly at his daughter.

He knows all right, she thought.

They showed Sven the blue exercise book and pointed out the drawing on the last page with its pencilled oval outline.

'Can you make out what this means?' asked Else.

Sven studied it for a few moments, then shook his head. 'I have no idea at all but the word looks as though it could be in Russian.'

'It is,' replied Erik, 'and I'm fairly sure it means "Russia". I tried to learn the language once but soon gave up as it is very difficult!'

They fell silent for a moment while pondering what to do.

'There's a bit of a mystery here,' commented Sven, 'and I think that we should chase this up and find out just what's been going on.

'It seems as though the old man found something extraordinary which probably had those hieroglyphics on it, and which he copied out. The Germans seem to have heard that something odd was found – something of great interest to them, or at least to their police. If it is interesting to them, it must be of interest to us as well. The question is: how did they find out about it? I think the answer must be that they intercepted Otto's letter.'

Over the next few days Else showed the mysterious marks to several people in Alta, but no one could help beyond saying that the letters seemed to be Russian Cyrillic script. Then, when passing the clockmaker's shop, she went in on the off-chance. She had always been fascinated by the shop with its thin brass window bars and its great array of clocks inside which stood on every shelf and table. The shop was filled with a constant ticking and whirring, and as a child she loved to go in near the hour to hear the bells and chimes all going off at the same time. She had come to know Jakob Danielsen, the owner, well and when she went in he had the entrails of a clock spread out in front of him on a white cloth and was in the process of examining the bits with a magnifying eyepiece. Ever since the Germans had invaded Norway, he had lived in fear as he had Jewish blood in his background. He never spoke about it, and so far had never been questioned by the German police.

'Hello, Else,' he said, 'What can I do for you today?'

'I'm afraid that I don't need to buy anything,' she

replied, 'but I wonder if you could help me with this,' and she produced the blue exercise book open at the last written page.

'Do you have any idea what these marks mean?' she asked.

Jakob took the book and peered at the pencilled symbols and letters for a few moments, then looked up.

'Where did you find this?' he asked. Without waiting for a reply he continued, 'Your query is most interesting, but give me a minute while I have a good look.'

The clockmaker fell silent as he peered at the drawing under a bright light, then he sat back and looked up at Else.

'I can indeed help you. I have a particular interest in hallmarks and that's what this seems to be. This is a copy of a Russian gold hallmark. The drawing is fairly rough but shows the head of a woman facing right looking towards the number 84 which represents what is called the "standard mark". Behind the head, to the left, is an indistinct mark which looks like a tiny triangle and, if that is the case, it means that the gold was produced in Moscow. This form of the hallmark, unique to the Moscow plant, has been used since the 1920s. With the older Tsarist hallmarks the woman's head faces left.'

For a few moments Else was lost for words. Here at last was some definite information, more detailed, in fact, than she could ever have hoped for. Her train of thought was broken when the clocks suddenly stirred into activity. Whirrings and wheezes broke into chimes – some serene and beautiful and others urgent, stentorian clankings. From every shelf and table the sounds competed with each other.

When the clocks fell silent, she thanked Jakob for his help, retrieved the exercise book and went out into the street, leaving the clockmaker with a puzzled look on his face. As she walked back to her father's yard, her mind turned over possible explanations for it all.

Could it be that old Otto had unearthed some gold object when searching for his sheep and, in the absence of paper, had sketched a copy of the marks onto a smooth stone with a pencil stub? Then, perhaps, he went home with the stone in his pocket and once there copied the mark into the exercise book? But what was it that he had found and what had he done with it?

The discovery of gold would certainly account for his excitement. So far that theory seemed reasonable to Else, but where did the Gestapo come in to it all? The Germans had somehow got wind of the situation and were clearly desperate to locate whatever Otto had found. However, their activities seemed wildly out of proportion to whatever importance it could possibly have. They would hardly go to such lengths for the sake of a gold ornament or similar object and Else could think of no military reason for their interest.

Else continued down to the boatyard, deep in thought. She went through the workshop and into the office, where a lamp was burning. Her father and Erik were talking together but broke off when they saw her.

'Well, how did you get on?' asked Sven, looking at his daughter enquiringly.

She told them about her visit to the clockmaker's where Jakob had been so helpful, and about what she had learned from the drawing in the exercise book.

'Extraordinary as it may seem, I think it just possible that old Otto unearthed some gold object. The problem is,' she said, 'the Germans seem to have heard about the discovery too, although we don't know how, but they are going to great lengths to find whatever it is.'

Then Sven came up with a theory.

'It's odd that the Gestapo alone seem interested. It's almost as though the mystery has no military relevance at all. If it had, the Wehrmacht would surely have put in an appearance. So I just wonder, now that the war is turning against the Germans, if the leader of a Gestapo group is starting to think about his own skin. Gold seems to be involved in some way and one can imagine the thought of personal enrichment supplanting the purely military aims which we have seen so far. We just may be dealing with a Gestapo criminal who has a bunch of Gestapo thugs behind him, and who wants to get his hands on enough gold to buy off the justice which he'll likely face, when the war ends. Alternatively, perhaps he is hoping to set aside enough funds to allow him to disappear abroad to some sanctuary of his choosing. I know that may sound far-fetched but I think it's worth considering.'

'How do you think the Germans heard about the possibility of there being gold in the first place? Do you think they intercepted Otto's letter?' asked Else.

Sven thought for a moment. 'Yes. I think the letter that old Otto sent to some unknown recipient was probably seen by the German censor who, realising its importance, passed it on to the "relevant authorities". I'm afraid that Otto's disappearance may have a more sinister explanation than a simple drowning. The Germans may have arrested him forcing him to reveal what he had found and then subsequently liquidated him.'

'I can't do better than that,' he said, 'as I don't see how else the Germans could have got on to it.'

21

THE TRANSMISSION HIDE

In early September 1944, as the weather grew colder, Bernt, together with Rolf, a new helper, had continued to monitor shipping in Altafjord from their observation post in the forest above the town. They had made a hide of spruce branches for the wireless operator, which provided good concealment from any chance passer-by. Rolf usually acted as the lookout but when on the odd occasion he was unable to do so, Erik took his place.

One Sunday morning while Bernt was transmitting, Erik, with a sten-gun beside him, was acting as lookout. He had found a spot thirty paces from the hide where he could sit half-hidden, while leaning against a spruce tree trunk. The drooping, lower fronds of the tree hung like a curtain in front of his face, almost concealing him. At his right hand lay a warning device, a length of fishing line, which, hidden beneath the spruce needles carpeting the forest floor, ran to the hide. Two sharp tugs on it would warn Bernt to stop transmitting and to keep utterly silent. Erik had been there for ten minutes when, to his alarm, he heard someone approaching through the trees. A man wearing a thick sweater, a forage cap and breeches, appeared, wandering slowly through the forest while looking about him. Now and then he stopped to pick one of the many forest mushrooms, which he dropped into a canvas bag hanging from his belt. Then he chanced to wander straight towards Bernt's hide. Erik crouched lower behind the spruce branches and gave two warning tugs on the fishing line, at the same time edging the sten onto his lap. At that moment the man suddenly caught sight of the aerial slung between the branches above him. He stopped and gazed up at it, his eyes following it down to where it emerged from the hide. He stood still for a few minutes obviously thinking and then again stared up at the aerial. As he looked up the shadow of the forage cap lifted from his face. Erik could hardly believe what he was seeing – Bjorn's face! It was Bjorn, his own cousin! There was no doubt about it, but what on earth was he doing here? Was he really hunting for mushrooms or did he have another motive?

Erik remained motionless, still clutching the sten, as Bjorn turned and started to walk back down the hill. Then after a short way Bjorn stopped and turned round to take another long look at the aerial and hide as though confirming to himself what he had seen – or perhaps marking exactly where it was. Erik was confident that he himself had not been seen but Bjorn's interest in the aerial showed that he had fully realised its significance. Then, walking quickly downhill, he vanished among the trees.

Erik thoughts were in turmoil. Was it conceivable that his cousin was a collaborator? If that turned out to be the case the Resistance would ensure that he paid the price and Erik knew what that would mean.

After five minutes Erik got up from his hiding place and, still clutching the sten-gun, cautiously went over to the hide and put his head inside. Bernt was anxiously waiting to hear what had caused the alarm. Erik told him what had happened without mentioning who the stranger was, but told Bernt that the transmission site had definitely been seen.

'The man', Erik told him, 'was undoubtedly a Norwegian in his early twenties and was carrying a stick which he used from time to time for support – as though he had discomfort in one of his legs – though he did not have a definite limp.'

Bernt was greatly alarmed.

'Even if he's a Norwegian, he may talk about what he's seen and, at worst, may be an active collaborator. Help me to get the aerial down and get rid of any sign that we've been here! We must be quick about it.'

The pair worked hard for fifteen minutes and when they had finished they swept the ground with spruce branches to remove signs of their activities and then moved off downhill and hid the rolled-up aerial and fishing line beneath a fallen log. Further down the hill they buried the Paraset transmitter deep beneath a heap of twigs and branches.

When they emerged from the forest, they went together to see Sven at the boatyard and told him what had happened. The moment Erik had been dreading came when Sven asked him to give a description of the man. Sven noticed the changed expression on Erik's face.

'Are you feeling all right?' he asked. 'You've gone very pale.'

Erik did his best to pull himself together. He couldn't bring himself to implicate his cousin but at the same time how could he justify deceiving Sven and the Resistance?

He blurted out a description of the man as best he could, also mentioning the slight limp. He said that owing to the man's forage cap he had been unable to see his face clearly. As he spoke he felt Sven watching him.

Sven was quiet for a moment, and then remarked, 'We'll have to find out who he is as it's quite likely he's a collaborator. He sounds like the man who was previously seen wandering in the forest and if he is proven to be a collaborator he'll have to be eliminated. Find a new transmission site well away from the last one. Leave it to me to make enquiries in the town about this man and I'll let you know what I find out.'

Erik's worst fears were realised later that day. Ominously, a trusted forester reported to Sven that a detachment of Norwegian police had moved purposefully up to the now vacated transmission site. They obviously knew exactly where to look and although Bernt and Erik had tried to remove all signs of their activities the forester said the police had noticed traces of recent disturbance of the carpet of dead spruce needles where the hide had been. Bernt knew that most Norwegian policemen would not betray their countrymen to the Germans – but some would.

Several weeks passed but, at first, Sven was unable to unearth any information about the stranger. In the meantime, Bernt set up a new observation site, higher in the forest, from which the whole of Altafjord could be monitored. During those weeks Erik was tormented by the certainty that Bjorn must be a collaborator and that it was he who was responsible for the police search of the vacated transmission site. As well as that it suddenly struck Erik that perhaps the questioning he had undergone in Harstadt three years previously had been related to Bjorn's recognition of him on the boat leaving Svolvaer harbour. Whose side was Bjorn really on?

Sven's breakthrough came five weeks after the police raid. He had started to make enquiries about Norwegians employed by the Germans in the Todt labour organisation.

Two of these, both drivers, possibly fitted the sketchy description given by Erik. One was in his twenties and had a barely detectable limp but the older man, who had a severe limp, was in his late thirties. Sven asked Erik to come to his office to discuss the two men.

Once Erik was settled in a chair Sven told him that he thought it just possible that it was one of them whom Erik had seen in the forest and who had informed the police.

'Bearing in mind their ages, do you think, Erik, that the older man can be discounted?'

Erik felt tension rising in him as he considered how to answer. It seemed to him all too likely that the younger man was Bjorn, but in the end he had to say, 'Yes, I think he can.'

'Good,' replied Sven, 'that leaves us with just one suspect. We've found that he lives in lodgings at Veidebakken in the outskirts of Alta and that he drives trucks for the Germans. Everything seems to fit and I think he's our man.'

Later that day, torn by conflicting loyalties, Erik tried to decide what to do. If he let events take their course Bjorn might well be shot by the Resistance, and his own description of him would, in effect, make him party to the killing. On the other hand if he warned Bjorn of the danger, then murder might be averted but, if the Resistance discovered what he had done, he himself might be next on their list. In the end, after much thought, ties of family, even although not of true biological kinship, decided the matter and Erik decided to try to find Bjorn and to warn him, even although this opened the possibility that Bjorn might actually betray *him*.

★

Veidebakken, two kilometres from the town centre and just off on the road to Kafjord, was a convenient place for Bjorn to live. It was not too far from the centre of Alta and was handy for his work for the Todt Organisation, which usually involved moving lorry-loads of supplies and machinery to the *Tirpitz* anchorage in Kafjord. He enjoyed the driving work, found himself getting on well with the Germans and had learnt a few words of the language. His lodgings were basic but comfortable enough and life there had assumed a pleasant tenor. The fjord shore was only thirty metres away and, along the intervening strip of waste ground, ran a rough footpath used by a few locals and their dogs. One evening he was on his usual stroll along this path when a sixth sense told him that he was not alone. It was nothing definite but he began to feel curiously uneasy. It was almost as though someone was following him in the dusk. There! Had he heard something or not? He stopped and looked around. There was complete silence but for a fleeting moment he thought he half glimpsed a dark shadow flitting off the path and melting away into the surrounding bushes. He continued to gaze at the spot but could see only an empty path stretching back into the evening gloaming. Was he imagining things? He could feel his heartbeat rising and the pleasure of the walk had vanished. He knew that many Norwegians harboured a grudge against Todt workers and that retribution was an ever present possibility. He had better watch his back on a lonely path like this.

Cautiously, in the gathering darkness, he turned and retraced his steps. He had almost reached the spot where he thought he had seen the shadow melting into the bushes when he felt the hairs at the back of his neck rising. His heart thumped in his chest as he walked slowly on, listening intently for any sound of danger, when, suddenly, a dark figure stepped onto the path in front of him blocking the way. He couldn't make out the man's features but caught the gleam of a pistol, or, at least, a weapon of some kind, pointing directly at his chest. Oh God, this is it he thought, expecting a bullet at any moment. Then, from the darkness, a voice quietly enquired, 'Bjorn?' For a moment he presumed that an assassin was simply establishing his identity before shooting him. But there was something oddly familiar about the voice which went on, 'Bjorn, it's only me, it's Erik!'

Bjorn suddenly felt weak in the knees with relief. He held out his hand to Erik but instead of a handshake his fingers encountered the steel of a pistol barrel. Erik lowered the weapon saying, 'The Resistance has ordered me to shoot you as a collaborator and they've given me this silenced Welrod to do it – but I can't, I just can't!'

The two cousins stood in the darkness while Erik warned Bjorn that if he remained in Veidebakken and continued working for the Germans he would undoubtedly be murdered.

'You are a marked man because the Resistance believes it was you who told the police about the transmission site in the forest. I may say they have no idea that we are related by family and I have simply come to warn you of the danger, but tell me, Bjorn, why in God's name did you inform on your own countrymen?'

Bjorn did not answer but responded by asking Erik how he came to be in Norway. Erik did not reply either. For a few moments there was silence then Erik said, 'You must leave Alta immediately. Tell no one where you've gone and tell no one that you met me.'

With that, Erik seemed to melt away into the darkness. Bjorn, in a state of shock hurried back to his lodgings and made up his mind to follow the advice and to 'disappear' without delay.

Erik knew that, later, he would have to lie to Sven saying that he had indeed killed Bjorn and had pushed the body into the river. Alone in the darkness, to show that the Welrod had been used, he fired a single shot into the undergrowth.

22

KUZNETSOV'S EXTRAORDINARY STORY

In October 1944, from the new site in the forest high above Alta, the watchers had been aware of increased naval activity in the mouth of Kafjord. For some days there had been speculation that the *Tirpitz* might be moved and then, on Sunday 15th the monster emerged slowly out of her lair into Altafjord and, accompanied by some smaller vessels, headed out towards the open sea. The ship had occupied the attention of the watchers for two years and Bernt lost no time in ensuring that the information reached his SIS contact in Britain. The flotilla, led by *Tirpitz,* gradually receded into the distance, until lost to view, as the massive ship steered to port and disappeared around Stjernoya Island.

A relay of other coast watchers observed and reported her slow progress westward for 200 miles, as far as Tromso, where she anchored in the shallow waters of the fjord close to Kvaloya Island, not far from the town itself.

Not long after the departure of *Tirpitz,* Sven asked Erik to come down to the boatyard to discuss some interesting information, but before going into the office Sven took Erik aside and asked if he had succeeded in eliminating the collaborator.

'Yes,' replied Erik. 'I did it on a riverside path above

Veidebakken and I simply rolled the body into the river. As the current is very swift it may well never be found. I've brought back the Welrod with me today to give to you.'

'Good – that's a job well done. Now come with me to the office,' replied Sven, as he took the weapon.

When they went inside Erik was pleased to see that Else was already present. She glanced at him, gave him a slight smile and, almost imperceptibly, raised her eyebrows. Then she settled down to heat some water on the primus and produced four mugs of ersatz.

'Erik, I would like you to hear this,' said Sven. 'Roald Bratland, who ferried you across from Valanhamn to Tovik two months ago, arrived here yesterday to get some parts for his boat engine. He is due round here, again, very shortly. He knows that the Germans have been searching for something along the Tovik coast, something to which they attach great importance. Out of the blue I asked him if he thought that there could be any question of gold treasure and, after some hesitation, Roald, whom I consider to be a reliable fellow, told me an extraordinary tale which I had not heard before. I have already mentioned to him that I would like you to hear it directly from him.'

Erik was intrigued but more than that Sven wouldn't say.

Ten minutes later they heard someone come into the workshop. Sven put his head out of the office door.

'It's Roald,' he said and called out a greeting as he beckoned the visitor to come in.

Roald nodded to Else and Erik as he took a seat.

'Glad to see you two again,' he said, and turning to Sven, asked, 'Did you manage to look out those second hand engine parts we spoke about?'

Sven assured him that the parts were set aside for him, but asked, before he took them, if he would repeat his curious story for Erik's benefit.

Roald accepted a hot drink and settled deeper into his chair. He was silent for a few moments as he collected his thoughts, and then began to tell his extraordinary tale.

'It's all of two years ago that this happened – back in 1942. I was returning from a day's fishing in my boat and was sailing close to the coast, about fifteen kilometres north of Valanhamn. By that time we'd got used to coming across debris washed up from ships sunk on convoy duty between Scotland and Russia. Occasionally the odd body turned up on the rocks too. After one sinking, the sea was covered with Russian timber and another time bales of fleeces of some kind were washed up. Only later did we discover that they were, in fact, reindeer hides.'

'On the day in question, I was passing a dangerous point when something caught my eye among the rocks at the water line. Something was flapping just at the point where the surf was breaking. I trained the binoculars on it and you can imagine my surprise when I saw that it was a tattered piece of canvas at the top of what looked like a makeshift mast. I immediately put into reverse and pulled in as close as I dared, and there in a crevice was wedged a battered boat, probably a lifeboat, and what I had seen was the remains of a sail.'

He sipped from his mug, drew breath and continued. 'There were no signs of life, but I decided to have a closer look and found a safe place to land a little further on. I tied up and scrambled over the rocks to the boat. When I got there I could see straight away that the starboard side of its bow was partly stove in and lying on the bottom boards were two bodies, both covered with heaps of clothing. I thought they were dead and, indeed, the exposed face of one of them confirmed that this was the case as it had that livid appearance which comes after death. I leaned into the boat and pulled at the clothing which was covering the head of the other. As I did so the "body" gave a groan and the eyes opened. The poor fellow was clearly in a desperate state and, if he was to survive, I knew that I had to get him into my boat and back to Valanhamn quickly. It would be his only chance. In the end I had to hitch him onto my shoulder and carry him to my boat. He was very thin and didn't weigh much, so it wasn't too difficult.'

'Once aboard I put him on the wheelhouse floor, heated some water and gave him a mugful, laced with schnapps. I had to hold the mug to help him to drink and after a few minutes he began to mumble a few, unintelligible words. Then I settled him as best I could and headed straight for home. On the journey he kept repeating the word – "Rossi" or something. Then it came to me that he was probably saying "Rossia" and he might, in fact, be a Russian. At any rate, he could understand nothing of what I was saying.'

'Back in Valanhamn, someone helped me to get him up to my house, and my wife and I put him into a bed. She gave him drinks and made sure that he was warmly covered, as he was still very cold. Over the next few days he took some food and revived remarkably well and tried to indicate his thanks in what did indeed seem to be Russian. Communication was difficult but then I noticed that he used a few English words. I speak hardly any English but there is a man in the community who does, and I asked him to come down to help us. He found that the castaway could speak passable English and I waited while the pair of them had a long chat. Then, through the interpreter, I heard the man's story which was remarkable to say the least, and this is what he told us.'

With that Roald leant back, taking a few moments to drink what was left of his ersatz and to draw on the cigarette that Sven had given him. Then he began to tell his story.

'Our shipwrecked sailor was indeed a Russian and his name was Vladimir Kuznetsov. He had originally been a professor in the Lenin Academy of Agricultural Sciences in Moscow, under Trofim Lysenko, but, in 1932, he was caught up in the purges of intellectuals and consequently lost his job at the Academy. The only work he was permitted to do under the regime was general labouring. He also lost his home, became separated from his wife and ended up as a dock worker in Murmansk up in the far north. Life really had turned sour for him but, nevertheless, he gradually got used to hard physical labour. "At least," he told us ruefully, "I wasn't shot!"'

'After 1941, when the war began for Russia, his status as a dock worker protected him from conscription into the army. The work became harder when the British started sending convoys of military supplies for the Red Army. Munitions, tanks and other vehicles had to be unloaded, and, once that was done, the ships often took on board Russian timber for the return trips to Britain.'

'But there was one particular occasion which Kuznetsov especially remembered because he had been given the job of helping to load small wooden crates into a different kind of ship; a British warship, rather than a freighter. It was a big vessel which he found was called HMS *Edinburgh*, and from his description it sounds as though it was probably a cruiser.

There were nearly a hundred of the crates, which had red stars stencilled onto them. Although they were small they were very heavy. A crane was being used to lift them aboard, when suddenly four of them broke loose and crashed down into the hold, narrowly missing Kuznetsov himself who was in the hold at the time. Two of the crates were smashed apart right in front of him, spilling their contents.'

Roald continued: 'When the story reached this part, I could hardly wait to hear what had spilled out but Kuznetsov confused the interpreter by repeatedly using the Russian word "*zoloto*". When at last he pointed to my wedding ring it dawned on the interpreter that it meant "gold" in Russian!'

'Each crate, apparently, contained five large ingots, each of which seemed to weigh about twelve kilograms. The hold was immediately cleared of workers, and the English sailors quickly repaired the two crates before work was allowed to continue.'

'And that,' said Roald, 'is the main part of the story as Kuznetsov told it, though there's still a bit more to come.'

'After he'd finished working on the *Edinburgh*, he was sent to load timber onto a freighter which was docked nearby. Loading was almost complete and he had just gone down into the hold for some task or other when the sirens started wailing. The Luftwaffe quite often raided Murmansk docks but this turned out to be a very heavy attack. From where he was, deep in the ship, Kuznetsov could just hear a lot of shouting accompanied by the rumble of bombers and intense anti-aircraft fire. Soon every other sound was blotted out by enormous bomb explosions and it was then that he was aware that the hold doors were being closed over him, locking him into what might easily become a steel tomb.'

Roald paused once again, while Sven rolled him another cigarette, and then continued:

'At the height of the bombing several ships which had steam up, Kuznetsov's freighter among them, started to leave the docks, to escape the bombing. Although now shut in the hold, the Russian could feel that they were getting under way but, with no means of attracting attention, he simply sat down in the pitch darkness to await events. After a long time he finally got to his feet and began to feel his way around his prison and by good fortune, stumbled over an object which felt like a crowbar. He picked it up and started banging on the bulkhead to attract attention. Presently he heard a hatch being opened above him and, as a shaft of daylight lit the darkness, a very surprised British sailor peered down at him. With the sailor's help Kuznetsov climbed out of the hold to find that the ship was already well clear of Murmansk.'

'He was an involuntary passenger on that freighter for two days, in convoy with other ships, including the cruiser HMS *Edinburgh*, on their way back to Scotland, when their luck ran out. They were spotted by a German plane in the Barents Sea and some of the ships were bombed and HMS *Edinburgh* was torpedoed by a U-boat. Shortly afterwards, Kuznetsov's freighter was also torpedoed, but, before she went down, he and one of the British crew managed to get into a lifeboat, only to find themselves alone on a sea covered with oil and floating timber. The cold was terrible and in the distance they could still hear the boom of naval gunfire.'

'You can probably guess the rest,' said Roald. 'Their boat drifted for several days and they managed to rig up a fragment of canvas on an oar as a sail, hoping that the north wind would drive them to Norway. The cold was the worst thing and after a day or two the British sailor died from exposure. Kuznetsov was too weak to push him overboard and he had to just lie there waiting for the end, with the dead body beside him. He remembers encountering rough weather but little else of his drifting voyage and the next thing he knew was when he was in my boat on the way back to Valanhamn.'

'My wife and I hid him in our house and, unknown to the Germans, he's been living and working with us ever since. The rest you know, except that I took the dead British sailor out to sea and sank his body weighted with a stone.'

No one spoke for a while as Sven, Erik and Else digested the amazing tale which they had just heard.

At last Sven broke the silence. 'Now, let's look at the facts. We know that the Germans are desperate to find something on that coastline and we know that old Otto found something of exceptional interest there. Judging by the drawing of the hallmark it really does sound as though he discovered some Russian gold. The unanswered question is; is it possible that the gold which he found came from the sunken HMS *Edinburgh*? If so, how did the ingot or ingots which Otto seems to have found, end up on an isolated stretch of Norwegian coastline? There is one final point which may be relevant,' he continued, 'and that is we've heard that in 1942 the *Edinburgh* did not sink at once after being torpedoed, but drifted for days before the British, themselves, intentionally sank her. That means that the British would have had the chance to transfer an item of *Edinburgh's* cargo to our coast by another vessel. Interestingly, it's said that around that time, a German photo-reconnaissance aircraft was seen snooping around our northern coast-line and I suppose it's just possible that they knew that something was taken from the *Edinburgh* and was hidden on the Tovik coast.'

23

THE TOVIK COAST

Erik decided to make a final trip to visit Ingrid at Tovik to see if he could glean any more clues as to where Otto's gold might be. Else agreed to come with him once more, but this time they did not stop at their place by the little stream. Recently their relationship had developed a new confidence and Erik did not fret at passing up the chance of love-making in their spot by the stream, as love-making had become a regular event anyway. As well as enjoying each other physically, they were also happy simply to be together. Erik found Else to be an exceptional young woman – both intelligent and emotionally perceptive – and it had become a 'love match'.

They spent that night in Valanhamn and, next day, Roald again took them in his boat over to Tovik where they found that Hans had moved in permanently with his aunt. Ingrid said that the Kriegsmarine vessel had made two more appearances and she had seen the crew examining the coastline with binoculars, but no Germans had actually landed. Apart from this she could think of nothing else that might help them.

Roald, having business to attend to, was in a hurry to get back to Valanhamn and before departing he promised to come back for Erik and Else in two days' time. Unable to think of anything else to do they asked Ingrid if they could take out Otto's dinghy and some lines, to see if there were any mackerel about. According to Hans, the summer catch had not been good and further supplies would be most welcome.

Before long, with Erik at the oars, they were rowing close along the shoreline, while Else trailed a weighted line with half a dozen silver hooks tied with white feathers. They caught a pollock but did not come across any mackerel; however, it was pleasant to glide along in the bright sunshine.

'You have such a beautiful country,' remarked Erik. 'It's difficult to believe that there's a war on right now: just look at the sun on those mountains!'

They had rowed about two kilometres from Ingrid's house and were passing a small cliff, with knife-like ridges of rock reaching from its base out into the sea. The cliff itself was scored with vertical crevices, which widened at the bases to form narrow caves. Here and there, fingers of sea washed along gullies and into the caves.

The water under the boat became quite shallow and when Else's hooks snagged on the bottom, she managed to tug them free and wound in the line. Erik continued rowing along the cliff face while Else absent-mindedly gazed at the patterns of sunlight on the water and rocks. Suddenly she exclaimed, 'Oh, look at how the sunlight's reflecting onto the ceiling of that cave: it's so beautiful!'

Erik rested his arms on the oars, leaving the boat to rock gently in the swell, and looked to where Else was pointing. There, sure enough, dappled sunlight was reflected up to form a most beautiful evanescent shimmering pattern on the dark rock ceiling. Erik nosed the boat further into the gully, leading to the cave, to have a closer look at the golden reflections, when other thoughts came into his mind. Else looked achingly attractive in her tight sweater, which emphasised her shapely breasts. Erik, driven by the primitive urgency by which nature ensures survival of the human race, shipped the oars, leaving the boat to bump gently against the rocks and came and knelt in front her. He felt the familiar urge rising within him as he put his arms around her and pulled her down beside him.

'Oh Else, come on; let's do it!'

It was uncomfortable in the boat and undressing was difficult. Erik loosened his belt and pushed his clothes off his hips. Only half undressed, they completed the act in a few minutes of urgent activity and then lay back against the hard thwarts. The boat continued to bump gently against the rock wall, while the reflections shimmered and wavered above them. They pulled on their clothes and Erik took an oar and poled the boat deeper into the cave until the water was no more than half a metre deep. Suddenly he gave an exclamation of surprise.

'Else! Look, what's that?' he exclaimed, pointing down into the water.

Then they both saw it. The bed of the gully beneath the boat was strewn with a jumble of sunken wooden crates, some broken. Scattered among them, gold bars gleamed and flashed in the sun's sloping rays and it was light reflected from these that they had seen dancing around the cave walls and ceiling.

For a few moments, they were silent with the shock of their discovery. They glanced at each other wide-eyed and peered down again at the gleaming bars, each of which seemed to be about a third of a metre long. This must be *the* gold! They had found it, or at least, some of it. There could be absolutely no doubt about it. There were scores of crates, some with red painted stars still visible on the splintered wood, littering the bed of the gully and, judging by the marine growth on them, they had been there for some time.

'Good God!' exclaimed Erik. 'I can hardly believe it but I think that must actually be the gold that Kuznetsov loaded onto the cruiser in Murmansk? We heard that the ship was sunk after being torpedoed in 1942, although how the gold got here, heaven only knows. Presumably all or some of it was removed before she went down. There must be millions of kroners worth of the stuff right here and this must be what old Otto found when he was looking for his sheep. If so he must have scrambled or waded along the bottom of the cave wall to find it. No wonder he was soaking wet and was in a state of excitement!' Once again they peered into the clear water, just as a shoal of little wrasse glided over the gold, their bellies gleaming in reflected glory as they swam over the sunlit bars.

Erik lay face down in the stern of the boat, rolled up his sleeve and stretched his arm into the water. With his finger-tips he could just reach the smooth surface of one of the bars which was lying half out of a broken crate. He sat up breathless from his uncomfortable position.

'This is some find!' he said with huge understatement. They were both stunned by the discovery and sat there thinking of the implications, while the boat continued bumping gently against the rocks. Then the spell was broken by Erik.

'Right, it's decision time!' he exclaimed. 'To start with we must tell no one except your father. This has probably been lying in here for two years and a little longer will do no harm, but, if the Germans get to hear about it, that will be the end of it. Let's get the boat back to Ingrid's landing stage and then we'll return to Alta as soon as we can – but first let's lift one of the bars to see if, by any chance, it has the same hallmark that Otto copied.'

The water was a little too deep to reach the gold from the boat, so Erik quickly slipped off his clothes, rolled them up and put them on a thwart. Else watched as he lowered himself off the stern into the achingly cold water and reached for the nearest bar. He manoeuvred his fingers around it, disturbing a crab which scuttled away from underneath, and, using both hands, lifted the bar to the surface. Once out of the water, its weight became all too obvious and he struggled to lift it onto the thwart. Carefully, Else helped him to lower it safely into the boat, then shivering, he clambered back on board, while Else helped to dry him with his vest. Once he got his clothes back on he turned the bar over and there, surprisingly small, was the hallmark: a tiny version of Otto's drawing of a woman's head facing the number 84. Nearby the Cyrillic letters 'Россия' were clearly stamped into the gold. It was all exactly the same as in the drawing.

'Come on,' said Erik, as he took one of the oars and began to pole the boat back out of the crevice. 'If we don't get Ingrid's boat back soon she'll be worried and Hans might come looking for us.'

At that moment the magic lights in the cave vanished as clouds obscured the sun. Reflections no longer danced on the ceiling and the gold lay darkly beneath them.

'Wait! What about this bar that we've got on board?' exclaimed Else. 'We can't just leave it there!'

'Of course not,' replied Erik. 'We must hide it somewhere close by. We can go ashore at that stony beach before the next point and we should be able to find a hiding place.'

Erik rowed about forty metres along the shore and pulled the boat onto the stones. The two of them picked their way over the shoreline rocks and up an easily climbed low cliff to the tundra above. They could see no obvious hiding place there and there was no depth of soil in which a hole could be dug. They had walked only a short way when Else's leg sank into one of the many tundra pools, which were covered with green moss.

'That's it!' Erik exclaimed, as he reached to pull her out. 'This is a perfect place and we could put a good few ingots in here.'

He took off his shoes and socks and waded cautiously into the moss-covered bog to see if there was a hard base. The pool was about four metres across and the water was no more than knee deep. Erik's feet rested reassuringly on solid rock and there would be no risk of the ingots sinking out of reach.

'Come on! Let's get the bar up from the boat and drop it in here right now.' They hurried back to the boat and, with some difficulty, lifted the gold up the rock face and over to the bog. There they carefully lowered it to the mossy surface, then let go of it where it sank with a plop into its hiding place. The floating moss blanket immediately closed over it, leaving no trace of disturbance. For reassurance, Erik reached down and felt the bar with his fingertips.

As they rowed back to Ingrid's landing stage they agreed not to mention anything about their find, but to return the next day to transfer as many of the bars as they could manage to the bog. When they reached the landing stage, they found that Ingrid's nephew, Hans, was waiting for them. He had been concerned by their long absence and he gave Erik a knowing wink as he helped to tie up the boat. Tactfully he did not ask how many fish they had caught.

The next morning, after breakfasting on bread, cheese and dried fish, they got ready to set off once again in Otto's dinghy.

'You seem very keen on rowing the boat around the place, so I hope you will catch some fish for me this time!' remarked Ingrid as they departed.

Once again they rowed to the cave and Else poled the boat along the narrow channel to the where the gold lay. On this occasion the day was overcast and there were no reflections shimmering on the cave ceiling. Erik gasped as he eased himself into the icy water. He could just make out the jumble of crates and loose gold bars at his feet and began to pass the bars up to Else. Within a short time he was so cold that, after having retrieved only four more bars, Else helped him to clamber back into the boat and, this time she had sensibly brought a towel. They estimated that each bar weighed over twelve kilograms, and it was tiring work carrying them one at a time up to the hiding place. When they had finished Erik stood back to memorise exactly where the place was. There were other boggy pools round about and it would be all too easy, with the passage of time, to become confused about which one was the gold's hiding place.

'We'd both better be sure that we could find this spot again, in case anything happens to one of us,' remarked Erik as they returned to the boat.

On the way back to Ingrid's, Else, remembering the old

lady's request, reached beneath the stern seat where the mackerel lines were stowed. She took one of the winders, freed the gut cast, with its half dozen feathered hooks and let the line out. Before long, she was rewarded with a pull and a pair of mackerel flashed their blue and green brilliance in the clear water as she wound them in. Later on, after rowing back over the same spot, they caught five more.

'That should please Ingrid,' she remarked as she lifted the flapping fish on board. They then returned to the landing stage, tied the boat up and walked up to the house with the mackerel. The old lady was, indeed, delighted with the catch.

Later that afternoon, a day earlier than expected, Roald's boat appeared to ferry them back to Valanhamn. Although it would mean that they would not be able to lift any more gold, Erik and Else were grateful to take up the chance to return. They thanked Ingrid for her kindness, said goodbye, and, after collecting their things, walked down to the landing stage.

24

THE ISLAND IN PORSANGERFJORD

When Erik and Else got back to Alta they went straight down to the boatyard where they found Sven welding a motorboat's broken propeller blade. Sven placed the welding lance on the ground, took off his face shield and smiled his welcome.

'What's up? You two look pleased with yourselves!'

Looking around to check that nobody else was in earshot, Erik replied, 'That's because we are. We've discovered something quite extraordinary, I mean *really* extraordinary.' He lowered his voice. 'I think we have found what the Germans have been looking for. We've found the gold and there is an absolutely unbelievable amount of it!'

Sven was speechless for a moment.

'What? Are you serious?' He looked at them intently and said, 'You are serious, aren't you? For goodness's sake, come and tell me about it, but not here. Let's go round to the slipway. We'll be able to talk there without being overheard.' They walked round the building and settled themselves on some upturned fish boxes.

'Well, come on, let's hear it and, by the way, I've got something interesting to tell you both too.'

Erik began with the account of their visit to Ingrid, leaving nothing out apart from some personal details. He explained how it had all started, when they had noticed that, when the sun shone in at an angle, one of the sea caves at Tovik became filled with eerily dancing reflected lights and he described what they had found when they nosed their boat right inside the cave.

'I am no expert on the value of gold,' he said, 'but there must be millions and millions of kroners' worth in there.'

Sven was obviously flabbergasted.

'It really must be some of the gold that Kuznetsov loaded into HMS *Edinburgh* at Murmansk, but how the heck did it land up in the cave? You haven't told anyone else, have you?' he asked anxiously. 'If this got out the news would spread like wildfire and the Germans would end up by getting their hands on it. Apart from the three of us – complete silence! We can decide on an action plan once we've had time to think. Meantime, well done, very well done indeed! I'm really absolutely astounded.

'Now,' he said, 'I've something interesting to tell you. Two weeks ago the British sent a Norwegian agent in a fishing boat from Shetland to a village not far from Bergen. He gave the Resistance there some highly important information about worries the British have about Russian intentions. Apparently the British, and Churchill in particular, are concerned about what will happen when the Germans are finally beaten, as I am sure they will be. Just now the Germans are facing the Red Army along the Litsa River, which is only seventy-two kilometres beyond the Norwegian border inside the extreme north of Russia. In the event of a German collapse there will be virtually nothing to prevent the Red Army from flooding into Norway. The Soviets would no doubt describe this as a "fraternal occupation", but the result could be a Soviet Norway: a communist state.'

'But, surely,' said Erik, 'the political power of the Big Four – Britain, America, France and the Soviet Union – will ensure that no one of them can take over another country when the war ends?'

'Don't you believe it, especially regarding the Soviets,' replied Sven. 'Anyway, a British agent who speaks Russian and Norwegian is being sent here to make contact with the Soviet military command at the northern front to find out just what they intend to do when the Germans surrender. The worry is that the Russian military just might slip the leash and act autonomously. If their forces penetrated into Norway it would be very difficult to get them out again.'

Else looked puzzled. 'How is this agent supposed to get through the German lines for his cosy chat with the Russian commanders?'

'They think that the agent should be able to get through the front without too much difficulty: they describe the front as "porous". Incidentally, the Soviets know about this initiative and will be expecting him.'

It was growing cold outside, as the late afternoon sun went down and the three of them moved back into Sven's office. Once settled inside, Sven continued the discussion.

'Bizarre though it may seem, Norwegian and German interests coincide in the need to prevent a Russian incursion into Norway, although obviously for very different reasons. Now what's relevant to us is that the British agent will arrive off our coast by submarine in ten days' time. Sending a small boat out to meet the submarine would be risky and difficult to coordinate so, instead, the agent will be landed on a remote, uninhabited island, at the entrance to Porsangerfjord. Shortly after he gets there we will pick him up and help with his onward travel. Here, have a look at the map.'

Sven pointed out Porsangerfjord and the tiny dot of the island, Finnsoya, near its entrance. Clearly the fjord, with its opening directly into the Barents Sea, would be suitable for submarine access.

'Who's going to pick up this fellow from the island?' asked Erik.

'You will, I hope,' replied Sven. 'Your perfect English will make communication with him straightforward. The pick-up's been arranged for ten days' time, on October 12th at 2 pm. It's most unlikely that you will come across any Germans in that isolated place and anyway, you will simply be a fisherman going about his normal business.'

'Does the agent have a name?' inquired Erik.

'They've called him Major Sands, though that's probably not his real name.'

'I'd like to go as well,' interrupted Else. 'It would be easier with two of us.'

Her father gave her a long look and Erik could see that he knew about his affair with Else. He did not seem to disapprove, in fact rather the contrary.

'All right then,' he replied. 'You can take my boat to Havoya, a village in the back of beyond and three-quarters of the way to the island. So that you can break the journey I've already arranged for you, Erik, to spend the night there with friends, Finn Olsen and his wife, Freija. If you want to go too, Else, I'm sure an extra person will not be a problem. They are good, trustworthy people. The next day you can carry on to the island which should take you only a couple of hours, do the pick-up and then return for another night with the Olsens at Havoya. They don't know anything about the agent, but will be expecting him as an extra passenger on your return trip. Staying a second night there will make the rest of the journey back here more manageable. Once you get him back here I want him to remain here on my boat till his onward travel is organised. As you know, the whole thing is not without risk and you will just have to be careful.'

25

AGENT PICK-UP

With a week to spare before setting off to meet Sands, Erik thought that he should try to get some idea of the value of the five gold bars which he and Else had hidden. He couldn't think who he could ask without revealing their secret, until Else came up with the idea of calling, once again, on Jakob Danielsen, the owner of the clock shop in Alta. After all, it was he who had recognised the drawing of the hallmark and he ought to know the value of gold.

They went to the shop together and found Jakob not at all his usual cheerful self. He looked worried and preoccupied.

'When I heard you coming I thought you might be the police again. They have been in twice to question me, and I have to report to the police station tomorrow.'

'Why?' asked Else, looking puzzled.

'I don't know, but they seemed to be interested in my parents' ancestry, and you know what that means. My grandfather on Father's side was Jewish, although non-practising. Our family have never given the matter a thought until the Nazis came to power. Now my wife and I are desperately worried.'

The clockmaker paused before continuing, 'However, I

mustn't talk so much about my own worries; what can I do for you?'

Else spent a few minutes talking and sympathising with Jakob about his predicament before moving on to the reason for her call.

'You will remember that I asked you about a drawing of a gold hallmark. My query is to do with that and I'm trying to find out the current value of gold – that is gold in the form of a bar rather than as jewellery.'

Jakob's face showed his surprise at the question, but he did not ask why she needed to know.

'Gold bars come in various weights; some are small, but there are also large 12.5 kilogram bars, whose value I would need to look up, but would probably be valued at around 33,500 kroner.'

After further discussion about gold valuations, Erik and Else thanked Jakob for his help and, leaving the clockmaker with a puzzled frown on his face, they made their way back to the boatyard. As they walked down the slope Erik sounded a cautionary note.

'Our five hidden ingots are obviously worth a lot,' he commented, 'but we should remind ourselves that it's not our gold. At the end of the war it will have to be handed over to the "appropriate" authority, whatever that turns out to be, but, at least, it won't go to the Germans.'

The next day Erik decided to take some locally caught codling up to Jakob's shop, as a 'thank you' for his help. However, when he got there he found an armed Norwegian policeman guarding the door. The shop was closed and the windows and door were covered with steel shutters. Erik had heard that many Norwegian Jews had been rounded up earlier in the Occupation, often by Norwegian police, and had been transported, probably to Germany, where, it was rumoured, they were later murdered. It was a terrible thought that the same fate might well have caught up with kindly Jakob Danielsen, who had thus far survived four years of the Occupation. Erik never saw Jakob again.

A week later at daybreak, Sven's boat *Odin* nosed out of Alta harbour with Else at the wheel and with plenty of spare fuel for the journey. It was a fine, November morning but with a marked chill in the air.

'I've just realised,' exclaimed Erik, 'that this boat's name is curiously apt because in Norse mythology Odin is the god-creator of gold! How's that for a coincidence?'

The course took them northwards up the channel, between the islands of Seiland and Kvaloya on the port side, and the mainland to starboard.

Gradually, the initial sense of keen anticipation faded and they settled down for the long journey. It was a good six hours later that Havoya came into view: a tiny settlement clustered around a sheltered harbour where six or seven fishing boats were tied up. Else cut the boat's speed and *Odin* quietly glided into a vacant berth. It had felt a long six hours and they were glad to have arrived. In the twilight they secured the boat and stepped out onto the deserted quay.

There was a light showing in a house overlooking the harbour. They knocked at the door, which was opened by an attractive young woman cradling a baby in her arms who pointed out Finn Olsen's house at the other end of the harbour.

Finn and his wife Freija were obviously expecting them and gave them a warm welcome without asking any questions.

'I think,' Erik said 'that Sven told you that I would like to stay for two nights. As you can see I've brought a companion with me and I hope that she can stay as well. For the second night there will be three of us to stay – I do hope that is alright with you.'

Freija accepted this without question, and, after producing a light supper, she showed them their rooms. Much to his disappointment, Erik found that his had a mattress on the floor, while Else had a proper bed. After a few minutes Erik knocked and peered into her room and whispered: 'It'll be a squeeze but it's big enough for two!'

'Get out,' replied Else, with a faint smile on her face.

The morning light on October 12th came slowly but, as it strengthened, sunbeams broke through the overcast like searchlights, revealing the full beauty of the Porsangerhalvoya Peninsula. To Erik it felt like the edge of the world. The mountains behind them were topped with new snow but there was nothing visible to the north except the Barents Sea, and beyond that was the North Pole.

They breakfasted on bread and slices of brown sheep's milk cheese which they enjoyed well enough, but the ersatz was as unpleasant as usual. Freija chattered away as they ate, while making sure that they had all that they wanted. 'The Germans', she said, 'don't bother us in this isolated place, and in fact I don't think that they have even been seen here. The only effect of the Occupation is the food shortage which affects everyone but fortunately we have plenty of fish.'

At noon Erik and Else went down to *Odin* to get things ready for the remaining twenty kilometres of the journey round the northern tip of the peninsula to the island in Porsangerfjord. They cast off on schedule, waved to Finn on the landing stage and set a course to the north.

Once clear of the shelter of land, they were exposed to the rolling swell and the cold wind of the open Barents Sea. It was not a comfortable part of the two-hour trip and they were relieved when they entered the shelter of Mageroysundet Channel. For seven kilometres *Odin* sailed through its calm waters, past a terrain of bare rock, and then quite abruptly they broke out into the seaward end of Porsangerfjord. Immediately, Odin's deck began to rise and fall under the influence of a massive swell funnelling in from the open sea. It was half an hour before the pick-up time when they felt rather than heard the deep throb of a powerful engine.

'Listen! Is that a plane?' asked Erik.

The engine noise grew louder and suddenly a fast-moving patrol boat emerged from behind a headland about a mile away. Its creaming bow wave exploded rhythmically into spray as it ploughed into the serried ranks of oncoming waves.

'That's a German patrol boat,' replied Else, 'and it seems to be in a real hurry.'

There was no evidence that they had been seen as the craft continued on its way westwards.

'It must have passed close to our island,' observed Erik. 'It's lucky it wasn't here an hour or two earlier or it might have caught the submarine dropping Sands off. I wonder what it's doing here.'

A short time later *Odin* approached Finnsoya. The island turned out to be little more than a rocky outcrop two hundred metres wide with scraps of greenish vegetation clinging on between the rocks, which were streaked with seabird droppings. Surf was breaking on the exposed, north shore while flights of guillemots skimmed low over the waves. Erik and Else trained their binoculars on the island but there was no sign of the agent. Else reduced speed and steered *Odin* around to the sheltered south side of the island. There, the sea was calm and they drifted slowly along the shore.

'Look at that!' Else exclaimed, pointing down to a piece of paper in the water close to the boat. It was an empty pink cigarette packet, floating on the surface.

Erik glanced at it and just had time to make out the words 'AVIATIR', 'Gute Privat' and '20 Zigaretten'.

'That was a German cigarette packet,' he remarked. 'It must have come from the patrol boat which must have come round this side of Finnsoya after all.'

Else steered *Odin* slowly along the sheltered south shore while she and Erik searched for signs of life. They began to wonder if Major Sands was there at all, but when the boat came to the island's highest point a figure stepped out from behind a rock twenty metres from the waterline and waved both arms above his head.

'That's him!' exclaimed Else, steering to port, and she brought the vessel gliding in to the shore. Moments later the stem grounded on a patch of shingle while the man, with a haversack on his back, walked briskly down to meet them. Erik jumped out to hold the boat and studied the approaching stranger. Sands looked about thirty years of age, seemed fit and had a thick-set, powerful-looking frame. He was not wearing a hat and had strikingly unusual crinkly, fair hair. The newcomer smiled broadly as he crunched across the gravel and holding out his hand, said: 'Hello, I'm very glad to see you. I'm Major Sands and you are Svensen?' The question was directed at Erik, who shook his head, while the man looked questioningly at Else.

'I'm Erik Knudsen,' he said, 'and this is Else, Svensen's daughter. We've been sent by her father to pick you up. Come aboard, it's cold standing here and we can talk once we get under way. It's a ten-hour journey altogether back to Alta so we've arranged to spend a night on Havoya, which is about twenty or so kilometres from here. That will make tomorrow's run back to Alta easier and Sven Svensen will be there to meet us.'

Else took the wheel while the two men went below to talk.

'Did you have a good trip over from England?' asked Erik. 'We were worried that a German patrol boat that we saw passing the island might have caught you landing from the submarine.'

'I set off from Scotland actually,' replied Sands, 'and I got here a good two hours before the patrol boat went by on the other side of the island. I had enough time to make myself scarce and I'm certain I wasn't seen.'

Erik studied the man opposite him. He could tell by his speech that had spent time in the Oslo region.

'You must be quite a linguist,' remarked Erik, 'what with your Russian and German as well as English. You sound as though you've spent time in Oslo.'

'You're quite right – you've a good ear,' replied Sands. 'I was seconded by the army to spend a year at language school in Oslo in '37. It was fun there and the girls were nice! Where in Norway are you from?'

'I was born in a little place in the far north-east near the Russian border, but I've spent some years in England.' The conversation then slipped easily into English.

During the journey they discussed the progress of the war and Sands talked about the problems he anticipated when it came to meeting the Soviet military commanders at the Litsa Front. Later they chatted about their interests before the war and it turned out that they both enjoyed country sports.

'I really love salmon fishing; in fact it's my favourite pastime,' Erik remarked.

Sands nodded. 'Yes, I quite like fishing too and I also did a bit of deer hunting in Scotland before the war and once bagged a fine twelve pointer stag on a snowy November day in a place called Glenmoriston.'

Erik glanced sharply at Sands. He noticed the use of the word 'hunting' instead of the more conventional 'stalking' and, knowing that October 20th is the last day of the stag stalking season, he wondered if the major was in the habit of shooting beasts out of season.

The overnight stop at Havoya was a welcome break for them all. Major Sands was given a mattress in Erik's room, and, next morning, they set off in good time for the final leg of the journey.

Darkness was drawing in by the time *Odin* finally turned into Altafjord. Sven had seen the boat approaching and was on the harbour wall to help tie up.

Erik told Sands to remain out of sight below, while Sven jumped aboard and went down to meet him. The two men shook hands and talked for a good half hour in the cabin. Sven stressed to Sands that he would have to stay aboard meantime to avoid being seen by the Germans and that, if things went according to plan, an agent would come to collect him next morning. Meanwhile, food and bedding would be brought aboard and help would be given for the onward journey to the Litsa Front.

Sven went back ashore to arrange for provisions for

their guest, and, on his return, found the major examining a Paraset transmitter, which he had taken from his haversack.

'I have a bit of a disaster here. It got wet when I transferred from the submarine,' he said, 'and I don't think it's working now. I doubt that drying will fix it but I need to let British SIS know that I've arrived and, for that, I'll need to make use of one of your transmitters. Where do you transmit from?'

'That's no problem,' replied Sven, 'I'll see to it and will ensure that SIS hear of your arrival.' With that he returned to the workshop and asked Else to organise a meal and bedding for Sands.

When she went into the cabin with an armful of blankets, she found their guest still going through the damp contents of his haversack. At the bottom of the bag she glimpsed the dull gleam of a Luger pistol.

'If the Germans catch you with that thing it will be the end of you,' she commented.

Sands, sounding a little testy, replied, 'Don't worry, they won't.'

He laid out some damp papers to dry, including an identity document made out in the name of Kristian Haagen. Peering over his shoulder Else saw that he was described as a forester with an address in Stavanger.

It was seriously risky having Sands on board and Sven decided to send him on his way as soon as possible. He had already warned the Resistance that its services would be required to pick up an agent from his boat and to pass him quickly along their chain of contacts, through Finnmark, to the frontier between Norway and Russia.

Sven spent the night on board along with Sands. On time, early next morning, the first contact arrived. The man was a local Norwegian and without mentioning his name, Sven briefly introduced Sands to him. The two men nodded to each other then, after a brief handshake with Sven, Sands muttered a word of thanks and was escorted away.

Sven was pleased to see the last of his guest and, anyway, he didn't much like the man. He knew that Sands faced a risky journey through the Soviet border and on for another fifty kilometres to where the Wehrmacht faced the Red Army. There was no active fighting there at that time and it was hoped that Sands would be able to penetrate the front without too much trouble. Extending through miles of a wilderness of Arctic forest and bog, the front itself had no precise demarcation and there should be plenty of reasonably safe crossing points.

The initial handover on *Odin* had gone smoothly, but, a week later a message reached Sven in Alta saying that Sands had disappeared on his way to the front. Apparently, he had got as far as Sirma, 200 kilometres from Alta, on the shores of the Great Tana River, where he had been lodged for a few days with a reliable Sami family. However, on the morning after his arrival his hosts discovered that he had disappeared without trace, along with his belongings. There was nothing to suggest that he had been abducted and no one had heard him leave. He had just gone.

There was nothing that Sven could do about it beyond ensuring that a radio message was sent immediately informing the SIS about the agent's disappearance.

26

OLDERDALEN.
THE REICHSKOMMISSAR'S INSPECTION

The proposed high level visit by Reichskommissar Joseph Adelbrecht, to the 'Lyngen Line', already put off from the previous year, should have taken place instead on April 10th 1944, the fourth anniversary of the German invasion of Norway. However, owing to the recent air attack on the *Tirpitz*, there was further postponement and the new date was to be July 30th. In spite of these changes, it seemed that the Germans were attaching considerable symbolic importance to the event.

Back at Lyngenfjord, preparations started a month before the inspection date. The anti-Russian defences of the Lyngen Line were to be inspected by General von Schirach, commander of German forces in Norway, together with Reichskommissar Adelbrecht, head of the secret police.

Two weeks before the date, the Larsens received notification that their house and store at Olderdalen were being requisitioned for three days, during the time of the visit, to provide accommodation for the General, the Reichskommissar and their staff. The whole dwelling house, part of the store and outbuildings were to be cleared and made available. The Larsens would not be able to trade during the three days and no compensation would be given.

The bulk of the food consumed by the visiting party would be provided by the German authorities, although any extras provided by the Larsens would be paid for.

Military and police units began to appear in the area a week before the visit and observation posts were set up in the woods and on high ground along the road leading to Olderdalen. Among the locals there was intense interest in the preparations and it was rumoured that the visitors would be arriving near Olderdalen in Storch floatplanes.

Five days before the visit, a police unit arrived to inspect the store and the Larsens' house. Hans and Hilder were told that their bedroom would have to be completely cleared of personal belongings; new sheets and bed coverings would be brought in. They would have to vacate the building in three days' time and, for the duration of the visit, they would have to find accommodation with neighbours. No apologies were offered.

Willi Schmidt had been returned to Alta for the winter months but now, in early July 1944, he was redrafted back to Olderdalen. Unusually detailed preparations were being made for the visit. Adelbrecht, being Chief of Police in Norway, did not have authority over regular, German Army forces and, while security was, in the main, to be provided by his police units, a Wehrmacht detachment with two snipers would be required. They would be Willi's responsibility.

Five days prior to the visit Willi arranged for a driver to take him from his billet in Olderdalen to the store to see for himself what potential risks the inspection party might face. His driver delivered him to the store and parked the vehicle on the gravel opposite the entrance. Willi did not get out at once and, recalling his earlier altercation with Hilder Larsen, decided not to go inside. The cooling engine clicked in the silence while Willi sat there admitting to himself that he was nervous of another confrontation with Hilder, but at last, he got out, stood outside the building and took in the layout of the surroundings.

He saw that the Reichskommissar and party would have to walk fifteen metres or so from their transport to the door of the store. From there, flat ground stretched to the fjord and there was no chance of an assassin being able to conceal himself on that side. Although there seemed to be no risk from that direction, one couldn't be too careful. There were many people in Norway who would relish the chance of killing Adelbrecht as he was the most hated of all the occupying Germans. He was responsible for the reprisal massacre in 1942, in which a village near Stavanger had been burnt to the ground and the inhabitants either shot or sent to Germany as prisoners.

Willi then looked up and down the road which went around the fjord. The birch woods gave plenty of cover in that direction but it was not his responsibility to provide security on the road journey to the store. That would be dealt with by police units.

He then turned to face inland – the most likely direction from which problems might arise. On the landward side of the road wooded slopes rose steeply to form two enormous rock buttresses a hundred metres high, topped with stunted birches. As far as he could see, the tops of both buttresses levelled out, each forming a flattish, lightly wooded area, about the size of a tennis court. These 'eagle's eyrie' vantage points would certainly give an assassin a good view of the parking place in front of the store and would have to be occupied by men under his command. Beyond the buttresses, the mountainside, almost treeless and rocky, swept upwards towards the distant summit.

After a difficult climb to the tops of the vantage points, Willi and the two Wehrmacht snipers assigned to him together assessed the field of fire. The men were armed with K98k sniper rifles with telescopic sights and would be able easily to observe and control the area surrounding the store and adjacent woods from the two high points. He watched as they selected the best observation and firing positions on each of the buttress tops.

From an aesthetic point of view, the panorama from where Willi stood was superb. The store lay far below and, beyond on the sunlit fjord, there was hardly a ripple except where a flotilla of eider duck troubled the mirror-like surface. His eye wandered along the shoreline to the left and he thought that he could see almost to the point where Lara lived. He fully intended to find a way to visit her again soon; not just Lara but his daughter too.

In the last six months his attitude to the war had changed, not simply because events were moving against Germany but because of the whole morality of the German position.

How could the treatment of the Jews be justified; there seemed to be no logical reason to regard them as 'Untermenschen'? Before the war he had been friendly with several Jews and had found them to be decent and often gifted individuals.

He sat on a rock and let his eyes wander, taking in the store far below. He watched as a distant figure emerged from the building and stood for a few moments looking at the vehicle. After half an hour Willi signalled to the two snipers to climb down with him and to return to the store. They were confident that they could cover the area including the car park where the visitors would leave their vehicles before entering the building. That, surmised Willi, would be the critical moment.

The weather on July 30th 1944, the day the inspection party was due to arrive, was perfect. That morning Willi and the two snipers again climbed to the top of the buttresses. He saw his men settled into their positions and then, on his own, climbed back down to the road and crossed over to the track leading to the store and stood waiting outside the entrance door.

The VIPs' arrival time was scheduled for 1400 hours, which meant that there were two hours to wait. It would have been pleasant for the two snipers high up on the buttresses but for the mosquitoes. The breeze had dropped and the pests swarmed out of the moist undergrowth, mercilessly biting every bit of unprotected skin. In their torment the men slapped and swore continuously. Perhaps for that reason neither of them heard a small stone rattling down the mountainside above and coming to rest among the birches thirty metres behind them.

Willi, standing at the store entrance, glanced at his watch as 'zero hour' approached. Fourteen hundred hours came and went and still nothing happened. Then, fifteen minutes later, two motorcyclists appeared on the road around the fjord, followed by three trucks carrying police guards, an open military vehicle which, in turn, was followed by a car with blacked-out windows. Finally, close behind the car, came an open truck carrying twelve armed soldiers. The small cavalcade led by the motorcycle outriders turned into the road leading to the store. Members of the police detachment spread out and took up guard positions around the building.

The car carrying General von Schirach and Reichskommissar Adelbrecht, the 'Butcher of Nordvik', crunched over the gravel and stopped opposite the store. Willi stepped smartly forward and opened the rear door.

Adelbrecht stepped out followed by the general. Adelbrecht, resplendent in greatcoat and peaked cap, looked around before returning Willi's salute.

'*Heil Hitler!*' he replied indifferently.

Willi studied him. He may be the Reichskommissar, he thought as he introduced himself, but he's a surprisingly ordinary looking man. General von Schirach on the other hand was a striking figure, tall, straight-backed and with a military air of authority.

Everything seemed to be going according to plan and, apart from the military and police personnel, the scene was peaceful. Beyond the flat foreshore, the surrounding mountains were reflected in the fjord, shimmering as the heat of the day built up. Adelbrecht had been travelling in the car for some time and clearly wanted to stretch his legs for a few minutes. Accompanied by Willi and an armed police guard from his own retinue, he walked over to the edge of the gravel to admire the view. He had just started to say something and had raised his arm to point towards the far mountains, when a violent shock wave and crack of an incoming bullet cut him short. A thick gout of warm blood hit Willi full in the face, momentarily obscuring his vision while the Reichskommissar's body fell against him. For a moment Willi thought that he, himself, had been hit but in the seconds that it took to wipe the blood from his eyes, he was aware of shouts of alarm from the police guards and found Adelbrecht lying at his feet with the base of his neck torn out by the bullet. General von Schirach had not flinched, but a bodyguard had immediately dragged him to the protective shelter of a wall.

Willi and the police guards at once took up firing positions against the walls of the store but there were no further shots. Shouts of consternation mingled with purposeful orders as the guard commanders gave orders to identify the source of the shooting. With a shouted exclamation one pointed up to the top of the nearest rock buttress where a figure could be seen getting up from a hidden position in the undergrowth but Willi quickly told him that it was one of his own men.

Together with the police commander, Willi bent over the Reichskommissar's body. It lay face upward, a congealing trickle of blood still flowing to join the crimson pool on the gravel. The entry wound was just above the tunic collar and, when Willi gingerly lifted the shoulders, a massive exit wound was revealed, between the shoulder blades. The position of the wounds suggested that the firing had come from the direction of the two snipers up on the rock buttresses.

The police commander immediately ordered all his available men to deploy in a fan-shaped race up the mountainside to intercept the assassin. At least twenty men ran from the store, crossed the road and scrambled, at speed, up the slope. Willi trained his binoculars on the mountainside, taking in the positions of his two snipers who were both now standing in full view trying to see what had happened.

Then something caught his eye far up among the rocks, well above the sniper positions. Was that a movement, there, among the jumbled rocks?

Someone, partly hidden by huge fallen boulders, was stealthily climbing up the mountainside. Just as the figure dropped out of sight into a ravine Willi caught a glimpse of what could have been a rifle in his left hand. The hunt was well under way, giving Willi a few moments to clean himself up. He turned on a tap on the outside wall of the store, cupped his hands and washed the blood from his face and cleaned his uniform as best he could. The 'Butcher of Nordvik' had met his just desserts and he, Willi Schmidt, was not going to go out of his way to help catch the killer. At the same time he reflected that, as the attack had been successful in spite of his precautions there was a real risk that he might well be accused of negligence. Mindful of this, he took high profile command of the hunt for the fugitive. All available troops were sent up the mountain to cut off escape routes from where the shooting had taken place.

Willi called an immediate emergency meeting with the aim of coordinating the search. Two officers of similar rank to his own and two senior members of the military police were included and seated themselves round a table in the store. None of them was under any illusion about the likely response of higher authority when their own roles as guards of the Reichskommissar were considered.

Meanwhile, high in the mountains above Olderdalen, the hunt intensified. One of the snipers had climbed straight up the slope avoiding the rocks from which the shooting had seemed to come. Within thirty minutes he had reached a saddle between two high points. The rocks now lay below him and he sat on the gravelly tundra to get his breath back and to examine the terrain below using the rifle's telescopic sight. The German sight gave a comparatively narrow field of vision and it took time to complete the task. The sniper was just about to move on when a movement caught his eye. It was a short way above the highest point of the rock fall where a cluster of stunted birches clung to the slope. He trained the sight onto the trees and at first saw nothing suspicious but one of the birches had a dark object at its base and, when he concentrated his sight on this, the clear figure of a man sprang into view. He was sitting, obviously resting, with his back to the thin tree trunk with his legs spread out in front of him. The German could see no sign of a weapon but if one was present it might well be hidden among the ground cover.

The sniper was certain that this was not a member of the German search party and must be the assassin himself. He made an assessment of the range, taking into account the dead ground which lay between him and his target. It would be a longish shot, nearly a thousand metres, but a hit was perfectly possible.

He adjusted the sight and lay prone with the rifle resting lightly on a bank of crowberry. He once again found the figure in his sight and made a slight allowance for the light wind blowing from the west. He relaxed and, breathing steadily, gently squeezed the trigger. At the moment of the shot his target seemed to give a start, rolled on its left side and was immediately hidden from view. The sniper kept the sight trained on the spot for a few minutes before standing up. He was sure that he had achieved a hit but at that range could not be certain if it had been lethal or not. He shouldered his weapon and raced across the mountainside towards where he hoped to find the assassin dead. When he was two hundred metres from the spot he approached with caution, rifle at the ready. He found the small birch tree and the flattened grass where someone had been sitting but there was no sign of a body. He worked out the trajectory of his bullet and found a deep furrow of the bullet track in the right hand side of the tree trunk from which a trickle of sap flowed down the white bark. But there, lower on the trunk, were some minute drops of sprayed blood. Clearly the fugitive was very much alive and, even if wounded, might well be dangerous.

There was complete silence on the mountainside and the German felt worryingly exposed. He quickly glanced behind him – nothing and still only silence. He had just decided to climb higher to try to locate his quarry when there was the deafening crack of a rifle shot. Instinctively he dropped to the ground. A bullet had struck a rock not two paces from him. He leapt up and raced for the cover of a patch of low birch scrub and threw himself down, crawling as deep as he could into the shade. He was an experienced sniper, having spent a year on the Western Front, and was not unduly worried about the turn of events, although it was never pleasant to become the hunted rather than the hunter.

After five minutes he got up and ran to a boulder outside the trees, from where he could scan most of the mountainside. Crouching down behind the shelter, he began systematically to assess his quarry's likely escape route. Away below him, the fjord stretched southwards towards its head, among the mountains. Nearer to him, along the shore, occasional small boats were moored near the scattered houses and, in the distance, he could just see a farm with a small river flowing into the fjord beside it. It looked a picturesque spot, with a small waterfall cascading over a cliff behind it.

For an hour the German examined this landscape, in which the fugitive had to be hiding, and realised that it amounted to an effective trap. At the head of the fjord a high barrier of mountains blocked the escape route and the most likely action of a wounded fugitive would be to take refuge in one of the farms along the shoreline. He decided to return to Olderdalen store to report to Major Schmidt and to say where he thought the assassin was probably hiding.

Down at Olderdalen the first search parties coming down from the mountain began to reassemble having found no trace of the assassin. General von Schirach, together with Willi Schmidt, called an urgent meeting in the store room to discuss developments. Willi's two snipers were brought in first to give their reports. The man who had fired at the assassin gave a good account of the stand-off between himself and his quarry. The general asked him why his shot had not been lethal, leaving him worried that he might be punished for his failure. Finally, it was decided to carry out a sweep of the ground along the fjord, with special attention being paid to farms and other buildings in which the fugitive, possibly wounded, could be holed up. An immediate start was ordered.

From the outset, Willi felt oddly anxious as the search would include Lara's home, although he could not see how she or the family could be involved in any way. The shooting must have been carried out by some misguided Norwegian patriot but might well be followed by terrible retribution. The destruction of Nordvik, which had followed the shooting of a Gestapo man in 1942, hung in Willi's mind like a black warning cloud.

The sweep operation lasted two days and, at an early stage, Willi decided that he would personally carry out the inspection of Gunnar's farm. His driver turned up the familiar track with the river on the left. When the car reached the house, Gunnar, looking anxious, emerged. Willi greeted him politely, explaining that it was necessary for him to search the building, as the authorities were looking for a wanted man. Gunnar nodded silently and gestured to the German to go inside. When the pair of them went in they found Birgitta standing at the kitchen table, anxiously twisting a tea towel in her hands. She called for Lara to come and as she did so a baby began to cry in a back room. Willi felt a wave of longing as he heard the crying. It was not just a baby, it was *his* daughter and he wanted to see her!

Lara, her face oddly white, came into the room and looked at him with a pleading expression. He went across and took both her hands in his and momentarily relapsed into German saying, '*Ich liebe dich. Du machst mich so glucklich!*' 'I love you. You make me so happy!'

'I know that I am here "on business" but can I see Little Lara, please?'

'All right, come on,' said Lara, and she took Willi's arm, while Gunnar and Birgitta watched as she led the German officer through to the back room. The crying stopped and was replaced by happy gurglings and the low murmurings of the two parents. Willi very gently lifted the squirming baby from the cot and held her to his chest, at the same time drawing Lara to him.

'My family!' he exclaimed. 'I love you both and one day we will all live together. You must never repeat what I am going to say.' He paused and looked at Lara intently. 'Germany has done some terrible things and will lose this war. Norway will be free again. I hope you will then marry me.'

Five minutes had elapsed when Lara emerged, carrying her baby, followed by Willi. To his surprise, Gunnar and Birgitta still looked shocked and frightened. He tried to reassure them and explained the reason for his visit. Suddenly they were startled by the sound of a small object being dropped in an attic bedroom overhead. Gunnar, Birgitta and Lara froze with shock. Willi looked questioningly at the terrified faces in front of him.

'You have a friend staying, yes?' he asked, but no one replied. 'You will permit me to go to see?'

Without waiting for a reply, Willi went up the stairs and, at the top, found two doors. He opened the one on the right which was obviously Gunnar's and Birgitta's bedroom and there was no one there He closed the door and opened the one opposite.

Bjorn made no attempt to hide. He stood against the opposite wall of the room with a look of defiance on his face. Willi stared in surprise at the young man in front of him who had recent scratches on his face and hands but most obvious was the dressing on the side of his neck. A small red stain had soaked through the centre of the square of white lint.

The sound of hurried footsteps approaching broke the brief silence and Lara burst in.

'Don't touch him, don't touch him!' she pleaded. 'He's my brother, Bjorn.'

Willi was speechless. He realised that he had found the Reichskommissar's killer, and he knew what he should do. All his military training dictated that he should take Bjorn back to Olderdalen under guard, after which summary execution would be inevitable, but instead he simply stood there. Then, on an impulse, he stepped forward, holding out his hand to Bjorn.

'I will tell them that I found no one here,' he said.

Bjorn, who expected to be arrested and shot, was stunned by this extraordinary turn of events. How could it be that he was being protected by a German officer?

'Please,' said Willi, still offering his hand which Bjorn, at last, shook.

'I hope that your wound is not bad. You must stay hidden until the searches are over and tell no one that I found you.' Lara, who had said nothing, ran to her brother, touched his hand for a moment, then threw her arms around Willi's neck, murmuring thanks.

Leaving Bjorn in the room, Willi and Lara went back downstairs.

'I have found no one here,' announced Willi to Lara's parents, who were waiting white faced, 'but please hide your son until the searches are over.'

The tension, which had been so obvious in both Gunnar's and Birgitta's faces, visibly fell away. Gunnar collapsed into a chair while Birgitta wept softly with relief.

'Thank you, thank you,' they said again and again.

'I am sorry about everything, about absolutely everything,' replied Willi, 'about this war and all the terrible things that have happened. I do not think that the war will last much longer and then I hope you will allow me to marry your beautiful daughter.'

There was silence in the room as neither of Lara's parents felt yet able to acknowledge that their daughter really might actually marry an officer of the Wehrmacht. Not so long ago it had seemed unthinkable but now… well…

'But now I must go,' said Willi, breaking the awkward silence.

He turned to Lara and her watching parents saw the

softness in his expression when he looked at her and how the attractive laughter lines round his eyes deepened as he smiled.

Yes, he did look a kind man.

27

RETRIBUTION

Early one morning two days after Adelbrecht's assassination
a detachment of German police along with a number of
Gestapo men arrived at the store in Olderdalen. Hans and
Hilder Larsen had not been allowed back into their home
as the Germans were still in occupation and they had been
staying with a neighbour just across the road. They watched
from the windows as the Germans posted a notice on the
store room door and anxiously hurried across the road to
see what it was about. When they got there several local
people were already reading it and their worst fears were
realised.

RECENT MURDER OF
REICHSKOMMISSAR ADELBRECHT.

In view of the outrageous murder of Reichskommissar
Adelbrecht, the community of Olderdalen is required to
provide two individuals who, unless the murderer gives
himself up, will be shot in reprisal in 24 hours' time. Then
a further two hostages will be required and they too will be
shot after 24 hours and this will be repeated on a daily basis.
This is intended only as a preliminary reprisal measure.

Signed: Herman Baumann
Chief of Police
0800 hrs. August 3rd 1944

As Hans Larsen read, his bowel seemed to drop as he took in the dreadful implications. He had always been afraid that a misguided Norwegian patriot would kill a member of the occupying forces, and now it had happened; but to kill the Reichskommissar was an act of utter folly: the retribution would be devastating.

For four years, Hans had acted as community spokesman and he knew that, at this terrible moment, it was his responsibility to arrange an urgent meeting to decide how to react to the order. The store would have been the obvious place to meet but with that now out of bounds, the only other place with sufficient room was a nearby boat shed jointly owned by six of Olderdalen's fishermen. Hans crossed over to the store and told the sentry that he needed permission to hold a meeting of the villagers in the boat shed. This, he explained, was necessary to work out how to comply with the demand made by the Chief of Police. Within an hour permission was granted, but on the condition that a police representative would have to be present. Hans returned to his neighbour's house and straight away spread word that an urgent meeting was to be held, at noon that day, in the shed. Meanwhile, he discussed the situation with Hilder and as many near neighbours as he could contact. Already an atmosphere of fear permeated the community.

Well before noon, thirty or forty villagers had gathered outside the boat shed. When the appointed time arrived, they filtered inside and stood among the coils of rope, nets and general fishing gear. They were followed in by two armed German police who stood guarding the entrance. The murmur of conversation among the white-faced gathering quietened as Hans walked to the front and climbed onto a packing case.

'I am sorry to have to ask you to come here to discuss such a terrible matter but I know that you will all have seen the notice on the store room door. I will set out our predicament, before opening the discussion to all.'

Hans continued, 'We have few options unless the killer gives himself up voluntarily. If he does not, there are two options: first, we can do nothing, in which case each day two of us will be shot. If, however, we offer two names then this killing of hostages just might be stopped. I have to ask all of you how we should proceed from here.'

A wave of consternation swept through the gathering. A murmur of voices filled the shed for a few minutes, before a loud voice spoke from the back: 'Does anyone know who the killer is? If they do then I think that we should either persuade him to give himself up or else we, ourselves, should give the Germans his name.'

Hans Larsen, who had remained standing, put the question to the gathering, 'Well, does anyone know who was responsible?'

There was a murmur of agreement with the proposal but no one knew who had done the shooting. That left the problem of how to select two people for execution, people of their own community, friends perhaps, or even relatives.

Hans called the gathering to order, held up his hand and slowly the agitated conversation died away.

'Will anyone volunteer?' he asked.

There was silence. People looked at each other, as though assessing who should die. Several standing near a simpleton, a mentally retarded young fellow of eighteen or nineteen, tried to hide their glances at him but their thoughts were all too transparent. 'He would do! What sort of life has he got ahead of him anyway?' However, he was well liked in the village and in his lack of understanding, he smiled and babbled, nodding at those near him, pleased to be at the centre of attention. His grey-haired old mother put her arm protectively, even defiantly, round his shoulder and put her finger to her lips to quieten him. Then some people felt ashamed of their thoughts.

The long silence continued and was broken only by the cry of gulls on the foreshore.

The very elderly shuffled uncomfortably, feeling their vulnerability and, perhaps, their guilt at not volunteering.

Suddenly Trond Torp, an elderly and emaciated fisherman, put up his hand. 'I'm willing to volunteer!' he said. 'I have an illness which, before long, is going to do for me anyway. I have a lot of pain and release from this would be almost welcome.'

A year previously the doctor in Tromso had told him that stomach cancer was the cause of his pain and weight loss and, recently, he had felt a cluster of lumps above his collar bones. The old man knew what that meant.

A murmur of appreciation followed Trond's statement and one or two of the villagers applauded gently.

Another volunteer was needed.

Hans quietly thanked the old man and looking straight ahead, he continued, 'I have acted as your representative for the past four years. This has been a privilege but it also obliges me to act in the interests of the community as a whole. Accordingly, having given the matter careful thought, I put forward my own name as the second hostage.'

The involuntary gasps which emerged from the gathering could have been astonishment or perhaps relief that no one else was going to have to volunteer.

A queue formed, while villagers shook the hands of the two brave and selfless men. In a corner, neighbours tried to comfort Hilder Larsen, who had broken down in tears.

Hans Larsen and Trond Torp spoke quietly together as the meeting dispersed and they decided to go straight to the store which was acting as the temporary headquarters of the German police. They were taken in and their details were recorded. They asked if they could return home for the rest of the day but this was denied and they were taken under armed guard to the store room at the back. The only furnishings were three chairs and a small table. Later a German police major came to inform them that 'sentence' would be carried out at 1000 hours the next morning, when they would be taken to a quarry in the nearby birch woods.

They spent the rest of the day guarded by a young non-commissioned Oberfreiter – a decent enough lad who was clearly uncomfortable in his role. The miserable hours passed slowly and in the evening two mess tins containing lumps of bread and sauerkraut were provided along with tin mugs of water. Later a bucket latrine was brought in along with two bedding rolls and the pair, fully clothed, settled down to try to sleep.

Hans and Trond spent a restless night. Their sleep was punctuated by disturbing dreams and, all too soon, the first light of the morning began to filter in through the window. Their guard put down the book which he had been reading during his watch and woke the pair at eight o'clock. Shortly afterwards, some more bread and two mugs of water were brought in.

No sooner had the prisoners finished eating than there was a commotion outside the store. Hans stood on a chair and peered through the high window to see what was going on. A prisoner guarded by two Gefreiters was evidently being questioned by a senior German officer but, before Hans could see his face, the man was bundled roughly away around the side of the building.

'What was that all about?' said Hans to his guard, who simply shrugged. Obviously he did not know, even if he had understood the question.

Shortly afterwards, their door opened and an Oberleutnant and an interpreter came in. The pair got to their feet to prepare for the worst.

'I have news for you both. The criminal assassin has just given himself up and, accordingly, you are both being released immediately. You may go now!'

Hans and old Trond could hardly believe their ears, and, with enormous relief, walked out into the sunlight as free men. Their joy, however, was tempered by the knowledge that some Norwegian, presumably the one whom they had just seen being questioned, was about to pay the price for the foolhardy act.

Bjorn had given himself up, having heard of the execution order. Bruised and beaten he was marched out of the storehouse and was placed with a guard in the back of a covered Wehrmacht vehicle. Six riflemen followed in a similar vehicle. An open car carrying an officer and driver led the way around the shoreline for half a mile, and all three vehicles turned in along the track among the birches. They slowed as they negotiated the uneven surface past a fern-covered clearing and continued for a hundred metres to a disused quarry.

The prisoner, ashen-faced, was made to stand, blindfolded, against the rock face, while the riflemen formed up opposite him. Then, at that eleventh hour, when all seemed lost for Bjorn, he heard the sound of a racing motorcycle engine approaching through the wood.

The despatch rider stopped beside the officer in charge of the execution party and handed him a note. The officer read the note in silence and then, visibly surprised, ordered the firing party to stand down and for the men to return to their vehicles. He then walked over to Bjorn, removed his blindfold and beckoned for him also to return to the vehicles.

Bjorn walked unsteadily after him, ashamed that his bladder control had failed in the expectation of the shots and the dark stain on his trousers was there for all to see.

The contents of the note were then revealed to him. It was signed by General von Schirach and stated that following the murder of the late Reichskommissar he, General von Schirach, representing the military forces, was now in charge of proceedings and that the prisoner should be transferred to his jurisdiction.

To Bjorn this was a staggering turn of events. Might his execution actually be cancelled rather than postponed? He was taken back to the vehicle that had brought him to the quarry, then driven back to the store and was placed once more in the back room. Oddly no guard was left to watch him, although he could hear the sound of one outside the door.

Fifteen minutes passed and then, to his surprise, General von Schirach himself, an imposing figure with an aristocratic face and silvery hair, came into the room alone. Instinctively Bjorn stood when the General entered, but the old soldier waved him to a chair by the table. The General continued to stand for a few moments, gazing thoughtfully at him. Then a Norwegian interpreter was brought in. What Bjorn heard disturbed and astonished him.

'I have something important to tell you in confidence,' said the General, 'which will explain why I gave orders for your execution to be cancelled. It is a very personal matter.'

'Many years ago, in 1921, my wife and I took into our home a girl to help with our four children. She was a very attractive, Norwegian girl with beautiful, blonde hair. We lived, and my family still live, in Schloss Adler in Bavaria, not far from München. This girl lived with us as one of the family and we became fond of her and our children adored her. She was satisfactory in every way except in one: she was too beautiful.'

'I am not proud of what I did but, in due course, she became pregnant. This became obvious to my wife, when the poor girl began having sickness in the mornings. My wife, naturally, was very angry when she realised that I was responsible and the girl was forced to leave immediately. The least I could do was to keep in touch with the home that she went to in Trondheim and where the child, a boy, was born. I found out what he had been called; his first name was your own. Later, he was adopted by a family on the shores of Lyngenfjord in Norway.'

'I have to tell you that I am your father and that, consequently, you are half German.'

Bjorn felt dizzy with shock. One minute he was about to be executed and the next he had met his true father and learned that he was part Norwegian and part German!

There was a moment's silence, while the old soldier gazed once more at Bjorn, as if searching for something of himself, perhaps for his lost youth or for a son he never knew. He then stepped forward, reached out his hand, and father and son shook hands. Without another word, the General turned his back and walked out of the room – and that was that.

Bjorn's mind was in turmoil. Clearly, von Schirach who, twenty-four years ago, had helped to create him, had just saved his life. His thoughts were interrupted when an aide came into the room and asked him to stay where he was until a staff officer had seen him.

It was midday before the staff officer arrived.

'General von Schirach,' he said, 'has instructed me to inform you that, as you were not involved in the recent assassination, you are to be freed immediately. Please go now!'

Bjorn, a free man, walked out onto the gravel in front of the store. A local resident was passing along the road and Bjorn asked him to take him to see Hans Larsen.

Hans was amazed to see him alive and well but his immediate assumption was that Bjorn had some connection with the Germans and was perhaps a covert collaborator. However, Bjorn told him of the extraordinary train of events which had led to him being freed, including his relationship with the General. For a few moments Hans was too surprised to speak and then remarked:

'That's difficult to believe; you really mean that the General is actually your father?'

'Yes, that is the case, whether I like it or not. I didn't have any choice in the matter.'

There was a long pause, while Hans collected his

thoughts. 'Bjorn, I must ask you if it really was you who killed Adelbrecht.'

'Yes, it was me and I would like to tell you why I did it. You must know that, for some time, I worked for the Germans in the Todt Organisation and, since then, I've been increasingly ostracised by my fellow Norwegians. Old friends won't talk to me any longer but I was really shaken when I discovered that I was marked for elimination by the Resistance – by my own people! On an impulse I decided to make a clear demonstration of my allegiance to Norway and I could think of no better way than to target the Reichskommissar. In retrospect I realise just what a bad decision that was and I am fearful of the repercussions.'

'Bjorn, please listen carefully. My advice is that you should tell absolutely no one about what Schirach told you and certainly not Gunnar and Birgitta. Keep this matter entirely to yourself; it saved your life and just leave it at that. I will never mention it but you must never, never again use violence against the occupying forces. If you were to do so it would only invite retribution against our community. Having said that, I concede that you managed to kill one of the most obnoxious of all the Nazis. Adelbrecht was a murderer many times over but I am afraid that reprisals are inevitable.'

Surprisingly, the German authorities did not immediately pursue the matter of further reprisals for the shooting. People in the community began to think that now that the war in Europe was going so badly for the Germans, they must be thinking about their own skins and it would be unwise to invite retribution when the war ended.

However, it was not to be and, a week after the assassination of Adelbrecht, the morning quiet of Olderdalen was broken by the sudden arrival of a small convoy of German police vehicles. Armed SS men disembarked and immediately fanned out through the village, banging on doors and arbitrarily dragging out twenty bemused, male villagers. They herded them onto the foreshore, near the boat house, and lined them up with their backs to the fjord.

Hilder and Hans had been allowed back into their home three days before, and now watched in trepidation from an upstairs window. It all happened very quickly.

An officer standing to the side of the six-man execution squad gave an order and the rifles were raised. Neither Hans nor Hilder heard the order to fire but the crackle of shots was unmistakable. Simultaneously, the hostages crumpled to the ground, whereupon the officer walked across to them with a drawn pistol. He glanced briefly at each, shooting in the head those who showed signs of life. As Hans watched, one of the shot men struggled to sit up, and, supporting himself with an outstretched arm, looked up at the approaching executioner. The image of the victim being finally despatched with a head shot would recur as a nightmare in Hans's dreams for years to come.

It was over. Hans bowed his head, as he said a quiet prayer to himself while Hilder sobbed beside him. Purely by chance they, too, had not been rounded up, but which of their friends and neighbours had not been so lucky?

28

TROMSO: NOVEMBER 12TH 1944

Eighty kilometres due west of Olderdalen, and just outside Tromso, lived old Leif Jessen's son. He and his wife had two children, Karl and little Anton, who, on November 11th had just celebrated his tenth birthday. Karl, his elder brother, had been almost as excited as Anton at what turned out to be a lively party with half a dozen invited friends. They had had to make do without cakes as there was almost no sugar available, but, to make up for it, the children had pastries, some cut into animal shapes, along with plates of pickled herring. On the mantelpiece stood a row of birthday cards, one of them from Anton's grandfather, Leif, who lived far away beside Lyngenfjord.

The next morning at seven o'clock, Anton was woken as usual by his mother to get ready for school. As he pulled on his clothes, he contemplated the excitement of the previous day's party and felt sure that today would be boring in comparison.

The family was having breakfast when they were startled by sudden thunderous gunfire from the fjord where *Tirpitz* was anchored near Håkøy Island, just beyond the outskirts of Tromso. The ship had arrived there in September after sustaining damage from repeated attacks in her lair near Alta.

The family stared at each other for a moment and, leaving the food uneaten, rushed out of the house to see what was happening. The surrounding houses hid the view of the fjord where the gunfire was coming from so, accompanied by numerous neighbours, Anton ran ahead down to the end of the street to get a clear view. As they ran they could hear shrieking of warning klaxons, coming from the direction of the *Tirpitz*. There, across the water, they saw the ship surrounded by coils of smoke from her guns, as they fired at some target invisible to the watchers, while puffs of the exploding shells pock-marked the pink morning sky. Within a few minutes a cluster of tiny dots appeared in the sky approaching from the south-east. Gradually the dots turned into about thirty big four-engined bombers.

'They are English Lancaster bombers, I know they are!' shouted Anton above the noise, as he danced with excitement. The boy knew his planes, both British and German, and had a model British Lancaster suspended by a thread from his bedroom ceiling.

The anti-aircraft fire redoubled as the first planes neared the ship and little Anton covered his ears with his hands to shut out the shattering noise.

In the weak morning sunlight the boy saw the sudden glint of an object dropping from the first plane. Almost immediately it became invisible as it plummeted down towards the ship. A few moments later a shattering detonation blasted the eardrums of the Norwegian onlookers, as a huge column of water rose alongside the *Tirpitz*. A second later the pressure wave of the explosion thumped into their chests. One after the other, the planes made their bombing runs, each dropping an enormous 'Tallboy' bomb which raised further great columns of water close to the ship but without actually hitting her. One of the bombs fell on land a short way from the water's edge, raising a huge black eruption of earth and rocks.

Anton was about to run away in fright when there was a deafening explosion. A furious inferno suddenly burst from the fore part of the ship, in a jet of smoke and flame, which climbed hundreds of feet into the air. A bomb had made a direct hit. It was an appalling sight and the memory of the explosion, far louder than all the rest, would stay with Anton for the rest of his life.

It was too much for a boy of ten and Anton burst into tears with the horror of it all. He did not hate the Germans and, only a few days previously, he had fallen when running in the street and had grazed his knees. A Kriegsmarine sailor from the *Tirpitz* had lifted him to his feet, comforted him and had given him a piece of chocolate, the first he had tasted for years. The kindly sailor told him that his name was Peter and Anton knew that his friend must be in the midst of all that fire and smoke.

A few minutes after the explosion a gasp arose from the watchers, as the great ship began to list to port. In a little over ten minutes the Lancaster bombers, having completed the raid, turned away and disappeared. The gunfire stopped. The ship listed more and more, while hundreds of sailors dived into the fjord waters and started to swim for the shore. Then there was one final, colossal, explosion which lifted one of the main gun turrets high into the air. The huge object rotated before crashing down onto the swimmers in the fjord. Then *Tirpitz* rolled over.

Almost at once, local people launched boats to rescue survivors, many of whom were covered with oil and were desperately badly wounded. Anton watched as a small boat came to the shore quite near to him with four German sailors, one of whom had lost an arm and was trying, white faced, to staunch the blood with pieces of uniform. He looked to see if it was his friend, Peter, but it was not. Scores of survivors, many of them little more than youths, were brought ashore, while local people did what they could to help them.

Anton Jessen's tender years had not prepared him for anything like this and he ran as fast as he could back home, with tears running down his cheeks. His young mind just could not take any more of the horror he had seen, a horror which he would never forget.

When he arrived home, panting for breath, he found his parents frantic with worry about him but, ignoring them, he rushed up to his bedroom and threw himself face down on the bed sobbing. After a few minutes, his father quietly opened the door, sat down on the edge of the bed and tried to comfort the boy. As he did so, he noticed that the model Lancaster bomber had been torn down from the ceiling and stamped to pieces on the floor.

Among the hundreds of bodies brought ashore that day was that of Seekadett Tomas Schmidt, whose elder brother, Willi, was serving with the Wehrmacht in northern Norway.

29

ALTA. THE GESTAPO

The news of the destruction of the *Tirpitz* was greeted with considerable satisfaction by Sven and the fjord watchers who had so assiduously observed her movements through Altafjord and in Kafjord. Sven reflected that, in spite of his involvement with the Resistance, it was beginning to look as though he might evade the clutches of the Gestapo altogether and live to see a free Norway. However, it was not to be.

At three o'clock one morning Sven was in bed asleep in his house on the slope above the boatyard when he was jolted awake by loud banging on the front door. For a moment he thought that it must be Else who was away staying with a friend for two nights. Perhaps she was back early and had found herself locked out. Alarmed, he swung his legs to the floor and reached for his dressing gown. Banging on the door at that time of the night might mean the one thing that he feared most – the Gestapo. Sven ran downstairs and, as soon as he unlocked the door, his worst fears were realised. There stood a grey-uniformed officer. The black patch on the right side of his collar and the death's head emblem on his cap showed all too clearly that he was indeed a member of the Gestapo. Behind him waited two armed policemen.

'You are Sven Svensen?' demanded the Gestapo man as he and his men barged in through the open door.

'I am, and what do you want at this time of night?' Sven replied, his mouth dry with fear.

'You are under arrest,' retorted the German. 'You have ten minutes to get ready. We will stay here to make sure that you do not do anything stupid.'

'What are you charging me with?' asked Sven as the men pushed him into the living room.

'You will find out soon enough. You now have only nine minutes left.'

Just within the allotted time Sven was dressed and the policemen shoved him roughly to the door and out to a waiting police vehicle. He was bundled inside and, with a guard on each side of him, was driven to the police station which he knew was staffed by some Norwegian police as well as by Germans. There he was taken to an interrogation room bare of all furniture except for a chair in the middle of the room and another beside a table against a wall.

Nothing happened for an hour which, Sven suspected, was intended to intimidate him. He wondered what the charge would be. He had been scrupulously careful to conceal his activities relating to the fjord watchers in the forest above Alta and he hoped that Else and Erik had not aroused suspicions on account of their activities. Presently footsteps approached the door and a different Gestapo officer came into the room. A picture of arrogance, the newcomer sat nonchalantly on the edge of the table with one foot up on a chair. He gazed at Sven in a silence broken only by a fly buzzing insistently on the inside of the window pane. The tense atmosphere went on for several minutes and then the questioning began.

'You are Sven Svensen and own the boat repair yard here in Alta, yes?'

Sven confirmed his identity and ownership of the yard.

'Have you recently had an unauthorised visitor staying on your boat?'

Fear permeated Sven's body as he realised that the Germans must know about Major Sands.

There was no time to think how to deal with the situation except to deny all knowledge of Sands and, for a moment, he did not answer.

'Why do you hesitate? You know Major Sands, yes?' his questioner persisted.

'I don't know anyone called Major Sands,' replied Sven.

His questioner was silent for a minute then stood up, went over to the door, opened it and nodded to someone in the passage. With shocked surprise, Sven saw none other than Sands himself walking in; at least the man whom he had known as Sands. The crinkly, fair hair was unmistakable, but now he wore a grey SS police uniform and on his face was an amused smile. Sven knew that the SS and the Gestapo frequently worked together.

'*Guten Morgen, Herr Svensen,*' he said, before reverting to Norwegian. 'My name is Standartenführer Richter. It was kind of you to have me to stay on your boat. We knew all about Major Sands whom the British were sending by submarine, as we had intercepted a message about him. It was a simple matter to remove him from the island and for me to wait there in his place. The British major has already paid the usual penalty for spying. Your daughter and Erik Knudsen will soon be joining you in custody. Tomorrow you will be taken to Tromso, where you will be further questioned.' Sven had no illusions about what this meant. He would be shot.

At least, he thought, there is no evidence yet that Else and Erik have been caught.

Sven's captors had no way of knowing what a 'big fish' they had arrested. Unknown even to his own daughter, Sven was commander of North Norway's active Military Resistance Organisation – the 'Milorg'. It was he who had been masterminding the coastal watchers and ensuring that information about *Tirpitz* and other ships reached Britain. It was he who had arranged the supply of small arms, particularly sten-guns and Thompson machine guns, to Milorg forces. In short, he was the key figure of the Resistance in the north.

The cell in the police station, with its sentry outside the door, was hardly a comfortable place. The window, small and barred, was a miserable affair high up in a wall, which let in little light and offered no chance of escape. A naked electric bulb, hanging on its wire in the centre of the cell, emitted a grudging yellow glow and, on the floor at the bottom of the wall, facing the door, some planks and a stained blanket served as a bunk. A bucket stood in a corner.

Sven's wrist watch had not been removed and he watched the time slowly passing, until it was obvious that no food was going to be supplied. He shook out the blanket on the planks, in readiness for night, when the cell door opened and a sentry passed in a tin mug of water. Then he settled down to try to sleep.

At seven o'clock next morning he woke, cold, stiff and hungry, but, to his surprise, he had slept fairly well. Soon afterwards, a plate with a lump of bread and a piece of smoked fish was brought in, along with more water. An hour later, the cell door was opened again and a German policeman beckoned for him to come out.

'Tromso,' he said by way of abbreviated explanation and marched him out of the police station, to a waiting

Wehrmacht lorry. He was helped to climb in the back and was followed in by two armed soldiers who sat, rifles between their knees, between him and the open back of the vehicle. Then, with two motorcycle escorts riding in front, they set off on the 300 kilometre journey.

Sven studied the two guards as they chatted between themselves without making any attempt to communicate with him. They were both young, little more than teenagers, and, presently, one of them brought out a packet of cigarettes, shook one out and offered it to him. It was a kindly gesture but, as he had never smoked, he simply thanked the youngster and waved the packet away.

As the journey wore on, Sven conceded that escape was not a realistic option and, resigned to his fate, he settled down to try to sleep.

★

One of the Norwegian policemen at the Alta police station, who was related to Sven, had reported the time of departure of the lorry, with its motorcycle escorts, to members of the Milorg. This gave enough time for an ambush to be arranged.

One hundred and twenty kilometres further on, near the shore of Lyngenfjord, four Milorg men made hurried preparations to ambush the vehicle which they knew was taking their regional commander to his almost certain execution in Tromso. They selected a bridge near the Lyngenfjord shore which the vehicle would have to cross and which would give them cover. It had the advantage of being only forty kilometres from the Swedish border, and that would give themselves and Sven at least a chance of escaping to neutral territory if pursued.

By 2 pm the men were crouching beneath the wooden bridge, across a river, not far from Gunnar Torkelsen's farmhouse. As they waited they carefully checked the cocking slots in their stens as 'stoppages' would be disastrous and there would be no second chances.

The turbulence of the river would mask the sound of an approaching vehicle so one of the men kept watch, while the others remained hidden. While they were waiting, a number of German vehicles drove across the bridge, oblivious to the gunmen hidden beneath it.

After having waited for an hour, the weak morning sunlight momentarily glinted on the windscreen of an approaching vehicle. At first, the birch trees prevented a clear view but then, half a kilometre away through a gap in the trees, emerged a Wehrmacht lorry with two motorcyclists riding in front. The watchman at the bridge hurriedly alerted his colleagues. This was it! This was what they had been waiting for!

Two of the Milorg men ran out from their hiding place and rolled a roadside boulder onto the approach to the bridge before ducking back out of sight. They were only just in time, as the lorry and escorts emerged from the trees, swept round a bend and headed for the bridge. Suddenly, the motorcycle escorts, seeing the obstruction, swerved and waved down the following lorry, which pulled up just short of the boulder.

Suddenly all four Milorg men leapt out from beneath the bridge firing bursts from their stens. Two of them shot out the lorry tyres and the other two rushed the escorts who were only yards away and who never even had a chance of using their weapons. They were quickly disarmed and made to lie face down in the road, arms and legs outspread.

Two of the attackers raced, one on each side, to the rear of the lorry but before they got there the guards jumped out and fired at them, hitting one Milorg man who spun round and dropped to the ground.

In the confusion, Sven leapt out of the back of the lorry and sprinted for the cover of the bridge.

Suddenly it was all over. The two young guards from the lorry had been taken by surprise and were overwhelmed by the speed of the attack. The driver, paralysed by fear, never even moved from his seat. The Milorg man who had been shot in the chest was dead.

The commander of the attackers shouted a terse order to Sven, who collected up the German weapons and flung them as far as he could into the fjord. Then, leaving their dead comrade in the road, the fugitives let loose a burst of sten-gun fire, close over the prostrate Germans and charged across the river. Once they were on the far bank two of them turned and fired more warning shots. Sven and his rescuers then ran for the wooded mountain slopes and, unsurprisingly, no one followed them. They climbed steadily up the slope for about thirty minutes then the commander called a halt to look for signs of pursuit. They stopped, panting, at a knoll from which they could look down on the ambush site. Seated on a rock, the commander scanned the area around the bridge with binoculars. The lorry had been pushed clear of the bridge and three newly arrived lorries were now parked nearby. There was no sign of the dead Milorg man. A number of soldiers walking around the site were obviously discussing what had happened. Two of them peered under the bridge apparently inspecting its structure but, most importantly, there were no signs of pursuers.

Sven, having got his breath back, was the first to speak.

'That was a highly efficient ambush and a credit to the Milorg. I'm very grateful, but am truly sorry that you lost one of your men on my account and I'm fearful that when his identity is discovered his family, if he has one, may be made to suffer. I hope I may somehow be offered the chance to repay you one day.'

The Milorg leader put down his binoculars. 'Look,' he said, 'since they don't seem to be following us, we can forget about having to try for Sweden and, in any case, we would be interned there if we did make it. I can only hope that as no German was hurt they may not be so determined to find us as they might be.'

The Milorg men huddled together for a quick conference, then the commander turned to Sven.

'We've done as much as we can for you. My men will disperse, and you'll need somewhere to shelter. On the way up we passed Gunnar Torkelsen's house but don't go there as it is too close to the ambush site. You'd be better going to Nils Anders, who is a good man. He lives half a mile further on down the fjord and may be able to hide you. Good bye and good luck!'

As they parted, Sven shook hands with the three brave rescuers.

30

LYNGENFJORD AND HOLBUKT.
THE MEETING WITH KUZNETSOV

For Lara, the reconciliation between Willi and her parents had brought her great comfort. Her mood was better and, looking back, she was unable to explain just why she had tried to commit suicide in the fjord. One morning, she was overjoyed when Willi unexpectedly called to see her. Willi was still nervous when he walked up the farm road and knocked at the door. However, he need not have worried and, when Gunnar appeared, the greeting was friendly enough.

'Oh, hello Willi! We were not expecting you, but come in,' he said, holding out his hand, and, for the second time in his life, he shook hands with a member of the Wehrmacht.

'Lara,' he called, 'there's someone to see you!'

After a few moments, the silence of the house was broken by the sound of a baby babbling happily, then Lara emerged carrying her daughter. She was overcome with surprise, rushed over to Willi and, depositing Little Lara into his arms, threw her own arms round his neck and kissed him on the lips in front of her bemused father. Birgitta, who had been tending the cow out at the back, heard the commotion and hurried around to see what was going on. She, too, seemed happy to see Willi, who was profoundly grateful for the transformation in Lara's parents' attitudes. He felt that he was gradually being accepted, but acknowledged the difficult road which Lara's parents had travelled to reach this point.

For a time, Willi sat at the kitchen table, with Little Lara on his knee, chatting to Gunnar and Birgitta about the joy and sense of purpose that she had brought into his life.

'Look!' he exclaimed, holding the child up high above his head, 'she's smiling down at me.'

He laughed when Lara asked him if he was still in the habit of buying great quantities of stokfisk at the Olderdalen store. Almost imperceptibly, the 'family' was beginning to relax and to take pleasure in having three generations gathered together.

Willi went on to tell Lara's parents about his life in Germany, about his old mother, about his lifelong interest in botany and nature and about the books he liked to read and the music he liked to listen to. He also said, quite openly, that he was ashamed of Germany's part in the pointless war with all its cruelty.

'However,' he went on, 'one good thing has come out of it: I have met Lara, and you should know that she and Little Lara have become the centre of my life and I will always be faithful to them.'

Willi was unable to stay for more than a couple of hours and, as he departed, he promised to write to Lara soon.

After he left, Birgitta took Lara aside as the devotion between her daughter and Willi was obvious for all to see. She agreed that he did seem a decent man and that she and Gunnar accepted that a permanent relationship existed between them. Once the war was over the question of marriage would have to be addressed. This lifted a great weight from Lara's mind. Ever since she had fallen in love with Willi she had been conscious of an oppressive cloud hovering over all, which she knew was to do with the acceptability of the relationship.

A week after Willi had returned to his unit, a new worry arose to trouble the young mother. Little Lara began to have distressing episodes when she cried and seemed to be in pain. Then Lara noticed that during the episodes, a cherry-sized lump appeared beside her tummy button and, when the crying went on for a long time, this swelling became bigger and quite hard. Naturally, Lara was worried and asked her parents to have a look at it. Gunnar took one glance and commented that he had seen a similar thing in his lambs and once in a calf.

'She's got a hernia,' he remarked. 'Usually, with farm animals, it gets better by itself but, since Little Lara seems to be in pain, I think you should take her to see a surgeon at the hospital in Alta. I don't think you'll need clearance to travel there since it could be considered an emergency, though it isn't really one.'

The bus service still ran to schedule and the next day mother and baby set off on the long trip to Alta. They found a space at the back of the bus, where Lara could cope with breast-feeding and nappy changes. Surprisingly Little Lara did not seem to mind the jolting journey over the gravelled road and her presence enchanted her fellow passengers.

At last, they arrived at Alta and got off near the post office, only a few hundred yards from the hospital. Lara was just passing the post office door when a young man, hurrying out of it, bumped into her. Seeing the baby he immediately apologised and smiled at the young mother. Then, with a gasp of surprise, he stared at her. Lara, momentarily startled by his reaction, could hardly believe her eyes. It was none other than her English cousin, Erik!

'Lara!' he exclaimed. 'What… what are you doing here? You have a baby! Look, we can't talk here; I have to be careful.'

'I am just going up to the hospital,' she replied when she had regained her composure. 'My baby needs a check-up and I'm on my way there right now. I don't expect to be kept waiting long. Why not come with me and, afterwards, we can go somewhere where we can talk privately?'

The consultation with the surgeon did indeed not take long. He was a pleasant young man and took a careful look at the baby's abdomen. Little Lara howled as he touched her tummy with a cold hand and the hernia immediately bulged out but then vanished again when he pressed it in with a finger.

'There is no need to worry,' he said. 'This is a common type of hernia in babies and will almost certainly disappear in time without treatment. It is only serious if the bulge stays hard and tender and you must come back right away if that happens, although I think it's unlikely to do so.'

Much relieved, Lara went back to the waiting room and, together with Erik, left the hospital and found a quiet café in the main street, where they settled themselves into a secluded corner. Little Lara, tired from the day's travelling, fell asleep on her lap.

'What in the name of goodness are you doing in Norway?' began Lara. 'It's great to see you, of course, but why haven't you been to see my parents? Tell me what's going on!'

'Look, Lara, I cannot tell you anything at all about me or what I am doing here.' replied Erik, 'and you can probably guess why I haven't been to see Gunnar and Birgitta. But first tell me about your baby and who the lucky father is – perhaps one of the Anders lads?'

'No,' Lara replied cautiously, 'it's not them or any other neighbour. Erik, what I am about to say will shock you. My baby's father is a German officer serving in the Wehrmacht.'

'Oh God!' exclaimed Erik, pushing back his chair in alarm. 'Oh no surely not! Are you being serious?'

Erik's agitation gradually subsided as Lara explained everything to him. While she assured him that her allegiance to Norway was unshaken, she explained her love for Little Lara's father.

'He's called Willi Schmidt, Erik. He's a Major in the Wehrmacht but is not at all like most people's idea of a German. He's very kind and thoughtful and wants to marry me when the war's over.'

'To marry you! Lara, you can't marry him – he's the enemy. No one here will speak to you again if you do. Please, please don't do it. What would your parents say?'

'I'm going to do it, Erik, whatever anyone says. I really have decided. Anyway, my parents know all about it and have said that they will accept Willi as my husband.'

The two cousins went on talking for some time and in due course, Erik asked after Bjorn.

'He's well but doesn't seem to have worked out his role in life. He puzzles everyone. For a time he drove vehicles for the Germans and his allegiance to Norway was openly questioned, but when he shot that monster, Adelbrecht, people briefly accepted him as a Norwegian patriot. However, since the reprisal shootings, public attitude has changed and Bjorn is now blamed for the twenty deaths. In fact he has become a figure of hate. He really is mixed up in his mind.'

An hour passed quickly and, when Little Lara became restless, they got up to go. Erik had been aware that a man eying him from four tables away stood up at the same time, came over and said quietly that he had some important to tell you. They followed the man out into the street while Lara, sensing that the information was for Erik only, moved out of earshot.

'Sven,' the man said, 'was arrested by the Gestapo but has been freed by Milorg. The Gestapo know about you. Both you and Else are in great danger and must leave your lodgings immediately. She has already cleared out. Don't go to the boatyard as it's being watched. Go immediately to this address where Sven will contact you.' He handed Erik a scrap of paper, before continuing, 'The house is empty just now and you'll have to fend for yourself but make yourself inconspicuous.' Without another word the man turned his back and hurried away down the street.

Lara saw that Erik had received disturbing news.

'What was that about?' she asked. 'You look pale.'

'I can't tell you anything Lara,' Erik replied abruptly. 'You must leave me at once and don't tell anyone at all that you met me, not even your parents. Now go quickly.'

With that, they parted. Erik looked at the address on the scrap of paper, on which was written 'No 6 Trydvang'. He asked a passer-by for directions and, doing his best to avoid the few Wehrmacht soldiers still in town, he managed to find the house within ten minutes. It was a dilapidated, wooden affair and looked unoccupied. Untended grass and weeds smothered the tiny garden and the unpainted gate was hanging by a single hinge. He pushed the gate aside and went to the front door and found that it was locked. He walked round to the back along a path trodden among the weeds and tried the back door. It was not locked and, pushing it open, he stepped into a damp, musty atmosphere of disuse. Cautiously he went along a narrow passageway and tried the first door. It opened easily and he found himself in a kitchen which, surprisingly, appeared to be very much used. There were some food supplies on the table, along with some pots and pans and a Primus stove. A mug containing the dregs of some hot drink stood on the window cill. Clearly someone had been staying in the house.

Erik stood for a moment thinking, when, suddenly he heard a floorboard creaking from somewhere in the building. He held his breath, listening, and then there was another creak, followed by the sound of stealthy footsteps coming along the hall. They stopped outside the kitchen door. The door handle moved, then slowly began to turn. Erik backed off behind the door and crouched down. Suddenly the door was flung open and Else leapt inside with a pistol in her hand, which she was clearly ready to use.

'Erik! Thank God it's you! I thought you might be one of the Gestapo men,' she said, as she put the Colt .45 into her pocket. 'A few days ago they arrested my father, but the lorry taking him to Tromso was ambushed by the Milorg and he escaped. He's holed up in a safe house in the town just now but he hopes to move in here later today. Erik, sit down and I'll heat up some soup; I've got a lot to tell you.'

Else, well used to the vagaries of Primus stoves, soon had a pot of soup bubbling away. She poured out two mugs and they sat together at the table, while she explained what had been happening.

'Things went wrong after the Major Sands affair. Father

was arrested one night and was taken to Alta police station. The next day the Gestapo decided to transfer him to Tromso with an armed escort but a Norwegian policeman in Alta tipped off the Milorg and he was rescued at Lyngenfjord. Ultimately, he found his way back here to Alta and sent a message to me saying that all three of us are on the Gestapo wanted list. Thankfully someone in the Resistance found this house for us. We can never go back to the boatyard or to our lodgings.'

Later on, in the evening dusk, Erik was startled by the sound of someone at the back door. Three quick taps were followed by three loud knocks.

'It's all right,' said Else as the door opened. 'It's Father; we arranged for that special knock so that I don't shoot him when he comes in!'

Sven appeared, looking pale and exhausted, after the stress of his arrest, but he was glad to see that Erik had found his way to the safe house. Erik mentioned the man in the café who had given him the address. Sven nodded.

'He's a very reliable Resistance man. We call him Axel though that's not his real name. He works in a garage behind the police station and services vehicles for the Wehrmacht and sometimes for the Gestapo too. He knows someone in the police and hears quite a lot of what goes on there. He says that the three of us are on the Gestapo's priority wanted list. They've been looking for us at the boatyard but are now widening the search to the town as a whole. That makes Alta too dangerous for us and we must move on as soon as possible.'

'Where can we go?' asked Erik.

Sven paused for a moment. 'I have in mind that isolated village, Valanhamn, where Roald lives. It has several advantages. First, few Germans ever go there and secondly it would not involve a long road journey. We can't avoid going from here to Holbukt by road but the rest of the journey could be done by boat direct to Valanhamn. I know that Axel could be persuaded to take us to Holbukt when he road tests one of the Wehrmacht vehicles.'

'What about road checks?' enquired Else.

'As you've seen, the Germans are leaving Finnmark in droves, now that things are going against them, and consequently there are fewer checks. There is a risk but I think we should make it all right.'

'Good,' said Erik. 'When do we go?'

'Hopefully, we can leave tomorrow morning; Axel knows to expect us at any time. Meantime, it's a risk staying here, but that's a risk we'll just have to take.'

The three of them scraped together a meal of sorts and Sven went on to tell them an odd story which he had heard from Bernt. Apparently, the Resistance had received a curious message from a source in Sweden, saying, 'Himmler orders Werewolves to occupied territories'.

'It's thought that these so-called Werewolves are to stay behind as terror units as the Germans retreat. No doubt they will not be subject to the usual rules of war. It sounds to me as if the Germans are getting desperate and, no doubt, they'll exploit the disturbing title with its undertones of the supernatural.'

'It sounds like another crazy Nazi invention,' remarked Erik.

'Quite, but we must keep in mind that such units may begin to operate right here in Norway.'

Early the following morning, the three fugitives, having just got up, were alarmed when a Wehrmacht lorry drew up outside. Else, armed with the Colt, waited just inside the back door, while Sven and Erik, keeping well back in the front room, watched the driver climb down.

'It's all right, it's Axel!' said Sven with relief, 'This must be one of his repair jobs which will take us to Holbukt.'

They gathered their few possessions and hurried out to the waiting vehicle. With a brief greeting to Axel, they climbed into the canvas-covered rear and, in moments, they were off. Mindful of the small chance of a road check, they pulled a tarpaulin over themselves.

The hundred and twenty kilometre journey was slow. The road was crammed with convoys of military traffic, as Finnmark disgorged its German occupiers, and Axel often had to trail along, behind a line of Wehrmacht lorries. There were no road checks: it was all almost too good to be true, but their luck held and they reached Holbukt in good time. Axel dropped them off near the harbour and drove away to continue his 'road test'.

Holbukt harbour was tiny but half a dozen fishing boats had managed to tie up there. Two men standing beside a boat were mending a fishing net, which was draped over some stacked fish boxes. Sven walked over to them and explained that the three of them needed someone to ferry them across the fjord to Valanhamn.

'That shouldn't be a problem,' one of the fishermen replied, 'Wait just a minute.'

He walked across to a nearby cottage and knocked at the door. A very old man emerged whose snow-white mop of hair matched his equally white beard, and, after listening to the fisherman for a moment, he glanced across at Sven before hobbling over to speak to him. He introduced himself as Odd Olsen. Sven was immediately struck by the old man's piercing blue eyes, as they shook hands. Sven explained to him that the three of them hoped to stay with Roald Bratland in Valanhamn and would like to set off as soon as possible.

'Oh, I know Roald. Yes, I can take you today if you want,' the old man replied, 'but I'll have to charge you a bit for the journey.'

Two hours later they set off. On the way across they chatted to Odd Olsen, who seemed curiously guarded when they mentioned Tovik.

'I would keep away from that coast if I were you as there's been quite a bit of German activity there. Besides, they say there's a curse on that area and I've heard that a German who landed there recently became ill with some terrible disease. I used to know Otto, who not so long ago disappeared across there. Apparently old Ingrid, his widow, also died some three weeks ago, apparently from pneumonia.'

When they arrived at Valanhamn, they thanked and paid Odd and walked up to Roald's house.

'Come in, come in. What a surprise!' Roald exclaimed. 'Welcome!' He ushered them through to the kitchen where his wife, helped by a stranger, was preparing a meal.

'This is my wife and I must also introduce you to Vladimir Kuznetsov who's been staying with us. He's the Russian I told you about whom I found wrecked and half dead on the coast. Being Russian he, too, has good reason to keep out of the way of the Germans. I may say he is doing well coping with the Norwegian language and will understand you if you don't speak too fast.'

'I well remember the extraordinary story of how you got to Norway,' replied Sven, shaking hands with the Russian before turning to Roald.

'We've had a difficult time with the Germans at Alta,' he explained, 'but I'll tell you about that later. Just now we really need somewhere to stay well out of the way of Germans. Can you suggest someone reliable who might give us lodgings, possibly for a month or two? It may not be for much longer than that as it looks as though the Occupation may be over before too long, but, just now, the Germans are making serious efforts to find the three of us. I had a feeling that this area might be as safe as any.'

Roald thought for a moment.

'I've an aunt who lives alone here in the village', he replied, 'and she would almost certainly be able to put you up. I'll take you to see her now if you like.'

The four of them walked up the steep slope to Roald's aunt's house. It was in an ideal situation. It stood on high ground at the back of the village with views over the rooftops and across the fjord to the distant Tovik coast. They could see the coastline where Ingrid's house was, but were too far away to make out the building itself. Roald mentioned that old Ingrid's nephew, Hans, had stayed on at Tovik after the old lady's death and had told him that, in the last two weeks, the Germans had been showing intense interest in that coast. He said that once, on returning from a fishing trip, he was securing his boat at the landing stage when he heard the sound of a boat engine and, scanning the sea, spotted a motor vessel heading at speed straight towards where he was standing. He had recognised it as a big German Schnellboot and when it neared the landing stage two of its crew began preparing mooring lines. Clearly their intention was to tie up beside his own boat. He waited on the landing stage as the vessel approached, undecided whether or not to help by picking up the thrown line. In the event he did pick it up and, securing it to a bollard, noted that a number of Germans were aboard the Schnellboot. A German officer stepped ashore, nodded, and announced who he was.

'I am Standartenführer Richter in command of this SS unit,' he said. 'My men may be here for two days to carry out a search of this part of the Tovik coast.'

He did not say what they were looking for. Without further explanation, Richter took ten men ashore, leaving one on board. At this point Hans left the Germans to it and walked up to the house with his mackerel. He stood for a time in the doorway watching what appeared to be preparations for a search.

★

In the German ranks there was a good deal of resentment at having to perform such a bizarre and apparently pointless task and the men also resented Standartenführer Richter, himself, who was the most unpopular of all the officers.

Starting at the harbour, the Germans formed an extended line stretching from the water's edge, with a number of men covering the shoreline rocks. The right wing of the line stretched to above the low cliffs to include a thirty yard strip of tundra. Once the men were in place, an order was given and the whole line began to move slowly forward in the direction of the open sea. The searchers on the rocky shore repeatedly slipped and fell as they worked while the others, walking slowly above the low cliffs, skirted round pools and boggy patches, occasionally probing the ground with what appeared to be metal rods. The whole exercise had made little sense to Hans and he went back into the cottage to start salting the mackerel.

The search had been under way for about twenty minutes when something among the rocks attracted the attention of the searchers. The line stopped and some of the men on the tundra moved over to the cliff edge to see what was happening below. One of the Germans below the cliff had stopped beside a white object wedged into a crevice just outside the mouth of one of the many sea caves. Using a stick he prodded what appeared to be the carcase of a long-dead sheep. As he did so, the inflated belly collapsed and a puff of gaseous corruption burst out, as greenish, semi-liquid filth poured onto the rocks. With an oath the man staggered away from the nauseous stench, covering his face with his hands. His comrades laughed at his predicament but backed well away from the area while the unfortunate man, still cursing, tried to clean off the foul liquid from his boots in a pool. Order was ultimately restored and the search continued but the men took care to avoid that part of the shore.

After four or five hours, the search ended and, from the cottage, Hans watched as the weary Germans returned to the landing stage and made preparations to leave in the Schnellboot. Hans expected them to return the following day, but they did not come back. Instead, Roald's boat appeared, approaching the harbour. Hans walked down to meet his friend and to help tie up and, as he did so, he saw another figure whom he recognised as Erik, standing in the bows preparing the mooring line. Hans was pleased to have unexpected company and, after welcoming the visitors, helped them to secure the boat and took them up to the house where he had been preparing lunch for himself. He added two more fish to the frying pan and, over the meal, they sat down to talk.

'It's good to see you both again,'remarked Hans. 'The Germans were here again last week looking for something, though goodness knows what. I was expecting them back the following day but they didn't reappear. I am beginning to think that they are afraid of this place – perhaps they have been spooked by its reputation.'

'What do you mean?' asked Erik. 'What sort of reputation?'

'Oh, it's an old story, which I'm surprised you haven't heard. A lot of people believe that this coast has a curse on it,' replied Hans. 'Some say it all began over thirty years ago in 1910 when a Lithuanian ship carrying Russian timber, reindeer hides and some cattle from Archangel to Vilnius was wrecked half a mile from here during a bad storm. Every one of the crew was drowned and, for a long time, the shore was littered with spruce logs, mixed up with dead cattle, and some of the crew's bodies. It happened long before my time but my late Aunt Ingrid used to tell me about it. She said it was a gruesome business because the local people had to tow the dead animals and the crew's bodies out to sea to get rid of them.'

Roald had heard the story before but it was new to Erik.

'But surely a shipwreck alone wouldn't give the coast such a reputation,' remarked Erik.

'No, you are right,' replied Hans, 'but you may have wondered just why this coast has almost no one living on it especially as it has such rich fishing and would easily support many families.'

'Well, go on, tell me why.'

Hans continued: 'After the shipwreck, several of the local fishermen, who had helped to dispose of the bodies, started to develop strange sores on their hands and three of them died of pneumonia. The sores turned into black ulcers and those men also started to die. That started a general panic and the people moved out. As far as I know, no one then knew what was causing the disease. However, the final blow came about eight years later when a couple, new to the coast, settled here. Within six months the man also developed the same sort of ulcers, which travelled up his arm, and he died a month or two later. That was the end of it, and now not many people like to spend much time here. I, myself, have never had a problem but Aunt Ingrid apparently died of pneumonia although no one knows whether or not it was caused by the disease. That doesn't alter the fact that most people give this place a wide berth.'

Hans paused: 'I seem to have done a lot of talking already but if you want to know the whole story I'd better tell you about the inquiry.'

'In about 1930 a medical inquiry was set up in Alta to try to establish what kind of disease it was. The official conclusion was that the cattle or the reindeer hides on the Lithuanian ship which went down here in 1910 were probably infected with anthrax – a disease which was widespread in parts of Russia at that time. The spores, apparently, can live for years in the soil and this, the report concluded, is why people became inexplicably ill and died so long afterwards. The troubling implication is that the infection is still lurking here and that's why I'm surprised to see you, Erik, coming here when most people avoid the place – literally like the plague.'

Hans continued: 'The other day a fisherman from Valanhamn called in at the landing stage. He didn't want to come ashore but we had a chat and he told me that a German soldier who had been involved in a search of the shore has developed what's being called "Tovik Coast Disease". Apparently it was the man who disturbed the carcase of a long-dead sheep on the rocks who developed pneumonia. That's the worst form of anthrax and is almost always fatal. Now that you know the facts, can't you tell me what it is it that you and the Germans are really after, because it must be something important?'

'I can't do that yet,' replied Erik, 'but I hope to tell you as soon as it's safe to do so, however, I am very grateful to you for telling us about the disease and about the German activities here.'

Hans looked disappointed, sensing that he was being excluded from some secret.

'As far as I know,' Hans went on, 'the Germans have found nothing special in spite of spending a lot of effort searching along the sea caves and I very much doubt they will come back in view of what happened to one of their men.'

Erik had learned all he needed to know – the Germans had not found the gold and perhaps the spectre of anthrax might well act as a deterrent against further searches. There seemed to be no point in staying on at Tovik and, shortly afterwards, he and Roald made preparations for the return trip to Valanhamn. Erik was pleased that he would be able to reassure Sven and Else that the gold was still safe.

31

THE ASSASSIN

When Roald steered his boat back into Valanhamn harbour, Sven and Else, who had seen it approaching, were waiting by the harbour wall.

'Glad to see you back,' said Sven. 'We have a visitor who has come especially to talk to you, Erik. He's waiting in Roald's house.'

'Who is it?' asked Erik.

'You'll see in a moment.'

The three of them walked across to Roald's and there in the living room, rising from a chair to greet them, was none other than Bjorn, whom Erik had been ordered to shoot with the Welrod on a path near Veidebakken. The shock of the meeting was all too apparent in Erik's face. Sven could see at once that the two young men were well known to each other and Erik, realising that he was in an awkward situation, decided it was time for him to tell the whole truth. He muttered an apology to the others, took Sven through to the next room and unburdened himself about his relationship to Bjorn.

'He's part of my family and a boyhood playmate and I could not shoot him. Instead one evening I confronted him with a pistol and told him that the Resistance had arranged for me to kill him and warned him to "disappear" immediately or face execution. Well, he disappeared all right and the next thing I heard was that it was he who shot Adelbrecht – a move which, I suspect, was intended to demonstrate his allegiance to Norway. I am sorry, however, that I misled you by telling you at the time that I had shot Bjorn.'

To Erik's relief Sven looked thoughtful rather than angry.

'That's quite amazing! I knew that you were half Norwegian,' he said, 'but I had no idea who your Norwegian relatives were. Our investigations into Bjorn showed that he comes from a farm on Lyngenfjord but I never suspected that his parents are your relatives. This brings the whole picture together.'

After talking for a little longer the pair went through to rejoin the others.

It was clear that Bjorn was not in good spirits. It had become common knowledge that it was he who had killed Adelbrecht and, while some locals at first applauded what he had done, the majority of Norwegians were appalled at what they saw as an act of gross stupidity, and held him responsible for the deaths by execution of twenty of Olderdalen's residents. Bjorn had become a pariah among his own people. Sven could see that Erik and Bjorn wanted to talk together and he suggested that they should be left alone to have some time to themselves.

'For goodness's sake, Bjorn, tell me everything,' exclaimed Erik once the others had gone out of the room. 'What have you been doing with yourself?'

Bjorn settled himself back in his chair and began a frank account of his activities over the past two years.

'Almost getting myself executed among other things –

and you'll be more than a little surprised to hear that I've discovered who my real father is.'

The startled look on Erik's face changed into a look of utter astonishment, almost disbelief, as Bjorn related what General von Schirach had told him.

'Yes, I thought that would startle you!' replied Bjorn. 'You see I'm not the cousin you thought you had. Being adopted, I never knew who my father was but now that I do know I feel like an imposter!'

Erik lapsed into dumbfounded silence, unable to think of anything appropriate to say.

'I've known that you were in Norway, Erik, ever since I saw you on that boat leaving the harbour in Svolvaer and I could see that you recognised me. I presume that you are back in Norway in some kind of covert capacity, though I know better than to ask you about that.'

They broke off the conversation as Roald's wife brought in a plate of sandwiches. He waited till she had gone and continued. 'Meeting you that night with a pistol really shook me. I've thought long and hard about it and I've come greatly to regret my past association with the Germans. Shortly before I abandoned my job with the Todt Organisation, I met a Wehrmacht officer who said that the Gestapo are after you. They believe you have certain information that they badly want and it seems that an SS unit, led by a certain Standartenführer Richter has been set up in order to hunt you down, and they want you alive.'

There was a short silence.

'Why are the Germans so keen to get you?' asked Bjorn.

Erik thought for a few moments – how much should he tell Bjorn? His cousin's recent actions had, after all, surely confirmed his allegiance to Norway.

'I think they want me on two counts. Firstly the awful truth is that they have been 'stringing me along' ever since you saw and wrote about me leaving Svolvaer harbour on a fishing boat. They hoped that I would lead them to a Resistance ring and unwittingly I have done just that. Looking back it did seem strange at the time that they released me after I was questioned in Harstadt. Secondly they think I know the whereabouts of some hidden 'war gold.' I'm not going to tell you where the gold is but we have stumbled on a hoard of ingots hidden on the Tovik coast. I'm not talking about a few ingots, but a massive hoard. It's been obvious for some time that the Germans know there's treasure of some sort somewhere round there but we're sure they don't know exactly where it is. We think the gold may have come from Russia on a British cruiser, the HMS *Edinburgh*, which was taking it from Murmansk to Britain, in payment for war supplies. The ship was part of a convoy which was attacked by aircraft or U-boats, and she sank somewhere in the Barents Sea in 1942. We have no idea how the gold found its way to the Tovik coast, but it's there all right.'

There was a stunned silence, as Bjorn took this in. 'How did the Germans get to hear about it?' he asked.

'We don't know for sure,' replied Erik, 'but an old fisherman seems to have stumbled across the hoard. Soon afterwards he mysteriously disappeared but before that his wife said that he wrote a letter to someone. I think it's possible that the letter may have been sent to Jakob Danielsen who, being a clockmaker and jeweller, would have been been well placed to give an informed opinion about the find. The letter was probably intercepted and read by a German censor.'

'By the way, you should know that Else and I are the only ones who know exactly where the gold is hidden. We are telling no one else. Sven and you are the only ones to know only about its existence somewhere on the coast and it's best to leave it at that.'

Bjorn nodded his agreement.

In the silence which followed, a gull cried mournfully somewhere out on the harbour. Erik could see that Bjorn was tormented by some inner conflict and was struggling to say something of importance.

'Erik,' he said at last in a troubled voice, 'I feel torn between two personalities. Most of the time I think of myself as a patriotic Norwegian, but then I feel a "tap on the shoulder" as my German half reminds me that it's a part of me as well and is waiting to be acknowledged. More and more, I feel it like a physical presence, waiting and waiting – but for what? Sometimes I think I'm going crazy. I know the consequences of Adelbrecht's shooting will always be held against me in Norway and that people here will never forgive me, but neither will the Germans forgive me for killing one of them. Either way I am damned.'

Erik was at a loss to know what to say or do.

After a pause, he asked, 'So what are you going to do now?'

'I don't know,' replied Bjorn, 'but I can't stay here. It's tormenting me and I feel really depressed about my future.'

Bjorn said nothing more but leant forward in his chair gazing at the floor in silence. He seemed to be choked up with emotion and his hunched shoulders began to shake, perhaps with suppressed sobbing. Erik leant forward and put a hand on his cousin's shoulder, and when Bjorn looked up, Erik could see tears in his eyes.

That was the last time that Erik had a serious conversation with Bjorn and, for the rest of his life, he blamed himself for his failure to talk through his cousin's emotional problems. Bjorn left Valanhamn the following day and Erik never saw him again.

32

FLIGHT FROM NORWAY: 1945

March 31st 1945 turned out to be the end of the peaceful time in Valanhamn. There was an illicit radio in the village and, judging by the news, the locals felt that the war could not last more than a month or two. It was almost as if the occupiers were losing heart, but the even tenor of life enjoyed by Erik, Else and Sven in Valanhamn then came to an end.

One morning, the engine note of an approaching boat dispelled hopes that it was all over as a Schnellboot emerged from around the headland and, moments later, a light aircraft appeared overhead and circled over the village.

'It's a Storch!' Erik exclaimed as the aircraft, its floats clearly visible, circled low over the fjord as it lined up for touchdown near the sheltered water of the harbour. After a short landing run it taxied over to the harbour wall where the pilot cut the engine, stepped down onto one of the floats and secured a line to a bollard. A second German, who looked like an officer, followed him and they both climbed the stone steps up the harbour wall.

A few moments later the Schnellboot reached the harbour and tied up not far from the rocking Storch. Leaving two guards in the Schnellboot, twenty armed SS men emerged and lined up on the harbour wall, while the officer from the plane gave them orders while pointing up to the houses. At once the men separated into two groups and ran round in what looked like an attempt to encircle the village. For a few moments Sven, Else and Erik watched with mounting alarm before realising what was happening.

'Oh God!' exclaimed Sven. 'Someone must have told them where to find us. It's us they are after – come on, let's get out of here!'

The three of them ran up a side street, which led to the highest point of the village. They had almost reached the last of the houses when they saw the SS men linking up on the high ground behind the buildings. They were trapped – encircled. They ran on, along a narrow street and, just below Roald's aunt's house, found an outbuilding where old nets and lobster traps were stored.

'Come on in here!' gasped Sven. 'We've got to decide what to do – and fast.'

Panting for breath, they ducked into the shelter and collapsed onto a pile of nets.

'We'll be lucky to get out of this one,' said Sven. 'My guess is that this is all about the gold and they want to take alive anyone who could tell them where it is; that means both you, Erik, and Else.'

For a few minutes each of them silently struggled to think of some way out of the trap. Sven was the first to come up with an idea – a desperate one.

'The only way of getting out of this is if one of us could fly the Storch. I can't think of any other way of doing it and that's for only two of us, not three, as it's a two-seater. Before that there's the almost impossible problem of how to get anywhere near it, let alone steal it. I think the plane's a better bet than the Schnellboot as it's closer to us.'

'Before the war in England I had some lessons on a Tiger Moth,' said Erik, the tension showing in his voice, 'but I don't know if I could manage a Storch.'

'Well, thank God for that! That's something and you may just have to fly it. Anyway it's our only hope. If, in the unlikely event we do successfully commandeer the plane, you will take Else and try to fly out of here. I've decided and that's final! I have a pistol hidden at Roald's house and we'll have to fetch it on our way to the harbour.'

The three of them cautiously emerged from the net store to find that the villagers had retreated into their homes, leaving the streets deserted. They could hear distant German voices up behind the village, as the searchers tightened their encircling noose but it was a slow process as they seemed to be checking each house.

There was no time to lose. Sven ran down to Roald's house, retrieved the pistol and twenty rounds of ammunition and caught up with Erik and Else. The three of them hurried down towards the harbour and stopped behind the general store which faced onto the water. They could see the Schnellboot a little way off but the Storch, hidden below the harbour wall, was close – very close. Two Germans stood, talking, by its moorings. Sven gave a surprised start. The officer had removed his cap and his crinkly fair hair was all too familiar. Yes, he was sure of it: it was none other than Standartenführer Richter of the SS, the man who had arranged the killing of the real Major Sands and who had interrogated Sven in the prison in Alta!

Sven grabbed Erik's arm.

'This is our only chance before the searchers get here. Listen carefully. I'll try to take out Richter with the pistol and, if possible, the guard as well. If I'm successful get Else into the Storch and see if you can manage to fly it. If it has enough fuel, head for eastern Finnmark which must be just about clear of Germans by now. Now go – and good luck!'

He gave his daughter a kiss on the cheek and then wandered nonchalantly from behind the store towards the two Germans. Richter turned as he saw the approaching Norwegian, who gave him a wave and called out a greeting. Sven looked so unthreatening that, when he pointed to the Schnellboot and said something in Norwegian, Richter glanced away at the boat.

In that instant Sven pulled the pistol from his pocket and fired two shots at Richter's chest at a range of no more than four metres. The German was thrown backwards onto the harbour stones without uttering a sound. The guard gave an exclamation of surprise as he struggled to free a rifle from his shoulder. Realising his own danger, he dropped to a crouch and fired several shots at the assailant. Sven, hit in the abdomen before he could again use the pistol, was hurled backwards and collapsed onto the ground, a crimson pool gathering beneath him. The guard cautiously approached what he thought was a dead body, but Sven was not quite dead. His vision began to mist over as haemorrhage caused his blood pressure to fall. He dimly perceived the outline of the guard standing over him and from beneath his body he pulled out the pistol and fired two shots at the fading silhouette. Then he slid into unconsciousness as he died.

Else gave an anguished cry of despair as she watched her father die, and was too shocked to resist when Erik pulled her across to the Storch. Erik ignored the guard, who was wounded and disabled but not dead, but kicked his Schmeisser into the harbour, before clambering down the stone steps to the plane. He freed the mooring and helped

Else to jump down onto one of the plane's floats. Precious moments were lost when he discovered that the only door was on the other side of the cockpit. Holding on to the struts they scrambled over onto the other float, opened the top hinged door and Erik pushed Else inside. He pointed to the rear of the cockpit while he settled into the pilot's seat and ran his eyes over the instrument layout. A red lever by his left hand had to be the throttle and the stick between his knees looked straightforward. He turned the generator and master battery switches to 'ON' and the fuel gauge on the console registered a three-quarters full tank. It was not so very different from a Tiger Moth after all. He pressed the starter button but nothing happened. Then he remembered that the ignition magnetos and the master ignition both had to be 'ON.' Once again he pressed the starter button and was rewarded by a cough from the engine, which then burst into life. The airframe shook as his feet found the rudder pedals. He jumped out again and, standing on a float, freed the mooring line and pushed the plane's nose towards the open fjord, then climbed back into the pilot's seat.

'Do you think you can do it?' shouted Else, from the rear seat. She was still white and shocked from seeing her father dying in a pool of blood. She had been very close to him.

Erik gave no reply, concentrating hard as he pushed the red throttle to 'FULL'. The engine howled as the plane started to move across the water, while Erik watched the rev counter slowly climbing to 1000 rpm. Then they were racing across the surface. Their speed increased further and, at 1800 rpm, he adjusted the elevator, said a prayer, pulled on the stick and, almost unbelievably, they were airborne. Miraculously, the fjord fell away beneath them even though the airspeed indicator read only eighty-six kilometres an hour.

'I've done it – what a plane!' he shouted.

Just when things were looking hopeful he was startled by a bang on the left observation window. He glanced at it and immediately saw a bullet hole in the plexi-glass.

'Are you all right?' he shouted to Else above the engine noise.

There was no reply and, thinking that she had not heard, he looked round. An appalling sight met his eyes. Else was slumped to one side, her head lolling on her shoulder. Crimson blood flowed in a steady stream from a hole in her left temple and onto the cockpit floor.

'Oh God, no, no!' cried Erik, sobbing with anguish.

He realised that the SS troops in the village must have discovered their dead commander along with Sven's body and had fired at the departing Storch. It was an unlucky, long distance shot that had killed Else.

Erik's thoughts were in turmoil. A beautiful girl, a girl whom he had come to love, was dead in the seat behind him and he had just seen her father killed. Else had become so much part of his life that he suddenly found he no longer cared much what happened to him. He loathed the war that had led to all this misery. He desperately wanted to get as far as possible from the Germans.

With a conscious effort he pulled himself together and turned his mind to navigation. The lower part of the cockpit windows, angled inwards at 45 degrees, gave a clear view of the terrain below and, using ground observation in the absence of a map, he set a course due east towards the wilds of Finnmark. After twenty minutes he caught sight of Altafjord and crossed it at a height of two hundred and fifty metres. Open tundra stretched to inland hills, strewn with patches of snow. In another twenty minutes he passed over the head of Porsangerfjord, recognisable by its many islands and, trying to remember the geography of the area, he adjusted his course a few degrees to the south in the hope of coming across the mighty Tana River which would guide him eastwards. He glanced at the fuel gauge in front of him; already the tanks were now only about a quarter full. He checked his watch and estimated that he had managed to fly the plane for about 240 kilometres. Below was a trackless waste of tundra and streams. Before long he would need an expanse of water, hopefully the Tana itself, for touch down.

Suddenly he saw it – it *was* the Tana! In the distance the silver coils of the great river meandered through the bare, winter, birch forest with a track running along its near shore. Within a few minutes, the river was beneath him. It looked about two hundred metres wide, with some winter ice still present near the shores. Erik circled the Storch, reduced altitude to just over a hundred metres and looked for a clear part of the river where the current was not too strong. He cut the airspeed to ninety kilometres an hour and slowly descended to the water. Just before the floats hit the surface Erik realised that he should have made an upstream approach, but it was too late to change. It was a basic error. The floats hit the water with a bang and the plane hurtled downstream.

Erik was just beginning to think that he had made it when a row of salmon net stakes appeared directly in his path. His speed and the current drove him inexorably on towards the stakes and seconds later the plane smashed into the obstruction. He had no safety harness and his head struck a dizzying blow on the instrument panel. With an almighty crash and a rending sound of tearing metal, the left float was torn away and the plane collapsed onto its side. Water poured into the cockpit, as the current took hold of the wreck and began to whirl it downstream. Erik lunged for the half submerged door. He took a despairing glance behind his seat. Else's lifeless body lay bunched behind him, the water in the cockpit already flowing over her face. Blood from the bullet wound had been mostly washed away and through the clear water her face looked up at him with a calm expression. He reached into the water and touched the face for the last time.

The plane, dragged downstream by the current, heaved and jerked as it snagged on hidden rocks. Erik wrenched open the cockpit door and leapt out into the river. The water came up to his chest but he managed to flounder obliquely downstream towards a distant shingle bank.

Minutes later, he emerged onto the dry stones, chilled to the bone and, with knees shaking uncontrollably, he looked back at the half-submerged plane. It careered on its way downstream, then as some snag took hold, a wing swung in a semicircle high out of the water like the sail of a windmill, before smashing down to be lost in the depths along with the rest of the wreckage. Into those depths the Storch took the girl that Erik loved.

He collapsed onto the stony beach, as a tide of nausea and shivering overcame him. He felt the cold sapping his strength and he knew that he had to do something to bring some warmth back to his body. He got up, took off his padded jacket and peeled off his shirt, wringing as much water from them as he could. Then, with great difficulty, he put the icy clothes back on again and set off downstream to see if he could find any signs of habitation.

Erik had stumbled along for half an hour when he caught the faint whiff of wood smoke and there, standing back from the river in the birch woods, was a rustic wooden cabin with smoke emerging from its chimney. Still bitterly cold, he staggered thankfully to the cabin and banged at the door. It was opened by a wizened old man who, on seeing Erik's predicament, gave an exclamation of surprise and beckoned him inside. Erik gratefully went in and was immediately enveloped by furnace-like heat from an almost red-hot stove which stood at one end of the room. Sitting beside it was an old woman whose yellowish, creased face was striking enough but, when she smiled, a single jutting gold upper front tooth gleamed from her otherwise bare gums. Her husband, for that was what he seemed to be, handed Erik a blanket from a bed in the corner and told him to get out of his wet clothes. Gratefully he peeled off his things and, shivering uncontrollably, wrapped himself in the blanket and collapsed into a chair in front of the stove while his clothes steamed on a rack beside him.

At first, owing to shock, he was unable to speak but after several minutes he revived sufficiently to explain how he came to be soaking wet with a bruise on his forehead on the Tana shore. The old man 'tut-tutted' at the strange story, while his wife wandered off to prepare something to eat.

It turned out that his hosts were river-dwelling Sami or Lapps who, unlike their reindeer-herding cousins, live mainly on salmon. The old man said that very few Germans were still in the area but that the Wehrmacht had caused terrible destruction before leaving, and had burnt all the buildings they could find. His neighbour, whose house had been burnt down, had gone to try to find shelter in the forest but had died of cold and exposure.

Presently, the old woman appeared with plates of hot, salted salmon and a little bread, which the three of them ate together. Revived by the food and warmth, Erik, overcome by drowsiness, dozed off in the chair and was only just aware when the old couple led him to a corner and laid him down on the floor on a pile of blankets and reindeer skins. There he fell into a deep, dreamless sleep.

★

In the morning Erik woke remarkably refreshed and put on his stove-dried clothes. Then, almost like a physical blow, the memory of Else's death struck him. He wanted to be alone and, excusing himself, he hurried out of the cabin and into the birch forest. Among the trees and overcome with grief he swept aside all inhibitions and wept until the emotional storm had passed. Else's loss, along with that of her father, had affected him more deeply than he could have imagined. Whenever he tried to recall his wife Anna's face, it was Else's features which floated in front of his eyes. He tried to think about his son Neil, who would be nearly five by now, perhaps playing in an English garden, but the little boy would have no recollection of his father.

After several minutes, his thoughts were interrupted by the old woman, who beckoned him back into the cabin and put a plate of bread and some brown cheese on the table, along with a large Sami knife and a jug of water. The old man sat with him at the table but seemed to have eaten earlier.

Erik explained to his hosts that he had to avoid Germans at all costs and that his best option would be to travel downstream through what he hoped would be a kind of 'no man's land' vacated by the Germans. He thought that it might even be possible to reach the Russian front. At this stage of the war it would be a pity to be caught and he was sure that because of the gold he would still be high on the Germans' wanted list. There was every possibility that remaining Germans in the vicinity might have seen the Storch approaching the Tana, and they might well come looking for him.

He asked about the chances of finding a boat and was relieved to hear that his host's neighbour had left his old boat in the trees near his burnt-out house and that Erik might as well take that if he wished.

'It's a very old boat,' warned his host, 'and is probably not very reliable, but, sadly, my friend will not need it any more.'

Erik thanked his hosts for their hospitality which, undoubtedly, had saved his life and, following their instructions, he set off downstream, along the bouldered shore. After about a kilometre, he came upon the ruin of the neighbour's burnt-out house, on some high ground, near the river. All that was left was the stone-built chimney stack and remains of the walls, within which lay the collapsed and charred roof timbers. An acrid smell of burning still hung over the ruin.

Erik looked around for the boat but could see no sign of it. He wandered a little way downstream and began to think that it must have been taken by someone.

He was desperately tired and underweight from malnourishment and felt that he could not carry on much longer. In despair, he sat on a boulder and looked across the river to the birch and pine forest on the Finnish shore. He searched for a sign of human activity but there was none, then, looking back at the river he suddenly caught sight of a line of salmon net stakes 200 metres downstream from where he was sitting.

If there are nets then a boat must be hidden somewhere nearby, he thought. With renewed hope he walked on and when he reached the stakes there, sure enough, were grooves in the riverside gravel as though a boat had been dragged into a thicket of birches.

33

OSLO TO BERLIN ON SS ATHENHORST

While, in that spring of 1945, Erik was struggling on the shores of the Tana, the war in Germany was approaching its climactic end. The Russians had already reached the outskirts of Berlin, now almost unrecognisable as a capital city, as it was pulverised by their shellfire and a storm of Katyusha rockets.

In desperation, the German High Command ordered Wehrmacht units in Norway to return to the Fatherland and to join the defence of what was left of the city. Willi was amongst those who received orders to report to Oslo, from where he and many others would be shipped to Kiel in Germany and then taken by rail or road to Berlin.

Willi was still grieving over the death of his young brother, Tomas, who had been killed three months earlier at the sinking of the *Tirpitz* near Tromso. The brothers had been very close to each other and he recalled fondly how he had helped to teach the boy to read and how, later, he had helped him with his school lessons. When Willi heard the news, he had found a quiet, private spot and had relaxed control of his emotions and let the tears run. He thought too about his mother and what the news would do to her. What an accursed war; what was it all for?

On November 1st a large number of Wehrmacht troops

congregated at the Oslo docks for embarkation into two vessels. The men were aware that the voyage through the Kattegat to Kiel would be hazardous, as the skies were patrolled by British planes and the sea by submarines. Knowing that it would be his last chance before leaving Lyngenfjord, Willi had left a message for Lara telling her of his recall to Germany. It finished, 'I hope, *mein liebchen*, that we will be together again some day soon. I will not be able to write to you for a time but, every day, I will pray for you and our Little Lara. Goodbye my love, goodbye.'

Willi's ship, the rusting SS *Athenhorst*, packed with troops, left the docks on an evening that was as sombre as his mood. He looked back at the receding coast of Norway, the land of his beloved Lara, and wondered if they would ever see each other again. In his mind they were already a family unit. He knew all too well that the Third Reich would finally die in Berlin, and, as the Russians steadily pulverised their way into the centre of the city, he, Willi Schmidt, would be in the middle of the carnage. He loathed what Germany had become, but readily conceded that she had brought this 'twilight of the gods' on herself. Hitler's dream was finished.

The voyage was made slightly more bearable when he discovered that some of his fellow officers from the Alta posting, including Hans Schreiber, were also aboard. He had not seen them since they had been together there.

'What happened to that Norwegian girl you were so keen on, Willi? I think that she was expecting your baby and I remember that article in *Germania* about two of our soldiers rescuing her from drowning in Lyngenfjord.'

Willi thought for a moment, as he wondered how much to tell about Lara.

'She is well and stays with her parents,' he replied. 'I have to tell you that we now have a daughter, Lilara, though we call her Little Lara. We are already a family. If I survive this crazy war we will get married and hopefully live together for always. What about you? Do you have relatives to worry about?'

'Just my elderly parents who live in Leipzig. They live in the south-west of the city and survived the big air raid of '43. There have been plenty of raids since then, but, as far as I know they are alive. What about your relatives?'

'Now that my little brother is dead, I only have my old mother in the Charlottenburg district of Berlin. As far as I know she is all right but I worry about her a lot. It looks as though the Russians will take the city in the end, and they really will pull the place apart. You can hardly blame them, but what will happen to people like mother I dread to think.'

The SS *Athenhorst* ploughed on through the night, down the Kattegat, between Denmark and Sweden but, at first light, the alarm suddenly sounded. The speck of a circling plane had been seen by the lookouts and its intention quickly became clear when it circled *Athenhorst* and then dived in a low-level attacking run from the stern of the ship. Some of the troops were on deck but dived for cover as the decks around them were raked by cannon fire. As it flashed overhead, some thought it was a Messerschmitt, an Me109, but the black and white stripes on the under-surface of the wings confirmed it as a British Typhoon. The attack lasted for only a few seconds and the plane then pulled out of the dive and disappeared to the north. For some reason it had not used the rockets for which the Typhoon was justly feared. The ship itself had got off surprisingly lightly, though four crew members were killed and some Wehrmacht personnel were wounded.

The rest of the voyage passed off without further attacks and *Athenhorst* duly docked at Kiel where the troops were transferred to trains and, from there, they set off for Berlin.

Willi was shocked to see the scale of destruction of the country, and, several times, they passed other, less fortunate rolling stock, which had been attacked from the air and lay beside the track in tangles of twisted metal. In many places, bomb damage to the track had been temporarily repaired and the train had to creep slowly over those sections.

Nothing had prepared Willi for the destruction of Lubeck. Almost all of the buildings visible from the rail track had been destroyed, leaving only shapeless lumps of masonry, whose crevices were already colonised by willow herb and other weeds.

The rest of the journey proceeded with numerous stops. Bomb damage to Schwerin was nearly as bad as that of Lubeck and it seemed to Willi that the whole of Germany was devastated.

How much longer will this madness go on? he wondered.

At last, through a wrecked landscape, the troops arrived at the ruins of Berlin.

On arrival, Willi and his brother officers were immediately put in command of what troops remained in the city. These were a mixture of Volkssturm, largely untrained older men, and boys of the Hitler Youth. The boys had been supplied with bicycles, each of which had two Panzerfaust anti-tank weapons fitted to the handlebars. There were no other weapons capable of stopping an advancing Russian tank.

As March turned into April, the sound of the Russian guns came to dominate the lives of the defenders. On April 20th shells began to land in the city followed, soon after, by Katyusha rockets, and Willi knew that the end was near.

34

THE GREAT TANA RIVER

Two thousand kilometres north of what was left of Berlin, Erik, looking for a boat, pushed his way into the birch thicket on the River Tana's shore. Clearly someone had been there recently. A coiled length of rope hung from a branch, and, nearby, were signs that something had been dragged into the trees from the water's edge. There, a little further in, lay what he was looking for. A slim, elongated river boat lay hidden in undergrowth, along with two ancient paddles and a long wooden pole. The boards below the seats were silvered with dried salmon scales and a short wooden gaff, with a curved, metal spike showed that it was, indeed, a fisherman's boat. There was no way for Erik to know if this was the boat that his Sami rescuer meant him to take or quite a different one, but, in the circumstances, there seemed to be no choice.

With considerable difficulty, he dragged the craft out of the birches, across the beach and into the water. He felt only passing regret as he acknowledged to himself that he might be taking a boat on which someone's livelihood depended. A glance downstream showed the river sweeping in a great curve before being swallowed up by endless birch forests. He stepped in and pushed off with one of the paddles. The current was swift and smooth, with occasional patches of broken water marking submerged boulders. He guided the boat out into where the current was fastest, and all he had to do was to keep the bows pointing upstream and the boat slid down, stern first. This was certainly better than risking being stopped by German road patrols.

Now and then he passed more salmon netting stakes, some of which were being attended to by Sami fishermen, who turned to watch as he passed. Far off to his left he caught sight of dust raised from the gravel road by retreating German vehicles driving south, putting as much distance as possible between themselves and the Russians. Ahead, a column of smoke spread into a huge black pall over a village recently destroyed by the retreating Wehrmacht. The whole countryside seemed to smell of burning, which was strongest around the blackened shells of houses near the river. The stone chimney columns were usually the only structures left standing; otherwise, the devastation was complete.

After an hour, Erik felt that the danger of encountering Germans had diminished, or, perhaps, even disappeared. There must come a point, he reasoned, when he would reach part of Norway which had been vacated by the Germans but not yet occupied by the Russians. It was clear that, as the war was moving towards its end, the greatest danger was probably now from lawless, marauding armed groups of partisans hiding in the forest. He continued floating downriver, sitting in the bow of the boat, gently guiding it with the paddle, when, suddenly, he was knocked off the seat by a violent blow to his left upper arm and simultaneously a rifle shot shattered the silence. For a few seconds, he lay in the bottom of the boat partially stunned by the shock. He turned to look at his upper arm and, although there was no real pain, there was a hole in his jacket and a warm trickle of blood was emerging from his sleeve and was running down his wrist. The arm felt numb but he could still move it and could still grip with his fingers. The impact of the bullet had made him drop the paddle which floated nearby, but out of reach. As he tried to sit up another bullet whip-cracked close overhead, forcing him to lie flat on the bottom boards. It was impossible to tell from where, or from whom, the shots were coming and clearly he would have to stay there on the bottom of the boat for a time and let the current take him.

Now and then he raised his head just enough to allow him to keep a lookout for more net stakes or other obstructions and he let at least five minutes pass before he gingerly sat up. When he did so, everything was quiet, as the boat continued on its silent way downstream but there was no sign of the paddle. Erik eased his arm out of the jacket to check the wound in the back of his upper arm. His fingers were sticky with congealed blood. The bleeding had stopped, but part of the back of his hand was numb. The bullet had passed through the upper arm but had evidently missed the bone, nicking a nerve on its way. It could have been a lot worse and the wound did not even seem to need a dressing.

He picked up the spare paddle but, with only one good arm, he found great difficulty in using it effectively and struggled to control the boat as the current quickened. Ten minutes later, the boat began to pick up speed and he noticed a figure on the Norwegian shore who looked like a Sami fisherman, waving to him. Erik raised his good arm in response, but the man continued to wave and beckon urgently. He seemed to be trying to warn of some danger ahead. Suddenly, to his alarm Erik remembered stories of the much feared Storfoss, on the lower Tana, where many boats had been destroyed in its violent rapids. He had heard that the Storfoss is almost a cataract where the river charges through a defile, for half a mile, to emerge downstream at a much lower level.

The surface was still glassily smooth, as the boat was swept faster and faster towards the defile, from which a low rumbling sound was coming. Erik tried desperately to paddle towards the shore but was quite unable to alter his course. Ominously, the low rumbling sound quickly grew to a bellowing roar as the boat entered the defile. Suddenly he was in it!

Huge standing waves, higher than his head, rose from the white water all around him. Time after time, the boat climbed enormous hills of water, the stern pointing skywards in front of him, before plunging down the far side and burrowing deep into the maelstrom. The boat was quite uncontrollable and it was all he could do to cling onto the sides while it careered downstream at a dizzying speed. There was no question of being able to keep the bow pointing into the current and, at times, the boat spun round and descended sideways. Water poured inboard and from the craft's sluggish movements, Erik knew that the end was near. Suddenly, a threatening wall of water appeared, rearing up in front him. It was by far the highest standing wave he had yet seen and, with a feeling of hopelessness, he watched the stern lift up the wave's face, until it pointed to the sky. For a moment the boat balanced precariously on top of the crest then the stern fell almost vertically down the far side, burying itself deep under water. The boat somersaulted and continued its chaotic journey upside down. Disorientated and half drowned though he was, Erik was aware that he was trapped under the boat, as a dim light revealed the bottom boards above his head. He inhaled water as he struggled to escape and, choking, he started to lose consciousness as his head crashed against something.

Oh God – this is it! he thought, half stunned, as his body was battered by the storm of water. Nothing seemed to matter any more and, mentally, he let go.

When he started to come to, he was lying on his back, at the river's edge on a stony beach, 200 metres below the Storfoss. Two armed soldiers, one with Asiatic features, stood looking down at him. Erik's head had cleared enough for him to realise that these were not Germans. One of them prodded Erik with a booted foot. Although he was still coughing water from his lungs it did not take him long for him to realise that these were Soviet troops, who must have advanced up to the right shore of the Tana which, at that point, was Norwegian territory. The men dragged Erik to his feet and clearly wanted to know who he was – then they made up their minds.

'*Pushli*', apparently meaning 'let's go,' said one of the soldiers. Erik, soaking wet, bone-chilled and shocked from his near drowning, could barely walk and his legs kept giving way under him but he was half dragged towards a small, well hidden rampart of boulders, which turned out to be a Russian observation post, at the edge of the riverside forest. The rough stone walls were roofed over with piled birch logs and, as they approached, two more Russians emerged from its narrow entrance.

Shivering uncontrollably, Erik was pushed into the cramped shelter. A log bench occupied the right wall and a number of tommy guns were propped against it. Through a gap in the wall a further weapon, which looked like a sniper's rifle, was trained on the river. One of the Russians produced a padded coat and indicated that Erik should get out of his soaked clothes. Although the coat stank of stale sweat, at least it was dry and, gratefully, he pulled it on, and threw his wet clothes outside. One of the Russians gave an exclamation as he caught sight of the wound in Erik's arm, and directed a tirade of incomprehensible Russian at him.

As Erik slowly recovered from his near drowning, he began to consider his new situation. He had become used to being a fugitive from German troops and although the threat from that quarter had, at least for the time being disappeared, the Russians looked far from friendly. One of them, who seemed to be in command, began to fire questions at him in Russian. He caught the word 'Fascist' at one point and, pointing to himself, Erik said 'English' which only seemed to make his questioner angry. He did not at all like the way things were going, as they seemed to take him for a Norwegian collaborator, who had been fighting for the Germans. Russian justice for that would be a bullet in the head.

For half an hour, he was left sitting on the floor of the shelter, while the four Russians discussed him among themselves, now and then looking his way. They were obviously deciding what to do with him and he knew all too well that his presence would be a problem for them. Finally, one of them picked up his tommy gun and pointing to the entrance indicated that Erik had to go outside. His heart pounded in his chest as he got up and his bowels suddenly felt as though they might give way. Was it to be execution? He turned to face the man who, he was sure was going to kill him but, instead, the soldier made him sit down on a nearby birch log and, to Erik's enormous relief, put down his tommy gun and started to prepare something to eat. Soon afterwards, the other soldiers followed them outside and, after lighting a small fire, they set a pot to boil. One of the men went into the shelter and emerged with some small fish which, to Erik, looked like grayling, on a tin plate. The Russian cut the gutted fish into fragments, heads and all, and dropped them into the pan, adding several pinches of salt from a small leather bag. He let the concoction boil for a few minutes, then poured some into four tin mugs. '*Ucha*', he explained, as he handed Erik one of the mugs of soup. '*Blini*', said another, as he handed Erik two hard pancakes. He noticed that because of his own presence there were not enough mugs to go round and that one of the soldiers had given up his own to let Erik drink first. The soup was delicious and the four Russians shared the food equally with him, showing him how to dip the blini into the soup. He was ravenous and did not take long to finish the food.

An hour later, one of the soldiers beckoned to Erik to come with him and waved his arm downriver. The Russian slung his tommy gun on his shoulder and they set off together. On the way Erik tried to communicate with his escort but was rewarded only with grunts and shrugged shoulders. They continued for ten minutes along the shore, passing two more well hidden observation posts at the edge of the woods, with one or two Russians standing beside them. One of these men evidently enquired who Erik was and, on hearing the escort's reply, gave a short laugh.

The command post was a larger structure but it, too, consisted of boulders with a birch log roof. Four Russians sat inside beside a pile of tommy guns and other equipment.

Erik was pushed inside and although he could not stand up straight he was not told to sit. The four seated Russians studied him, while his escort evidently described how they had come across him. The commander, a powerful-looking man with broad Slavic face and high cheekbones, seemed far from welcoming. He got up and, standing in front of Erik, tried to communicate in fragmentary Norwegian. Erik replied, also in Norwegian, that he was a British soldier of the Special Forces, had landed in Norway in 1941 and had been living as an undercover agent ever since.

'Impossible!' retorted the commander.

Erik became increasingly worried about what was going to happen to him and his fears were not calmed when he was taken under armed escort to yet another command post thirty minutes' walk downstream.

'*Stavka*', which evidently meant headquarters, said his escort as they reached the post, which was surmounted by a tall aerial. Four more soldiers and an officer who appeared to be a political commissar sat inside. None of the Russians could speak Norwegian but the commissar could manage a few words in English. He attempted to question Erik and tapping him on the chest said, 'You partisan.'

Erik knew that partisan fighters were usually summarily executed by the Russians and he again tried to tell them who he was but clearly was not believed. It was at this point that he heard Murmansk being mentioned, as his captors discussed what to do with him. His own clothes were still draped in a tree at the first observation post and he was grateful at least to be given a rough shirt and padded trousers. If, by any chance, he was to be taken to Murmansk 200 kilometres away in north Russia then he would need all the warm clothes he could get.

35

TRANSPORTATION

Erik's first night following his arrest by the Russians was spent in the open, beside the command headquarters' bunker. A youthful soldier with an Asiatic face, who was detailed to guard him, spent the night picking his nose and whittling at a birch stick with a knife while watching his prisoner.

Sleep did not come easily, but Erik must have dozed off at some stage as he was woken by the Russians moving around the bunker as they prepared for a new day. He lay on his back looking up at the thin tracery of the birch trees. They reminded him of his parents' garden in Surrey, that sunny garden he still dreamed about and where he had enjoyed all the security of a protected childhood.

Breakfast, such as it was, consisted of two small, dried, smoked fish eaten with his hands and a slab of greyish bread, washed down with river water. At least he was being given some food, although not enough to sustain any level of physical activity.

For about an hour, nothing much seemed to be happening at the command post until, to Erik's surprise, he heard the sound of a vehicle approaching through the trees. He had seen no sign of a vehicle track this side of the river but, nevertheless, after a few moments, an

American-made jeep appeared threading its way through the woods. He thought that it must have arrived on one of the Arctic convoys which delivered war supplies from Britain to Murmansk. It stopped at the command post and the Russian driver and another soldier got out and conferred with his captors. Erik was uncomfortably aware that he was, once again, the subject of discussion. After five minutes, they seemed to come to a decision. One Russian remained, guarding him, while the others disappeared into the command bunker. Evidently some vodka was produced and Erik, through the entrance, caught a glimpse of a bottle being passed round. The Russian conversation became increasingly animated and was punctuated with raucous laughs. They were getting drunk!

Half an hour later, the men emerged unsteadily. The senior officer beckoned to Erik, prodded him in the chest with a finger and, in a slurred voice, said, 'You Murmanshk.'

He was led over to the jeep and told to get aboard along with the two men who had arrived in the vehicle. They set off through the woods and, to Erik's surprise, came across a track leading eastwards only fifty yards in from the river. The going was rough and the driver, emboldened by vodka, charged ahead at a crazy speed. They careered along, without hitting anything for nearly two hours, before coming to the head of a long fjord with distant views to what Erik presumed was the Barents Sea. They were certainly taking him to Russia and, although Russia was an ally, Erik had serious misgivings about what would happen to him on arrival. So far, at any rate, he had been treated with suspicion but not with outright hostility.

The results of the German scorched-earth policy were all too evident as they drove along the south shore of the fjord. Every house had been destroyed. The timbers and roofs had been burnt and only bits and pieces of standing masonry remained, while an occasional, local inhabitant poked amongst the debris looking for something to salvage.

Finally, the jeep approached a town that had been utterly destroyed by a combination of burning and explosives. They had reached Kirkenes, a Norwegian port recently vacated and largely destroyed by the Germans and only a few kilometres away from the Russian border. They drove through what had once been normal busy streets, now scattered with debris and deserted apart from groups of Soviet soldiers. On the way, they passed more American vehicles and several parked British-made, tracked, bren-gun carriers, before turning down to the port. It, too, was largely destroyed, but what caught Erik's attention was a wired-off compound near the waterfront, containing a considerable number of prisoners. Most of them seemed to be Germans but there were also men in fragments of Russian and other uniforms, supplemented with a variety of odd articles of clothing and footwear. All were desperately thin and a ring of bored-looking, armed Russian soldiers guarded them.

The jeep pulled up outside a partially destroyed warehouse, not far from the compound, and Erik was escorted into the building which, apparently, was being used as a Russian army administration centre. Papers and maps lay around on rough, wooden tables. Russian personnel sitting at the tables looked up with curiosity as Erik was marched in and made to sit at a vacant table while his guard remained standing behind him. For half an hour nothing happened, then an officer appeared, sat down opposite him and stared at him in silence for a few minutes. The silence and unrelenting gaze were disconcerting and Erik suspected that this might well be one of the feared NKVD political commissars. The man's brass buttons embossed with a star were common to most Soviet troops, but the diagonal brown leather belt showed that this was no ordinary officer and the crimson piping at the collar reinforced Erik's suspicions. In accented English the questioning began:

'Your name?'

'Captain Erik Kingsnorth, No. 4 Commando, British Army.'

'Where have you come from?'

'From England and I have been in Norway since our raid on the Lofoten Islands in 1941.'

'I do not know of such a raid. Why were you in a boat on the Tana River and why were you trying to get behind the Soviet front line?'

'I was trying to get away from German occupied territory.'

'You are a collaborator.'

'No.'

'No? We have proof: your membership card of the Nasjonal Samling Movement. You are lying and you are a fascist spy attempting to infiltrate behind Soviet lines.' With that he slapped Erik's NS membership card onto the table.

Erik was amazed and appalled. Here he was in the hands of Russian allies accused of treachery while, for three years, he had been risking his life to maintain the safety of the Arctic convoys to Murmansk. Possession of the NS Party card was the problem and when his interrogator got up and walked out of the warehouse, he felt that final judgement had already been passed with no possibility of appeal. The guard standing behind him poked him with a finger and directed him outside.

He was marched along the wrecked waterfront and was greatly alarmed to see that they were heading for the prison compound. His escort spoke to the two soldiers guarding the gate which they swung open and he was pushed inside. Dejected prisoners wandered about or sat listlessly on the ground, some glancing up at Erik as he joined them. Most of the inmates were Germans but others were emaciated Russians who, presumably, had been prisoners of war in Germany.

Erik was swept by a tide of hopelessness. To have evaded the Germans only to end up here, along with German prisoners, was an almost unbelievable turn of events. The Soviet authorities, such as they were, were clearly not interested in reviewing his situation. Gloomily he recalled stories about Russian prison camps where inmates were used as slave labour and worked to death or executed.

He wandered over to a low, bomb-damaged building inside the compound next to the waterfront. He looked inside and was immediately struck by the foul smell of stale urine and filth. Along the only intact wall, two tiers of planks serving as bunks were partially occupied by prostrate figures covered in rags. Some were so still that they might well be dead but others stirred restlessly, scratching at lice-ridden limbs. Shocked, he went outside. Clearly there was no chance of escape over, or through, the wire fence which, anyway, was patrolled by armed soldiers.

Two days passed, which were among the most distressing that Erik could remember. The only meal each day consisted of a slab of grey bread and a scoop of soup, containing fragments of fish and a few vegetables. When he first joined the food queue he saw that the other prisoners each held a tin can for their soup ration. Hurriedly he broke out of the line to search for a utensil of some kind. In desperation, he went into the bunkhouse and, with only a momentary pang of conscience, took a tin mug belonging to an ill-looking, sleeping German. By the time he re-joined the queue the soup was almost finished and he was lucky to get a scoopful along with his bread. These were clearly starvation rations. The days were still cold and the lack of bedding or blankets added to the misery which the bare sleeping boards in the bunkhouse did nothing to alleviate. On the second day his body had begun to itch and he found with disgust that he, too, had acquired lice.

On the third day, a small, ancient-looking steamship entered the harbour and slowly approached the only undamaged part of the waterfront not far from the compound. It was a run-down vessel, streaked with rust with its name, in Cyrillic Russian, on one of the lifebelts. A Russian prisoner standing near him read out *'Vologda: Murmansk'*. None of the Russian prisoners seemed to speak English or Norwegian, therefore Erik was unable to glean any information from them about what was likely to happen to them all. Several Germans could speak some English but were uniformly gloomy about their prospects. They thought that they would be used as slave labourers somewhere in Russia, with little chance of survival.

After his third night in captivity, Erik was woken early in the morning by guards marching through the bunkhouse and shouting to the prisoners to get outside. There they were marshalled into four lines and counted by a junior officer. There seemed to Erik to be about 100 prisoners and, when the officer was satisfied, they were marched out, through the compound gates and down to the waiting ship. Without a pause, they were directed up a gangway, across the deck and through a steel door which led below. They continued down a second gangway, deep into the hold and another steel door was closed behind them. There were no portholes and the only light came from six bulbs, each protected by a wire grill. For a time nothing happened, then gradually the vibrations from the engines increased and, within ten minutes, the vessel seemed to be under way, although, without any way of seeing out, it was difficult to be sure. After time, a gentle sway of the deck underfoot confirmed that they had left the port. There was nowhere to rest except on the steel deck. Ten buckets stood along the bulkhead and were already being used by some of the prisoners to relieve themselves.

Erik tried to question some of the Russian prisoners to find out how long the voyage to Murmansk would take but either they did not understand, or else did not know. The Germans had no idea either.

As the ship emerged into the swell of the open Barents Sea, some of the prisoners became seasick. The condition was no respecter of nationality and both Russians and Germans lay retching on the steel floor united in misery. Erik, who, hitherto, had only once suffered from seasickness, began to salivate as nausea, and then vomiting, overcame him. The miserable journey lasted fourteen hours, during which two drums of water were provided but no food.

When the vessel finally docked, the prisoners were removed from the hold and were escorted, by armed guard, onto the quay. Murmansk at midnight was, for the non-Russians, their first sight of the Soviet Union, and it looked a hellish place. The darkness was, to some extent, relieved by arc lights strung along the waterfront illuminating workers unloading cargo from one of a number of grey-painted ships moored nearby. As they waited on the quay, Erik glanced at the ships and, with a start, realised that they might well be part of a British Arctic convoy which had, at great risk, delivered war supplies to the Soviets. Not only that, but it was right here, in Murmansk, that Vladimir Kuznetsov had helped to load the gold bullion into HMS *Edinburgh*.

Before long, two covered Russian army lorries drove up and stopped beside the prisoners, while an officer in charge of the guards walked along the line of men. He ignored the Germans but pushed about twenty of the most ill and weak looking Russians out of line. These people were then herded onto the waiting lorries and driven away.

About ten minutes later, while Erik and the remaining prisoners stood wondering what was going to happen, they were startled by a sudden volley of rifle shots followed by a number of irregular single shots. On the dockside, a low moan arose from the waiting prisoners who knew all too well what the shots meant. Erik knew that the Soviet authorities regarded those of their countrymen who had allowed themselves to become prisoners of the Germans to be ideologically contaminated and unworthy of returning as citizens of the Soviet Union. The unfit would be liquidated, while the rest would probably end up as slave labourers somewhere in Russia.

'*Entschuldigen Sie bitte!*' The German voice broke into Erik's thoughts as he gloomily contemplated his probable fate. He looked round to see a Feldwebel of the Wehrmacht standing beside him. In the new circumstances and for the first time, he did not feel threatened by a German in uniform.

'I do not understand German; I am Norwegian, I – I

mean English,' he replied. The Feldwebel looked surprised.

'All right,' he said, 'I can speak a little English but are you English or Norwegian and why are you a prisoner of the Russians? Perhaps you were fighting on the side of Germany – yes?'

'No,' replied Erik. 'I was a British military agent in Norway for three years.'

Erik was conscious of the relief at no longer having to maintain the fiction of his life as a simple Norwegian who had been working on fishing boats and, before long, the pair established a reasonable rapport. The German had been part of the garrison in Kirkenes and had been taken prisoner by the Russians when they had crossed into Norway in October 1944. Until recently he and Erik had been enemies but now things seemed so different; there was a new enemy common to them both – the Soviets.

'I must introduce myself to you. I am Franz Bekker,' said the Feldwebel.

'I am just Erik.'

They did not shake hands but the German just nodded and went on: 'I have heard that we are all being sent to a place called Pechorlag, which is about one and a half thousand kilometres away in Arctic Siberia. It's near Vorkuta where, during the war, the Russians started a huge coal mining enterprise using slave labourers, which is exactly what we may become – if we survive.'

36

MURMANSK TO PECHORLAG

Five hours later, the prisoners were marched to a railway siding where a train of cattle trucks waited behind a huge, black locomotive. Wisps of steam rose from this monster as its crew shovelled coal into its furnace. The prisoners, herded by Red Army soldiers, were pushed into the trucks, thirty in each, and the sliding doors were slammed shut and bolted.

Erik looked about him. A pile of straw-filled sacks and two buckets were almost the only furnishings. A water-filled bucket with a metal scoop tied to its handle completed the inventory.

Not much, he thought, for a journey of several days in a cattle truck. His fellow prisoners were a mixture of Germans and Russians and, he discovered later, several Lithuanians. Bekker happened to be in Erik's truck and, as the men sorted themselves into two national groups, Erik pushed his way to him and sat down on a sack to await events. Not surprisingly there were no other British or Norwegians aboard, and Erik was glad to be able to speak in English with the Feldwebel.

With a sudden clanking and jerking the train, at last, started to move. The only view of the outside world was through a two-metre long horizontal ventilation strip adjacent to the door. It at least allowed the prisoners a limited view of their surroundings, but, in the half light, what Erik saw filled him with depression. The world was grey, the docks and shabby warehouses, and, later, the concrete blocks of flats, epitomised, for him, the gloom of Soviet Russia. He was being drawn into the maw of one of the most awful, dehumanising systems on earth. He doubted more than ever that he would see his family or the green fields of England again. Once the train was moving, the cold air quickly penetrated the men's clothing but, in spite of that, they gradually fell asleep on the sacks, huddled in whatever clothing they could manage. The jolting rhythm of the truck kept Erik awake for an hour until he finally lapsed into a half-frozen sleep: a sleep troubled by confused dreams of pursuit and of Else – or was it Anna, his wife? Sometimes the shadowy figure of a child had seemed to flit at the edges of his dreams.

Several hours later, Erik woke when the train shuddered to a halt. He got up, relieved himself into one of the already half full buckets and peered through the ventilation opening. Armed guards patrolled alongside the train which had stopped beside a small settlement of impoverished-looking houses. The reason for the halt became clear when the truck doors were opened, allowing the prisoners from each truck in turn to disembark. Under armed guard, they were escorted to the head of the train, where cabbage soup and bread were distributed. Fortunately Erik had kept the tin bowl which he had acquired in the compound at Kirkenes. All of the prisoners were virtually starving and, although the food was meagre, it helped to bring some warmth to their bodies. They stamped and flapped their arms to restore the circulation, thankful to be able to move about again. Then, all too soon, they were herded back to the truck to allow the next group to take their turn.

In due course, the train continued its slow progress, past great lakes, forests and swamps. Twenty-four hours later, they reached a junction at the town of Konosa where, for once, a reasonable amount of bread and soup was provided. The prisoners were transferred into another train which set off on a branch line towards the north-east and, after a seemingly interminable journey of nearly three days and sustained by the same diet, they reached Pechorlag, a camp by the Pechora River.

Erik discovered that the camp lay only 500 kilometres from the icy Kara Sea and only sixty kilometres west of the Ural Mountains. It was one of three camps in the complex. A barbed wire fence four metres high, interrupted by watch towers, enclosed the huge compound with its rows of identical accommodation huts. A few distant figures, muffled against the cold, shuffled between the wooden buildings, while the dismal scene was swept by flurries of dry snow, driven by the biting Arctic wind.

The prisoners were marched from the railway, past the main guard house and into the prison compound. It was there that Erik discovered he had been sentenced, under 'Article 58', to ten years' hard labour for 'anti-Soviet activities'. It came as a terrible blow and he felt ever more certain that he would die in this awful place, this place of greyness, of cold and misery. In his mind, all hope faded and he settled into a deep depression. The barrack huts, each about thirty metres long, were lined with two tiers of bare board sleeping shelves with no bedding of any kind. Two stoves in each hut served to take the edge off the cold, which permeated the whole camp, and in each hut, a bare table stood in the centre of the living space. The stark scene was lit by two weakly glowing electric light bulbs hanging from the roof.

The only familiar face that Erik could see was that of Franz Bekker. The rest of the prisoners were German or Polish with some Russians, some of whom, Erik discovered, were common criminals.

'This is where we will die,' remarked the German, and Erik was unable to disagree. Their situation did, indeed, seem hopeless. It looked a hellish place.

'This camp,' said Bekker, 'is not far from the Vorkuta gulag, which supplied the Soviets with coal during the war, after our armies captured the Donbas coalfields in the Ukraine. It seems that Pechorlag was set up to house prisoners who built and maintained the railway line on which the flow of coal from Vorkuta depended. Unfortunately, all this was beyond the range of our bombers!'

Pechorlag, beside the ice-covered Pechora River, was surrounded by an interminable wilderness of tundra and spruce forest, defaced by mining detritus. It had an air of devastation, in which there were no colours, just an all-pervading greyness.

Around Erik, a milling crowd of fellow prisoners gloomily surveyed the desolate scene. Guards in watch towers stamped their feet in the minus 20 degree Centigrade cold, while observing them dispassionately.

Before long, an announcement in German was made over a loudspeaker. Most of the prisoners had been in the Wehrmacht, but there were many Poles and Balts too who, like Erik, understood nothing of what was said. Later, Erik asked Bekker what the announcement had been about.

'Some of us', he replied, 'will be assigned to railway

repair and maintenance work and the rest of us to timber operations. Camps upstream do the tree felling and, after the river ice breaks up in mid-May, they float the logs down to us for processing here in the camp.

'At least we don't have to go down the mines,' he added. 'We have to work a twelve-hour day and, if we don't fulfil our "norms", our daily ration of 600g of bread will be cut and you can guess what that means.'

The following day the prisoners were organised into work parties, not all of which were attended by guards because, quite simply, there was nowhere for the prisoners to escape to. Overall supervision was carried out by a gulag boss, a 'nachalnik', whose function seemed to be to harry the prisoners into ever greater productivity. Erik's work party of fifteen 'politicals' included Franz Bekker, several other Germans, some Russians also sentenced under 'Article 58', for alleged anti-Soviet activities and there were two Uzbek 'basmachi' – common criminals.

37

LYNGENFJORD: MAY 1945

Two thousand kilometres away in Norway, the morning of May 1st 1945 began normally for the Torkelsen household, but, when one of the Petersen twins came running up the farm track, it was clear that something unusual was afoot. Per ran straight in through the open door, his face red with excitement, and gasped out the momentous news to Gunnar.

'Hitler's dead!' he said, panting for breath.

'What? Are you quite, quite sure? I mean, really sure? How did you hear this?' asked Gunnar.

'It's definitely true,' the boy replied. 'Father heard it on his wireless just now.'

Gunnar turned and shouted through: 'Birgitta, come and hear this!'

Gunnar knew that his neighbour had kept his wireless throughout the Occupation, at some risk to himself and his family, and consequently the Petersen house had become a focus for news gathering and discussion amongst the neighbours.

Both Birgitta and Lara hurried through to see what the excitement was about. Gunnar and Birgitta hurried down to the Petersens' house to hear if there was any more news, but Lara would not come with them.

Arne Petersen greeted them with a broad smile and,

ushering them inside, produced four glasses of akavit from a bottle which he had kept hidden for five years.

'Well, we have some rather good news today I think! We must drink to Norway!'

And they did.

In due course, having heard the rumour, more neighbours arrived including Nils and Helga Anders with their sons, Lars and Kristian. The akavit bottle was quickly emptied and soon a great party was under way, filling the room with jollity.

People expected that an official announcement would soon be made but they knew that the war did not necessarily end with Hitler's death. However, that did not detract from the general rejoicing in the communities all along the fjord, and in Norway as a whole. The national flag sprouted on houses and in gardens and people laughed and waved to friends and to strangers alike.

The next few days brought more good news:the German armies had begun to collapse throughout Europe, as the war drew to its end. German soldiers remained in the Lyngenfjord district, but they made themselves as inconspicuous as possible. It was almost hard to hate them now in their furtiveness.

Lara's parents tried to encourage her to go out more and to see people and suggested that she might mark the occasion with a visit to Hans and Hilder Larsen at the Olderdalen store.

'They were so good to you when you were working there,' said Birgitta. 'They'd love to see you again, especially with Little Lara.' The little girl had captivated the hearts of both of her grandparents, who had almost forgotten about the nationality of her father.

At last Lara let herself be persuaded to go out, and, a few days later, she set off on the bus with the baby in her arms.

She enjoyed seeing the beautiful outside world again. The mountains were capped with snow, yet the day was comfortably warm. As the bus passed the spot Lara looked up towards the track leading to the quarry and imagined the bed amongst the ferns.

She alighted from the bus by the store and pushed open the door. Hilder was standing at the counter chatting to a group of locals.

'Oh Lara!' she exclaimed, 'Oh, and you have brought Little Lara too! How lovely to see you both.' The kindly soul took the baby and enveloped it in her ample arms, cooing to it in her delight. However, the moment was spoilt when some of the locals, who had been chatting in the store, pointedly picked up their things and walked out. Two others made perfunctory excuses and also left, leaving Rolf Nordhus, the roadman, as the only customer who remained. Lara could not miss the effect that her presence had on folk, some of whom she had known all her life. She was being rejected – she knew it. Everyone knew about her German lover and that the child was his and, in their eyes, she was damned. Tears began to glisten in her eyes and she wished that she had not come to the store. After Rolf had left, Hilder took her and Little Lara into their own house and sat them down and made a hot drink. Lara breastfed the baby while Hans and Hilder tried to console the unhappy young mother but it was difficult to know what to say and, privately, they doubted that opinion in the community would change in the foreseeable future.

In due course, Little Lara fell asleep and Hilder suggested that she would look after her for a time to give Lara an hour or two to herself. It seemed a good opportunity to go for a walk and Lara accepted the offer. With some trepidation she looked out to the front of the store and was relieved to see that no one was about. She set off at a brisk walk along the fjord, knowing, though hardly admitting it to herself, that she was going to look one more time at the bed among the ferns. Twenty minutes later she came to the track and turned off along its stony surface. The birch wood seemed especially quiet around her, as though it understood the emotional agonies which had become part of her life. It was as though the wood was watching and listening; then she came to the 'place'. There was no mistaking it, with its overhanging birch branches and the ferny bed. Today, however, there was no willow warbler to observe her presence. It and its companions would only just be leaving Africa on their migration back to Norway.

While she stood there, Willi seemed to come alive in her mind. She could feel his presence, his gentleness and could see his face; that beloved face which so often seemed to be smiling and those curved lines round his eyes when he laughed. She could smell the manliness of his body. Spiritually, he was there with her, she was sure of it.

It was all so real that she felt uplifted and calm in a way she had not felt for a long time. It did not last. Although her imagination had brought Willi to her again, reality returned on the walk back to the store. The cruelty of some of the locals at the store confirmed her growing fear that she and Little Lara would never again fit back into the community. She often seemed to be crying these days and, once again, tears began to well up in her eyes and then the dam burst. She sank to her knees on the damp mossy ground and wept.

When she arrived back at the store, her tears had dried but

her eyes were still red. Hilder understood; her sympathetic mothering, not only of Little Lara but also of Lara herself, was comforting, and the emotional upset subsided. The two women played with the baby until it was time to catch the return bus, but, as Lara closed the store door, she was suddenly reminded of the awful red-painted word which she had seen daubed on it: 'Tyskertoser' – German whore.

38

EMBATTLED BERLIN. LARA'S ORDEAL

While Lara was struggling with her emotions in those final days of the Occupation, Willi in embattled Berlin knew that the last days of the Third Reich had arrived and that he would probably not survive. The Soviets were attacking from almost all sides, and the centre of the city, now little more than a heap of rubble, was being saturated with Russian shell and rocket fire. Over this ruined landscape hung the stench of decaying human flesh as shells uncovered, and then reburied, hundreds of corpses. From his bunker in the midst of this hellish scene, Willi, crouching in the rubble, watched as a splintered but heroically flowering cherry tree in the remains of a garden showered pink snow as shells landed.

Perhaps, he thought, beauty may after all outlive National Socialism, but then he noticed, high in the tree, part of a dismembered body and pieces of clothing caught up among the blossom.

Soviet tanks began to pour up Unterdenlinden, while isolated German troops cowered in doorways or any other available shelter. Some were elderly Volkssturm but many were simply boys of the Hitler Youth who had been conscripted into the Waffen SS. Mere boys they might be, but some of them fought with desperate ferocity, using grenades and anti-tank Panzerfausts. Many were blasted to pieces by shell and Katyusha rocket fire. Others burst into tears.

The orders to make these boys fight to the end seemed, to Willi, cruel and pointless. On the evening of May 1st he decided to try to lead them in a breakout through the Tiergarten, and over the Charlottenbrucke Bridge spanning the Havel River, towards the American lines in the west. But it was not to be. It was in the ruins of the Tiergarten that he came face to face with a Soviet T34 tank. The monster halted, while its gun traversed towards him. He was aware of a momentary silence before the shock wave hit him, then, for Willi Schmidt and many of his young charges, the Battle for Berlin was over.

★

Mercifully Lara knew nothing of this. Her parents emphasised that home on Lyngenfjord was always there for her when she felt rejected by the community. She still avoided meeting people but she felt the need to confide in old Leif Jessen. He was such a wise old man and she trusted his advice. She got her bicycle out of the shed and set off on the four-kilometre ride to his house. She found that he, like many other neighbours, was flying the Norwegian flag on a hastily erected pole in front of his house in celebration of the momentous events.

'Hello Lara. Come away in and tell me about everything,' he said, clearly pleased to see her. 'Have you any news of your man? How is your baby?'

'Little Lara's fine,' she replied, 'but I have had no word from Willi since he was recalled to Berlin at the beginning of April. I'm so worried as he will have been in the thick of the fighting in the city. What makes it worse is that, even if he is alive, and I don't suppose there's much chance of that, he'll be a prisoner of the Russians.'

'Did he have relatives in Germany whom you could contact?'

'Yes, I sent a letter to his mother who lives in the outskirts of the city, though I don't suppose it'll get through. He told me to contact her if I needed help – and I do.'

Then Lara poured her heart out to this kind, old man. She told him about being ostracised by the locals and of her love for Willi.

'He may be a German but he's so gentle and considerate. I know that he loves me too and we made a vow to get married after the war.'

Leif was silent for a few moments.

'One day,' he said, 'Germany will rebuild itself as a civilised nation and the horrors of Nazism will be consigned to history. If you do make contact with Willi's mother, would you ever consider taking Little Lara there and making Germany your home? I say this because I think you are going to have difficulties here in Norway, not only for you but also for Little Lara. Did you know that the Germans set up what they called Lebensborn homes here in Norway for Norwegian women pregnant to German soldiers? The dreadful thing is that now the babies are regarded as "German trash" and are treated as such by Norwegians!'

'My advice is, Lara, if you can get away from Norway with your child then you should do so as soon as you can.'

Lara was shocked by hearing what she really knew was the truth. She couldn't make a decision yet and still hoped that her fellow countrymen would relent and come to accept her and her baby. For a time she stayed talking to Leif about the old days, the days before the Occupation, when everything had seemed so uncomplicated, and then it was time to leave. She felt better for having opened her heart, as she set off home on her bicycle.

On Lyngenfjord, the first week of May passed in a furore of excitement and people clustered round any wireless sets that were still available. The news of the fall of Berlin to the Russians on the 2nd of May was followed by what everyone had been waiting for. It came five days later – Germany's unconditional surrender!

The population went wild with joy and a big celebration party in Olderdalen was announced and those who could, hurried to join in the fun. Birgitta volunteered to look after the baby if Lara wanted to go too. The Petersen and Anders families would certainly be there and perhaps even Leif as well.

Lara, at first, said she was afraid to go but changed her mind and she set off with her father on their bicycles. When they arrived at Olderdalen, the scene around the store was one of jubilation. People were dancing and singing and waving Norwegian flags, while bottles of liquor miraculously emerged from their hiding places, serving to fuel the joyful pandemonium.

After an hour or two, things quietened down and people started to go home. Gunnar decided to leave but Lara wanted to go along the street to the café, which was part of a small shop. Groups of locals were talking quietly together outside the building and one or two looked up as she passed. Some nodded to her and some ignored her, but one youth said 'Tyskertoser' at first quietly and then loudly, 'Tyskertoser, Tyskertoser!'

Everyone looked up to see what would happen next. A

woman stepped forward and grabbed at Lara's sleeve and swung her round, followed by another who pulled her other arm. The sleeve tore. Lara looked around for help. In panic, she saw the shopkeeper's wife watching, a woman whom she knew quite well.

'Help me please, please!' she pleaded but the woman turned away muttering that Lara wasn't a friend of hers. Several bystanders walked away, looking at the ground as they went.

Poor Lara was subjected to increasingly rough treatment as more bullies joined in. She was pulled and pushed until she fell to the ground while a chant of 'Tyskertoser' rose from the mob. A man emerged from the café, carrying a chair, which he placed beside the prostrate girl. Her tormenters lifted her up and forced her to sit, surrounded by the jeering mob. Lara, wide eyed with terror, could do nothing while tears smeared the mud from the road down her face. A girl with whom she had been at school spat on her. The grip on her arms tightened as a woman tore her blouse open, exposing her breasts. Some people walked away; others laughed as she struggled, but still the frenzied mob had not finished. A middle aged woman emerged from the café with a pair of scissors and, grabbing handfuls of Lara's beautiful hair, cut at it until the she was nearly bald. As if that was not enough, a girl, a mere schoolgirl, tried to daub a swastika in ink on her forehead.

Then they let her go. The onlookers quickly dispersed, many shaking their heads at the dreadful thing that had happened. Some were ashamed at what the mob had done and others at their own failure to help the victim, but still others had enjoyed watching the brutality.

Lara was in a state of near collapse when Hilder came

running from the store to see what was happening. She had heard the noise and was appalled to discover Lara slumped on the chair in tears, only partially clothed and with her hair gone.

She helped her to stand and put a coat round her and, after giving her a few minutes support, helped her to walk round to the store.

'You should be ashamed of yourselves!' she shouted at some lingering bystanders.

Lara was shaking with shock and, at first, could not speak. Hilder took her upstairs, laid her on a bed and comforted her while sponging her face and removing the remains of the inked swastika, then she rummaged in a drawer and found a replacement for the torn blouse. Gradually Lara recovered enough to go downstairs and share a simple meal with Hans and Hilder. She was shattered to have encountered a degree of savagery and hatred that she had never seen displayed even by the Germans. When they had finished the meal Hilder glanced at her husband, who nodded his understanding. They got up from the table and helped Lara upstairs to her old room. Hilder put her to bed below the sloping ceiling then unobtrusively removed the mirror from the dressing table, took it out of the room and returned with a woollen hat. Finally she closed the curtains.

'If you want anything, just call. I'll be downstairs. Now try to get some sleep.'

39

A LETTER FROM GERMANY

When the Occupation officially ended on May 10th 1945, Lara could see no alternative to leaving Norway. What had happened to her was bad enough but she could not bear the thought of such vilification being directed at Little Lara. She was fully aware of how children born to Norwegian girls made pregnant by German soldiers were regarded and she made a firm decision to try to find out if Willi's mother was still alive in Berlin. If she managed to find her she would ask if she and Little Lara could settle permanently with her in Germany as soon as travel to that country again became possible. Lara loved her parents and knew that leaving them would be a dreadful wrench and she would also miss the neighbours whom she knew so well. They and Lyngenfjord had been her life, but now there was a new life to consider – Little Lara's.

Lara had never stopped loving Willi and often dreamed of being reunited with him, but could he really have survived the murderous shell fire of Berlin's last days? She had to try everything. To begin with she wrote a letter to Willi's elderly mother, hoping that she would still be alive. She did not know if the letter would ever be delivered, or even if the street and house still existed. In the letter she told her about Little Lara and of her love for Willi and how he had said that she should come to Germany after the war and that one day they would be married.

She told her parents about the letter and arranged for it to be posted. As an afterthought, she decided to visit old Leif Jessen again to tell him as well. She pulled on the woollen hat given to her by Hilder Larsen to hide her almost bald head and set off on her bicycle.

Lara looked about her as she rode up to the little wooden house. The pony gazed impassively at her as she went past. She stopped to give its soft nose a stroke and was rewarded with a snort.

'Hello, Lara!' said Leif in surprise, as he appeared from behind the house. He saw her patting the pony and remarked, 'The poor beast has a girth sore just now and I can't use a saddle till it's healed. Come and sit here with me and tell me how things are with you.'

The two of them sat together on a wooden bench outside the front door and looked out over the fjord. It was so peaceful again with no Wehrmacht vehicles on the road to disturb the silence, but Lara almost wished they were there as it would mean that Willi would still be in Norway too.

She started to tell the old man about everything, unburdening herself of all her pent-up emotions. She told him about the terrible thing that had happened to her at Olderdalen and found it a relief to talk freely to someone so much older and wiser than herself. She always seemed to be on the verge of crying these days but managed to stop the flood and covered her eyes with her hands. Leif understood and put his arm round her shoulders and quietly comforted her.

'You know,' he said, 'it is just possible that your Willi is still alive, so don't give up hope yet. I think your decision to leave Norway is for the best, though it will be sad for us to see you go. I do hope you get a reply from Willi's mother. Isn't it strange that you are trying to get into Germany when most people are trying to get out!'

Two months later, when Lara had almost given up hope of a reply to her letter, Gunnar called to her to come downstairs as something important had arrived. As soon as she saw what it was Lara took the envelope and, with trembling hands, tore it open. Inside was a single sheet of paper which, to her frustration, was covered with German script which she was quite unable to read. She studied the strange writing to see if she could glean any meaning from it. She couldn't; not one single word. Her anxiously waiting parents saw her disappointment and suggested that she take it to Knut Haas in Olderdalen who had worked in Germany before the war and was known to speak a little of the language.

Lara wasted no time in following up the suggestion and she set off on the familiar bicycle ride. She knew where Knut Haas lived and had seen him in Olderdalen from time to time, but they had never spoken.

Knut was very kind and there was no hint of the rejection which she had experienced from other villagers when she was last there. He said that, of course, he would try to help with translation, and ushered her into the house. The two of them sat at a table while Knut smoothed out the sheet of paper and started to read.

Dear Lara,

I am very happy to hear from you as Willi wrote to me telling me about the wonderful Norwegian girl he had met. The censor had blacked out the name of the place in Norway where he had met you but that doesn't really matter. Most important of all he told me that the two of you have a beautiful baby girl whom you call Little Lara and who must be over a year old by now. I, therefore, have a granddaughter and I am so happy about that but I do not know if I still have a living son.

Willi was wounded here in Berlin in the last days of the war and was taken away by the Russians. After two months, I managed to find out that he was sent to Russia with many other of our troops but I have heard nothing since.

Sadly, my youngest boy, Willi's brother, Tomas, was killed when the *Tirpitz* was sunk in north Norway. It was a terrible blow to me and I do not suppose that I will ever recover from it.

You will understand then how important it is for me to know that I have a granddaughter and, of course, almost a daughter in law. You are now my family.

If you could both find a way of getting here I would give you a warm welcome; however, I know that there are restrictions on travel to Germany. If you can come, there is room in my flat which was damaged by the bombing, but it is safe and there is a home here if ever you want it.

I should warn you that much of Berlin is in ruins, the streets are filled with rubble and food is short. That's Hitler's legacy to us.

Please keep in touch. I am longing to see you both.

With fond love to you and to Little Lara.

Gerda Schmidt.

For the first time Lara caught a glimpse of a new future – admittedly a strange future – but Gerda Schmidt's welcome was almost more than she could have hoped for. She thanked Knut, took the letter and set off on the bicycle to tell Hans and Hilder Larsen at the store.

'Come in, Lara. It's always good to see you,' said Hans, looking at the piece of paper Lara held out.

'And what's this? A letter from Germany!'

'Yes,' Lara explained. 'It's from Willi's mother, and I've just been to see Knut Haas who can read German. He translated it for me and it says that she survived the war and is offering me and Little Lara a home with her in Berlin. I know it seems strange to want to go and live in there, but not all Germans can be bad and I'll never, ever give up hope of seeing Willi again.'

Before she cycled home she looked into the store. There was another girl behind the counter now but, otherwise, it looked just the same as it used to when she had worked there. She glanced into the back store room, where Willi had kissed her for the first time. Then she said goodbye to the Larsens and set off back home.

40

PECHORLAG, 93RD CAMP UNIT, PROVINCE OF KOMI, ARCTIC USSR

There was blood on his bread! Erik looked more carefully but there was no denying that the bite marks were bloody. It was only six weeks since his arrival at Pechorlag: early for scurvy to make its appearance, but scurvy it had to be as his gums had been feeling tender for some time. To try to prevent the condition some of the prisoners chewed on spruce tree needles for their vitamin C content, but best of all were the bilberries which carpeted the tundra during the brief, arctic summer.

For a month Erik's work party had been detailed to repair the single track railway along which coal from Vorkuta travelled through Pechora and Kotlas, and had fed the Soviet Union's mighty, wartime appetite for energy. The track had been laid in a hurry, by slave workers, in the early years of the war. The urgency at that time meant that all manner of short-cuts in construction standards had been taken, and some sections had simply been laid on frozen lakes. When rivers rose with the spring thaws, embankments and bridge approaches were constantly being washed away and the often long gaps had to be filled with stony spoil, brought by the prisoners using wooden barrows.

The work was exhausting and all the prisoners, sustained

on near starvation rations, lost much of their body weight. As summer warmed the pools on the tundra, millions of mosquitoes emerged, adding to the misery as they feasted on any uncovered skin.

On one fateful occasion, in order to let a coal train pass, the prisoners took a brief rest on an embankment where Erik found himself sitting beside Franz Bekker and some other Germans. He had removed his pea jacket and Bekker pointed to Erik's neck and asked,

'What's the string round your neck for?'

'It's for my wedding ring. If it was on my finger the basmachi would chop my finger off to steal it. It's been round my neck ever since I landed in Norway.'

Another tall German listening nearby said, also in English, 'I spent most of the war in Norway too. It's a lovely country and I was lucky to be there.'

Erik glanced at him. He looked a pleasant fellow, tall and with wrinkles round his eyes as though he used to laugh a lot, but a war wound had torn away part of his right cheek and he was blind in his right eye.

As soon as the train passed, a guard shouted to the prisoners, '*Rabotate, rabotate!*' – Work, work! The men got to their feet and resumed carting the unwieldy barrow-loads of gravel, which they were using to fill the gap in the embankment.

That evening, after the prisoners had returned to the barracks, Erik went to find the German with the face wound. He was sitting on his bunk talking to some other ex-Wehrmacht men. Erik introduced himself and asked where in Norway the German had served.

'Up north in Alta and also in a small settlement called Olderdalen, over 100 kilometres to the west. My name is

Willi Schmidt – you sound English but with your fair hair and blue eyes, you look Norwegian.'

Erik introduced himself and explained how he had come to be serving in Norway and that he was, indeed, half English and half Norwegian.

'Before the war I used to spend summer vacations with my Norwegian uncle and aunt on the shores of Lyngenfjord.'

He noticed that Willi Schmidt gave a start on hearing this. The German sat forward in his seat.

'Have you heard of a girl called Lara Torkelsen who lives on a farm there?'

It was Erik's turn to be startled. 'Yes, of course I have, she's my cousin – my uncle and aunt's daughter!'

Willi, quite agitated, leapt to his feet.

'How is she? When did you last see her? She's my fiancée.'

Erik was momentarily speechless, as he remembered his meeting with Lara in Alta, when she had told him about a German officer, who was the father of her baby.

'It was about two months ago in Alta,' he replied, 'and she has a little baby now.'

'That baby's my daughter!' exclaimed Willi, now visibly agitated. 'She's called Little Lara.'

For a moment the two erstwhile enemies lapsed into a stunned silence. Old enmities had become irrelevant, in the face of these new realities. A year ago they might well have been trying to kill each other, but now they were linked by family ties whether they liked it or not, and, imperceptibly, a bond began to form between the unlikely pair.

Life in the camp became even more miserable as time went on. The food was not enough to sustain a body subjected to constant hard labour in the cold of the Arctic tundra. Even in spring, the thermometer routinely fell to minus 15 degrees Centigrade but in winter, it would be much worse, with temperatures of minus 40° being commonplace. On two occasions Erik had been physically unable to carry out his work 'norm' and as a result his daily bread allowance of 600g had been reduced to 400g. Although his gums had stopped bleeding, his weight had fallen dramatically and he wondered if he could be suffering from tuberculosis which was common in the camps. To make matters worse the criminals in the camp, mostly Russians and Uzbeks, were a constant threat and were in the habit of stabbing anyone who offended them. Sometimes, just for amusement, they drew lots to select a fellow prisoner whom they would kill. Even the camp bosses were afraid of the criminals and did not dare to force them to work.

Two months after the defeat of Germany, conditions in the camp worsened and the seriously inadequate diet endured by the prisoners was the trigger which provoked talk of open rebellion. The grumbling started first among the criminal prisoners but the mood was taken up by the 'politicals' as well, including some of the Germans. Matters came to a head when they were working on a railway embankment not far from the camp. An exhausted German prisoner suddenly downed tools and sat on the ground. A guard shouted at him to get back to work. '*Rabotate!*' he ordered, but several other prisoners joined in and also sat on the ground. Two more guards appeared and threatened the striking workers with their rifles but the men remained sitting. Two guards with rifles stayed watching the prisoners while a third went off to fetch the work unit boss.

After half an hour the guard returned with the boss

who, aided by an interpreter, demanded that a spokesman be put forward to present the prisoners' grievances. By this time, about twenty prisoners had joined the revolt, among them Erik. As the seated men put their case to the boss, others gathered round until there was a small, restless crowd surrounding the negotiators. Suddenly, and without warning, the work boss drew his pistol and shot the spokesman in the chest. The body rolled down the embankment, accompanied by a howl of protest from the crowd. Some prisoners stood up and moved threateningly towards the guards, who panicked. A volley of shots rang out and ten prisoners in the surrounding crowd fell, either dead or wounded.

That ended the revolt, but worse was to come. The guards forced the fifteen men who had started the insurrection, including Erik, to remain sitting on the ground. They were then made to move and to sit in a row on the edge of the embankment facing away from the rail tracks. The boss reloaded his pistol and walked along, behind the prisoners, shooting each man in the back of the head while a guard, with a shove from his boot, sent each body tumbling over and over down the embankment. Erik, at the end of the line, had a few moments to contemplate his inevitable fate. The prisoner on his left was shot and rolled down the slope. Then the crunch of the executioner's footsteps stopped behind him. It was his turn – but there was a pause. Erik felt his heart thumping in his chest as he heard the executioner reloading his weapon, then the gravel crunched once more as the man stepped up behind him. A vision of Anna, his wife, who seemed to have Else's face, flashed through Erik's mind. It was the last thought that he would ever have, as the shot brought abrupt oblivion, then his body, too, rolled down the slope.

A work party of prisoners was made to drag the bodies to a hole in the embankment which had been eroded by floods, and to bury them with gravel and stones.

Willi Schmidt had watched the massacre and was one of those detailed to dispose of the corpses. He had been appalled at what he had seen and went straight to Erik's body, which he dragged to the hole. As he did so, he caught a glimpse of the string round Erik's neck, which he remembered held the golden ring. He broke the string with a jerk and as he did so there was a gleam of gold as the ring tumbled into the gravel at his feet. Quickly he retrieved it and hid it in his clothing.

★

The death rate among the remaining prisoners was such that, by 1953, eight years later, nearly two thirds had died. The salvation of the rest, which included Willi, came with Stalin's death on 5th March 1953 and from that time foreign prisoners were gradually repatriated. Willi Schmidt, gaunt and ill, reached West Berlin on August 1st 1954.

41

EDINBURGH: 1960

A freezing evening fog drifting in from the North Sea had enveloped Edinburgh, making it difficult to read the bus numbers. Outside the Edinburgh Royal Infirmary, the young, fair-haired medical student standing in the cold at the bus stop, was relieved to see a Number 23 appearing out of the gloom and, climbing aboard, he found a seat and settled his books on his knees. He wiped the condensation from the window with his duffel coat sleeve, but could see only gleaming black cobblestones as the bus descended to Tollcross. The shop lights lining the route, dimmed by fog, barely lit the darkness and, to Neil Kingsnorth, Edinburgh in November looked a thoroughly depressing place.

His gloom lifted a little as the bus continued through Tollcross and up to Bruntsfield. There he disembarked and walked across the grassy Bruntsfield Links to his 'digs', which were run by Mrs. Sinclair. As Edinburgh landladies go she was alright but was a strict adherent of her 'Wee Free' church's principles. From the outset she had made the house rules crystal clear.

'I will not have wein or women in the rooms!' she had said in her unmistakable Morningside accent, which had largely replaced her Hebridean lilt.

She had come originally from the Isle of Lewis in

Scotland's Outer Hebrides and, in common with many of the islanders, was a devout churchgoer. In her eyes a good Christian lived frugally, with few indulgences and should not even think about sex. Neil had a room to himself which was furnished only with a bed, a chair, a table with a lamp and shelves for his books. The only heating was supplied by a small, electric bar heater with a coin meter, which always seemed to be running out. Two fellow students, sharing an adjacent room, provided some company, and after studying in the evenings they sometimes enjoyed an illicit beer or two together in their rooms or went out to the Golf Tavern on the edge of the Links.

When Neil let himself in through the front door that day he was met in the hallway by Mrs Sinclair, who handed him a package which, she said, was addressed to him and had arrived by registered post that morning. Neil thanked her and took it up to his room. He dumped his books on the table, switched on the electric heater and, sitting on the edge of the bed, slit open the package with a penknife. Inside was a letter from the family lawyer, along with a small, wrapped object and a photograph protected by two pieces of heavy white card. Both of the items, the lawyer wrote, had been found together among his late mother's possessions and he thought that Neil would want to have them.

His curiosity aroused, Neil unwrapped the object, which turned out to be a gold wedding ring. It had a small label tied to it which, in his late mother's handwriting, simply stated, 'Erik's Ring'. The outer surface was deeply scored, as if it had been abraded by rocks and, on the inner surface was a set of tiny engraved initials – those of his father and mother: E.K. 1939 A.F. There could be no doubt about it: it was his father's wedding ring all right. After gazing at it for a few moments, he put it on the bedside table then eased the photograph from between the pieces of card. From out of the picture his father, Erik, then a young man, looked back at him laughing, while wrestling with a black Labrador dog on a sunlit lawn. He was holding the dog by the scruff of the neck and on a finger, half hidden in the black fur, was the gleam of a ring – almost certainly the one lying in front of him on the bedside table.

Neil did not remember Erik, his father, but knew that he had disappeared without trace somewhere in north Norway while serving in the war as a commando. Then, quite unexpectedly, in 1955 his ring had found its way from there, through Germany and finally to Neil's mother in England. It was only then that she knew for certain that her husband was dead. She never really recovered from the bereavement and had kept the ring locked away.

Neil looked at it again. He had no way of knowing that its golden circle encompassed a tale of desperation, treachery, capture, final transportation and execution in Pechorlag, the far Russian Arctic gulag, where his father was shot and his body dumped into the foundations of a prison railway. It was as well that Neil did not know of these terrible events that the ring had witnessed.

Neil pushed the ring onto his right fourth finger and was surprised to find that it fitted well so he kept it on. Then he forgot about it but, during the next day's lectures, he felt oddly unsettled, as if the focus of the feeling was the ring itself. In the afternoon, when he was working in the dissecting room, he glanced again at it just as a ray of winter sunshine from one of the high windows glinted on it with a flash of reflected gold. He was not in the least superstitious but it was almost as though the spirit of his dead father had just said, 'Hello'.

One Wednesday afternoon Neil was again working in the anatomy dissecting room. It surprised him how quickly he had become used to dissecting the preserved human cadavers, two rows of which were laid out on tables down the length of the hall, the shrunken, mahogany-hued faces and torsos covered with thick green canvas drapes. Students huddled over the bodies as they worked in pairs, referring now and then to brightly illustrated anatomy books propped against the cadavers. The smell of formalin nipped Neil's eyes, as he painstakingly teased out the recurrent laryngeal nerve in his cadaver's neck. It was a tricky piece of anatomy. Sometimes one of the students would wander over to one of the black, lead-lined chests along the wall, to pull out a dissected arm or leg, with its nerves dangling like cords, to refresh his memory about some anatomical detail.

On that particular Wednesday, a group of more junior students was ushered into the hall, as part of their introduction to anatomy. As they were escorted round the tables by a white-coated demonstrator, one of the students, a girl of about eighteen, paused and watched as Neil gently retracted a small muscle to display the recurrent laryngeal nerve beneath. He glanced up to find a very attractive girl looking quizzically at him from across the body.

'Hi!' he said, putting down his scalpel. 'I'm doing the head and neck this term and it's fiendishly difficult.'

'The stink of formalin's horrible,' she replied, wrinkling her nose and looking a little pale. 'I suppose I'll have to get used to dissecting, though thankfully we don't start till next year.'

Neil noticed a hint of a foreign accent in her speech, though her English was perfect. They chatted for a few minutes, during which Neil became increasingly curious about her faint accent.

'Where do you come from?' he asked at last.

'Germany, West Berlin.'

Was it her limpid brown eyes and striking auburn hair or, perhaps, the slightly foreign intonation of the words she used that attracted him? Neil, intrigued, pushed his instruments aside, sat back and looked at her. She was nice, very nice.

Before he could ask anything else, her group moved on. She hurried to catch them up, but turned around to smile at him as she went.

'Hey! Meet me for a coffee in The Doctors today at five o'clock,' he called after her, though he was not sure if she had heard him.

Shortly before five, Neil washed the formalin from his hands, although the smell of the stuff still clung to them. He tidied himself, and, with a selection of books for that evening's studying, he crossed the road and went in to the warm, smoky atmosphere of The Doctors. The place was packed and the windows were streaming with condensation. He found a seat in the corner from which he could watch the entrance. The cafe was, as usual at that time of day, full of cheerful groups of chattering students, most of them medics. He waved to a few friends and settled down to wait.

Ten minutes passed and he began to think that the girl was not going to turn up. Then the door opened, she stepped inside and stood scanning the tables. Neil jumped up.

'Over here,' he called, pulling out the chair opposite him.

Her face, flushed in the sudden warmth of the crowded room, broke into a shy smile as she sat down.

'I'll get two hot chocolates, or would you like something else?' he asked. 'I'm Neil,' he said, 'Neil Kingsnorth. I'm from the south of England which, by the way, is a good bit less cold than Edinburgh. What's your name?'

'I'm Lilara, Lilara Schmidt.'

For a time, the pair chatted about their medical studies and about their hobbies and interests.

'You really do speak good English,' commented Niel, 'and Lilara is a beautiful name. It almost sings.'

Lilara smiled. 'Yes, my name is unusual; it's a shortened version of Little Lara. You see, Mother's name is Lara.'

They went on chatting for half an hour and Neil found himself more and more attracted to this girl who was so unusual, with her occasional funny use of words and who looked so fascinating with a rim of foam from her chocolate drink on those delightful lips. Those lips! He was determined to see her again soon and invited her to come to a modest Italian restaurant for an evening meal on Friday. After they had parted, Neil thought about her lips a lot and the way the tip of her tongue emerged to lick off the foam.

After the last tutorial on Friday, Neil took a bus for a mile to meet Lilara at her halls of residence, on the south side of the city. In the gathering dusk, the great crags of Arthur's Seat, surrounded by the twinkling lights of Edinburgh, reared blackly against the evening sky. A short walk from the bus stop brought Neil to the halls of residence. He pushed open the door and there, in the hallway, was Lilara already waiting for him, looking attractive in a flared blue coat with a mauve scarf around her neck. They greeted each other a little shyly and set off together to the bus stop. The restaurant, near Tollcross, was modest but warm and after ordering spaghetti Bolognese for two, they settled in at a quiet table by the window. Only two other tables were occupied and for a few moments they peered, in silence, through the window at the passers-by wrapped up against the winter chill, as they hurried along the pavement. Their initial awkwardness quickly resolved and soon they were chatting easily about their medical courses. They had nearly finished the spaghetti when Neil asked Lilara if there were any medical connections in her family.

'No,' she replied a little abruptly and seemed to become oddly wary of the direction the conversation was taking. It was almost as if she did not want to talk about herself, or, perhaps, about her family. They were quiet for a few moments, then Neil explained that his grandfather had been a general practitioner in Surrey but had died a few years previously, in 1955. As a boy, he had been very close to the old man, as he had never known his own father who had been in the commandos in the war.

'We never really found out what happened to him,' he said. 'Near the end of the war he was posted "missing, presumed killed on active service" somewhere in north Norway.'

The evening passed well enough, though Neil still felt that Lilara was withdrawn and was holding something back from him. Once they had finished their meal, he escorted her back to the halls of residence, puzzled by her mood change. Before he said goodnight he asked her if she would meet him again the following week and suggested that they might take a bus out of the city, to the Pentland Hills, and go for a walk. Lilara seemed happy with this idea and in the shadow of the door way, he drew her to him and kissed her gently on the lips. She did not pull away but neither did she respond much.

As the weeks went by their friendship developed into something more and their university friends came to recognise them as a couple. It was shortly before the Christmas vacation that they again decided to go for dinner at the Italian restaurant near Tollcross. They took the same table by the window and, during the course of the meal, Neil again asked Lilara about her parents. Once more there was that hint of evasiveness, but this time he persisted.

'All right, I'll tell you everything,' she replied and added, 'but you may not like it.'

'My mother,' she said, 'is Norwegian, but lives in Berlin. She was brought up on a farm in north Norway and met my father, who was a serving German officer there during the Occupation. When she became pregnant all the locals knew that my father was responsible. Mother had a terrible time because of this and was rejected by everyone, except her parents and immediate neighbours. Did you know that children born from a relationship with a German were called "Nazi spawn" and were, and indeed still are, treated accordingly in Norway? In the spring of 1945, Father was recalled to the final defence of Berlin, which was being assaulted by the Russians, but, before he left he gave her his own mother's address in Berlin and said that when the war ended Lara, my mother, must come to live in Germany and they would get married. They were very much in love.'

Neil, moved by the tragic story, leant across the table and took Lilara's hand in his own. She looked up at him and there was a tear in her eye. After blowing her nose and muttering an apology, she took a deep breath and continued.

'The disgrace of having me as a child made life impossible for Mother in Norway. When the war ended and travel again became possible, she took me to Germany

347

to see Father's elderly mother, to try to find out what had happened to him. It was thought that he had probably been killed in the final defence of Berlin, or just possibly, had been transported as a prisoner to Russia. Mother and I lived with "German Granny" for several years and I took Father's name of Schmidt. In 1954, the year after Stalin died, Mother suddenly received some almost unbelievable news. Father was alive after all and was about to be released from a prison camp in Russia! Sure enough, on August 1st, a date which I will never forget, he was sent across from Potsdam to West Berlin on the Glienicke Bridge. Mother was overjoyed. I was just thirteen years old and you can imagine my excitement when I found that, suddenly, I had a father after all! Father was dreadfully thin and weak but Mother became a changed person – happy and cheerful – and I began to hear her singing about the house and, within a few months, the two of them were finally married.'

In a flash the truth dawned to Neil! Everything became clear. He knew all about his Norwegian relations who lived on Lyngenfjord, where his father, Erik, used to stay for summer holidays, before the war. He remembered that his Norwegian great aunt Birgitta and great uncle Gunnar Torkelsen had a daughter called Lara. This girl sitting in front of him must be none other than Lara's daughter and, therefore, his close cousin!

Neil's head swam with the extraordinary and disturbing new reality which faced him. He was in love with his close cousin and they had shared their love physically on numerous occasions. If they were to marry and have children might they be affected, possibly mentally or physically, by a union of close cousins?

The shock of Lilara's revelations had almost

overwhelmed him and, when he looked up, he was surprised to find himself still in an Edinburgh restaurant.

It was ten o'clock, all the other diners had left and the waiter was hovering with the bill. Neil paid him, adding a good tip and saying that they would like to stay for another fifteen minutes. He proceeded to tell Lilara everything – about his Norwegian cousins and how closely he was related to her.

Lilara's face, across the table, showed her emotion at these revelations and a single tear ran down her cheek.

Suddenly the waiter's voice jolted them back to reality: 'I am afraid that we are closing now. I have to lock the door!' The man could not know how disturbed and distraught the young couple were as they got up and went out into the cold Edinburgh night.

★

At the end of that term, many of the students packed up for the journeys home. Lilara departed for Berlin to stay with her parents and elderly granny, while Neil took the train south to his own grandmother's at Chiddingfold in Surrey. As they parted, they still had not decided what to do in the light of their unsettling discovery.

During the vacation Neil had time to ponder about marriage between close relations and recalled hearing about a related couple who had lived near the Torkelsen's farm on Lyngenfjord. Their first child turned out to be severely mentally retarded and, tragically, had drowned in the fjord by the boat anchorage. At the time people living round about thought that the parents being related was the cause of the child's condition and had said that relations should not marry.

*

Two weeks later, at the beginning of the new term, Neil and Lilara returned to Edinburgh and an emotional reunion. After they recovered their composure Lilara produced a creased letter from her shoulder bag. Her mother had given it to her and it was from Granny Birgitta Torkelsen in Norway, to her daughter, Lara, Lilara's mother. It was written in Norwegian and had been addressed in capital letters to –

MS. LARA SCHMIDT

FLAT NO.5

HORSTWEG

WEST BERLIN

'I'd like to go somewhere quiet to read the whole of this to you,' said Lilara.

They found a seat in a café and she began to read:

Dearest Lara,

Now that Gunnar, your father, has passed away, I want to tell you something that I could never have divulged when he was alive, but I have to tell you now before it is too late. The doctor has told me that I have leukaemia and, therefore, I may not have another chance.

You know that your father and I were very happy together on the farm beside Lyngenfjord but our one disappointment was our inability to have children.

We were thrilled to adopt Bjorn, and he brought us great happiness. In spite of that I still yearned to have a baby growing inside me, but that seemed impossible. I did not know if it was my or Gunnar's body that was at fault and, secretly, I went to see Helga Anders our dear neighbour on the next farm because she and Nils had two healthy boys. Perhaps you can guess what I asked. Over the following few weeks she discussed the situation with Nils and at last he agreed to try to help just once. When it was done I fell pregnant straight away and Gunnar never knew about it.

Your natural father is Nils Anders but you know that Gunnar loved you as his daughter with all his heart. Perhaps what I did was wrong but I really cannot believe that it was. Please be careful with this secret and on no account tell the Anderses what I have told you.

I know what a terrible time you had in Norway after you became pregnant and nothing can excuse the behaviour of our fellow Norwegians. I think you did the right thing at the end of the war by going to live with Willi's mother in Germany. From what you told us about Willi we knew that he was a kind and decent man but just happened to be on the wrong side.

You must know that I have never stopped loving you and you are always in my thoughts and I still think of Lilara as 'Little Lara' my beloved granddaughter.

God bless you both.

Your loving mother,
Birgitta

Lilara handed the letter to Neil, her eyes moist with barely suppressed tears.

'Neil,' she said, looking into his eyes, 'this means that we are not biologically related at all!'

42

CHIDDINGFOLD, SURREY, ENGLAND

The marquee shone white in the summer sunshine beneath the enormous cedar on the lawn at the Kingsnorth family home. The marriage ceremony had just taken place and in front of the tent were more than a hundred chattering and laughing wedding guests, champagne glasses in their hands. The men, grey, black and white in their morning suits, contrasted with the blaze of colour of the ladies' dresses and hats. Staff, with bottles of champagne, moved among the guests, topping up the emptying glasses.

Neil and his radiant bride, Lilara, circulated among the guests. She wore a magnificent white wedding dress, the veil thrown back to reveal her stunning cascade of auburn curls amongst which glowed a circlet of diamonds and rubies, presented by her many Norwegian and German friends. As she shook hands with the guests, a diamond solitaire ring flashed on her left fourth finger but a second very special ring of plain gold nestled there as well, specially adjusted to fit her finger. It was a much travelled and deeply scored ring. If one had been able to look at its inner surface, the initials of Neil's parents, 'E.K. 1939 A.F.' would have been seen encircling Lilara's delicate finger. She carried a wedding bouquet of freesias, sweetly perfumed gardenias and orange blossom. Proudly displayed amongst the blooms were three tiny flags – one Norwegian, one West German and the Union Jack.

At the marriage ceremony, in the small village church, there had not been room for many guests but, at the front sat Alice, Neil's grandmother, now a fine old lady who still retained a hint of her Norwegian accent even though it had been all of sixty years since she had left her homeland. Sadly, Willi's mother, Gerda, who had survived the bombing raids on Berlin had died five years after the war's end. Beside Alice, on a symbolically empty pew seat, rested a discreet wreath of dark leaves with scarlet poppies representing Erik and Anna, Neil's late parents. Alice had adored Erik, her lost soldier son, and when, later on, during the marriage ceremony, the vicar had intoned the solemn words, "until death do us part", a careful observer might have seen the old lady's eyes glistening with tears. It was then that, for Alice, time suddenly stood still: the familiar mustiness of the church, the smell of prayer books and old Bibles, the glow of the brass wall plaque commemorating her late son and the candles brought it all back – 'Erik! Oh Erik!' Her old shoulders shook with long-suppressed, hopeless grief as a tide of emotion swept over her.

Separated from Alice only by the vacant pew with its wreath of leaves and poppies sat her niece, Lara Schmidt, the bride's Norwegian mother, newly arrived from Germany with her husband Willi. She had become an attractive middle aged lady, her dark hair streaked with a hint of grey, which her simple hat did not quite hide. Beside her, his hand on hers, sat her German husband, Willi, silver-haired but still tall and military-looking. His facial scarring did not hide the laughter lines around his eyes and, somehow, he had managed to find a ghost orchid for a buttonhole.

The unlikely couple had overcome almost insurmountable problems in their wartime relationship and, still in love, they were triumphant on this, their daughter Lilara's wedding day.

Some other men were missing, but that was a legacy of the war. Bjorn, Lara's adopted brother, was one of these. He had always been something of an enigma. Throughout the Occupation, his loyalty to Norway had been ambivalent. He famously shot and killed Reichskommissar Joseph Adelbrecht, one of the most hated of the Nazi occupiers, but he had also worked intermittently for the Germans and may have betrayed a Resistance radio operator, who was transmitting in the forest above Alta. In the last stages of the war, he had shocked his fellow countrymen by joining a Nazi SS ski battalion and had been killed fighting the Finns in Lapland.

At the back of the church, behind the pews, where some extra chairs had been brought in, sat Arne and Inga Petersen, farming neighbours from Lyngenfjord, and Hans and Hilder Larsen from the store at Olderdalen, all now well into their sixties. Nils and Helga Anders, also neighbours of the late Gunnar and Birgitta Torkelsen, were there too. At the altar rail the bridegroom and his best man, a friend from Edinburgh University, fidgeted nervously as they waited for Lilara to appear

Just before the service began Willi rose quietly from his pew, gave his wife, Lara a quick kiss and disappeared towards the church door. Then, to the sound of Mendlessohn's 'Wedding March', he returned leading Lilara, veiled and in a cloud of white tulle, down the aisle to where Neil waited. Just then, a sunbeam shining through the colours of a stained glass window projected a ring of gold onto the couple and when, during the ceremony, the vicar pronounced the couple 'man and wife', old Alice could hardly believe her eyes – it was a miracle! Neil had changed into her late, beloved soldier son! Erik was there, right there, standing at the altar rail; she was sure of it – Erik! Tears, which had glistened in her eyes at last ran freely down her face.

At the end of the ceremony the newly married couple walked back in triumph along the aisle to the thunderous chords of Widor's 'Toccata'. The very rafters of the church shook.

Outside, in the sunshine of that glorious July day, the guests lined up to offer their congratulations to the couple. None of the other guests, except his wife, could know just why Nils Anders looked so proud, as he first embraced Lara, just as any father would – and then kissed Lilara, his granddaughter, the bride.

Of course, Nils's wife, Helga, had known the truth from the very beginning and she gave her husband's hand a reassuring squeeze.

EPILOGUE

While researching material for this book, the author travelled extensively in northern Norway and on numerous occasions visited Arctic north-west Russia. The Svolvaer War Museum in the Lofoten Islands has a wide range of original exhibits and provided invaluable information about the Occupation. A visit to Kafjord in northern Norway showed just how impregnable an anchorage it must have seemed to the German naval planners of the time. In spite of that, the *Tirpitz* was badly damaged there in a British midget submarine attack and in attacks from the air. There is an excellent museum beside the fjord detailing what happened.

Many of the main events of the novel are historical facts, but the names of Reichskommissar Adelbrecht, General von Schirach and others are invented, as are some of the geographical place names.

In 2009 the author met an elderly Norwegian, who happened to be waiting for a ferry near Tromso, 150 miles from Kafjord. In conversation he revealed how, as a young boy living in Tromso in 1944, he (Anton Jessen in this story), had watched the final lethal attack by British Lancaster bombers on the *Tirpitz* near Tromso. He had watched as the ship rolled over after being struck by enormous 'Tallboy' bombs, designed by Barnes Wallace, and had, with considerable distress, seen the rescue of dreadfully wounded survivors who were given Schnapps by the local

Norwegians. His account, which he wrote down for the author's records, forms the basis of the description of the destruction of the *Tirpitz* in Chapter 28 of this novel.

★

In the nineteenth century, two French psychiatrists were the first to name a rare psychosis, '*folie à deux*', or 'madness of two'. It is characterised by psychotic delusions shared between two close, emotionally stressed individuals.

The mentally traumatic events experienced by Erik during his war in Norway are entirely credible and would have been stressful in the extreme. Near the war's end, he and Else Svensen formed a deep emotional and physical bond and from that time a hint of surrealism creeps into their shared experiences, particularly the dancing reflections in the sea cave. The reader must decide if this was, in fact, an expression of *folie à deux* in the minds of two war stressed young lovers or whether the reflections were real.

It is left partly to the reader's imagination to decide how, in 1942, an enormous amount of Stalin's gold bullion could have found its way from the stricken HMS *Edinburgh* in the Barents Sea to deep in a sea cave in remote north Norway. Historically the presence of the gold on the ship is beyond doubt: it was on its way from Murmansk to Britain in payment for arms shipments to the Soviet Union. It is also a historical fact that in 1981 a deep sea salvage venture recovered 460 ingots from the sunken ship with a value then of over forty-five million pounds. However, the novel exploits the fact that a further five ingots remain missing to this day and readers will note that this is the precise number of ingots that Erik and Else claimed to have hidden in a bog.

EPILOGUE

On the other hand perhaps there never was any gold at all on the Svartfjell Peninsula.

In the novel, the only gold to emerge from the tragedy and to carry any meaning at all for Erik's family was his wedding ring. In the far Russian Arctic it was removed from Erik's dead body by a German fellow prisoner, Willi Schmidt. After Stalin's death in 1953 Schmidt was released and he returned the ring to Erik's family in England.

MAIN CHARACTERS

Dr.Andrew and Alice Kingsnorth of Chiddingfold, Surrey, England.

Erik Kingsnorth, their son (b.1920, m. Anna Forteith 1939).

Neil Kingsnorth (b.1940), son of Erik and Anna. After the war he became a medical student in Edinburgh and married Lara's daughter, Lilara (Little Lara) 1962.

Gunnar (Norwegian brother of Alice Kingsnorth) and Birgitta Torkelsen, his wife, Lyngenfjord, Norway.
   Two children, Bjorn (adopted) and Lara.

Nils and Helga Anders, neighbours of the Torkelsens.
   Two children, Lars and Kristian.

Arne and Inga Petersen, neighbours of the Torkelsens.
   Twin boys, Per and Pal.

Leif Jessen, elderly widowed neighbour of the Torkelsens. Grandfather of Anton Jessen of Tromso.

Hans and Hilder Larsen, proprietors of Olderdalen store.

Sven Svensen, Resistance leader and owner of the Alta boatyard.

MAIN CHARACTERS

Else Svensen, Sven's daughter.

Roald Bratland, Norwegian fisherman, Valanhamn.

Olav Birklund, Resistance member, Svolvaer, Lofoten Islands.

Magnus, Resistance member, Tromso.

Vladimir Kuznetsov, Russian dockyard worker, previous intellectual, subsequently shipwrecked.

Major Willi Schmidt, Wehrmacht officer and Lara's lover.

Hans Schreiber, Wehrmacht officer.

Standartenführer Richter, SS officer.

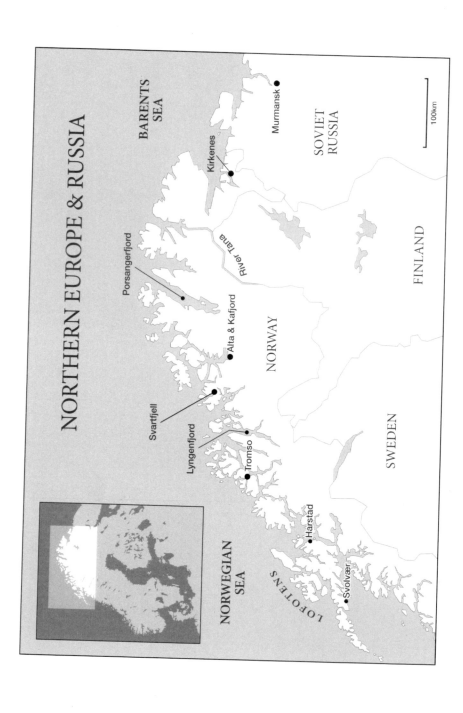

NORTHERN EUROPE & RUSSIA

NORWEGIAN SEA

BARENTS SEA

SOVIET RUSSIA

Murmansk

Kirkenes

River Tana

Porsangerfjord

Alta & Kafjord

Svartfjell

Lyngenfjord

NORWAY

FINLAND

Tromso

SWEDEN

Harstad

LOFOTENS

Svolvær

100km